Lilac Mines

Lilac Mines

a novel

Cheryl Klein

Manic D Press

San Francisco

For
my dad
Chris Klein
who taught me how to ghost-hunt

The author gratefully acknowledges the following excerpted lyrics from songs recorded by Bessie Smith:
p. 120: "Kitchen Man" by A. Razaf and E.B. Pinkard
p. 124: "Haunted House Blues" by J.C. Johnson
p. 176: "Frosty Mornin' Blues" by E. Brown

Published by Manic D Press. For information, contact Manic D Press,
PO Box 410804, San Francisco CA 94141   www.manicdpress.com

Vintage cover photograph © Duncan Walker
Printed in the USA

Library of Congress Cataloging-in-Publication Data

Klein, Cheryl.
  Lilac mines : a novel / by Cheryl Klein.
      p. cm.
  ISBN 978-1-933149-31-8 (trade pbk. original)
  1. Lesbians--Fiction. 2. California--Fiction. I. Title.
  PS3611.L443L55 2009
  813'.6--dc22

                              2009016004

I

BORDERLAND
Felix: Los Angeles, 2002

This will become the place they broke up. Felix tries to see it in the past tense: the exposed brick, the goddess painted on the bedroom door, the stack of legal books by the couch. This was Eva's fabulous downtown sublet, above Liberty Bail Bonds and across from a hotel where you could buy your own private sushi chef. Eva moved into this place last month, and Felix had pictured many more good months spent here, in artist loft bliss.

"But you just liked that she had so many sex toys," Felix pleads. "Remember, you said, 'She's fun to mess around with, but I could never be in a relationship with a musician.' You said the hours wouldn't work."

Felix hopes that if she can create a precise history—and back it up with quotes, as her professors always said—that Eva would reconsider. She'd renew the vows of their non-monogamy and agree that, while Kate Mendoza-Lishman might have a great drum kit and an industrial strength vibrator and sweet slim hips, Felix is the only one she calls her girlfriend.

Eva perches on the arm of the couch, angular chin resting on knees, arms wrapped around long thin legs. Normally she moves like a dancer, as if a pirouette could be spun at any minute, but upset, she pulls in and gets very still. Kate probably doesn't even know this.

"I guess accommodations are made when you really want to be with someone," Eva shrugs. "We haven't worked out the details. I just wanted you to know—that's what we agreed on, right? That as long as we are honest, no one could really get hurt?"

"That's so… lawyerly of you. You're totally twisting it around," Felix says, wishing she sounded less desperate. "Anyway, I accommodated *you* with this whole open relationship thing because *I* really wanted to be with *you*."

This is partly true. It was Eva who said that monogamy was archaic and doomed to failure, that it pitted women against each other. And Felix liked the idea of infinite possibility, of trying on different women like outfits in a giant walk-in closet. Others might be the too-high heels she strutted in for a few hours; Eva would be her comfy jeans. She liked the idea of being at the forefront of something. In practice, Felix sat at home liking various ideas while Eva went out and met Kate and Vanessa and Donald, the bail bondsman. The latter has been a bit inconvenient. Donald has seen too much porn. He keeps knocking on Eva's door and asking if she and her girlfriend want to "hang out." Felix has endured it all—because she is determined to be progressive; because in their year together there have only been three side-whatevers, all seemingly casual; because she loves Eva.

"Hey, isn't Kate going on tour this summer anyway? In Europe or something?" Felix asks. She realizes she's looking for a loophole.

"Actually, yes." Eva looks at the goddess. Her blonde hair, straight and capable and chin-length, hides her face as much as possible. "That's another thing I need to tell you. I'm, um, thinking of going with her. I might take a semester off or, or…." Eva never stammers. This is big.

"Do you love her?" Felix suddenly is following the script of a movie she would never pay money to see.

Eva considers. "I like her enough that I have to figure out if I love her."

"I always thought that if you left me for someone, it would be a guy," Felix admits. "Not Donald, but some guy."

Before Eva, Felix never dated a bi chick. She had no particular bias, had never been ditched for a man, but the possibility worried her. And bisexuality trumped Felix's mere gayness in terms of sheer postmodern cool. To slip one's sexual identity on and off like a sleek coat—it was a little intimidating. Eva referred to herself as queer, or sometimes pomosexual (she had dated transsexuals of the male-to-female *and* the female-to-male varieties, so Felix supposed she'd earned the title), but rarely bi. Eva was post-bi.

"You said that like I was going to run away to the suburbs and pop out 2.5 kids," Eva says, gaining confidence. Her sentences flow. Her eyes flash.

"It's a moot point now," Felix snaps. She stands up feebly and grabs the backpack she brought because she thought she was spending the night. She figured they would drink wine on the metal staircase outside, have sex, walk down the street for post-coital udon. Felix struggles with the backpack straps, and Eva, with the instinctive movement of someone who's still her girlfriend, untwists them.

"Fuck you. Don't touch me," Felix growls.

Eva's blue eyes widen behind her glasses. Now she looks hurt. Felix wants to comfort her and hates Eva for making that impossible. "Stop making it all sound like some fated *thing*. You decided to fuck her and now you're *deciding* to go be, like, her Eurotrash groupie."

Felix is not sure she's using "Eurotrash" correctly, but Eva's too tearful to call her on it. Standing there with her backpack, almost a head shorter than Eva, Felix feels childish, the naive butt of a joke she doesn't even get.

"But we *said*," Eva protests. "We always said, if it's meant to be, it's meant to be, and if not we should find out and not waste our time."

"I'm a waste of fucking time? I'm *so* sorry, Eva. Don't worry—I won't waste any more of your precious time." She has to unlock three heavy locks before she can leave and the door slams behind her, but what is lacking in dramatic timing, is made up for in strength. The old building shudders. She pounds down the stairs. Donald is standing at the bottom with a tray of lemon bars.

"Aw, you're leaving? I was just gonna see if you and Eva wanted to hang out."

"I've gotta run, but I'm sure Eva would love to see you. Go on up."

Felix wants to run, for real. She wants to sprint through the streets of downtown like one of its after-hours residents, give herself over to the world of addicts and schizophrenics and cautionary tales. She wants to run until her bones shake apart and collapse in pieces. But her blue Bug beeps politely when she instinctively presses the keychain button. She drives away, glaring at Donald's hand-lettered sign, *No Free Parking Any Time!!* as she rounds the corner.

After two weeks, Felix gives in and calls. But a voice on the machine says, "Hello, you've reached Tim and Crystal." The owners of the loft are back. Eva's cell number yields a disheartening three notes followed by, "We're sorry, the number you have dialed—" Felix hangs up. She tries to think what people did in the days before phones. Probably what they still do in movies—run after trains carrying their true loves away, fall on their knees outside bedroom windows. All gestures that, in real life, would result in restraining orders.

She begins to hear rumors. At clubs. At the park where they walked Eva's brother's border collie mix. From the friends of their mutual friends: *They went to Europe. They flew into Berlin. Or maybe it was Prague.* "They" makes Felix cringe. No one knows exactly where they went, exactly how long they'll be gone.

After three weeks, Felix starts to see Eva everywhere. Eva is getting her hair cut at a retro barbershop in Silver Lake. Eating at the sandwich shop across the street from Felix's office. Walking a big yellow dog. Getting on the bus. The longer she's gone, the more she pops up in Felix's peripheral vision.

Unnerved, Felix stops going out. She goes to work in West L.A. and drives straight home to her gray shoebox building in Koreatown. Her roommates worry. Usually they spend their free time in Silver Lake, where they would live if the commute were endurable. Usually they are all about ditching here-and-now for somewhere better-and-next. But once Felix hunkers down in her apartment—with the white walls their landlord won't permit them to paint, the vintage movie posters and inflatable easy chair—she decides home isn't so bad. She watches decorating shows on cable and rearranges her closet three times. She will live in a neat and stylish shoebox. Her roommates will report from the outside world so that she can remain cutting edge without having to spend any time on the edge.

Now it's late Friday afternoon, and Felix is cross-legged on the couch, flipping channels and eating Arctic Kiss ice cream. It's basically chocolate mint.

"Oh my God, you are so chick lit right now!" her roommate admonishes, barging through the front door.

Crane Mitsubishi is a small girl with a big pink walking cast and big hair. Currently her dark, laboriously achieved dreadlocks are corralled into a thick ponytail on top her head. The cast followed a seemingly minor fall from the elevator into the hallway of the building where she and Felix work for separate Time Inc. magazines. She was carrying a cake to celebrate her magazine's Summer Movie Preview issue; she never made it to the party.

Crane limps over and snatches the ice cream from Felix's hands. "Are you going to drink a bottle of wine and sing... what's that Bridget Jones song?"

It doesn't sound like the worst way to spend an evening, but Felix just snaps, "I don't know. I never read it."

"Well, me neither, I just saw the movie," Crane admits. "It had its charms." She stops before launching into full pop critic persona. "You're better than this. There are other fish in the sea and all that bullshit. There are other Evelyns and Avas and *Evangelines*. Let's find you an Evangeline."

Crane is referring to Felix's first and only other girlfriend, Evie, also known as Jia Li. When she and Felix met, during their politically outraged college senior year, she'd just returned to her Chinese name after years of going by Evie. Sometimes she forgot to answer to Jia Li.

"Maybe I'm *not* better than this," Felix challenges. "Maybe I'm meant to eat ice cream and spend the rest of my life missing Eva. When we were together, I imagined us as this sort of power-couple-in-training. But she was the one on her way to a real career. She was the one who introduced me to all the good bands."

"And introduced herself to them," Crane interjects.

Felix ignores her. "I'm just some wannabe who writes about Nadia Sellars dyeing her hair back to its natural color and how that's such a brave move."

"Who's Nadia Sellars?"

"Some chick on the WB. See? Who cares, right? Maybe I should quit my job. Today sucked. Renee kept harassing me about this stupid lipstick chart I finished weeks ago. She said, 'Felix, you used the word 'fun' *three times.*' She always uses people's names when she's pissy." Felix adopts a high, chirpy voice that sounds nothing like Renee's. "She was like, 'The reds are 'fun.' The glosses are 'fun.' And here you say that the Revlon product is 'perfect for a long night of fun.' I'm pro-fun, *Felix*, but this suggests a lack of creativity.' " She sighs. "I spent so much time thinking about different words for red, you know: scarlet, crimson, carmine... (whatever the fuck that is) that I didn't realize. I don't know, I guess I believed in the power of fun." She smiles weakly.

"You're insulting my job too, dude," says Crane.

"At least you write about actual movies that movie stars are in. I just cover, like, the ephemera. Maybe Eva saw how lame I really am."

Crane sits down next to her. Her voice shifts from its normal semi-shout to a gentle tone. "She wasn't with you because you have a cool job. Eva's not that shallow. I mean, she's a moron for dumping you, but she's not stupid."

Felix closes her eyes. Eva is here, too, behind her eyelids. Pink-cheeked, a quizzical look on her face. Eva dreamed of working for Amnesty International. She would have loved if Felix had extended her activism beyond a long list of product boycotts, but mostly, she just loved Felix. She called Felix's brown eyes hazel; she adored the awful poem Felix wrote her for their six-month anniversary; she glowed when Felix praised her term paper on "Last of the Famous International Playboys: Decision-Making Institutions and International Human Rights Law." Felix had struggled through it with a legal dictionary in one hand and a very strong cup of coffee in the other. *She* is the one who's shallow. While she was striving toward some hipster ideal, Eva was losing herself in the dark wet beats of Kate's band, the Manly Cupcakes. Really feeling it.

Felix wants something equally loud. Something distracting and real.

"We're going out," Crane announces. "Tonight. This is the part where the fun girlfriends take the sad, dumped girl out and get her smashed. I'll see if Robbie can come, too."

It's a good night to go out. The building where Felix, Crane and Robbie live has been invaded by a film crew. The roommates sidestep cameras, wires and Teamsters in the hallway.

"Why would they want to film anything here anyway?" Robbie asks. He pulls a brown plaid flannel over his white T-shirt. "We live in a pit."

"Our landlord makes more money renting that apartment out to film crews for a couple of days than he would from renting it out to some poor Section 8 family with, like, three kids," says Crane. She crosses her arms and look like an angry elf. She's 4'11" and wearing an Anpanman T-shirt. Anpanman is an anime superhero with sweet bean bun for a head; when people are hungry, he gives them a bite. Then his friend the baker toasts him up a new head. Felix appreciates the simplicity of his heroism.

"Besides, I think they're making a movie about the 'hood," Crane adds.

"Come on, you guys," Felix says impatiently. "We have to hurry if we want to find parking."

They're off to West Hollywood, where you go when your girlfriend disappears from the continent. Where you go when you've had a terrible day at work. Where you go if you can't stay home.

The first stop is Sourpuss. There's no sign exactly, just a neon lemon over the entrance, so they suspect it's a good club. Better than that sweaty, shirtless boy club (what was it called?) that occupied the same space until a few months ago. Sourpuss is a girl club so Felix, Crane, and honorary lesbian Robbie feel duty-bound to check it out. Otherwise they'd be in Silver Lake, where no one even bothers with distinctions like gay and straight. Silver Lake is gritty and funky and underground whereas shiny WeHo nearly pulses with its ache to be mainstream. So they also feel duty-bound to make a few comments to reassure themselves that while they are *in* West Hollywood, they are also beyond it.

"Robbie, please tell me you did not just check that guy out. He was such a FOB," Crane hisses when Robbie's eyes linger on a pale-haired man wearing an Old Navy T-shirt tucked into tight, light jeans.

Robbie shrugs. He is the gentle offspring of the forested Oregon college at which he spent his pre-transfer years. "He had a nice body." Robbie's weakness, hardly original. "What does that even mean, FOB?"

"Fresh off the boat." Crane's Japanese. She has *positionality*, a term seemingly coined by one of their activist professors; at least, Felix hasn't heard anyone else use it in the three years she's been out of college.

"I know, but how does that apply to *him*?" Robbie wants to know.

"Fine. Fresh off the bus. From, like, Iowa." Crane smiles. "He's so in love with WeHo, you can tell."

Sourpuss is sort of... sour. Brushed aluminum surfaces, aloof bartenders. Too new to have settled on a look, it's a crazy quilt of lesbians and near-lesbians. Slim glittered bellbottoms, swingy flowered skirts, work pants, cargo pants, and giant raver jeans all cradle animated asses. Hopeful swinger couples work the margins of the dance floor, and gay boyfriends grind like the place is theirs. It's times like this that Felix loves West Hollywood. It's just cheesy enough that she doesn't feel self-conscious. She's wearing one of her dykiest outfits: black Dickies, black wifebeater with red silk-screened lips that hover between her boobs, steel-toed boots, and a choker that looks like a handful of ball bearings strung together. Her short brown hair is gelled into chunky spikes. For the sake of juxtaposition, she carries a purse adorned with a white poodle appliqué. The ensemble makes her feel angry-happy.

The three friends shimmy into a platonic triangle. Near the bar, Felix spots Eva putting the moves on some neo-butch dyke, a woman with cut-off sleeves and sinewy biceps who probably loves knitting and getting fucked with a strap-on. One of Eva's many types. A few minutes later, Felix catches Eva whispering to the DJ, a pixie-faced girl with a German accent who keeps welcoming the crowd to "Sow-ah-puss." The real Eva could be doing almost exactly this thousands of miles away. She could be hunting for the side-whatevers to her relationship with Kate—or worse, what if Kate is so fabulous that Eva doesn't need anyone else? Felix calculates the time difference and realizes that Eva is most likely sleeping. Her arms thrown over her head, as if she's dreaming of roller coasters. Kate trying to spoon her un-spoonable body. In Berlin or Prague, it's already tomorrow. Eva is living in the future, and she's not calling Felix to tell her what it's like.

Felix wishes she had backpacked through Europe after graduation instead of working at an internship that became a tedious editorial assistant position. Then she would know what early summer weather was like there, how it would touch Eva's skin. Is the light buttery or sharp? Are the toilets the same? Is it true there are no homeless people? Who will Eva give her change to?

"I am hoping everyone is having a good dance," the DJ purrs over a techno pop song.

"She's cute," says Crane.

"You have a girlfriend, lady," Felix reminds her. Sandy and Crane are very monogamous, but Sandy hates to dance.

"I mean for you. You're free, remember?"

"Oh. Right."

Felix doesn't know how people meet in clubs. She doesn't know how to make the transition from looking hot and dancing well to actually hooking up the names and numbers and body parts. She keeps moving, her fists punching at the ceiling. For now it's enough to be in a new place.

Crane buys her a ginger ale/vanilla Stoli, Felix's drink since she decided she needed A Drink. It was the perfect beverage—pale and unadorned enough to make her think of detective fiction, but still wet with sugar. Crane sways as she hands it to Felix, sloshing her own apple martini as she balances on her cast.

Robbie drinks beer, preferably micro-brew, but he's not a snob about it. "Hey, lushy," Robbie yells to Crane over the music. "When do you get that thing off?"

"Couple more weeks still. My brother told me that I probably broke it because I broke it before, in gymnastics when I was little. Something about how once you kill the nerves in a certain part of your body, they don't regenerate. Like, I can't feel the ground quite right with that foot, even though the bone is strong. Everyone thinks it's the bone that's the problem, but really it's the nerve."

Felix feels faraway from the conversation. She sees Eva enter the club, wearing big Elton John glasses and trailing two hip-hop chicks. She decides to try out an idea, the way you can try out things in a bar. "Hey, you guys, what would you think if I ran away?"

"Not to Europe!" Crane says. "I forbid it. I don't want to hear any more about her tonight."

"It's okay to miss her," says Robbie. "Crane, have a little sympathy. I remember when Andrew and I broke up—"

"I'm not talking about Eva," Felix insists, although she wants to let the name linger in her mouth. The small, neat bite of it, like tapas. "I just sort of want to go somewhere. I want to do something more interesting, more creative or whatever." Even through her drink's shimmer, she can feel the cliché of her statement. Everyone she knows is thinking about quitting. To Do Something More Creative or To Give Back A Little. But unlike Felix, they're too busy being successful. Felix hates being a cliché, longs for a world not divided between mimics and reactionaries. *Where would that be,* she asks herself, *the womb?*

"Maybe I'll do a little traveling. On *this* continent, don't worry. To, like, New York," Felix says, thinking, *Sure, I could just break into fashion design.* Her secret, uber-cliché More Creative Thing.

"You should, you'll love it," Crane says excitedly. They believe that New York is better than Silver Lake. They believe that there's truth in brick and verticality. New York says, *This is where it's at,* and they nod, awed. Collectively, Felix and Crane have spent six and a half days there.

The club's roving blue spotlight hits a posse of newcomers. "Is that what I think it is?" Crane leans in like she's whispering, but she's yelling over the music.

"A mullet," Felix confirms. "A real, live mullet." The woman is on the older end of the Sourpuss spectrum, in mailbox-blue jeans and a tucked-in T-shirt.

"Do you think it's retro?" Crane asks. Felix can see her brain trying to accommodate this oddity, the way if you saw an alien walking down the street, you might rationalize: costume party, film shoot.

Felix shakes her head, "Not with that outfit. It's gotta be the real thing."

"I hope she doesn't ask the DJ to play 'Achy-Breaky Heart,' " Crane giggles.

"It's 12:30!" Robbie exclaims. His roommates turn to look at him. He's squinting at his watch.

"Are you going to turn into a pumpkin?" Felix asks.

"Are you trying to distract us from our cattiness?" Crane laughs.

"No, we have to feed the meter," says Robbie, annoyed. "It expires in, like, two minutes."

"It is so oppressive that West Hollywood has 24-hour meters," grumbles Crane.

The cattiness and the vodka are making Felix a little queasy. "I'll go," she volunteers. "I could use some air."

She passes Billy Ray on the way out the back door. Felix brushes against her, the softness of the woman's upper arm touching her own arm.

Crane's yellow Volvo is parked on one of the side streets between Santa Monica Boulevard and Sunset, in the borderland between boystown and fratboystown. Felix hikes up the hill. The night air, chilled as a beer glass, bites at her cheeks.

Eva is here too, lurking behind manicured bushes outside Spanish-style cottages. Handing money to a homeless guy. Punching her code into the security gate outside an apartment building. Two old men pass Felix, speaking Russian, which makes her think of Europe, which makes her think of Eva.

She tries to step back and assess the situation rationally. Is she in one of those movies where two people are destined to be together but are kept apart for years as a result of wacky plot twists and tragic human flaws? Or is she in one of those movies where the girl is dumped by Mr.

Wrong early on—winning the audience's sympathy—only to free her up to find Mr. Right? If there were more gay movies out there, maybe she would know.

Here comes Eva again, trailing behind a broad-chested Sunset guy at the end of the block. When they get closer, Felix sees that this Eva is in fact a young man with blond surfer hair. Eva would appreciate the genderfuck, Felix thinks.

"Hey," says the more masculine of the two. He has centimeter-long brown hair and a tan that promises to turn cancerous by middle age. They probably thought she was checking them out.

"Hey," she says with a lips-no-teeth smile.

"Hey, are there any good clubs around here?" They're closer now, and they smell like college. Pabst Blue Ribbon. He flashes white teeth, and Felix pictures a toothpaste-commercial "ping!" accompanied by an animated sparkle emanating from his grin.

The only straight clubs Felix likes are in Silver Lake. These two would hate places like Good Luck Bar and Gabbah and Zombie Lounge. But maybe it's her mission to expand their horizons.

"If you keep going down Sunset—like, *way* past Dublin's—past where the neighborhood starts to seem kind of shady, there's this great little bar called First Base. It used to be a cop bar, back in the day, but now it's pretty cool. I guess *because* it used to be a cop bar, right? They have this one DJ—"

"You wanna come with us?" says the Guy Guy.

"Dude, we're not gonna drive," whines the Eva Guy. "How about somewhere around here?"

"All the straight bars around here suck," Felix says. She's feeling done with these two. She digs in her pocket for quarters. "Sorry, but you're on your own."

The Guy Guy takes a step closer. He is nearly a foot taller than her. She can see the stubble on his chin. Everything about him reminds her of meat. Felix is suddenly aware of her surroundings. They're on a dark skinny street, midway between Sunset and Santa Monica. An alley stretches off to her left. Crane's car gleams half a block away. The Eva outside the apartment building has long since turned in for the night. Felix clutches her purse and tries to keep looking bored.

"Dude, just look at her shoes. Those are dyke shoes," points out the Eva Guy. As if Felix is not there. Normally, she might wonder what kind of closet case analyzes women's fashions in this manner—but right now her heart is whirring too loudly in her ears.

"My buddy here really needs to get laid," says the Guy Guy. "How 'bout you do him a favor, just this once?"

"Shut up," laughs the Eva Guy. But he touches the strap of her tank top. The gesture is almost tender, like he plans to stick up for her. His fingers are thick and fumbling. *He is nothing like Eva. Nothing,* Felix thinks.

"I've got to go," she says. "My friends are waiting." She tries to step past them, but the Guy Guy is a mountain. The Eva Guy is a mountain lion, skittish and aggressive at the same time.

The Eva Guy grabs her wrist. Her bones are impossibly small beneath his grip.

"What the fuck!" Her voice is small. She doesn't know how to be intimidating, only ironic. She tries to twist free, but the Eva Guy's grip tightens. His friend steps in and pushes her against the cinderblock wall behind her.

"Who do you think you are?" the Guy Guy hisses, his breath potent and hot in her ear. She has no idea. Her back scrapes against the wall, her bare shoulders pinned. Her clothes are no help. They can't stand up to strong hands and cement. Her poodle purse slides to the ground with a clatter of lipstick and change.

She kicks. The steel toes of her boots hit shins, but her feet feel so heavy. She can't find the guys' groins, even as their square hips press against her pants.

A hand or a knee slams into her ribs. Her body is wracked with surprise. It wasn't made to bend this way, to take this.

She opens her mouth, and suddenly there's a tongue there. It's not hers.

"Dykes like tongue, right?" chuckles whichever guy is not choking her with his tongue.

Her own tongue crouches in the back of her throat. Hidden and useless. She should bite down, she half-thinks, but she's too shocked. All of this is so surprising. *No, you don't understand, I'm not—* she thinks. She's not what? Pabst Blue Ribbon mingles with ginger ale in her mouth. Then blood.

Teeth are biting her bottom lip. Her head knocks against the wall with a hollow thump. They are saying something, but they are saying it to Felix's clothes. She is elsewhere, floating, searching for the circus or for New York, her eyes landing on the street sign on the corner. It says Cynthia Street. She focuses on the font, the sound, white letters on blue background. Cynthia. If she can keep saying it, she will be okay.

The word creeps up from her stomach. Past the screaming pain in her ribcage, past the storm of alcohol in her throat. "Cynthia!" The scream bursts into the world.

"You are Cynthia? You are Cynthia?" repeats one of the Russian men she saw earlier. They are here, somehow, and Felix is back, sort of. She sits on the sidewalk, slumped against the brick wall. She pats her body to make sure it is here with her. The neck of her tank top is stretched and torn. The top button of her pants is undone, but the zipper remains zipped.

"I'm Felix," she whispers hoarsely. Is this even true?

The man's friend is further down the street. "You boys shoo!" he yells, as if they were cartoon birds eyeing a pie on a windowsill. Felix watches them flee. The Guy Guy has an uneven, duck-footed gait.

"They are bad boys," mutters the man closer to her. "You should not be out alone, a young good girl. My friend, he call doctor."

Felix nods. The man has wide flat cheeks and ice-blue eyes. He extends a hand to help her up. She takes it, and immediately recoils. His fingers are as rough as the Eva Guy's. She struggles to stand on her own.

When she hears the sirens as they get closer and closer, it seems like a coincidence that two bad things are happening on Cynthia Street tonight. Then she realizes the sirens are for her. When a police car appears at the top of the block, the Russian man says hurriedly, "I go now."

"Wait, you have to tell them—" Felix protests.

"My friend and me, we have no papers, you understand?"

"Papers?"

"Polizia, they send us back, you understand?" he says quickly, moving away from her.

Slowly, Felix does. She has no strength to fight him. To fight anyone. He follows his friend down the alley, two more broad male backs in retreat.

Sitting in an emergency room bed, Felix listens as Dr. Julia Muto lists her injuries: cracked rib, lacerated tongue, strained neck, non-concussive bump on her head, slightly abraded skin on her shoulders and arms.

"That's all?" Felix says. It feels like more.

"We should be glad that's all," says Dr. Muto brightly. She has a swingy black ponytail, and entirely too much bedside manner.

"Are you sure she wasn't raped?" Crane demands. A nurse called Crane's cell phone, then Felix's parents, who are now on their way up from Hermosa Beach. "That's how hate crimes work, you know. Assholes like those goddamn cracker fratboy homophobes always have to fuck someone. She might have blacked out. She might have already repressed her memories." Crane is a firecracker of rage and color in the sterile room.

"I should have gone with you to the meter," Robbie laments. He touches her forearm so lightly she can barely feel it.

"Nah," Felix says over her fat lip. It's all she can muster.

There are too many people in the room. Crane, Robbie, Dr. Muto, a nurse, and two West Hollywood sheriff's deputies. All looking at her, still in her torn clothes, lipstick smeared around her face. Messy and broken.

The deputies had plenty of time to quiz her in the Cedars-Sinai waiting room, as heart attacks and strokes and a seizing baby cut in front of her. One of the cops is so tall and blond that it's hard to believe he's the real thing, not a stripper ready to handcuff a bachelorette. The other is a compact Latino man with a hooked nose. He speaks slowly and earnestly, as if he is choosing each word from a textbook. They take turns making her tell the story, again and again, as they scrawl words in skinny notebooks. Clubs. Parking meter. Tank top. Of all the stories in Felix's head, this is the last one she wants to tell. Can't she talk about her road trip to San Francisco last summer? Her idea for a music magazine column called *The Jaded Raver?*

Deputy Salvatierra turns to his partner. "You'd better call Windus." To Felix he says, "We have a special Hate Crimes unit. But I'll level with you. If we're going to pursue this as a hate crime, there needs to be some suggestion that the individuals assaulted you because you are gay. And it doesn't help that the two witnesses also fled, although we'll try to track them down. Now," he looks at his notes, "we already determined that your wallet was missing from your purse shortly after the individuals fled the scene."

Felix has no recollection of either guy reaching into her purse, but when the officers suggested she inspect its contents in the waiting room, her wallet was indeed gone.

"Is there a chance that this could have been a robbery?" Deputy Salvatierra asks.

"I don't know," Felix says, "I don't know." She can't get enough air in her lungs. She doesn't know if that's a result of her cracked ribcage or the bandage that corsets it.

"*Look,*" says Crane. She thumps her pink cast against the tile floor. "It's not like people say, 'I'm going to go rob someone, but I'm going to really respect their sexual orientation.' Or, 'I'm going to go commit a hate crime, but when the chick's wallet falls on the ground, I'm going to let her keep her money.' "

The deputies circle and circle. The nurse gives her a pill. People begin to slide away. Dr. Muto's voice chirps on, but Felix stops listening. At the foot of the bed, there is a folk art print of multicultural children holding hands. Lederhosen next to kimono next to some kind of Rastafarian poncho. The last thing Felix thinks before she falls asleep is, *What a bunch of bullshit.*

Moments later, someone is nudging her awake. The nurse's face is inches away. Pink plastic beads click at the ends of her black braids. "You have to wake up, you sleep too long." She has an accent, maybe Caribbean. "We need this bed. Your mama take you home."

Her body creaks when she tries to move it. Felix can't quite turn her head to look around the room, but she sees that the nurse is right. Her parents are both here, two worried faces at the foot of her bed. Her friends are long gone.

"Oh, Felix, honey," her mother, Suzy Ketay, whispers. Her dyed brown-blonde hair sticks out at odd angles. Martin Ketay blows on a cup of coffee.

They help her to her feet. Dr. Muto breezes in, hands her a prescription and some instructions and takes off again, smiling like it's not four in the morning.

"I don't get to stay the night?" Felix slurs. Her tongue takes up too much space in her mouth, making her sound drunk.

Her father scratches his beard with his free hand the way he always does when he's annoyed. "I thought this was supposed to be a good hospital, but obviously they're cutting corners just like everyone else. Someone's going to hear from me about this." His arm still around Felix's shoulders, he looks around for who this person might be.

"Where am I supposed to go?" Felix whimpers.

"Home," Suzy Ketay says with forced brightness. She sounds like she's doing a bad impression of Dr. Muto. "First we'll stop somewhere and fill this prescription, though."

Felix doesn't know which home her mother means. Her apartment or the house where she grew up in Hermosa Beach. Both places seem wrong. The hospital does too, with its too-bright lights and freeway-loud hallways, but now that she's being kicked out, she wants to stay. She could find a small white space and crouch there forever.

But now her parents are leading her to the street. Her mother's blue nylon tracksuit crinkles as they walk. The sky is too tall out here. Every step hurts. Getting in their big Ford Explorer, which she has always referred to as The Smogmobile, requires an act of contortion. Her father drives too fast and honks at every other car between Cedars-Sinai and the Koreatown Walgreen's. Felix's stomach lurches. She lays down in the backseat while her father sprints toward the drugstore.

Her mother twists around to face her and says what she has probably been waiting all night to say. "I *told* you L.A. wasn't safe."

"Mom. Not L.A., West *Hollywood*." Her side aches at the emphasis. "Do you know what that means? I mean, like, about the world?"

Her question is only half rhetorical. If what happened tonight (last night?) can happen in West Hollywood, where is she supposed to hang out? In college she read essays about how the whole world was a construct, a big lie everyone told themselves to cover up the fact that the only truth was that there was no truth. It sounded glistening and mysterious, a conspiracy theory. Felix would trip out for a while, then close her course reader and go sing Spanish karaoke with Jia Li at a semi-scary bar on Hollywood Boulevard. They'd stop at In-N-Out for hamburgers-sans-burgers on the way home, and sometimes they would see movie stars there. All of this, too, seemed to have something to do with postmodernism. She wasn't sure what because she didn't read that carefully.

But tonight (or last night), her big, colorful adventure turned sour and real and unbearably old. She's been sentenced to walk the dangerous streets of a land that is suddenly as foreign as a dream.

Suzy answers Felix's question. "It means I have to worry about you! I *already* worry about you. I know you won't even consider coming home and staying with us—I know that would be horribly 'uncool'—"

"Mom, I'm not in sixth grade. I'm not really worried about looking uncool." Although Felix does feel very uncool at the moment. Her head and neck throb, and all she can see from the car window is a billboard inviting Korean people to move to Valencia.

"So won't you reconsider what I said about visiting your aunt?"

This has been a running theme of their conversations for nearly a year. Suzy wants Felix to spend time with Anna Lisa, who ran away from home at 19 to go be a dyke in some town in the elbow of California. Felix usually responds by accusing her mother of thinking that all lesbians are the same.

"Just for a couple of weeks," Suzy persists. "You'll make her so happy. Lilac Mines is one of those safe, sleepy little towns. Nothing ever happens there."

"Exactly!"

"Someone needs to help you change the dressing on your wounds," Suzy continues. Felix hates the words 'dressing' and 'wound.' It makes her sound like a Civil War casualty. "And who better than your Aunt Anna Lisa? She's a nurse, for goodness sake."

"Fine," she says. "I'll think about it."

She does not think about it. She does her best not to think about any of it. As soon as she can, she goes back to work. Her regular doctor, whom she has actually only seen once before, insists that she wear a hideous plastic-and-foam neck brace.

"I think maybe I should do a write-up of the summer's hottest medical accessories," Felix tells her editor, Renee Salt. "This would be just below 'colostomy bag.' " She is wearing a loose embroidered blouse, but the bandage around her ribs makes her feel fat.

"God, Felix, you shouldn't joke about that stuff," says Renee. She purses her fuchsia (magenta?) lips in concern. "What happened to you was really terrible. I hope you know how terrible we all feel about it."

Felix wants to tell her that she just used "terrible" twice in one breath. When Jessi Menaster, the West Coast photo editor, got a nose job last winter, it wasn't nearly this awkward. Felix wishes she could tell them she was mugged instead. That would be very New York. But Crane called Renee the Monday after the attack and relayed every detail. Felix realizes that, until now, being out at work has meant being lesbian-chic. She wore leather wrist cuffs before anyone else did. Now she's A Lesbian, a victim in a neck brace, and no one knows what to do with her, not even Felix herself.

When she goes to the break room at lunch, Jessi Menaster and an editorial assistant named Shana are making fun of an actress's dress at a recent awards show.

"She looked like a birthday cake," Jessi is saying. She is tall and slim, and always wears black pants and perfectly pressed, button-down shirts.

"Or a porn star," Shana says. "The star of, like, *Bedtime for Boobsy*."

"Oh my God, Shana, you are so fucking hilarious. Sometimes I wish we weren't such a classy magazine. Then we could publish comments like that."

When they see Felix, they clam up.

"Hey, Felix," Shana says sheepishly. "Sorry."

"For what?" It's not like they were making fun of her. Do they think that she's too pathetic to have fun now?

"Um, just, I don't know..." Shana trails off.

Felix feels her face turn red above the neck brace. She leans into the refrigerator. Her sack lunch is right in front of her, but she huddles in the cool air as long as she can. She wants to tell them that blood, when it is in your mouth, does not taste scarlet or crimson or carmine. It tastes metallic and evil. But, of course, they don't want to know this. Maybe that's why they don't want to talk to her.

After eating by herself, she slouches down in her cubicle, as far as her neck brace and bandage-bustier will permit. She wishes she could call Eva. Eva would be fired up, ready to litigate. Felix doesn't know which hurts more, the persistent ache of her ribcage, or the ache inside it.

She tries to fact-check a piece on platform sandals, but her mind wanders, and soon she's searching the Internet for flights to New York.

SQUARES
Anna Lisa: Fresno, 1965

Anna Lisa climbs the ladder to the attic store room above Hill Food & Supply expecting to find what she always finds: crates of canned goods and complete silence, except for the train whistle she hardly hears anymore. When she and her sister Suzy were little, they thought the room was haunted, and somehow Anna Lisa assumed Suzy was still afraid. It wasn't hard for Anna Lisa to claim the space as her own, since no one else wanted it.

But today there is a red wool hat bobbing up and down between the window and a box of stewed tomato tins. And there is moaning. *A ghost?* Anna Lisa thinks. Oddly, the thought doesn't frighten her. She could use some company.

The voice that says, "Oh God. Goodness," however, is Suzy's. Self-correcting, demure after the fact. "Anna Lisa, what—" Suzy sits up and pulls the hat further down on her head, even before checking to see whether her white sundress is covering the parts of her body it should be covering. Even before glancing at the moaning ghost next to her, a disheveled boy Anna Lisa vaguely remembers as Kevin Zacky. He was a sophomore when she was a senior, a kid whose white-toothed yearbook picture preceded him. He looks far less confident now.

Suddenly the frozen Kevin Zacky and the flustered Suzy switch roles. He becomes a flurry of movement, as if executing a play on the football field, and she stares at Anna Lisa from beneath the brim of her hat. He mumbles his way to the end zone—the square of light above the ladder—and disappears. Anna Lisa hears herself ask, "Why are you wearing a hat?"

"Why are you *here*?" shoots Suzy, as if the attic is hers.

And it is, Anna Lisa realizes. The way Suzy leans against the splintery wall with just the right amount of caution gives her away. She's been coming here for a while. Her sweat and perfume fill the air like tea in water.

"This is my—" Anna Lisa begins, but it sounds stupid. "I was going to read," she says. It sounds like an apology. She makes sure the back of the book is facing out, the cover tight against her chest. "Things were slow at the store."

Suzy pulls the hat off her head. Her blonde-brown hair, previously prone to schoolgirl braids and the occasional Swiss Miss crown, now stops abruptly just below her ears. Hence the hat in the 95-degree heat. For the first time, Anna Lisa notices her sister's delicate shoulders, the naive pout of her chin.

"Please don't tell Mother and Daddy," Suzy says.

"About your hair or the boy? Because they're going to notice the hair."

"About Kevin, obviously. Oh goodness, Nannalee, what am I going to do?" Anna Lisa hasn't heard Suzy's childhood nickname for her in years. She wants to melt into it, to protect Suzy from attic ghosts. But the girl in front of her is two severed braids away from Anna Lisa's help. She's suspected it since Suzy graduated in June. As her classmates got engaged and packed for college, Suzy began to stand taller. She started polishing her shoes. She stopped singing along (badly) to the radio, and started dancing to the songs instead—better and better, more hips and winks in front of their bedroom mirror. And the boys whose girlfriends were away at school picked up on her scent and edged toward their house, a phone call here, a slow-driving Chevrolet there.

The haircut proves it. Suzy's life is dynamic and sexual. Anna Lisa takes it personally. They've never quite been close, but people tend to confuse the two of them, or lump them together, which is almost the same thing. The Hill Girls. Squares with B- averages and home-cut hair. You can find them behind the counter at their parents' store; they're not going anywhere. Except now Suzy is. It wasn't until Suzy's graduation that Anna Lisa realized that she herself had not "just graduated." She was 19, two years into the so-called real world.

"Well," Anna Lisa considers, "do you like him?"

"I do... Not as much as Roy, though."

"Roy?"

"You know, with the white Buick, the convertible? He works at the real estate office. He says Fresno is due for a boom." Suzy glows. Her life is a convertible.

"Then why were you... with Kevin?" Anna Lisa blushes, as if it were her indiscretion.

"I don't know, I just... oh God, I'm awful, aren't I? I seem to like whoever I'm with. Not who*ever*, but, well, I keep thinking that it will all sort itself out. *Please* don't tell Mother and Dad," she repeats. This is her most urgent concern. This is what she wants from Anna Lisa more than advice on her over-popularity problem.

"Fine," Anna Lisa says curtly. "I'm not six years old, you know. I'm not some tattle-tale."

From there, they retreat to the safe territory of haircuts. Their mother came of age during the Depression and cannot imagine why anyone with a pair of scissors and a mirror would pay a stranger to do the job. Suzy skipped the Lovely Dove, she tells Anna Lisa, for fear of seeing someone who knew Eudora Hill, and ventured across town to Lola Felix's Beauty Shoppe.

"I think she was a Mexican," Suzy whispers. "But it was amazing. She was so kind. I just love saying it, *Lo-la Fee-lix*. And her fingers in my hair during the shampoo part... glorious!"

It's several days before Anna Lisa is alone again with her book. She surprises herself by feigning illness and skipping church.

"Poor dear," says Eudora Hill, pausing as she fastens her pearl necklace. "And the day we're planning the picnic, too." Her expression tells Anna Lisa this is something she should be sad to miss. Anna Lisa wishes she liked the things she was supposed to like. *The first time I saw your father, in his crisp white shirt....* Eudora has told them the story many times. How she met Gerald Hill at the annual Fresno Presbyterian picnic. Anna Lisa knows she will never find love at a church picnic, no matter how much she loves cold fried chicken, no matter how starched the boys' shirts are. For her mother's sake she tries to be disappointed.

Her parents tell her to drink plenty of orange juice, and leave with Suzy, who looks as wholesome and sinful as a white orchid in her blouse and skirt. Despite the fact that Anna Lisa has the house to herself, she does not feel safe. The old farmhouse sits in the middle of fallow fields (lettuce or wheat once grew there, depending who you listen to) without a single tree to provide shade.

Anna Lisa settles for the west corner of the room she shares with Suzy. She unfolds the pink nylon nightgown that one of her spinster aunts gave her for Christmas. It shimmered in the sentimental tree-light, but now it just seems flammable. From its pink yards, Anna Lisa rescues her book. Beneath "Valerie Taylor, Author of WHISPER THEIR LOVE," red block letters announce "THE GIRLS IN 3-B." Beneath that, the girls: the jaded blonde with the cigarette watching the brunette in the black slip pull on a stocking, and the girl with her back to the reader. Anna Lisa likes her best. She has wavy black hair and is about to pull off her sweater. The pale valley of her back shows, just a few inches.

Since buying the book at Secondhand Sam's—her heart pounding as Sam scrawled the receipt she would immediately shred—Anna Lisa has not read more than the back cover. She knows that the story takes place in Greenwich Village. Apartment 3-B, apparently, contains a number of potted ferns and windows that the girls don't bother closing when lounging about in their lingerie. Maybe that's how it is in Greenwich Village, which Anna Lisa thinks is in New York or London. She will wait to see whether "favorite" is spelled with a U. Apartment 3-B looks cramped—the girls may even share a bed—but somehow it is the most spacious place Anna Lisa has seen. A place where things happen. She logs the necessary ingredients for such a life: a tall building, a possibly-velvet bedspread, ferns. Fresno has none of these things. Only whores have velvet bedspreads, Anna Lisa can hear her mother saying. Are the girls in 3-B whores?

She doesn't know what she'll do if it turns out she is just like them— a girl who could fall for her own roommates. If their red-lettered desires are just like hers, whatever hers are. And she doesn't know what she'll do if the girls of 3-B are nothing like her.

The book is dog-eared, its spine creased to the point that the title is almost obscured. Who else has read this book? Everyone she knows is upstanding; their outer lives mirror their inner lives, Anna Lisa is sure of it. She corrects herself: Suzy has proven capable of rebellion, and she wears it like a new dress.

Maybe there is a way. Anna Lisa opens the book. But before she can even find out what the girls' names are, her gaze is snagged by a black splotch in the middle of the page. When she flips to page two, she sees its cause. A large square of ink has taken up residence over the third paragraph. Nervously, she fans through the pages. Black square after black square jumps out until it's like a flipbook, a cartoon about a dancing box. The girls of 3-B are lost, a blur of text.

Her stomach clenches. The crossed-out passages confirm what she is: a pervert who dared to wonder what was underneath. The strength of her wanting has revealed her to herself, more than if the main girl were named Anna Lisa and had thick brown hair and loved strawberry ice cream.

The doorbell rings. Her parents! Anna Lisa becomes a tidal wave of obliteration, clapping the cover shut, smothering the book with the nightgown and plunging the bundle into the hamper in one movement. She will erase, she will deny.

She pounds down the stairs, not realizing until she opens the door and sees Roy that her parents have no reason to ring the doorbell.

"Hi," he says. His hands are in the pockets of brown dress slacks. He extracts one to raise his palm. "Anna Lisa, right? We were in the same geometry class. Three years ago, can you believe it?"

Boys blend together for Anna Lisa. Roy could have been in her geometry class. Circles and parallelograms dance in her head.

"Uh, is Suzy around?" Roy wants to know. His Buick is a stretched-out summer cloud in their driveway. Roy is a sky-blue boy who likes a flower-pink girl.

"No, she's at church. I stayed home. I'm sick." She says it too quickly. She thinks, *I'm sick.*

"Okay, well, tell her I stopped by." Roy returns to his cloud and floats off down the gravel road.

Anna Lisa makes her decision in the dark. A twin bed away from her, Suzy's silhouette breathes up and down, a girl unafraid of her dreams. In the wicker hamper, the book waits. The shades of 3-B are shut tight, and Anna Lisa suspects this makes the girls sad. More than worrying that the book might be found, she begins to think of it as a lost puppy. She will rescue it, find it a home.

She puts her bare feet on the rag rug. The floor conspires with her, squeak-less, as if she were a ghost moving across the room. Mining her way through Suzy's deflated church clothes and her own moist socks, Anna Lisa's hands hit gold. As soon as she picks it up, she lets out a deep sigh.

But where will the book be happy? Greenwich Village? She likes the sound of this, a green witch specializing in something wilder than black or white magic. Even if she knew where this magical village was, though, she doesn't have the money to get there. San Francisco is not so impossibly far away. She thinks of fog, bridges. They went there on a family vacation when she was little—she remembers cold wind. This appeals to her, the opposite of Fresno stillness, where the scent of onions lolls in the air for days after a harvest. She remembers the immense, frightening ocean and the sea lions that played there. *I will be a sea lion,* Anna Lisa thinks.

Before the sun can rise and convince her otherwise, Anna Lisa packs. The suitcase is half Suzy's, but she imagines her parents will replace it. Suzy will get married and they'll buy their good daughter a set of matched luggage for her honeymoon. There's surprisingly little to take. Thin gauze of dress, arc of shoe. It's as if she barely existed until now.

HUNGRY, HOMELESS, NEED A JOB?
Felix: Lilac Mines, 2002

Felix pictured a train station reunion. Somehow she would acquire a steamer trunk. The tracks would lead to Lilac Mines, a town of 2,000 on the eastern edge of Calaveras County. Anna Lisa would greet her with a doughy, dykey hug, and before long Felix would admit her mother was right: they *did* have a lot in common.

After perusing New York apartment listings online, Felix quickly realized there was no way to move there without a job or a hefty student loan. And as much as she tries not to fall for stereotypes, the thought of living in a city known for muggings terrifies her now. All Lilac Mines has going for it, really, is that it's not L.A., but she's determined to make the best of it. Somehow, her aunt will transform her from a middle class girl in an overpriced peasant blouse into a back-alley wrestler, passionate enough to do real damage with her steel-toed boots.

But Felix's journey has been an endless stretch of chaparral punctuated by gas stations masquerading as towns. Not even the *Best Road Trip Compilation in the World* (as Robbie labeled the CD spinning in her car stereo) can glamorize the 7-Elevens and Burger Kings.

 She insisted on driving herself, despite her mother's protests. She crammed a summer's worth of clothes into her baby blue New Beetle, and pasted a rainbow sticker on the bumper. She used to think they were lame, but she's feeling militant at the moment. Nevertheless, every time another car tails her too closely, she worries her car's ass has offended him. When she stops for gas, she looks around nervously.

The neck brace is gone, thank God, but her ribs are still bound and painful, and she moves stiffly. Still, it feels good to be out on her own. Eva won't be the only one to spend her summer traveling. Felix has had enough of hovering, too-nice roommates and coworkers and doctors, and sheriff's deputies who never have anything new to report. Felix described her attackers—again—to a hate crimes specialist and to a sketch artist, who drew two beautifully detailed portraits of two generic looking white men. Her words were so inadequate (blond, brown, straight nose... no, his eyebrows weren't like that). If she spoke the same words to a different artist, a completely different person would appear on the page. And yet she knows she would recognize either guy in an instant.

Lilac Mines erupts out of nothing. The skyline promises snowcapped mountains, but the town begins in yellow foothills, as if to get a running start before climbing the mountain, which it does, impressively. She studies her map, printed from the Internet. It seems funny that the Internet and Lilac Mines know about each other, but look, there between the Gold Rush Tavern and Nugget Gifts, a sign that says "Internet Café, Cappuccino." As if there might be a cafe that does *not* have cappuccino on its menu. Felix quickly surmises that this is Lilac Mines: one foot in the Gold Rush and one in 1997.

She clutches the print-out. Her hands are chilled from the car's air conditioning, her armpits are sweaty. She hopes the map will not lie to her.

But the meandering, pixely lines don't match up with the roads unfolding in front of her. She's supposed to be on North Main Street, but the signs say West Main Street, suggesting an entirely different orientation. Is this like Little Santa Monica and Big Santa Monica, something only locals know? Is the key to her map trapped in an oral history?

Felix punches Anna Lisa's number into her cell phone. In the weeks Felix spent planning the trip—quitting her job, subletting her room, shopping to the point of numbness, emailing Eva and not getting a reply—she and her aunt spoke on the phone twice. Short, cordial conversations. Felix told herself that it would be different in person.

Anna Lisa picks up in the middle of her own recorded voice. "Sorry, I was gardening," she says, slightly out of breath. Felix is somehow surprised that her aunt's day had substance prior to Felix's arrival.

"Sorry to bug you, but I think I'm a little lost," Felix says.

"You're what?" The phone crackles and skips.

"Lost!"

"Where are you?"

"West Main and, uh..." She cranes her neck to look for a sign. "Inga Lunaris Road? Who's Inga Lunaris? The map says I'm supposed to be on North Main."

"There are two Mains," Anna Lisa says. "I know, it's strange. The north-south one used to be called—" Her voice sputters out, and Felix can only catch dashes of words.

"HOW DO I GET TO YOUR PLACE?" Felix shouts.

Anna Lisa talks her through it, with much repetition. She turns left at the intersection of Main and Main, passing an art deco theater with a marquee that reads: "JUNE: LATE NIGHT CATECHISM, AUGUST: LOVE LETTERS, EVERY SATURDAY: GOLDRUSH MELODRAMA." She supposes that *Gold Rush Melodrama* is to Lilac Mines what *Rocky Horror* is to the indie theater on (Big) Santa Monica Boulevard. North Main propels her uphill. Usually, driving a stick shift makes Felix feel tough. Now she hopes she won't roll into the mud-freckled truck behind her.

On the right side of North Main, there is dust. Thick, Steinbeck-style dust turns the bald half of the hillside into a sepia picture: small brown houses, trailers, structures that appear to be frozen on the verge of collapse. The other side of the street is like a giant Christmas tree lot. Some of the pines grow straight up out of white desert sand, as if they don't need water or soil or any of the things that trees need. And as her gaze travels west, the mountain turns a preppy green. Lush and still as a wall calendar.

Anna Lisa's house is just a few blocks into the green side of town. Like the other houses on Juliet Street, it's a sort of a modern cabin. The structures Felix passes are naturally colored and pimped out with uncabin-like amenities: satellite dishes, air conditioning boxes, mail boxes built to match the homes. Felix is thankful that Anna Lisa has limited her decorations to a "Beware of Dog" sign and a bush of yellow flowers. In the window, a motley row of purple glass bottles do their best to shimmer in the 6 p.m. sunlight.

Gripping the smaller of her suitcases and fighting her fluttering stomach, Felix knocks.

The sound of furious barking makes Felix snap her hand away from the door. Anna Lisa opens it with one hand, wrestling a black standard poodle with the other.

"*Stay*, Coal," she says sternly. The dog reluctantly obliges.

Her aunt's hug is light, but it still aggravates Felix's bruises. Afterward, Anna Lisa stands in the doorway for a nervous moment. She's wearing jeans that hug her sizeable hips, a T-shirt advertising "Lilac Mines Festival 1997."

"You're here," she says. "That was fast." She has that lesbian voice, not quite deep but flat where a gay man's would be punctuated and italicized. "Well, uh, come in. Dinner's almost ready."

She shows Felix to the sparse guest room at the back of the house. There is a bookcase stocked with gardening books, and a twin bed. Felix turns in a slow circle, the dog's black eyes following her. She feels like she's standing in a museum, in an installation called something like, "Anonymous Slept Here." She unpacks her hats and shoes and hurries to rejoin Anna Lisa in the kitchen.

Her aunt removes a pot roast from the oven with lobster-shaped mitts.

"Wow, check those out," Felix says.

"From a student," Anna Lisa explains. Felix remembers that she's a nurse at an elementary school. *The* elementary school, Felix supposes.

The pot roast sits in the pan, a big brown lump steaming angrily. Felix can't believe anyone still eats pot roast. Even her mother makes things like chicken-and-black-bean burritos. Even her friends on all-protein diets eat cheeseburgers wrapped in lettuce. Disgusting and cruel, but contemporary.

Actually, the pot roast smells delicious. Heavy and savory, carrots and onions swimming in gravy. It smells like her childhood, which takes her by surprise. She sees the old black and gold linoleum, the plates bordered with rosebuds. There must have been pre-burrito days, she realizes. What other dishes have been lost?

Unlike many of her fellow vegetarians, who claim that a sip of chicken broth will make them ill, Felix loves the smell of bacon and fish sticks and, apparently, pot roast. She eats so many veggie burgers and pseudo-sausages and fake McNuggets that she occasionally forgets that other burgers and sausages and nuggets are made out of real dead animals. She has nearly ordered them from menus by accident. There's relatively little process involved in pot roast, however. There's no forgetting here.

"Um, Aunt Anna Lisa, that looks great, but—well, I don't know if my mom mentioned that I'm a vegetarian?" She's not sure why this should be her mom's job, but that seems right. Grown-ups feed, kids eat.

"Oh. Well, shit." If Anna Lisa were Felix's mother, this is the part where she'd apologize and offer to grill up a cheese sandwich. Anna Lisa just stands there thinking, lobsters on hips. "There's one health food kind of place in town, but they close early on Sundays. Could you find something to eat at a lunch counter-type joint?"

"Sure, yeah, no problem," Felix says eagerly. Anna Lisa is butch in that older-woman way. Short hair, the same brown as Felix's, clothes you could change a tire in. You can't quite tell if she's fucking with gender or is just fed up with pantyhose. And really, should anyone have to wear pantyhose more than five or six times in a lifetime? Felix wants to make her aunt feel as comfortable as white-kneed jeans would, even as she wants to be the newcomer in moon boots, footwear no one here is advanced enough to understand.

The lunch counter place has a tin ceiling, a dark-wood-and-marble soda fountain and, Felix counts, 32 wall-mounted signs saying things like, "Hungry, Homeless, Need a Job? Call the Sierra Club & ask about Their no-growth Policy." Felix bristles at the sentiment and the sloppy capitalization. Over a bowl of limp spaghetti Felix asks her aunt, "What are the politics like here?" She's learned to call the red parts of the map "fly-over territory." That way she can dismiss them before they can hate her.

Anna Lisa shrugs. "Like anywhere, I guess. A little of everything."

The shelves behind the counter where they sit are stocked with canned soup and different types of ore, labeled with kindergarten-teacher handwriting. Silver. Gold. Copper. It's hard to tell what's for sale and what's not. What Felix meant was, *How are you a lesbian here?*

The only other person here is the waitress, who leans against the soda case, smoking. Felix is pretty sure that's illegal, but she's not about to call her on it. She looks older than she is, 40 going on 50. She has stringy orange hair and penciled-in eyebrows. She watches them, and Felix tells herself that the woman is probably just bored. Still, it makes her nervous. Now that the rules have changed, anyone might turn on her—say something that will cut into her, pull her down a dark alley.

Felix says, "That dog of yours wasn't very happy to see me," meaning, *Why do you have a poodle when you're so butch?* And, *But* you're *happy to see me, right?*

"Coalie? Oh, he's not as bad as he sounds. Or as goofy as he looks. He's great at hunting mice, and he chases rabbits out of the yard. He's smart, too. I got him at the shelter when he was six weeks old, this little fluff-ball. No one knew where he came from."

The dog conversation runs out quickly, and Anna Lisa seems content to sit there eating her cheeseburger. Forks clink against plates. The noise reminds Felix of movies about unhappy families. She wants to make pithy comments about the plaques on the wall, but what if Anna Lisa *does* hate the Sierra Club? They haven't talked about the attack. Suzy told Anna Lisa, but when Felix and her aunt talked directly, they spoke of the trip as if it were strictly a vacation. Felix doesn't know what to say. Her questions are too big, and she feels tiny, ignorant. A stupid Red Riding Hood who spent too much time talking to wolves about nightclubs.

"I'm thinking of going to New York after this," Felix volunteers.

"After this?"

"After, you know, after staying with you for a while. I'm going to send away for some applications to fashion design programs and apply at the end of the summer."

Anna Lisa brandishes a pickle spear. "So you could use the free room and board, and the peace and quiet?"

"I didn't mean it like that," Felix says hurriedly. No-bullshit people scare Felix. They seem capable of anything. And Anna Lisa is proving to be a no-bullshit lady. Felix *likes* a little bullshit; she likes her conversations safe and accessorized.

After another pause, Anna Lisa says, "You healing okay?"

Felix swallows. "I'm still kind of sore. Really sore, actually. And I think this thing on my lip is going to leave a scar, but, yeah, I'm okay."

As soon as she says it, though, her eyes fill up with tears. Before she can put her crumpled napkin to her face, they spill over, and she's making gulping sounds that echo throughout the store. Is it her imagination, or does the waitress roll her eyes?

"It's freaking me out," she admits between sobs. She glances at the waitress and lowers her voice. "I thought those times were over. I mean, maybe not in, like, Wyoming, but at least in West Hollywood. Every place I go in L.A. reminds me of my ex-girlfriend, and now, to top things off, I'm looking over my shoulder all the time for guys with baseball bats."

"They had bats?" Anna Lisa raises an eyebrow.

"No, but...." She's avoided talking about any of it with her roommates and coworkers, but with Anna Lisa, it all comes rushing out. She wants her aunt to see the attack as a badge of courage. She wants to fall into her arms and be saved. "I was trying to be useful! I was suggesting some good clubs to go to, and then they just turned on me."

"Yeah, well, people do rotten things," Anna Lisa mutters uncomfortably. She squints at something outside of the window. "Don't try to be useful, that's my advice."

Felix nods. She feels like she's just been kneed in the stomach again. When Felix catches her breath after an interminable awkward silence, she throws out a new topic. "When was the last time you were in L.A.? I must have been six or seven."

"You were pretty little. Leigan wasn't even born yet, and Michelle was potty training, I remember." Felix's sisters, now a freshman at Caltech and a hostess at a pseudo-French restaurant, respectively. "Your poor mother was so frazzled. You were in your button stage." Anna Lisa wipes mustard from her hands with a thin paper napkin.

"My button stage?" Felix rubs her eyes.

"Mm-hmm. You would only wear clothes with buttons. The bigger and more colorful, the better. You had a little shirt with plastic, whale-shaped buttons that you wanted to wear every single day. And Suzy just about tore her hair out trying to get you to wear elastic-waistband pants."

"Really? I don't remember that at all. Buttons?"

"Number-shaped buttons, fake pearl buttons, you name it. You were an obsessive kid, that's what your mom always said. When you were in fifth grade or so, she wrote me about how you were obsessed with the *Titanic*. Every report you did for school had to be about the *Titanic*. You wanted to change your name to Molly Brown."

Slowly, it comes back to Felix. She used to lie awake thinking about how terrible and romantic it would be to lie at the bottom of the sea. She didn't know that her mother thought she was "obsessive," though. But now that she thinks about it, there were other phases. When she was in seventh grade, girls started greeting their friends in the hallway with dramatic hugs instead of shy smiles. Felix would keep a tally— small and coded in the back of her notebook—of how many hugs she could accumulate from popular girls in a given day. Her record was 13. In college, long before it dawned on her that she might be a dyke, she became obsessed with gay male culture: dance music, drag queen fashions, anything ironic. It seemed a tad pathological in retrospect. Felix is embarrassed to discover that these passionately adhered-to trends were, apparently, a lifelong pattern. "Well," she says breezily, "I'm just Felix now. Not Molly Brown."

"And I'm just Anna Lisa." She peers into Felix's half-empty bowl. "Are you all finished?"

Why is she in such a hurry to leave? Trying not to sound insulted, Felix says, "Sure, I guess."

"You can take longer if you want."

"No, no, it's fine."

They wait in silence for the waitress to put out her cigarette and give them the bill.

Coal has a vet appointment Monday afternoon, and Anna Lisa asks Felix to drive the poodle to Lilac Mines Elementary, where Anna Lisa is on duty for summer day camp. Then they'll all go to the vet together. Felix would like to be treated as a bit more of a guest, but she tries to pretend that this is Europe and she is one of those travelers who forgoes snapping pictures in front of the Eiffel Tower for picking grapes at a vineyard with locals and fellow adventurers, the ones who want the *real* experience. Eva could be tangled in vines right now, scratches on her arms, Frenchmen flirting with her. Germany is a beer country, but if Kate's on tour, they could have moved on.

Eva, I know you made your decision. You made that really clear, Felix emailed before she left. *Not to get all psychobabble on you, but I need some closure—can you just write back and let me know how you're doing? As for me, some crazy shit has been going down. If there's any way that you could give me a call, that would be cool.*

She hit "send" and the message zipped into the abyss, along with her where-are-yous and her what-is-it-about-Kates and her do-you-think-there's-a-chances. The arc of her breakup floats somewhere in cyberspace.

In this case the "real experience" involves chasing Coal, who wants to play with a chewed-up tennis ball, around the house until she can lasso him with a nylon leash. Coal looks like a dog who would relish riding in a Volkswagen, but he growls and twists and distracts. By the time he's inside, he's covered in dust, as are Felix's silver-studded jeans.

The school looks like most schools, gray and fortress-like, and Felix feels her outsider status acutely among the waist-high children jumping rope and greeting parents. She's drawn to the one unique feature of the donut-shaped campus, the one-room schoolhouse in the middle of the schoolyard. Maybe because it's older than her. A bronze plaque announces that this is the original Lilac Mines School, built in 1881. But a length of chicken wire stretched across the schoolhouse's sagging porch tells her that this bit of history is for looking, not touching.

"I never knew there would be so much *paperwork* in divorce," an older woman's voice is saying. Felix rounds the corner of the nurse's office and finds a big woman in an honest-to-God muumuu talking to her aunt. A wispy little boy sits on the bed across the room, gnawing on the pale pink sheet. Anna Lisa is refilling a jar of Q-Tips. The smell of rubbing alcohol makes Felix queasy.

"You hear about 'divorce papers.' You hear people say, 'I got the final divorce papers' and you think, y'know, it's just a *symbol*," the woman booms. Her thin hair is pulled into a tight bun that seems to anger the rest of her head. "You figure they're really happy or sad about their divorce. But it's not true, Anna Lisa, it really is the paper that makes you sad, the paper that makes you happy when it's the last one. You know your marriage is over long before anyone says 'divorce,' so all that's left to torture you is paper, paper, *paper!*" She throws up her flabby arms in a gesture Felix finds embarrassing.

Anna Lisa looks up from her cotton swabs and sees Felix and Coal. "Blanca, this is my niece, up from L.A. till Halloween. Felix, this is Blanca Randall. And her grandson, Telly."

"Telly's in a little bit of *trouble*," Blanca stage-whispers. She winks, but Felix doesn't know what the joke is. She does not want to be complicit with Blanca Randall; in the minute Felix has observed her, Blanca appears to be the exact opposite of everything Felix strives to be. She even wants her own heartbreak to be different from Blanca's. She recoils from the woman, until she is pressed against the balloon-printed wallpaper alongside Telly.

"I know what you mean," Anna Lisa continues to Blanca. "It was the same with my ex."

Felix holds her breath. Will her aunt play the pronoun game? It's easy to be out-and-proud in a world of adults. In kid worlds, you risk the wrath of grown-ups who think the little ones should be fed neat and wholesome narratives. She wants Anna Lisa to accept the dare.

Felix feels her summer hinge on whatever her aunt says next. If Anna Lisa resists the urge to be vague, Felix's bones will knit. The woodsman will make capes out of Guy Guy and Eva Guy's pelts, and Felix will wear her inheritance with ass-kicking confidence.

"He was out of my life by... good God, by 1974, I guess," Anna Lisa says. "I moved to another town, but the mail followed me to my new post office box. There were so many documents, it kind of made him bigger than he actually was."

No, Anna Lisa will not sprinkle her speech with "they" and "them" and "my ex." She will straight-out lie. She will just stand there, not even looking ashamed, her face serene and memory-glazed. She won't even drop a Q-Tip. Felix's legs bend beneath her.

Blanca turns to her grandson. "Take that sheet out of your mouth, Telly. Are you a baby or are you a young man?"

"Neither," whispers Telly. The wet sheet falls to his lap. "I'm a little boy."

"Little boys grow up to be young men," she snaps. Then she speaks over the top of his head to Anna Lisa. "Why can't he just get in fights like other boys? Why does he have to get in trouble for *coloring* in a *library book*, for goodness sakes?"

Felix is breathing hard and fast, trying to think. There is something to be said here, but Blanca gathers up her grandson quickly and adjusts her purse. On her way out, she seems to see Felix for the first time, despite Anna Lisa's introduction.

"Don't let our moaning and groaning get you down, dear. We're just a couple of bitter old broads, God help us. There are lots of nice men out there, and if you're lucky, you won't make the same mistakes your aunt and I did."

Felix and Anna Lisa drive home from the vet's in their separate cars. By the time Felix has a chance to talk to her aunt, the incident is far away, a debatable history. Maybe Anna Lisa said "she" and Felix misheard. But Felix's stomach remains rubbery, and she spins this feeling into a pearl of anger. How is she supposed to transcend gaudy, rainbow flag-waving parades if Anna Lisa hasn't even worked up *to* them?

"I couldn't believe you lied to that woman," Felix says as her aunt changes from her comfortable nurse shoes to even more comfortable sneakers, like a lesbian Mr. Rogers.

Anna Lisa looks up, perplexed. "What are you talking about?"

"Saying your ex was some guy you divorced."

Anna Lisa stares for a minute. "Wow, your mother hasn't told you *anything*, has she?"

"My mom told me you were gay." Actually, she'd talked about "your aunt's husband" when Felix was little, but she explained the truth when Felix was in junior high. That was the first time Felix paid attention—fascinated, horrified—to a story about one of her dull and distant relatives.

"It's the 21st century, you know," Felix says defensively. "People, like, died and stuff so we could be out."

"I never asked anyone to die for me." Her aunt is clearly annoyed. Is she belittling Felix's injuries? Not that Felix's sacrifice was intentional, but she wants someone to tell her she is brave, even if it's a lie.

"Who's Blanca Randall, anyway?" Felix retorts. She leans forward for emphasis, which makes her side hurt. "Some loud woman in a muumuu? You don't need to be afraid of her."

"Some of my best friends wear muumuus, Felix."

"I'm just saying it's not like she can judge."

"Only supermodels have the right to judge?" Now the conversation has been hijacked—it's about clothing and attitude.

"I'm just saying you should tell the truth!" Felix is surprised by the volume of her voice. Her face is hot and tears hover at the corners of her eyes. She waits, silver bracelets clinking on her shaking wrists, for Anna Lisa to respond. She wants her aunt to tell her that there *is* such a thing as truth, but Anna Lisa just gives her a parental look that says, *You clearly cannot be reasoned with.*

"Look, don't assume you know everything," Anna Lisa says quietly. "If you go through life jumping to conclusions, you'll never get the real story." She pads out of the room in her quiet shoes, a promise that, no, Felix will not get the real story, at least not from her.

THIS AIN'T SAN FRANCISCO
Anna Lisa: Lilac Mines, 1965

There were no direct buses from Fresno to San Francisco within Anna Lisa's price range. This one curves up the arched spine of the state into towns with names like Angels Camp and Lilac Mines. At each stop they pick up a few more people until, by Lilac Mines, Anna Lisa feels like an old timer. The girl next to her—who got on in Modesto—bounces a red-faced baby on her lap. She sings songs and plays pat-a-cake, but the child keeps crying. A few people grumble, but most shoot mother and child looks of tired sympathy. Anna Lisa doesn't feel sorry for them. *The world loves you*, she thinks. The woman is doing what women are supposed to do. In Lilac Mines, a barely-there town at the foot of a mountain, she steps out to give her ears a break.

She's scared to leave her suitcase—the one that sat, packed, in her closet for three weeks while she worked up the courage to leave, saved her money, composed a note that explained as much as she could without explaining too much—in the bus, so she lugs it to the drugstore, where she scans the menu for cherry cola. It's not there, so she settles for regular. Her throat and stomach welcome the icy sweetness. Even though she's wearing her thinnest dress, blue-flowered and nearly transparent, the heat is sinister in its persistence. At the other end of the soda fountain, a young man takes his own soda from the shopkeeper. When he sits down next to Anna Lisa, she sees that there's a cherry in his.

"I thought they didn't have cherry cola," she says. "It wasn't on the menu."

"Just gotta ask," he says, smiling. She recognizes him from the bus. He has thick hair that grows in several different directions, or maybe that's just the legacy of napping on the road. There's a gap in his smile. "I'm John."

What a horribly dull name, Anna Lisa thinks. Boys so frequently have dull names. She likes the way girls' names sound like flowers, even names that aren't Rose or Daisy. Even names like Christine and Delia and Phoebe.

"Anna Lisa," she says.

"Nice to meet you, Anna Lisa. Can I buy you cherry cola?"

"Oh, no, thank you," she says quickly. She's only gone on one date before. She didn't know what to do with her hands or where to look, afraid of what each gesture might mean to this creature who opened doors and twisted his class ring on his finger. She's not sure if John is trying to turn their bus break into a date, but she doesn't want to take any chances. She lifts her glass. "I'm almost done with this one anyway."

John is unfazed. The world is full of girls thirsty for cherry cola. "So why are you going to Eureka?" he asks.

"I'm not, I'm going to San Francisco." She didn't pay attention to where the bus went after that. She hopes he won't ask why she's going to San Francisco.

John frowns. "Not on this bus, I hope. This bus goes through a few more small towns and then on up to Eureka. I'm going to get a logging job."

"No, it goes to San Francisco first." Her voice is thin, existing only in her mouth, as if her lungs have deserted her.

Now John smiles with half his mouth. The look is part pity, part righteousness. "You can check at the bus station if you want."

Anna Lisa leaves her soda in its ring of condensation and runs out of the drugstore, slamming her suitcase into a rack of magazines that she doesn't bother to pick up. It's late Saturday afternoon; the sign on the single window of the tiny bus station informs her that it closed an hour ago and will not re-open until Monday morning. But a yellowed schedule confirms that John is right: the bus she's on will snake through the Sacramento Valley and stop in Eureka, skipping San Francisco. The next bus to San Francisco departs Wednesday. She has enough money for a ticket, but not if she spends four nights in a hotel. The next bus to back to Fresno costs less and leaves Tuesday, which she can manage if she doesn't eat over the weekend. She reaches into her purse and touches the stack of bills curled like a snail in hopes of divining an answer. She can't believe her own stupidity. She replays her original ticket purchase over and over—her question whispered so low that the woman at the window made her repeat it three times.

Maybe, Anna Lisa concludes, she is not meant to go to San Francisco. Maybe San Francisco is for girls like the girls of 3-B, girls who smoke and wear black stockings. Destiny is laughing at her for thinking she could have a big, wild life. She should call her parents now. She can hear her mother's voice: *I don't know what got into you.* Anna Lisa will repeat it back: *I don't know what got into me,* affirming her mother in herself, her promise to live a life more like her mother's from now on.

But for the moment there's no leaving Lilac Mines. She checks into the first hotel she finds, the Lilac Mines Hotel, quite possibly the only one. As soon as she rattles open the door to her room with a skeleton key, she flings herself on the bed. Her sweat-drenched dress clings to her torso and legs, and the comforter is itchy, but her lungs have returned to her. A giant sigh leaves her body. She relaxes into the secure sleep of a decision made for her, if just for tonight.

When she wakes up, the room is dark. For a minute she's not sure where she is. Her hands grope for something familiar. They land on her watch. It's 10:15. Outside her window the moon is a copper penny demanding to be spent. This may be her only night away. She can't imagine sleeping through till morning.

Downstairs the restaurant-and-bar is sparsely populated, but somehow it glows enticingly. She thinks of saloons in Westerns, swinging doors, girls in ruffles and garters. This must be what those bars look like in color, when you're *in* one and not just watching. She has changed from her wilted dress to a pair of slacks. Now her thighs don't stick together; she feels vaguely like a cowboy. She sits at a small round table in the corner, hoping the waiter won't see her for a while, since she can't order anything. She touches the round slump of her belly, wondering how long she can go without food. Already she is hungry, but maybe her body will give up hope of being fed if she waits long enough.

Anna Lisa finds herself gazing at the broad back of a man at the bar. He's wearing a work shirt; his hand rests on a bottle of beer the same light amber as his hair. Mushrooming over the barstool, his hips are large for a man's. There are so many things Anna Lisa doesn't know how to do: talk to boys, order a drink, buy a bus ticket apparently. Are these skills a matter of time or destiny? What would happen if she transformed herself into a person like Suzy? If she walked up to the man at the bar and said something friendly? She reminds herself that nothing will come of it—she's returning to Fresno in a few days—and this emboldens her.

She slides onto a stool near the man with the beer, leaving a stool between them. The bartender is on the other side of the square bar, twirling a rag on his finger with a blend of boredom and intense concentration. The man glances up at her, then back down. Anna Lisa wills herself to look at him. She takes in his profile: small straight nose, soft chin, freckles a shade lighter than her own. Blonde eyebrows that fade out at the edges. And somewhere in these details lies a revelation. The man is a woman.

"Hi," she says, which is what she'd planned to say to a man, too. She did not know a woman could look like this. She did not know that girl hips could find a home in straight brown trousers. As alien as the ensemble is, she's the right alien for it; on her planet, this must be what women look like.

"Hey," she says. Her voice is dark ale.

"Do you live here?" Anna Lisa needs to know where this planet is.

"What's it to you?"

"I just wondered..." Anna Lisa stutters. "I was going to San Francisco," she adds, as if this explains her presence in Lilac Mines.

The woman makes a face not unlike John's, but it's just a stopping point on her way to a full smile. "Well, this ain't San Francisco. But sure, I live here. It's not so bad."

"I'm Anna Lisa."

The woman laughs. "Seriously? You sure don't look like an Anna Lisa."

Anna Lisa has never thought about what she looked like, name-wise. It's just something she was born into. Now she has a burning desire to know what she *does* look like, but she can't ask; it would seem flirtatious.

"Name's Jody." Indeed, Jody looks like a Jody: Irish, tough, friendly, boyish. "Hey, what're you drinking?"

"Um, I'm not. I'm too young, and besides—"

"Gotta start sometime, right?" Jody waves to the bartender. "A Pabst for my friend, *Anna Lisa*." She says it in that inside-joke way, and in this faraway bar with a woman who looks like a man, Anna Lisa feels like one of the girls. The warmth in her chest is so strong and rare that she can't send back the bottle that lands in front of her, an uncapped twin to Jody's.

Is it possible that Jody is buying the beer *for* her? She's not sure if she wants this to be the case or not, but when the bartender—his fingers tickling the rag at his side, promising to return to it—says, "Sixty-five cents," Jody doesn't reach for the wallet that bulges from her back pocket.

So Anna Lisa extracts her coin purse, which she suddenly wishes were a real wallet. She touches the coins it would take to pay for the beer. She touches the sleeping bills next to them. Blood races past her ears. "Can I also get a ham and cheese sandwich?" she hears herself saying. The words make her hunger rear up, stomp its feet. "And a side of mashed potatoes?" she says. "And a strawberry shake?"

"All right," Jody says. "That's what I call a real man's appetite." If Anna Lisa's mother said she was eating like a man, she'd be telling her daughter to slow down, chew 20 times before swallowing. But from Jody it sounds like a compliment.

Jody washes dishes at "this bar down on Calla Boulevard" four nights a week and is helping a man fix his barn. What Jody really wants is a job at the sawmill, she says. That's where the good jobs are. Jody shakes her head and runs her fingers through her short, fuzzy hair. Jody says there are ghosts in the mines above town if you're stupid enough to believe in that stuff. Jody smells vaguely like wood. Jody is intimate but guarded. Jody seems to be inviting Anna Lisa somewhere, but she's not about to give away the directions.

When Anna Lisa's shake is half gone and there is only an inch of bitter-tasting beer left in the bottle, a Negro woman walks into the restaurant. She wears a red dress that matches her lipstick and clutches her purse with both hands. When she spots Jody, she lets her purse slide down her arm and swing on her elbow.

"That's my girl," Jody says to Anna Lisa without taking her eyes off the woman.

Can a girl have a girl? Can a white girl have a black girl? The possibilities make Anna Lisa's head throb. Could *she* have a girl?

Jody makes introductions: Imogen, Anna Lisa. Anna Lisa, Imogen. There were three Negroes at Lincoln High School. Anna Lisa knew each of their names and never had occasion to talk to any of them. Imogen is standing so close Anna Lisa can see the clumps of mascara on her eyelashes. And she's Jody's girl. Anna Lisa feels slightly dizzy. Maybe it's the beer.

"We're going over to Lilac's," Jody says. "It's the bar where I work, 'cept I'm off tonight. Wanna come?"

Imogen looks at Jody, alarmed. "Is she cool?"

Jody smiles. "I've got a hunch."

Imogen has not touched Jody, but from the way she rolls her eyes beneath her mascara and her night-blue eyeshadow, Anna Lisa knows they have been together a long time and that they are in love. "*Your* hunches are always getting *us* in trouble. But I'm not one to be rude. Anna Lisa, you said your name was? Come on with us."

They leave Main Street behind and begin climbing Calla Boulevard, a steep street with older buildings and shorter streetlights. Anna Lisa studies the figures in front of her on the narrow sidewalk. Jody's love handles, her echoing work boots that hint at hollows beneath the pavement, her hair that might be called strawberry blonde if the title didn't seem somehow undignified. Imogen clicks along next to her. Thin waist and unashamed breasts wrapped in rose print. Her black hair is curled in a controlled and intricate pattern. Her arm swings next to Jody's, occasionally brushing it. As if this were all perfectly natural.

Anna Lisa's breath quickens as they climb. And we're going to a *bar*, she thinks.

Jody stops abruptly in front of a squat, wood-sided building. There's no sign over the closed door, but a rectangular halo of light surrounds it. The night has turned chilly, and Anna Lisa imagines it's warm inside. When Jody halts, Anna Lisa bumps into her.

"Okay, here's the rules," Jody says. "No putting the moves on somebody else's girl, but I don't think you're dumb enough to do that. No nursing one beer all night—you're in a bar, you drink. And if Caleb flashes the light, it means stop dancing or switch to a guy, 'cause the cops are coming."

Imogen puts a hand on Anna Lisa's shoulder. It's warm and heavy. "We don't have cops. We have one sheriff who bothers with us maybe once every two months. Just breathe, honey."

Anna Lisa doesn't know what the insides of regular bars look like. She doesn't know the names of beers. She thinks 90 cents sounds expensive, but she can't be sure. She's never danced with anyone besides her own relatives at weddings.

The first beer has already rendered the night twirly, but she follows Jody's lead and orders a Rheingold. Her voice is so quiet that Caleb, a thin man with dark, center-parted hair and a blue turtleneck sweater—what Anna Lisa imagines a poet might look like—makes her repeat it twice. She hands him her money and silently says goodbye to her trip home.

"You gotta tip, honey," Imogen whispers.

The bar is dark with low ceilings. But the people: Anna Lisa's entire body tingles like a sleeping limb awakening. There are more women like Jody. They prop elbows on the bar, extend booted feet into walkways, emit low whistles at pretty girls. Upon seeing these women who act like men, Anna Lisa is startled by just how differently the sexes carry themselves. The women who look like Imogen—except white—slide into the gazes of the Jodies. They figure-eight around tables and pull their limbs inward in a way that somehow exposes as it conceals: crossed legs revealing a sliver of thigh, crossed arms summoning cleavage. None of them look like the girls of 3-B, but Anna Lisa realizes this bar is nevertheless her book. The black ink has lifted; she's been invited to look and look.

LILAC
Felix: Lilac Mines, 2002

When Felix wakes up, her side hurts so badly she can barely sit up. Last night she ordered pizza and ate it alone in her room. Her dreams were threaded with Eva and hot-breathed men who looked like Eva. Both seemed out to get her. It's late morning now, and she's thankful that Anna Lisa is already at work.

She rises slowly, swallows a handful of Advil, and takes her sketchpad out to the deck. She tries to draw the mountains. But what appears green-brown and majestic in person becomes gray and lumpy on paper, and soon all she has to show for her efforts is a pile of eraser crumbs. Nature is the opposite of fashion, which always looks sleeker and funkier before it's translated into cloth and thread.

Her pencil moves clumsily and her head pounds with questions. Where is Eva right now? Where is *she*, really? What is this nearly vertical town—will the thick-trunked trees and rows of cabins protect her? Anna Lisa won't, that much is clear. But what other choice does she have? An art student named Genevieve Barilla has sublet her room in L.A. through October. She doesn't want to live with her parents. She can't afford to move to New York.

Felix gives up on the mountains, goes back inside and takes a shower. She puts on a pair of knee-length cargo shorts and a sleeveless T-shirt that says, "Dump Him." But when she studies herself in the guest room mirror, she decides against the outfit. She doesn't want to encourage anyone to dump anyone right now, she tells herself. There's nothing funny about getting dumped. That's what it is.

But the ensemble she settles on is decidedly less dykey: a royal blue secondhand cheerleading skirt, an asymmetrical tank top and tall reddish-purple legwarmers. She poses, tugging at her top to make sure it covers her bandage. She feels a little better, although she is now officially all dressed up with no place to go.

So she goes to Kate's Kappuccino, even though it reminds her of Kate Mendoza-Lishman, even though she hates dorky misspellings. There's only one woman working at the small shop, so there's a line. Felix waits behind a chubby man wearing overalls and a bowl cut. *What self-respecting hairstylist would agree to give him that awful cut?* she wonders.

The bell dings and two teenage girls enter. They're 14 or 15, an age when girls dress alike without even knowing it: flared jeans with faux fade marks bleached across the hips, ponytails, baby tees in bright colors. The air conditioning is blasting. Felix wraps her arms around her bandaged body and wonders if she should order a hot drink instead of an iced "frappukato." As she studies the menu, she hears the girls giggling.

"What is she *wearing?*" one of them whispers. At first Felix thinks they're talking about the man in the overalls, but no, she definitely heard "she."

"Hello, *Flashdance!*" the other one giggles.

"What's *Flashdance?*"

"Remember I told you—that movie my mom made me watch when she did that mother-daughter slumber party thing?"

Felix feels her face turn red. Her legs start to itch beneath the legwarmers that these little Lilac Mines teenyboppers are not advanced enough to understand. She looks around. No one here is. She is completely defenseless.

"Maybe she's a cheerleader—from Beedleborough or something."

"No, their colors are red and silver. Besides, she's, like, old."

"Shh… she'll hear you."

Felix might as well be naked. Her thighs feel like a map of ugly blue veins. In a shaky voice she orders a grande black coffee. She can't drink coffee without a lot of accessories, but she's not about to hang out by the cream and sugar bar, so she shuffles out of Kate's, head down.

In the safety of her car, she peels off her legwarmers and tries not to cry. *I hope they remember me when legwarmers are all over the Gap a year from now,* she thinks, but she knows they won't. Is that even what she wants to be remembered for? She wipes her eyes with a wadded-up legwarmer. *Fuck all of this. Fuck Lilac Mines and Anna Lisa.* She wishes she could live in her car. She wishes she had the strength not to care what people thought. She takes a deep breath and turns the key in the ignition. Maybe she'll just drive around.

Fiddling with the radio dial, she finds three country stations and four Bible shows. "Well, ma'am, I'm glad you asked. As you know, God has a plan for each of us. As the Lord Jesus Christ said in…." *Why do Bible-thumpers always refer to Jesus by his full name?* Felix wonders. But there's something appealing about the man's voice. It is rich and comforting and self-assured. As if he knows exactly what God's plan is. She envies the caller: just phone in and receive God's prescription, then go to the nearest church and fill it. But if Felix called in, the man would quote from Leviticus (she's pretty sure that's the God-Hates-Fags part) and prescribe some sort of conversion program. She's screwed in all worlds.

Sighing, she turns off the radio and pulls into the nearest parking spot. Looking up, she sees she's in front of the Lilac Mines Visitors' Center, a log cabin sandwiched between an auto shop and a café that, of course, promises cappuccino. At least a government-funded educational facility is likely to be free of preachers and too-cool teenagers. She gets out of the car and pours her coffee on the ground, making a thin black river in the dust.

Inside, Felix is greeted by an assortment of stuffed dead animals. Apparently posing them in "natural" positions and surrounding them with dried plants—instead of mounting their heads on wooden plaques—makes them scientific rather than artifacts of machismo.

She must have quite a look on her face because the ranger behind the counter says kindly, "Most of 'em were roadkill."

"Uh, I guess that's good," Felix offers.

"Doing the Gold Rush country tour?" She has two yellow braids, a Midwestern accent, and a badge that says "Ranger LeVoy." She leans forward enthusiastically, her plump arms folded on the counter.

"No." Felix doesn't feel like talking, but Ranger LeVoy waits for a more complete answer. "I'm visiting my aunt."

"Oh? And what's her name?"

"Anna Lisa Hill."

"That's right, I should have known, you look just like her." Ranger LeVoy nods energetically. "She works search and rescue, you know. Of course you know."

"She's a nurse. Maybe you're thinking of a different Anna Lisa?"

"This town's not that big," Ranger LeVoy laughs. "She works for the volunteer squad. You didn't know? She saved a couple of crazies who tried to hike the Sierras in the wintertime just a few months back."

"Seriously?" Felix tries to picture her aunt hoisting herself up the face of a mountain, or whatever search and rescue people do.

"Yeah, all those search and rescue folks are great. But super modest. Don't let her get away with not telling you about it."

Felix sighs. She tries to concentrate on the sepia tone photos and blocks of text interspersed with the carnage. Bearded men with pickaxes stare back at her, as if *she* sent them down in the deep black mines. Here and there a testament to the gargantuan nature of mining: a rusted bolt the size of her fist, a slice of the beam that held up a stamp mill, cut from a 200-year-old tree. Things that could crush her to dust.

She follows the story on laminated cardboard. Lilac Mines, a silver town in Gold Rush country, did its best business from the 1860s through the 1890s, when it was still referred to as East Beedleborough. Mineshafts shot through the mountain like bullets, and the mountain bled silver. Teams of mules lugged the ore to a V-shaped trough that snaked down the mountain to the stamp mill. Once crushed, the ore stewed in vats of cyanide until the silver let go of the rock.

"Still cyanide in the ground water," Ranger LeVoy says cheerfully. "I'd stick to bottled Arrowhead if I were you. We all do." Six days a week, the town shook to the rhythm of the stamp mill. Immense iron wheels engraved with their places of origin—Los Angeles or San Francisco—pounded out the shape of a new place.

There was also a sawmill on the eastern side of town, just above the mining camps, where the less glamorous half of mining took place. Trees were felled, planed square, and more mules pulled them up the mountain, where they shored up the mine, making a hole in the rock look like a saloon entrance. Rustic but welcoming. Miles and miles of wood lined the mines, and as the trees vanished from the eastern half of East Beedleborough, the mountain was, in a way, turned inside out.

The town became a boomtown, which was not unlike a city, except that everything was the same age and everyone thought they'd be leaving soon, even as they hung curtains and planted telegraph poles—in a straight line, because who knew if electricity could bend? The women held quilting bees at the church. The men joined E Clampus Vitus, the miners' fraternal order. "Both good places to gossip," says Ranger LeVoy.

Then, in 1899, the 16-year-old daughter of mine foreman Harold Ambrose walked into a mine entrance at the top of the town and never walked out. No one knew why Lilac Ambrose had gone there in the first place. Her father wasn't even working that day. No one knew much about Lilac Ambrose at all. For 20 days, the men and the mules searched the hollows of the mountain. Lanterns swinging and voices calling as loudly as was possible without causing a cave-in. They found a few artifacts. Girl things—a shoe button, a hair ribbon. The latter hangs on a nail behind glass. But they didn't find Lilac or Lilac's body. They started calling the town Lilac Mines. They even wrote it into the hillside, a giant LM made of tiny white pebbles, but Harold Ambrose was still broken-hearted.

Within ten years, the mine dried up. The mountain was like a person who'd cried so hard he had no more tears. The people who'd talked about moving back—to Chicago, Hartford, Iowa City, to the tenements of New York—finally did. Or they moved forward.

History stops at the 1920s. Lilac Mines becomes a ghost town. The end. But there are people here now, plenty of them. Still, Felix concedes, it would be weird to see color photos from, say, the 1960s alongside the stuffed snakes and rusty pickaxes. History has to be black-and-white and rust-colored.

"The sawmill re-opened in the '40s," Ranger LeVoy volunteers. "But they ripped most of the mine equipment apart and used the metal in the War. Hey, did you see our collection of scented bath products?" She gestures to a basket next to the donation box. "They're all-natural and all the proceeds go to E Clampus Vitus."

"The fraternal order? It's still around?" Felix is feeling just slightly more sociable.

"Oh yeah, except now it's just a bunch of old guys who want to preserve mining history. I doubt any of 'em were actual miners."

"And they're selling lotion?" Felix picks up a bottle. "And eucalyptus-scented bath oil?"

Ranger LeVoy nods happily. "All natural."

The hair ribbon draws Felix back to the glass case devoted to Lilac Ambrose. A nail pierces the ribbon like an exotic insect, but it's limp and frayed, and Felix can't tell what color it was originally. It's embroidered with tiny rosebuds that remind Felix of the old flatware her parents had before they upgraded to a Southwest pattern. Pink rosebuds freckling the rims of plates and the tops of mugs. Most of it's gone, but a few pieces migrated to Felix's apartment. She closes her eyes and sees one of the mugs on Eva's rickety end table. She can't remember why she took a cup to Eva's loft. Just that it teetered there, so feminine and precarious in its hip surroundings.

Did Lilac leave the ribbon behind as a marker, like that guy in the myth about the maze? Or did it slip from her braid? Felix touches the back of her own head, as if she might find answers there. She wants to tie the ribbon in a bow. She wants to know more. Why did this girl go into the mine, why didn't she come out, when did she make the transition from exploring to panicking? There are obvious questions, and more basic but elusive ones. Who was she, besides Harold's daughter? It takes a certain kind of girl to venture into a dark tunnel alone.

She wills herself to chat with Ranger LeVoy. "Did she go in there all by herself?"

"Guess so. They say her ghost still haunts the town." Ranger LeVoy's eyes get Halloween-big, but her mouth keeps smiling. "We're not allowed to put that in the literature, though. Just the facts."

"Has anyone ever looked for her body—well, her bones, I guess—in recent times? I mean, now that there's more technology and stuff?"

Ranger LeVoy shrugs and smiles.

Felix looks at the panoramic pictures blown up so big that they are a swarm of Georges Seurat dots. She cannot believe that the bald spot on the mountain wasn't always desert. There were no sign of tree stumps when she drove through. She can't believe that kind of erasure is possible, as if the trees never happened, as if killing them never happened.

There are no pictures of Lilac. There's a group photo of sour-looking miners with a red arrow glued next to Harold Ambrose's head. He has a thin face and deep-set eyes. He looks older than the father of a 16-year-old. Felix's eyes roam the rows of miners. Collectively, the haggard men look like they could use a union. Except for one in the front row. He is young and shirtless, with bulging pecs, a straight nose and a cocky smile. Oddly white for pre-fluoride days.

Felix knows that smile. It's the kind that asks, "How 'bout you do my buddy a favor?" Her stomach drops. Maybe it's the kind of smile that lures a 16-year-old into a mineshaft.

"It sounds fishy," Felix says in a small voice. "She just *disappeared?* People either leave, or they're taken."

"Lot of people in this town would agree with you," Ranger LeVoy says.

As a journalist—sort of—Felix believes that all information is available to her if she has the will to dig for it, if she gifts it with her curiosity. She's no longer willing to give her curiosity to Anna Lisa, who won't do her part. She's had enough of Eva's evasiveness. But Lilac— Lilac *needs* her. Lilac is a lonely girl waiting in a cold, dark mine for Felix to rescue her. She will devote her immediate future to the past, and free herself from the present, populated by People Who Don't Get It.

She glares at the shirtless miner. *Watch out, fucker. I'm going to track you down.* It feels good. Looking at a real photo, not a pencil sketch. It's a little like that coming-out rush: the sense of a world unseen but knowable.

BAPTISM
Anna Lisa: Lilac Mines, 1965

Gossip reigns at Lilac's. After a few hours in the bar, Anna Lisa will learn its name and many others. Imogen links up with a half-circle of skirted women peering out from beneath their eyelashes near the jukebox. Anna Lisa wants to join them—they seem as if they're exchanging important information, and Anna Lisa is full of questions: *Who are you all? How did you get here?* The bar seems like an oasis, lush and improbable, but she knows its patrons were not just conjured by the desert. Before Anna Lisa can float over to Imogen's crescent of girls, Jody pulls her to a table with two other trousered women. There are more rules at work here than the ones Jody announced, but Anna Lisa would need a pad and pen to begin to make sense of them.

"She's not gonna show up. She wouldn't dare," says a square-jawed woman named Shallan.

"Why not? I showed up," says Jean, who has sloping, sorrowful eyebrows and shoulders to match.

Anna Lisa tries to keep up without intruding too much. "Who?"

"Jean's femme," Jody says.

"Former femme," clarifies Jean. "Well, she's still a femme, she just ain't mine."

Femme means *girl* in French, Anna Lisa remembers. Are they French? It doesn't quite add up, but nothing tonight has.

"Meg's a gutsy broad, though," Jody says. "If anyone would show up, Meg would."

"This place is too damn small," says Jean. A wispy beer-foam mustache lingers on her top lip. "I guess I can't stop her from finding a new butch if she wants, but I don't want to *see* it, you know?"

Once Anna Lisa's father found a tortoise in the road and named it Butch. Anna Lisa and Suzy fed him lettuce and dog food and called him Butchy. They assumed the tortoise was a him, but really they had no way of knowing.

"You'll find someone before she does," says Shallan. She's as tall as a man, with dark hair slicked back into a tiny ponytail at the nape of her neck. She has green, green eyes and long black lashes that look wrong on her boxy face. Her voice nearly shakes with loyalty. It's sweet even as it etches invisible lines across the bar. Butches. Femmes. Couples. Singles.

"That's Shallan's girl over there." Jody gestures with her chin to a compact, black-haired woman dusting her face with powder. "Edith. She's a catch. Never says a bad word and likes low-cut dresses."

"Watch it," laughs Shallan.

"Do You Want to Know a Secret?" is playing on the jukebox. Jean is watching the door, and Anna Lisa is watching Jean. When Jean's worried expression cramps even further, Anna Lisa follows her gaze. Her pain is Anna Lisa's initiation: this is what loving a girl can do to a girl.

The woman who crosses the doorway and beelines for the bar is not quite pretty, but still the word *gorgeous* enters Anna Lisa's mind, because gorgeous is big bold colors, a little over the top, a bird of paradise. Meg is taller than Caleb, and he leans forward on his toes to take her order. She jingles a key chain on one finger. She's dressed in a pleated plaid skirt, a loose, sleeveless blouse and high heels that tilt as threateningly as the mountain. Meg is a femme, clearly, but she doesn't immediately join Imogen and friends in their designated area. She takes a long, slow sip of her drink, rolling her keys in her free hand.

With a clatter, the keys hit the floor.

"Shit," says Meg. When she bends down to get them, a strand of shiny brown hair escapes the twist at the back of her head. Anna Lisa sees a night not going according to plan, and she wants to tell this woman everything. About how three days ago she was weighing oranges and thinking about how, if the world were the size of a fruit, it would be smoother than an orange and rougher than an apple (a distant fact from school). At the table with Jody and Jean and Shallan, Anna Lisa wishes she could drink her drink faster. She wishes she had boots instead of worn loafers. But for Meg, she wants to peel an orange and put it in her smooth, slightly trembling hands.

"Just ignore her," Jody says to Jean, but it might as well be to Anna Lisa.

Jody and Imogen are dancing to "Paper Roses." No particular step; they're just a knot of arms and legs swaying to the music. Imogen's chin rests on Jody's shoulder. Jody closes her eyes, and Anna Lisa can see the rest of the day drift away. One of Imogen's pink-nailed hands finds its way into Jody's back pocket. Jody touches one of Imogen's sculpted curls, and Imogen pulls her head back and smiles, as if to say, *I love you, but hands off the hair.* Together they are like a centaur, a mythical creature. Anna Lisa can't help but stare. Awkward and graceful and rare. By the time the song ends, she's a little in love with both of them.

Caleb has replaced her beer, and Anna Lisa is doing her best with her third drink of the evening, but the swiveling bar stool is starting to make her dizzy. Hoping for the curative powers of fresh air, she heads for the door.

Shallan grabs her arm. "You leaving?"

"No, I was just stepping out for some air."

Shallan laughs. "You can't just stand out in the street, kid. If you need to need to fend off puking, go out the back door."

Anna Lisa is embarrassed that her new and rocky relationship with alcohol is so obvious, but she turns around and heads out the back door, crossing beneath the red light bulb that has not yet flashed. The alley is narrow and dark, crisscrossed with telephone wires. The row of overflowing trash cans a few feet away do nothing for her cartwheeling stomach. She sits down with her back to the stucco wall, pulls in her knees, and bows her head. *Just stay still,* she tells herself. *Make it go away.*

She's not entirely sure what "it" is. Breathing through her mouth, she imagines herself at home in bed. The house will have finally cooled down by this hour. She'll pull her hair off her neck and fan it behind her on the pillow she's had as long as she can remember. It's indented with the shape of her head. It cradles her through all her dreams, the pleasant ones and the ones that nudge her into a dreading wakefulness. Right now she wants to wake up in her ordinary life. She wants to see her mother in curlers, extending a glass of water, her head cocked in concern.

"Got a light?"

Anna Lisa looks up and sees pink and orange pleats. Above them a shelf of breasts, bare hands twirling an unlit cigarette like a miniature baton. She struggles to stand, bracing herself against the rough outside wall of the bar.

"Sorry to bug you. It's just there's no one inside I particularly feel like asking right now," says the woman who is Meg, who is so close Anna Lisa can smell her shampoo.

"I don't smoke," Anna Lisa apologizes. She wants to learn, she wants to breathe this air, even if it makes her sick.

Meg rummages through her white, faux leather purse. It seems to be a deep and messy place. She does not find matches, but she does pull out a wad of paper. When she unfolds it, Anna Lisa sees that it is stationery. A row of pink daisies runs along the top edge. She finds a pencil stub with a squashed eraser and begins to scrawl on the paper in big, oblong letters. Anna Lisa catches *Dear Petra, Do you remember how I told you that Jean—* before Meg looks up at her.

"I'm sorry," Anna Lisa gulps. Bizarrely, she finds herself envying Petra, whoever she is. She wants Meg to spend five cents on *her* for a stamp. She wants that slanting, outraged handwriting.

"Do you ever feel like faraway people understand better than the ones close by?" Meg says. Her eyes are the color of rust. She looks hard at Anna Lisa and then past her, deep into the alley.

"Maybe," Anna Lisa says. She doesn't know any faraway people. "Why did you come here?" she asks, meaning Lilac Mines. She's still in her dream—she doesn't know which kind it will be yet—and she wants to know what sort of real lives her fellow dream-world citizens left behind. Or were they here all along, waiting for her?

"I have a right to be here," Meg says fiercely. She steels her free hand on her hip, and Anna Lisa finds herself thinking, *Yes, of course, that's all there is to it.* Her need for comfort recedes in Meg's tough, sleek wake. "Don't let Jean tell you otherwise."

"Oh—no, she didn't. I mean—I'm Anna Lisa."

"Anna Lisa," Meg repeats. The letter and pencil return to her purse. "I'm Meg. That's a lot of name, you know. And kind of prissy. You could shorten it, say, to A.L. … Al."

Anna Lisa's stomach begins to feel less like an impending storm and more like a flock of birds preparing for migration, preening their feathers before the flight south. She tries on the name. "Al." In her head, she tries Al-and-Meg.

Meg looks more cheerful now, too. "Hang on," she says. She slips back into the bar and returns with a glass of water. Her smile is full of answers and secrets. She dips her hand into the glass, a pale aquarium creature. When she extracts it, she flings a spray of water at Anna Lisa. The drops are ice-cold. She gasps, as if Meg herself put her fingers on Anna Lisa's skin. Did Meg know she was sick?

"I hereby baptize you," says Meg. "Al of Lilac Mines."

Anna Lisa doesn't know what to say. But she knows the answer to one secret: it's just as hard to talk to girls, the flirting kind of talk stitched with meaning. But she wants more. Whereas John from the bus made her tired and nervous, Meg makes her want to try. Anna Lisa rubs her wet face. Meg mines her purse again and this time finds a single, splintery match. She lights her cigarette: a tiny, bright fire in the dingy alley.

THE OFFICIAL STORY
Felix: Lilac Mines, 2002

"How do you feel about used clothes? Do they ever, um, scare you?" Until now, all of Tawn Twentyman's questions have been fairly normal: Do you have retail experience? Can you work Saturdays once in a while? Felix responded cheerfully and confidently, suppressing her vague annoyance. Wasn't it obvious to this girl that she was overqualified on all fronts? Felix is wearing an old jean skirt that has been merged with an old patchwork skirt by a Melrose seamstress. There's a small astroturf heart sewn on her tank top, just to the right of her real heart. All this *and* a college degree.

Having a job will get her out of Anna Lisa's house and, she hopes, give her night-brain something better to dream about. The frat boys are always more sinister than they were in reality, because in her dreams she knows what's coming. As for Dream-Eva, she's perfect: she never stresses out or rolls her eyes the way Real-Eva did. Felix hates her subconscious for idealizing her.

Tawn, the thrift shop's manager, is wearing a baggy T-shirt with a stretched-out neck over black jeans that do not flare in the least. The regulation blue smock doesn't help. Her waist-length black hair is tangled in a manner that might be interesting if Felix could be sure it was the result of a style choice, not a misplaced hairbrush. Tawn looks like she could be gay, in a frumpy sort of way, but the rules are different in Lilac Mines.

"What do you mean by 'scare me'?" Felix asks.

"Well, would you be comfortable doing intake? Unloading and organizing all the stuff that comes off the truck?"

"Oh, sure, that's the best part, I bet," Felix says. "I'm not all prissy about clothes that are old or smelly. You have to sift through a lot if you want to find the treasures, right?" She reminds herself that she's interviewing, not shopping, and adds, "And I would love to help with window displays. Have you ever read *Confessions of a Window Dresser* by Simon Doonan? It's really smart."

Tawn looks at her blankly. It figures, but Felix hopes she wins points for research. The Lilac Mines Goodwill is not Barney's, but Felix vows to find the realistic mannequins lounging in too-big togs as bizarre and ripe as Simon does.

"I really love vintage," Felix continues. "There's such an art to it, compared to, like, mall shopping. I'm a total thrift store hound. Every time I see something kind of interesting, I immediately start thinking about how I could work it into my wardrobe. My roommate has one of those old BeDazzlers—remember, from the '80s? She found it at this flea market. And we both had our own BeDazzlers back in the day, but of course we got rid of them when rhinestones went out of style the first time."

"But you're okay doing intake?" Tawn repeats.

"Yeah." Is there something Felix should know about this task?

"You wouldn't have to price stuff or anything, just kind of organize it."

"Oh, I'm really organized. It's just my personality."

Tawn looks down at her clipboard. "Okay, lemme see if there was anything else I was going to ask you." She's Felix's age, maybe younger. She has a round white face, significant cheekbones and dark eyes that open a little too widely, as if everything Felix says is troubling or surprising. It makes Felix feel like even more of a city girl, as if she has a full-face tattoo instead of just a small silver ball below her bottom lip. These big-fish possibilities please her, but she's also struck with a desire to make those scared eyes laugh.

"Nope, those are all my questions," Tawn concludes. "Is there anything you want to know?"

Felix swallows. "Well, it's not really a question, but I should probably mention... I had, um, an accident before I came here, I broke a rib. So I'm not supposed to lift anything heavy for another few weeks. So I probably shouldn't rearrange the furniture area or anything for a while." She usually goes to the gym three times a week—well, at least twice a week—but feels like an 80-year-old, talking about her aching bones during a job interview.

"That's okay," Tawn assures her. "I make Matty do most of that stuff anyway." She scratches her head. "I should probably think it over a while and then call, but I think I'll just hire you now. Can you start Friday? That's when the truck comes."

Before she leaves, Felix buys a preppy V-neck sweater and a stack of old postcards. Tawn gives her the employee discount.

"I could have gotten you a job at the school," Anna Lisa says. Felix is still angry at her aunt, but she'd half hoped that Anna Lisa would be impressed by her new blue-collar job. "It would probably pay better, even though it would just be clerical, most likely. At least you wouldn't have to move around too much."

"I'm not *that* delicate," Felix protests.

After a day that melted her eyeliner, giving her a sad clown look, it's finally starting to cool off. They're on Anna Lisa's balcony with the lemonade of Felix's fantasies and strawberry ice cream, handmade by her aunt. Felix thinks of ice cream like she thinks of pasta, candy, and almost any kind of sauce—as elements that cannot be broken down into simpler parts. But knowing that the pale pink ice cream sweating in her bowl did not enter the world fully formed, that it took milk and sugar and salt and labor, makes it delicious. Still, their week of monosyllabic exchanges is bitter in her mouth.

"I can pay rent now, and buy groceries and stuff," Felix offers, thinking about Anna Lisa's free-room-and-board comment the first night.

"I'm doing fine, you know," Anna Lisa bristles. "I've supported myself for 40 years."

"Right, but you've never had to support an invalid niece."

"Felix, I said it's fine," Anna Lisa snaps. "Buy yourself some records or something. CDs." She looks over Felix's interview ensemble. "Some new clothes."

Felix takes a long swallow of lemonade and wipes her hand on her skirt.

"Hey, Anna Lisa?"

"Mm?"

"Do you have, like, a girlfriend?" She's never sure what older gay people call their significant others. You have to outgrow "girlfriend" at some point, but "partner" is so serious and "lover" is scandalous and "ladyfriend" is comical, though fun. Felix doesn't really know any older gay people.

Anna Lisa doesn't look uncomfortable, but she also doesn't seem like she plans to answer. She just focuses on the patchwork mountain in front of them. Eventually, she says, "No... No, not now. There was—" She pauses and seems to switch directions. "There was a woman I met at a nursing conference. We dated for a little while. But nothing recently."

"What was she like?"

"It was really just for a short time."

Felix waits for Anna Lisa to ask if Felix has a girlfriend. The story of Eva's disappearance waits just behind her teeth. She wants Anna Lisa to sympathize and promise her that there's a new love on the horizon, that pain will make her grow stronger and all that. Crane and Robbie and Jia Li promised those things, but they were all in their mid-20s too, blindly guessing what might be around the corner. Anna Lisa just keeps taking small bites of her ice cream, shaggy brown hair blocking most of her profile.

On her way to the library Wednesday morning, Felix drops three postcards in the mailbox. She hasn't looked through even half of them yet, but she did address a few of the blank ones. She's not sure what to say to her friends or even her parents and sisters. She knows they need to know she's okay, so she peppers the cards with sarcasm and exclamation points.

This morning, as Anna Lisa searched for the pooper-scooper, Felix told her she was going to check out a book. Summer reading. The truth is, she's beginning her search for Lilac. Maybe it's the rosebud hair ribbon. Maybe it's the miner's white smile and brown chest muscles that stick in her head, merging with Guy Guy. Lilac doesn't even get a photograph. Doesn't even get a dress, just one lonely accessory.

The library is in the brown, treeless part of town, just above East Main Street. It's a prefab structure that looks elegant compared to the exhausted trailers and shacks fanning out behind it. The yards here are marked by sun-cracked Big Wheels, fence posts adorned with inverted purple bottles, dishwashers put out to pasture. When you're poor you live in the open, a life exposed.

A library window poster promises, "Reading answers all your questions!" Below the slogan, children clutch books, looking satisfied. But when she tries the door, it's locked. As far as she can tell, the hours aren't posted anywhere. She sits down on the top step. It's too hot to begin the walk back right away. She was excited that the library was so close, but Lilac Mines miles are longer than regular miles. Sweat drips between her smallish boobs, the bandage makes her hotter. For the first time since she cut her hair, she wishes it were long enough to put in a ponytail—the inch that rests on her neck is far too much. The dust has turned her black toenail polish to gray.

"It's not open Wednesdays."

Felix's muscles tense, ready to run. Some redneck from one of the trailers will slaughter her for trespassing on this forsaken land. She looks up. A man with a ruddy, stubbly face shadowed by a blue baseball cap peers down from the back of a tall, muscular mule. The mule pulls a handmade metal cart with a bumper sticker: *I brake for mules*.

She exhales slowly. "I couldn't find any hours posted."

The man shrugs. "Gary Schipp, the guy who runs it, pretty much keeps the hours he feels like. But he never feels like coming on Wednesdays, seems like."

"What kind of library doesn't have regular hours?"

"This kind," says the man.

Felix hasn't been to a public library since high school. She went to the university library in college and now she frequents bookstores because she likes to drink coffee while she reads. Now that she's made the effort, she believes the library should be open.

"Nice mule," Felix says. "What's his name?"

"Lilac," says the man. He removes his hat and wipes his forehead with the back of his hand. "Kind of a long story. When I got him, I didn't know nothing about mules. I was apprenticing with this old welder—that's what I do for a living, since raising mules don't pay much. I was apprenticing with this old guy, a Clamper, and he was just brimming with trivia about this town. The lost girl and the silver and all that. Most of it didn't interest me much, but I've always had a soft spot for animals and when he said that they used to lose a mule a day—or even two—in the mines, well, that really struck me. Said it took two more mules to pull the body out of the mine shaft, this 1200-pound animal dragged down the mountain by its own kin, like some kinda mule funeral procession. The thought of it just disturbed me, I guess, and I found myself wanting to do right by mules." He looks up. "You look like a city girl... I must be boring you."

"No, not at all. I mean, I am—I'm from L.A.—but I'm not bored."

Lilac waves his ears and flutters his silver-brown lips. He appears a tad bored, but in an understanding way, as if humoring senile grandparents.

"Yeah? You don't say! I grew up in Hollywood." The man looks like he was swaddled in horse blankets as a baby. Felix cannot picture him in Hollywood. "Never did anything but get in trouble there, though. It's not for me."

"I'm not sure it's for me either," Felix says. "So... the mules?"

"Right, the mules. Well, Lilac here was my first, this little runty baby, and I didn't know nothing about them then, like I said. I thought it would be cute to name her Lilac, like a whatchamacallit, an homage. I thought all mules were girls, like calico cats, so I didn't even think to ask about the sex. But the name had stuck by the time I found out he was a boy, and I couldn't bring myself to change it to Lyle or nothing. It's wild, though—'stead of thinking of my mule as a girl, I started to think of that little girl that got lost as a boy. Like Lilac was a boy's name. And when I picture her wandering around all lonely down there, I picture her as this tomboyish kinda girl."

Lilac shakes his head. The man adds, "I'm Ernie Janss, by the way."

"Felix. Ketay. I've got a boy's name, so, well…it's really spooky, the whole Lilac Ambrose thing." Spooky is not the right word for the alchemy of loss and fever and mystery in Felix's stomach.

"I've heard people say they found bones up in the mine. Just here and there. I don't know about that—this place was fulla hippies in the '60s and '70s, and I figure that if there was anything to be found, they made off with it a long time ago. Probably left a lot of crap, too. Probably had barbeques and sing-alongs and whatnot up there.

"Nice meeting you, Felix," says Ernie, touching his baseball cap. "If you ever want to take a ride on a mule, I'm at all the fairs. Me and my daughter'll be at the Lilac Mines Festival come spring. You enjoy your stay."

"Thanks."

Lilac and Ernie make a wide turn and crunch up the gravel road, the cart clattering behind them, toward a cluster of trailers.

She returns to the library Thursday afternoon; this time she called ahead. An old woman sits at a center library table with a stack of large-print mystery novels. When she finds a couple she likes, she checks them out and waves good-bye to the librarian, leaving Felix alone with Gary Schipp. She feels highly conspicuous, her Doc Marten Mary-Janes squeaking loudly as she crosses the floor. Everything here is on a small scale: the low ceiling, the narrow stacks, the miniature-golf pencils held by a juice glass.

In the back corner, there's a computer. A sign next to the monitor says, "Internet access: Visit the circulation desk to put your name on the waiting list." Felix looks around the empty library. Gary Schipp, a 50ish man in librarianesque half-glasses and a loud, not-so-librarianesque Hawaiian shirt, hunches over a book. He has not acknowledged her presence.

She clenches her fists. She's checked her email once since arriving, at a café in town. But it's been over a week. What if Eva was staying in some shady hostel in a former eastern bloc country, cut off from the Internet? Maybe she's only recently made it to a developed city and has finally emailed her remorseful thoughts to Felix. Maybe she's wondering, at this very minute, whether Felix will forgive her and take her back.

A few feet away, the computer stares blankly at Felix.

She takes what her *Rock-Hard Abs 'n' Enlightenment* DVD would call a cleansing breath and turns her back to the computer. She tries to imagine herself as one of those kick-'im-to-the-curb girls on *Rikki Lake*. *You are not even worth booting up for, Eva*, she tries to think.

She walks over to the circulation desk and clears her throat. Gary Schipp lowers his glasses.

"Do you have, like, a local history section?" Felix asks.

Gary Schipp sighs. "You don't know how to use a card catalog, do you?" His voice indicates he's resigned to this fact. He gestures to an ancient set of cherry-colored drawers.

"No one does these days," he continues. He is losing his hair an atypical way. A ring of gray-blond wisps remains, making him look like a monk with bangs. "Part of it, of course, is that there's no money to overhaul the old system, but I have to admit, I like the old girl. All those delicate drawers and the typed cards. Each one is a little gem, don't you think?"

"Like how sometimes an artist's sketches are more interesting than the final painting or sculpture or whatever?" Felix considers.

"Exactly like that," Gary agrees. "Now, you're looking for local history? It's in the third aisle, see where the *Sweet Valley High* display is? In back of that."

Felix seats herself behind a cardboard cutout of the Wakefield twins and begins scanning the shelves. There are lots of books on the Gold Rush. Hikes to take in Gold Rush country. Maps to ghost towns in California and Nevada. Mechanical histories of the mining industry. Felix grew up in a world of soft, Spanish-derived names: Hermosa Beach,

Rancho Palos Verdes, Santa Monica; she and Eva had their first date at a vegetarian co-op café called Luna Tierra Sol. Now she encounters harsh tumbleweed names, mineral-sounding names: Chemung, Chloride City, Rhyolite, Leadfield, Salt Springs, Calsun. Places that promise a hard life.

The books favor Wild West tales and well-preserved towns. If a sometime boomtown is now a few crumbling foundations, it doesn't seem to matter what happened there. The books conflate history and tourism. Most have exactly one paragraph about Lilac Mines: girl got lost, town got its name. Make sure to visit the old soda fountain and see the *Gold Rush Melodrama* at the old theater.

One book stands out, perhaps because it does so little to announce itself. It has a thin, taped spine with no title. When Felix dislodges it from the others, she sees that it's staple-bound. The cover is hand-lettered: *A Brief History of Lilac Mines* by Lucas Twentyman. Felix smiles. The title sounds like that Stephen Hawking book her dad read, *A Brief History of Time*. She likes to think that the town's history might be as objective and as profound as the laws of physics. But the book—which appears to be self-published—was copyrighted in 1974, so Lucas Twentyman pre-dates Stephen Hawking.

The book is missing many of the trappings of regular history books. There's no index, no "about the author," no intriguing blurb on the back cover. Felix pries open the stiff cover and starts with the foreword.

Dearest Readers,

I write this as our town is in danger of, once again, succumbing to the whitewashing sands of time, of becoming a ghost town for the second time in its unlikely history. This, dear readers, is precisely *why* I write: to preserve, to fight the Powers That Be. Let little Lilac tell her story, from the earliest settlers to the tragic fate of Miss Lilac Ambrose to the noble folk that manned the sawmill in the industrious nineteen-forties.

The '60s-revolutionary-meets-doddering-historian tone calms down after the first few pages. Without an index, Felix flips. She is hungry for something, and she can't devour the pages fast enough. She learns that Lilac Mines gets up to 15 feet of snow in the winter. That the remaining trees are sugar pines. That, before the town was East Beedleborough, it was Ragtown. When travelers made it over a particularly difficult pass in the Sierras, they washed out their clothes and spread them out to dry wherever they could. Only rags remained, spider-webbed over the sagebrush like a warning. Finally she finds Lilac.

> Little is known about Harold Ambrose or his daughter, Young Lilac. As he was a working man (though, as foreman, he did better than some), it is not surprising that his name fails to appear in society registers or, in fact, much of anywhere besides mining documents and a grocery tab before he made unwanted headlines after Lilac died (presumably). Ambrose left his native Milwaukee in the mid-eighteen-eighties, when Lilac was a baby. Although newspaper accounts would later list her mother as "deceased," there are no records of a female Ambrose being born in Milwaukee in eighteen-eighty-four. There is, however, record of a Lilac Zaide, born to a "Gertie" Zaide in April of that year. The father is listed as "unknown." This leads us to conclude that Lilac was either an illegitimate child or not born in Milwaukee after all. I was hoping to travel to Milwaukee to investigate this matter in person, but I am of limited means at the moment.

Well, at least he's honest, Felix thinks. Lucas Twentyman wins when it comes to Lilac Ambrose minutiae—her hair was "said to be a golden-brown shade;" her father was promoted to foreman just a month before the accident; an elaborate funeral was held, as if an abundance of flowers could compensate for the lack of a body. For the first time since arriving in Lilac Mines, she feels like she might have a place here. As she reads, she is at Lilac's funeral, inhaling the soapy sweet smell of lilies and throwing herself on the empty coffin, her broken body embracing Lilac's missing one.

At the same time, the gaps and question marks send chills down her gauze-wrapped spine. The story is the same as in other books. The holes are the same. The book includes the same group photo of the angsty miners that was in the visitors' center. The caption says, "Miners circa 1898. Silicosis, a lung disease, was a common ailment." No names. She's angry and intrigued.

She tucks Twentyman's book and the one that had the best photographs under her arm and returns to the circulation desk.

"What about local newspapers?" Felix asks. *A Brief History* has grainy reproductions of the more sordid headlines from the *East Beedleborough Examiner*.

"We've got the *Lilac Mines Chronicle* going back to 1983, but if you want anything older than that, you'll have to go to the main branch in Columbia. They've got some originals and some issues on microfiche," Gary says. He stamps the cards in her books. "Luke Twentyman, eh? This one hasn't been checked out in quite a while. He's sort of a local eccentric," Gary explains.

"You mean he's crazy or something?" Felix wants the book to be true. She wants *books* to be true.

"No, no—at least not by small town standards," Gary smiles. "You know how we are out here."

"Mm." Twentyman—when she hears it aloud, she remembers: This is her new boss's last name. There can't be too many Twentymans in town.

"Anything else?"

Felix means to say no, but she hears herself say, "Can I use the Internet?"

Finally, the name "Eva London" lights up her inbox as if accompanied by a small red flag icon. Nervously, Felix clicks and reads:

hi everyone,

berlin is amazing. a welcome change from prague, which was beautiful, of course, but so touristy already. if i'd been born even five years earlier, i know i would've been chillin' with all the other ex-pats, but c'est la vie.

but berlin—this is a real city. this morning we went to the jewish museum—so powerful—and took a walk by the spree river, which is overrun with these adorable little black ducks. haus am checkpoint charlie was pretty cheesy (lots of berlin wall for sale), but it was cool seeing the funky cars people built to sneak across the border. they managed to smuggle someone in an *isetta*! it's amazing what people will do to get to a safe place.

an interesting fact about the city: a huge percentage of the "historic" buildings here are actually replicas. the originals were badly damaged in the war, and afterward, the re-builders just made a giant photocopy. maybe the citizens felt better surrounded by history, or what looked like history. between the dreary communist apartments in east berlin and the new "old" buildings in west berlin and the club we went to last night (abandoned storefront-turned-pool hall), it's a totally schizo city. i love it.

everything's covered in graffiti, even the graveyards.

next stop: munich.

till then,

e

Felix gulps. Apparently, Eva has forgotten to take Felix out of her address book; now she's just one of "everyone." The two vague "we's" in the email dance and gloat. For the first time since the break-up, Felix seethes. How dare Eva relegate her to travelogue reader. She deserves a personalized story, a real explanation, a confession: *Kate snores. I miss you.* How dare she think that Felix will be content with the official story.

She looks at the books in her bag. More official stories getting her nowhere. She needs to rake her fingers along the floor of the mineshaft until Lilac's ghost asks, *What's all that noise?*

SQUATTERS
Al: Lilac Mines, 1965

On the ride to Beedleborough, Jody and Imogen debate who should get the clerk's attention, and who should avoid it.

"We want to get in and out of the store fast, right?" says Imogen. "And if I'm the one asking for help, I'm going to be waiting behind every white person who walks in there."

"But at least you look normal," says Jody, steering the Edsel down a street bigger than Calla Boulevard but smaller than most of the avenues in downtown Fresno. From the back seat, Anna Lisa watches taverns and barber shops roll by. Her palms are sweaty. "When people see you, they think, 'There's a Negro'—it makes sense, even if they don't like it. They don't think, 'What is that freak of nature?'"

Imogen pets the blonde fuzz on the back of Jody's neck. "You're not a freak, you're my handsome butch."

"I'm just telling it like it is. And put your hand down. Someone's gonna see."

They have chosen a department store in Beedleborough as their destination because Lilac Mines is too small to shop for menswear in. People talk. A boy that Edith dated when she was dating boys works at the one apparel shop in Lilac Mines. He threatened to hurt Shallan, Edith's butch, if Edith or her friends came in there again.

In the end, they decide Imogen will take the lead. Jody and Anna Lisa hang back by the ties and socks, as if working their way up from accessories to meatier items: shirts, suits. The men's section is paneled with dark wood and smells like shoe polish.

"Go talk to him," Jody says, gesturing with her chin to one of the clerks. "He looks like family."

Imogen shakes her head. "Naw, he's a bigot."

"How do you know?"

"I can tell, okay?"

Imogen waits while another clerk helps a thick-waisted man select a belt. Then she approaches.

"Excuse me, I'm looking for some nice shirts for my husband's birthday."

While the thin-lipped clerk talks to Imogen, Jody and Al load their arms with clothes and sneak off to the fitting room. Al's heart feels as if it might burst out of the first cotton shirt she tries on.

A few minutes later, there's a soft knock on the dressing room door. Al freezes. "Imogen," Jody mouths, and opens the door.

"*Smooth.*" Imogen nods approvingly, and slips inside. The three of them are inches apart.

"We gotta get Sylvie to cut your hair, though," says Jody, keeping her voice low. "That'll be the finishing touch."

Al sees herself in their faces, but she turns toward the mirror behind her to check if it's true. The crisp white shirt makes her shoulders look square. The black slacks are sleek and formal. They make Al think of dance floors. Her shoulder-length brown hair crouches in a low ponytail at the back of her neck.

Jody slips it inside Al's collar. "See? All gone."

"The pants are too long," Al worries, wagging a foot.

"One of the femmes will hem them," Jody assures her.

"Really?"

"'Course."

"*If* you ask nice," Imogen clarifies.

Al thinks of her father's slacks. He takes them to the tailor down the street from Hill Food & Supply. Even if Al could afford a tailor, she can't just walk in and say, *Shorten these pants to fit a 5'4" woman—and let the hips out a little while you're at it.*

"All the femmes are going to swoon," Imogen whispers.

"You think?" Al says, stifling a smile. She has seen Meg at Lilac's two more times. All the other regulars seem to be more… regular. Jody and Imogen keep singing the praises of Sylvie, a femme who lives with them and a few other women in an abandoned church east of Calla Boulevard. Sylvie has delicate features, silent-film-star lips, a funny way of wringing her hands. She's okay, but something about her is too familiar. Al prefers to watch Meg in profile as she sips her drink. There's a bump in the middle of her nose. Al wonders if it's been broken.

"Wait till Sylvie sees you," says Jody. Jody has a way of making things sound like the final word. These clothes. This girl. Al wonders if this is what it's like to have an older brother—someone fiercely on your side and mostly uninterested in your opinion. "Okay, put your old clothes back on and Imogen will go pay for these," Jody instructs. "Did you want the blue shirt too?"

"No, this is already more than I can afford," says Al.

"Don't worry, we'll chip in. Right, Jo?" Imogen says. "We're like the Homosexual Welcome Wagon."

Al slides out of the slacks, catching sight of herself in white underpants and bra, suddenly a girl again. Opening her body as little as possible, she puts on her women's brown slacks. In the fluorescent light of the dressing room, she can see how dusty they are. She's worn them almost every day during the weeks she's been in Lilac Mines. She's reluctant to unpack her other clothes—the circle skirts, the secretarial blouses—for fear that they'll mop up all the town's magic like old rags.

Imogen gathers Al's new clothes and eases out of the dressing room. Twice as fast, she pulls back in. "Damn it," she hisses. "I think he saw me."

"Who?" mouths Jody.

Imogen's voice is barely audible. "Some man. Some customer. Damn it, *damn* it." Her blue-shadowed eyes are wide. Jody is breathing heavily, combing her hands over her short, red-blonde hair as if it will coax a plan from her head. The fearless centaur of the other night looks panicked, slightly wild.

Peering through a narrow gap in the booth's structure, Imogen whispers, "All right, he went back out. You two gotta make a break for it."

Al doesn't know exactly what this involves so she follows Jody, who walks briskly down the hall of dressing rooms, past a rack of shiny leather shoes, and toward the make-up counter. Behind them, the clerk's voice calls out, "Ladies? Ladies!" a reminder of what they are or should be.

"He's on to us," Jody says. "I hope Imogen doesn't try to pay for that stuff now. She'll get hassled something awful."

They linger nervously by a poster of a dark-haired woman powdering her face. It says, "Ladies: what could be more foolish than choosing a foundation based on your hair color?" Al, who only wore make-up when Suzy pinned her down and attempted to obliterate her freckles, didn't know that this was something ladies did. She has to agree it seems foolish.

Finally, Imogen trots up to them. "I took it upstairs and paid in Children's," she says. "I don't think that clerk in Men's was about to leave his post, but we better get outta here just in case."

"Sounds good to me," Al says. She takes the bag from Imogen and clutches it tight to her body as they exit the store and hurry toward Jody's grinning Edsel. Al has never worked so hard for a pair of pants. She's never had a pair that fit so well.

The church is a plain wooden building with peeling paint and a rusted-silent bell in its steeple. Nevertheless, Al considers it a holy place. When Jody explained that they were squatters, Al asked how they got away with it. "Think of us like church mice," Jody said. "Everyone knows they're there, but no one cares until one of them runs up some old lady's leg." And so by this blessing they are left alone with their functional altars: the wood-burning stove; the long table Jody and Shallan built; the old pews pushed together to form beds, appropriated as shelves, arranged in every formation but straight rows.

Al's new clothes are folded neatly on the pew that holds her suitcase. The white shirt is dappled gold and purple in a stained-glass shadow.

"Where's Imogen?" Al asks. "I need to pay her back for the clothes."

She peels the last bills from her wallet. They're dog-eared, soft as a peach.

"She's getting dinner started," Sylvie says with a giggly grimace. Of the femmes, Imogen is the worst cook. Jody has asked that she not cook meat because it's expensive and she always renders it un-chewable.

Al finds her in the church's tiny kitchen chopping vegetables. Zigzags of hair escape her carefully molded bun. The ostensibly white countertop is stained and missing tiles, like a bad smile. Imogen's coffee-brown forearms ripple as she knifes a yellow squash, as if pure determination will summon the proper picture of domesticity.

"Ten seventy-five, right?" says Al. "I'll leave it over here." She puts the bills under a saltshaker shaped like a chubby farmer. His chipped wife holds the pepper. "I need a job," Al sighs.

"We all do," says Imogen, although she's just being sympathetic. She has a regular job at a doctor's office—technically as a receptionist, although the doctor frequently asks her to clean the examining rooms, and occasionally asks her to kiss him. She gives in to the former to make it easier to refuse the latter. "The end of the month is the toughest. But don't worry too much. We know you do your part. Maybe you're not working yet, but you swept up and set those mousetraps and helped Jody with..."

With a start, Al says, "The end of the month... wait, what's the date today?"

"August 24th."

"Oh *no*. It's my sister's birthday." Al can't believe she forgot. Usually she is vigilant about deadlines. Her school papers didn't always earn A's, but she invariably turned them in on time. But so many things are different in Lilac Mines. Maybe time is too.

"You still talk to your family?" The hard and longing look on Imogen's face says that she does not talk to hers.

"Well... I don't know. I haven't really decided anything yet, not officially." Hot afternoons of around-the-church work with Jody have stretched into evenings of scanning for Meg, which have cooled into yellow-gray mornings waking up on her mat. The floor pressing into her back makes her feel resilient, ready for another day with her tribe.

Imogen wipes her pulpy hand and reaches into the pocket of her skirt. She drops two dimes into Al's palm. "Go to the drugstore and give her a call." Her voice is so sure, so parental, that Al doesn't dare turn her down.

Al could walk to the drugstore, buy a soda, and page through movie magazines for a while. She could buy a newspaper and read it at the counter. But she's not a good liar. If Imogen asks her how her sister is, she won't be able to invent an answer. This is why she cannot live in Fresno and love girls at the same time. She can't imagine looking at her father's expectant, mustached face and telling him that she was out with a nice boy last night, nothing serious, no, she doesn't think she'd like to bring him home.

The first dime tinkles into the pay phone. The operator asks for another, and Al remembers that this is long distance. She's not sure she's ever made a long-distance call before. She blows a small O of air from her lips and drops in the second dime.

Suzy picks up on the third ring. Al's first reaction is relief that it's not one of her parents on the other end of the line, but her stomach quickly clenches again. She will still have to explain.

"Anna Lisa?" Suzy exclaims when she hears her sister's voice. "Oh my God, Nannalee, I'm so glad you called. Are you okay? Where are you?"

"I'm fine, I'm in..." Al hesitates. She wonders if her family is the type to form a search party, and if she'd want them to. She decides to say she's in San Francisco—big, un-searchable, home to Alcatraz—but when she opens her mouth, she says, "I'm in this little town. It's, um, kind of northeast of us." She is still placing herself with them: "Us" is Fresno, slow days, the hum of the ceiling fan in the family store, crops lined up the way church pews are supposed to be lined up.

"Why did you run away?" Suzy wants to know. It's a fair question.

Al recalls the vague note she left. "I... when I tried to picture the rest of my life, nothing came up. Does that make any sense at all? It was so frightening. Just a blank, like all the old fields around our house."

To Al's surprise, Suzy says, "Yes! It *does* make sense. Oh, Nannalee, they both broke things off. First Roy, because he found out about Kevin, then Kevin because he's just a copycat. Now I don't know what to do— they're both spreading rumors—and I can't exactly tell Mother and Daddy about this sort of problem."

Suzy's voice is twisted with despair. Somehow Al thought that things would stay the same in her absence, that liking boys would be enough to guarantee Suzy a future in Fresno.

"What should I do? Couldn't you come home?" Suzy begs. Her questions are no longer about Al's motivations and safety; now they demand things from her. Al's fraction of a moment in the spotlight burned her, then left her cold.

"Let me think about it. I'll call you again soon, I promise." Their phone time is almost up, and Al is out of coins. "Happy birthday," she adds feebly.

DIFFERENT STORIES
Felix: Lilac Mines, 2002

For her first day of work, Felix wears a '70s sundress over skinny-legged jeans. She's aware that she's been femming it up lately. She's always worn dresses and skirts and chunky jewelry, but she's alternated them with butcher days: long shorts and boyish T-shirts and knit beanies. Lilac Mines is a town of sweatshirts and sneakers, androgynous and utilitarian, but she doesn't want to take any chances. And she hates that she doesn't want to take any chances.

At Goodwill, she winces when Tawn hands her the requisite blue apron, and winces again when she pulls the strings around her waist. The ache in her side has dulled, but it's far from gone. Its persistence irks her. *Okay, I get it, you've made your point,* she tells her injury. Pain—she would never have suspected this—is boring.

"I feel like I should be baking," she jokes, smoothing the apron over her thighs.

"I hate baking," says Tawn. She seems immune to Felix's humor. Today she's wearing the same black jeans that she interviewed Felix in, with a different baggy T-shirt. This one says *I Love to Ski Mammoth Lakes* in puffy letters. Felix doubts it's ironic, but she can't picture Tawn—with her resigned posture and fearful expressions—actually skiing, either.

"The truck comes today," Tawn reminds her.

"You said."

"I'll be working on payroll, but Matty can help you with any of the heavy stuff." She gestures to the other employee working the shift, a chubby, 30ish blond guy in a very sincere-looking marijuana leaf T-shirt. Tawn tugs at her rope of black hair—somehow braided without being untangled—and retreats into the back of the store.

"It's Matt," says Matty as Felix follows him outdoors. It's already hot. "Tawn and I grew up together, I mean, she's eight years younger than me, but I was still Matty when she was a kid. Old habits die hard. I still can't believe she's my fucking boss."

But it's too late: Matty is Matty to Felix. They sit down on an old bench, someone's discarded patio furniture, and wait. Felix is surprised that they're not expected to do anything in the meantime, but she has no complaints. The sky is cloudless, the sun unapologetic. She can feel new freckles erupt on her shoulders.

"Tawn says you're from L.A.?"

"Yeah, I'm visiting my aunt Anna Lisa for the summer." She holds her breath. There's no reason that this explanation shouldn't suffice, but she lives in fear that someone will call her on it.

"Cool," Matty nods vigorously. "I'm probably gonna head down to L.A. sometime. Or up to Portland. I gotta get out of this place." He lights a cigarette.

Felix doesn't think he'll leave. He doesn't seem like the motivated type. "I'm going to New York in a few months," she says. She did visit the Fashion Institute of Technology website. There was a photo of the street sign for 7th Avenue, with the words "Fashion Avenue" above it. But the only graduate program that's vaguely related to fashion design is "Museum Theory: Costume and Textiles," which sounds stuffy and irrelevant. She clicked "Send me an application," just in case.

"What do you think of our lady Tawn?" Matty challenges.

"She's interesting."

"She's a trip, isn't she?"

"She's really hung up on getting me to unload the truck. Is it that hard?"

Matty's mouth forms a half-smile, half-smirk. "No. It's not hard at all. It's a bitch when it's this hot, but that's not why Tawn tries to get out of it whenever she can." He pauses dramatically. "She's afraid of the clothes."

"What do you mean?"

"I mean, she has a fucking phobia of other people's old clothes."

"Well, it's probably not a bad idea to wash your hands after——" Felix allows.

But Matty cuts her off. "No, not like that. Get this: whenever Tawn sees, say, a pair of baby's pajamas, she immediately pictures something awful happening to the kid who wore them. Like he turned all cold and still in his little baby crib and his parents came in and freaked out, and his pajamas ended up here, eventually. Or she sees some jeans with a weird stain on them and decides it's blood, that the person was in a car accident and lost his leg and can't bear to look at the jeans he was wearing when it happened. How fucked up is that?"

"Wow," is all Felix can say. For her, thrift stores are a chance to have what no one else has. It never occurred to her to think about the lives that shirts and scarves and jeans had previously.

The truck pulls up: a huge 18-wheeler, a football player at a tea party. Matty leads the way, and with the driver's help unloads five cardboard boxes. He shows Felix how to sort the clothes into blue plastic bins taller than she is, labeled "Men's Pants," "Women's Blouses," "Undergarments," etc. It hurts to lift her arms too high, but it's a hurt she can deal with. She feels good when sweat darkens the flowered print beneath her arms.

"What do you think?" she asks holding up a pair of gray wool pants. "Men's or women's?"

"Men's," Matty says definitively.

Felix tosses them into the appropriate bin. They strike an acrobatic pose in the air before joining the other golf pants and jeans and Dickies. For a second they look alive.

"How about these?" She holds up a petite pair of light pink leggings. "Women's pants, or tights?"

"Women's pants." Matty is immune to doubt.

"Not kids'?" They make no allowance for hips. They'd probably be small on Eva, who is 5' 8" and wears a size six.

"Nope."

The leggings arabesque into the Women's Pants bin.

Felix sets aside a tank top decorated with what is either a yoga symbol or a Farsi word. Either way, her sister Michelle, who can fold herself like a cinnamon roll and has a Persian boyfriend, will like it. But as she folds the shirt, she takes a minute to smell it, something she'd normally avoid. Beneath the generic used-clothing smell, there's a hint of something sweet and foody. A thread of soapy perfume beneath that. The smells give nothing away, but Felix starts to think. She sees a girl walk through the kitchen of a family restaurant, grab a snack, kiss someone on the cheek, the fat of love stretching her tank top.

Tawn says Felix can help with the front window's back-to-school display. This is clearly a prize for touching the clothes at their most raw. After excitedly combing the store for plaid skirts, Felix says, "What I don't get is why you always assume that something *bad* happened to the people who wore the clothes."

Tawn opens her mouth, then closes it. Her face turns tartan-red. "Matty told you?"

"Was he not supposed to?"

"God, I hate him." Her vigor surprises Felix. For someone so timid, she is steadfast about her dislikes. "I should fire him."

"There's nothing wrong with that," Felix says kindly. "I thought it was sort of an interesting theory—I mean, I'd never looked at clothes as having their own histories before."

"But I'm in the wrong job," Tawn laments. She strips a smooth-skinned male mannequin of its pants, shaking her head sadly. "When I was a kid, I took this field trip to Washington, DC with my class. I went to prom. I almost went to college. Now I can't imagine any of that stuff. I can only think about, like, how the guy who wore those brown shoes over there was a traveling salesman who cried between houses."

Felix frowns and sets down the stack of skirts as Tawn's feet, like an offering. "Well, maybe it's just a matter of re-appropriation."

"Huh?"

"Different stories."

"What, he was a salesman and he *laughed* between houses? He worked so hard because he really loved his children? Doesn't work. I wouldn't buy it."

"Neither would I," Felix admits. She likes that Tawn is a tough sell. "But... what if he wasn't a salesman? What if he was, um... how about a tap dancer? He was a tap dancer, but he lived in an apartment building in New York, and he practiced in these shoes instead of the ones with the taps so it wouldn't bother the people living downstairs."

"So why'd he get rid of them?" Tawn says, arms crossed. She's cute when she's skeptical—one dark eyebrow raised, T-shirt pulled tight over young-girl breasts.

"He moved into this apartment building and lived above the woman who had the best hearing in the world. Like it was actually measured by the *Guinness Book of World Records*. And she could hear him tapping away on his wood floors, even in these normal, non-tap shoes. So he had to switch to sock feet."

"That's still kind of sad."

"No," Felix assures her. "It's not, because he and the woman hooked up. They had, like, really amazing sex. Both of them in their sock feet. She said she could hear his heartbeat when she put her ear to his elbow. It didn't work out in the end, but that's okay, 'cause it wasn't really love anyway. The woman moved to a different building, and the man moved into *her* apartment, and it was on the first floor. The first first-floor apartment he'd ever had—because New York is like that, you have to take what you can get—and he finally got to tap in his actual tap shoes. He bought a new pair to celebrate, and sent this pair to Goodwill."

Tawn has paused in the middle of putting knee socks on a female mannequin. The look on her face says she's not sure if she buys it, but she'll play along.

So Felix tells her about how the socks belonged to a girl who bought her entire uniform for the prep school her parents wanted her to attend, and decided at the last minute to go to public school with her friends instead.

"On the first day of class," Felix says, "she tore off her socks and stuffed them in her backpack. She ripped the sleeves off her stiff white shirt. But she kept the cute plaid miniskirt because those get trendy every fall anyway."

"You're really into what's trendy, aren't you?" says Tawn.

"No," Felix says, "but the schoolgirl is." She smiles, volleying Tawn's mischievous look back to her.

They dress the mannequins in plaid. Tawn looks a little green when they discover a brown stain on one of the skirts. They give their school kids backpacks and books. A romance novel for the boy and a coffee table book about hot rods for the girl. Felix tells Tawn about the pants that starred as the "before" pair in a weight loss commercial before being donated by their newly svelte owner, and the golf cap given up when its owner discovered a hidden talent for gymnastics.

The store is open now and Matty helps the customers, who are few and low-maintenance. By the time their mannequins are ready for school, Tawn is ready to try her own story.

"So this ugly purse," she begins, picking up a shapeless leather satchel, "was actually used, uh, to carry three little kittens—"

"Who lost their mittens?"

"Shh, I'm trying. Fine, *four* kittens, from under the overpass on Washoe Street to a lady's house. And she took care of them and everything. But got them fixed when they were old enough, of course."

"Kittens," Felix nods. "That's good. You can't go wrong with kittens."

"Are you making fun of me?"

"Yes."

"*Anyway*," says Tawn, flinging the golf cap at Felix like a frisbee, "the kittens peed all over the purse. So the lady couldn't wear it anymore, which was a good thing for everyone. The end."

"*Much* better."

When Felix gets back to Anna Lisa's house, there are corn muffins cooling on the counter. Crispy on the outside, cakey inside, flecked with little bits of real corn. She wonders where her aunt learned to bake. Felix's mother is an add-some-real-cheddar-to-the-mac-and-cheese-mix cook. But Anna Lisa, once again, is not around to ask.

After rinsing her plate, Felix retreats to the guest room. According to Crane, Robbie adores Genevieve, the subletter. Apparently, Genevieve makes marinara sauce to rival her namesake. (The residents of apartment 414 are hopelessly branded: Genevieve Barilla, Crane Mitsubishi, Robbie McCormick, and Felix Ketay share their last names with a pasta, a car company, a mortuary, and a literary agency, respectively.) Genevieve has Betty Page bangs and crazy art school friends. Genevieve makes abstract papier-mâché sculptures because she believes in the return of beauty.

Felix vows to make her reluctant sublet a little more her own. She retrieves the stack of old postcards from the nightstand; she could tape them around the dresser mirror. It would be a start. Flipping past a black and white landscape and a portrait of a stoic Native American man, she selects one of the oldest looking postcards, an illustration of a poppy, as intricate and vulnerable as a page from a sketchbook. Unlike the others, it has writing on the back. The handwriting is heavily slanted, anxiously pushing forward.

> *My Dear Cal, Why must you be all the way 'cross town? (I'm kiding with you of course, but its fun to write, is it not?) Father was in a bit of a mood to-day. I never thought I would say it, but some times I miss school. Time is slow as soup with out it, and with out you. But we'are going berry picking in just a few short days! I am praying for sun but not too much of it, and wilde straw-berries galor! All my love, L.*

Felix studies the last letter. It is a joyous loop of an L, written in faded pencil. And she can't help but think, *L is for Lilac.* Of course she *would* think this, she reminds herself—the way Cookie Monster would think, *C is for Cookie.* The ancient postmark is local, dated August 1899. It would have been just a few weeks before she died. The handwriting is youthful—well formed but not yet set in its ways. Not weighed down by anything so dull as correct spelling.

Who is Cal? Is he really such a dear? There's no last name, just an address: *319 Washoe Str., E. Beedleborough, Calif.* Felix thinks of the young, bare-chested miner. It's just a hunch, of course, but today stories come easily to her. Maybe Dearest Cal invited Lilac to go berry-picking. Maybe he promised that the best berries were farther up the mountain, just a little farther still. The next thing Lilac knew, the air was thin, and the August sun burned a red line into the part of her hair. Dearest Cal took his shirt off. He seemed too perfect to be real, and she felt far away from him. When he suggested going in the mine, she agreed to it, hoping that in the dark, it would feel like they lived in the same world again.

Felix shakes her head. Tawn is rubbing off on her. It's just as likely that Cal was sweet and gentle, the kind of guy who takes his dates berry-picking. It's likely that "L" is not Lilac Ambrose. And it's *very* likely that Cal is not the scary-studly miner from the photo. What are the chances?

The postcard becomes an artifact in Felix's hands. Suddenly she feels guilty touching it, like she should be wearing gloves. But she can't quite let go either. She holds it gently, Maybe-Lilac's words between her own purple-glitter thumbnails. Out loud, she says, "All my love, Lilac."

A + M FOREVER
Al: Lilac Mines, 1965

Al assumes she'll go back home and Lilac Mines will fade into a strange, distant episode, but she's not quite ready to be sure of it. So she gives herself a few more days, another week, to pretend that Lilac Mines is real. She tries not to think about the fact that the days now add up to nearly two months.

On Fridays and Saturdays, the women eat dinner in a hurry, dress in a drawn-out frenzy and head for Lilac's, where they look at each other as if half of them didn't walk over together. As if the butches' DAs weren't sculpted from spit on palms, as if the femmes didn't have to pay for their own drinks. Al has consumed more beer in the past eight weeks than she has in her life up till now. She's gone out more in the past seven days than during all of high school. She's compressed a lifetime into a handful of weeks and, for now, it's Fresno that is fuzzy and unreal.

One night, she touches Meg's hair. She's playing darts next to Jody, whose arm slices through the air like a tractor-trailer rumbling through the hot valley—not quite graceful, but accurate and unstoppable. The frayed dart pricks a ring near the middle.

"You should see her when she's sober." Caleb the bartender is sweeping coins from the bar into his palm. Al has learned that Caleb smiles only with his eyes. At first she thought he was unfriendly, but now she knows she just has to look closely. This is a world of looking closely: handkerchiefs peeking out of men's pockets mean different things depending on whether they are orange or green or light blue. A girl off limits yesterday might be available today, but you have to move in oh so slowly. Al has to still herself to sense the movement, like a rabbit with its ears up.

Jody is frustrated that the dart is not closer to the bull's-eye. She throws her head back and shakes out her arms. She takes bar games very seriously.

"Your turn," she says to Al.

Al is less sober than Jody, and probably got worse marks in Phys Ed. Her strategy in dodgeball was always to avoid the ball at first, comfortable in the throng of fleeing students, then—when it was being thrown by one of the milder members of the other team—throw herself in its path and get tagged out before she became a real target. Jody probably played like a boy, actually *trying* to catch the ball.

Al rolls the dart in her fingers, the dartboard swaying like a happy moon. She lets go. Suddenly Meg is where the moon was, and the dart is heading toward her neck. Meg turns, her lips forming a dark red O.

But Meg must have been a P.E. ace as well. She puts her purse up as a shield. The dart pierces it with a *thwip*.

Al lunges toward Meg. Her vision has proved untrustworthy, so her fingers take over. They land on Meg's dark hair—shiny, somewhere between ash and chocolate. She's wearing it down tonight, and it falls just below her shoulders. Somehow Al is cupping a handful. It is so heavy it feels slightly obscene—hair this thick should be regulated. It's just a little wet. Bordering on coarse. And the combination of weight and texture is undeniably real.

"Careful there," says Meg, and Al lets her hair drop and bounce. "I want to keep both my eyes if you don't mind." Her voice is smooth and wide, like her lips. She's smiling.

"Sorry. That was some move. With the purse."

"Likewise. Except for the purse part." She plucks the dart from her bag. There's a pinhole in the satin.

"Did I damage anything?"

Meg snaps open her purse and peeks inside. "Dildo's okay."

Al feels her ears turn the color of Meg's lipstick.

"I'm just joking around," Meg says. "I didn't mean to embarrass you. Butches can be such prudes."

Does this mean there *isn't* a dildo in Meg's purse? Al has only recently heard about them. Maybe butches use them but femmes carry them? Al is happy to be called a butch, one of the gang. She's less happy to be called a prude. But gangs are slippery like that. There are benefits and consequences of membership.

"But—well, I think you're sweet," Meg clarifies. When Al fidgets, Meg plants a kiss on her cheek, as if to prove it.

Now Meg's lipstick takes over Al's whole body—the red, the heat.

Al fumbles, drunk and floating toward the old tin ceiling. "I want to keep both of your eyes too," she says.

The second kiss happens during the tenth week of Al's unemployment. She has already traipsed Calla Boulevard and Main Street in her black slacks and white shirt. Lilac Mines Green Grocer is not hiring, nor is Main Street Market. All Al knows how to do is work in a grocery store, but she has tried the butcher shop and coffeeshop as well. The latter had a "Help Wanted" sign in the window, but the owner studied her for a minute, then said, "Sorry, that sign's old. We filled that position two weeks ago." Al suspects her clothing is to blame, but if she left the church in one of her schoolgirl skirts, Jody would call her a Saturday night butch.

Today she's trying Washoe Street, a less commercial stretch of town. So far the real estate office and tailor don't need anyone. It's late afternoon now, late fall. The air has taken on a crisp urgency. Exhausted, Al sits down on a wooden bench outside a two-story brick building with a faded ad on its side for Dr. Bell's Scientific Cough Suppressant. For the hundredth time, she contemplates returning to Fresno. She wants her father to direct her toward a case of canned lima beans and say, "Give us one of your eighth-wonder-of-the-world pyramids, kiddo." She misses his voice. She misses not having to say anything herself, sitting for hours among the undemanding vegetables and earnest grains of Hill Food & Supply.

"You're not bad-looking in the daylight, either."

Al looks up. Meg has appeared, like Glinda the Good Witch in her pink bubble. She's wearing a tight brown skirt and a yellow blouse, silk or at least silky. Her lipstick is even redder, if that's possible. She props a stack of papers and books on her hip like a baby and carries a paper cup of coffee from the shop that's not hiring in her free hand. She's not bad-looking in the daylight herself.

"Meg, hi!"

"Don't sound so surprised. I don't live at Lilac's, you know."

"I know." Al blushes. As much as she's heard Jody and Imogen and the other women discuss jobs and local landmarks, a part of her thought they *did* live at the bar; the bar and the church, maybe, but nowhere else. That they were magical enough to pull it off, while Al had to recite her cash register skills repeatedly. But now it appears that Meg is real. Al doesn't know if she wants her to be real or not.

"I work upstairs," she explains. "For a crazy Indian named Luke Twentyman. I'm helping him research a book about Lilac Mines. At least, that's the idea. Really I'm listening to his stories and reminding him to pay the phone bill."

"Wow," says Al. Although Meg is nonchalant, her job sounds important, academic. She's never known a researcher before.

Meg gets a mischievous look on her face. "Want to see the place? Luke is down the street at the post office."

Al follows Meg's curvy hips and muscular calves up a narrow staircase and down a hallway that smells like old newspaper. Luke's office is cramped and hot. Two hand-lettered signs lean against the bookcase: TWENTYMAN FOR MAYOR '62 and VOTE TWENTYMAN 1963. Two maps of Lilac Mines curl from the walls, one of the streets and one of the underground tunnels, which look like streets on paper. Luke's big desk is strewn with papers and sepia-tone photos. Meg's smaller desk seems to be growing its own junior mess. There are stacks and stacks of books, so much paper that it seems all the answers in the world must be stacked somewhere in this office. Meg is shiny and young in the middle of it. She smells like fresh coffee.

There is nowhere to sit—the chairs are piled high with papers, as well—and Al doesn't know where to stand. She leans from one leg to the other, hands in her pockets. "So, um, what are you researching? You know, specifically?"

Meg laughs. "Oh, who knows. Who ever knows with Luke." She talks about him like he's her favorite eccentric uncle. "One day it's the mining days, another it's the Clarksons. Today it's the Clarksons."

"The Clarksons?"

"The guys that own the mill. They bought up all the land when it was worth nothing, and now it's worth, well, more than nothing, I guess. Luke always calls them 'robber barons.' He uses words like that."

"Jody would kill for a job at the mill," Al says.

"What butch wouldn't? Hell, I'd work there myself if they'd hire me."

As difficult as it is to picture Meg doing manual labor, it's just as impossible to imagine anyone turning her down. Everyone, it seems, would want to spend as much time in Meg's radius as possible. Right now Al is trying to figure out how to do just that.

"How come you don't live in old church with everyone else?" Al asks.

"It's not everyone," Meg says. Her whole face becomes smaller for a minute, pinched together. "This town has a really narrow definition of 'everyone.' Anyhow, I did. I lived there for a while when I first moved here. But some people don't like it if you don't do every little thing their way. And I had enough money to rent my own place. My dad sent me a check for tuition every month. Or so he thought."

Half of her mouth relents. Her semi-smile lets Al know that she— Al, who is always the last to know—is in on the joke.

Al nods. Meg is standing so close to her that she can see how her gold hoop earrings pull at her earlobes. Al wants to touch her dewy, end-of-the-day skin. Thumbtacked to the wall just over Meg's shoulder is a photo of two girls holding hands. They are probably 15 or 16, but they wear serious pioneer expressions and busy, grown-up hats. Their slightly blurry, clasped hands are the only hint that they're still young girls. Or maybe it's a hint of something else.

Al opens her mouth to ask who they are. But something stops her. They are already the thing she needs them to be, which is the thing that gives her the courage to lean forward and kiss Meg on her red lips.

Meg's whole body responds, her tongue and her breasts and her hands, which cup Al's chin. They say, *This is okay, this is good.* Al has never kissed anyone before, but her body seems to know the story. Her hand knows how to reach around to the small of Meg's back, to rest lightly on the waistband of her skirt. Her pores open up. Her tongue circles. She's suddenly conscious of her underwear. But her ears pick up footsteps in the hallway, and her head pulls away.

What was she thinking? This is an office, not Lilac's. Meg looks at her as if Al is the person who could turn an office into Lilac's. But Al presses her face against the frosted glass in the door. She can't see anything.

"Was that him?"

Meg seems unconcerned. The sound fades. "Guess not. I took you for a goody-two-shoes, but wow." She sighs happily. Her sepia-brown hair is trying to escape its up-do. "This innocent girl from... Fresno, right? But you don't kiss like a goody-two-shoes."

Al shakes with excitement and nervousness. She wants Meg's words to be true. She wants to disappear before anything can ruin what just happened. Before what just happened can ruin the rest of her life.

"I should go," Al laments. "He'll be back any minute, right?"

"I could say you're my cousin, come to visit."

"I should go," Al repeats.

Meg puts her hand on Al's shoulder. It is a ten-colored tropical bird, perched there. "See you at Lilac's then?"

"At Lilac's." Al slips down the empty staircase and onto the empty street before anyone can discover which world she has sneaked into, and which she's slithered out of.

Weeks later, the row of women at the bar goes: femme, butch, butch, femme, femme, butch. More specifically: Meg, Al, Jody, Imogen, Sylvie, Jean. So that each woman can be seated between her love and her confidante. It's been three weeks, 17 kisses and one half-naked romp.

Meg and Al are official. So are Sylvie and Jean, Meg's ex. The two new couples slid together easily, and it feels like destiny.

Meg is tracing circles on Al's slacks with her red-polished finger. Al is finding it difficult to concentrate on what Jody is saying, something about President Johnson, how he will never measure up to Kennedy, who would have ushered in a new era if he had lived. "He understood young people, he thought the way we think," Jody says.

"Sounds like he's got your vote," Shallan jokes.

"Politics according to Jody," says Imogen, rolling her eyes. She turns to Sylvie, who is ignoring Jean the way women ignore their husbands, and Jean is left dangling like a husband, drumming the bar with her fingers.

"I'll tell you what else about President Kennedy," Jody says, fist meeting shiny wood bar in emphasis. "Everyone was so worried about him being more loyal to the Pope than to the Constitution, right? Well, this is what I say: they didn't need to worry because the Pope is overseas, far away, in Europe or wherever. And the Constitution is right here. I mean, maybe not framed in the presidential bedroom or nothing, but he was still surrounded by it. He woke up every day in the White House, met with Congress, maybe listened to a Supreme Court hearing now and then, ate some nice American lunch. You can't just *forget* all that, no matter how much you love Invisible God and Invisible Pope. You do what the people around you do."

"I think you're wrong," says Imogen. "I liked him too, but I think if he were still alive, people'd be picking on him same as Johnson. He'd be a little better looking, but he'd do dumb things, too. He'd mess with Asia and Cuba some more. It's just 'cause he's dead that everybody loves him. People like living in the past, especially white people. They can look back on five, ten, a hundred years ago and say, 'Aw, look how pretty and golden everything was back then.' And that pretty picture guides whatever they do in present times."

Meg has ceased to make circles on Al's thigh and is now scribbling something else. A code! Al's skin perks. Her love is sending her a message. "Start from the beginning," she tries to whisper out of the side of her mouth. Jody and Imogen don't seem to notice.

"What?" Meg whispers.

"Start from the beginning."

L... And then, another L? No, wait, two horizontal slashes: E.

"And Jackie, she's a cool cat... really classy, don't you think?"

Down, across. T. LET. Curve like, like Meg's profile. Ssss.

"She's really exotic looking. I wouldn't mind her as my first lady, if you know what I mean."

"God, Jody, don't be disgusting. You're making all the white girls blush."

LETS G, another E, another T. LETS GET. What, another drink? Ice cream?

"And no one's gonna buy your dumb soapboxes when they come *after* Johnson's been president for almost two years. You're a little behind in your speeches there, Jo."

LETS GET O-U-T O-F—

"Yes, let's," Al breathes in Meg's ear, and they exchange secret smiles and they're off down Calla Boulevard, forgetting to drop hands, climbing into Meg's pale yellow Ford, moonlight buttering its curves, spitting twin rivers of gravel as they wind toward the mountains, thinking about where they're going only after a bit of necking.

Al is behind the wheel, squinting at the road and trying not to let Meg's fingers on her earlobe send her careening into a ditch.

"Lilac Mines needs more streetlights," Al complains.

"Are you kidding? That means more getting caught. In the dark you can totally pass for a guy."

Al perks a little. Even with clothes that fit, she's not sure *she* fits. She believes that Jody and Jean and Shallan are butch down to their bones, but Al is short, with small hands and hesitant, fluttering insides.

Meg has a fabulous way of folding her legs on the passenger seat. Smooth white feet in a delightful tangle of sandal straps, toenails a pearly moon color. After wearing men's clothes for a time, Al has also developed a removed fascination with women's clothes, as if it takes a particular talent, a particular stoic grace to wear them.

Driving in Lilac Mines is a vertical experience. Up and up, loop and loop. Meg wants to show her something. She navigates from the passenger seat: turn here, turn here. The pine trees shoot out of the ground beside them, quiet arrows aimed at the sky.

Then: *thunk*. The car rattles and skids, not off the road, but its confidence seems to be shaken. "What was *that?*" breathes Al, foot to brake.

"Just a pothole. It's a gravel road. There are gonna be more, darling."

They're stopped now. "Still. I don't know this road well enough. Can you drive?" She's worried Meg will roll her eyes. She's patient and all— 21 to Al's 19, a virtual divorcée—but there are certain things a butch is supposed to *do*. But Meg's fingers are already around the door handle, her enticingly sandaled foot is already on the ground.

Before getting out, she leans back in and kisses Al on the cheek: "I *love* you."

Al gasps at Meg's casual passion and at the random gestures that prompt it. She feels as if she's only a few blocks away from love herself, but miles from comprehension.

Meg tears up the switchbacks, trees blurring, only blackness in the rearview mirror—as if there is nothing at all behind them, no past, no nothing—and Al wills herself not to clutch the safety handle above the window. This is her way of I Love You, this is I Am Putting My Life In Your Slightly Tipsy Hands. She looks at Meg, who leans into the steering wheel and the accelerator. There is something reckless about her, like she is capable of big, forbidden love and of other, darker things. Al saw that look in Suzy's eyes in the weeks before she boarded the bus. But on Meg, the look is not fleeting. She brushes a brown curl away from her face, as if nothing will come between her and the road.

And before Al can figure anything out, they are there. The Place. It looks like any other slight flattening of the mountain until Meg aims the headlights at a row of boards, seemingly nailed directly into the hillside like a giant eye patch.

"Lilac *Mines*," Meg says.

"Wow," is all Al can say.

Outside the car, it is mountain-cold: thin-aired, red-nosed, Christmas-scented. Dutifully, Al holds Meg's insufficient coat as she slips into it. Al feels Meg's arms animate the cloth with her warm, wriggling body. If this were the city, they would see lights stretched out below them and a gray sky above. But this is Lilac Mines, so they see the reverse: a vast black valley beneath an upside-down city of stars. It all feels upside-down to Al. She is a speck in the middle of nowhere… but that's the thing, it's the *middle* of nowhere: the absolute, pulsing epicenter of it.

Behind her, Meg has broken two fingernails prying boards back, revealing the socket beneath the patch. "Wanna see the mine?"

"Aren't there… aren't there, I don't know, coyotes or mountain lions in there?"

"Nothing bigger than could fit through these boards. Besides, it's true, you know… about them being more scared of you than you are of them."

Meg kneels in her dress, which was pink in the bar but now, like everything in Al's view, is just another shade of gray.

"It's warmer in here, that's the main thing," Meg says. Then she continues her history lesson. "Actually, I don't think there ever was a Lilac Mine. That's just what they started calling it after the little girl died. I think the mine itself was called something horribly dull. Western Mining Company Mine or something. This isn't the main entrance. We passed that on the road five miles back. This one is sort of hidden away."

They huddle together on the other side of the boards. *We are sitting in someone's eye*, Al thinks. The vast brain of the mountain thinks its secret thoughts behind them. Strings of dusty light squeeze between the boards, the only reminder of the car and the world outside.

"What do you mean, 'when the little girl died?' " Al asks.

Meg is quiet for a minute. Al studies her flat white cheeks, the large hands and sturdy arms that pull her knees to her chest.

"In 1899," Meg begins, "the mine was doing really good business. The town was one big silver factory. There was a miner named Mr. Ambrose, I think his first name was Gerald, or Harold maybe."

"Gerald is my dad's name," Anna Lisa says, but this interrupts Meg's once-upon-a-time tone, so she clamps her mouth shut.

"And he had a daughter, Lilac, who was 16 or 17. She was beautiful, with dark red hair, and she had little freckles like yours."

"How do you know what she looked like, if it was in the olden days?"

"That's just what people say, that's just how the story goes. Anyway, one day Lilac disappeared. A few people said they had heard her talk about going up to the mine, so pretty soon everyone in town was in the mine looking for her. They lowered themselves down in buckets and lit up the whole place with candles. They looked and looked for weeks. But they never found her, not in the mine and not anywhere else."

Meg's dark eyes are candles, too. She speaks as if Lilac Ambrose were her sister.

"Finally they gave up," Meg says. "They had to. It wasn't only sad for Gerald, it was a tragedy for the whole town. Can you imagine? It was just exhausting going about their lives with this big question hanging in the air. So they decided to have a funeral. Of course, there was no body, so they filled the coffin with flowers—little white wildflowers and big white calla lilies. And when they put it in the ground, it was so, so light."

There are tears like snail tracks on Meg's face. Al didn't notice her start to cry, but here is the evidence. Al pulls Meg toward her and whispers, "What happened to her? Does anyone know? I mean, now?"

"No. People talk about her, but personally, I think they like keeping it a mystery. My boss, Mr. Twentyman, he's done a little bit of research. He probably knows as much as anyone. But no one but Lilac knows why she decided to kill herself."

"You think she killed herself?"

Meg looks surprised. "Well, she must have, don't you think? Look, a miner's daughter knows how dangerous a place like that is. She didn't go in there—here—to have a... tea party. But she probably didn't want to bring shame to her family, so she couldn't just hang herself."

"I can understand that," Al says. Meg's body is warm. She's shaking, and Al holds on tighter.

"Sometimes I can feel her," says Meg, looking around the mineshaft. Al squints into the dark corners, as if something will manifest and she will be able to share it with Meg. "I'm not crazy," she adds. "Everyone says her ghost haunts this place."

It's too cold to have sex, but they do anyway. Not right away, but after they turn off the headlights, after they carve *A + M Forever* into the rafters with Meg's car key. This time Al starts things. Last time Meg held Al's hips above her: move like this, move like this, her fingers said. Now Al pushes Meg's shoulders against the dirt-rock floor of the mine. Meg breathes in sharply.

Al works her way down Meg's ribs to her soft belly, brown-pink dress bunched around her hips like an overripe rose. Al keeps a knee between Meg's legs, where it's warm and wet. She's not exactly sure what to do next, and she hopes Meg's body will tell her. One of Meg's garters has already fallen below her knee. Her thighs are big and muscular and shaking.

"I'll save you from ghosts," Al says into her ear. She means it like a promise, but it comes out coy, and Meg makes a gulping noise that could either be a giggle or a half sob.

Al wants to lean into Meg the way Meg leaned into the road: hard, unflinching. Hands on flexible legs, teeth biting into darkness. There is heat between them; a fire burns in this mountain's eye. As if Al can create radiance out of friction. As if she can butch away Meg's worst thing, even as she's dancing in the wound.

MORE OF A LEGEND THAN AN ANIMAL
Felix: Lilac Mines, 2002

For nearly a month the postcard sits on Felix's nightstand beneath her F.I.T. application. Every time she sits down to work on the application, she finds herself staring at the postcard. She thinks about New York, about the mountain of rubble in the middle of the city from the day it snowed hot paper ash, and her breath gets caught on her ribcage. She can't breathe until she reads the postcard again. Just one person lost here, one little story. It's an innocent and manageable sort of darkness.

"Where *is* the mine?" she asks Anna Lisa one morning in mid-October. Felix only has a few weeks left in Lilac Mines, and things between them have been polite and neutral. She accepts this as progress. On Tuesday night Anna Lisa invited Felix to dinner at a vaguely Mexican restaurant with the school secretary and a playground attendant. One woman mentioned her husband, but mostly they gossiped about school.

Anna Lisa fills Coal's water bowl. When she puts it down, Coal looks disappointed that it does not contain food.

"The mine is everywhere," Anna Lisa says. "All around us."

"Do you mean, like, metaphorically?"

"No, I mean the tunnels run under the entire town. There are a few different entrances, but the main one is at the end of North Main Street. If you follow it up, it turns into a dirt road and then there are some switchbacks and then you're there."

Recently, Anna Lisa has spent most weekends gardening vigorously in the Indian summer heat. She trims the leathery birds of paradise and plants black icicle pansies, delicate goth flowers that she dotes on like a helpless lover. She has gone on one search-and-rescue call this season, bringing water to an ATVer trapped beneath his illegal dune buggy. The man had a cell phone, so it was just rescue, no search. They chugged Crystal Geyser together and waited for the helicopter.

"Would you take me to the mine?" Felix ventures. "I mean, to the entrance?"

"I'm kind of busy today," Anna Lisa says, "really busy, actually. I need to take care of those snails—they're destroying what's left of the roses. I want to be prepared when the cold weather sets in."

"What if I helped you with that stuff now and then we went to the mine later? We could get the gardening done before it gets hot."

"No, that wouldn't work. Besides, I've been up there before. It's just a hole in a mountain."

Voice tight, Felix says, "Okay. Well, I think I'll go anyway."

"I'm not stopping you."

Felix wants bones. An architecture to hang her story on. Bones are truth—they can be broken by sticks and stones and other bones. No one doubts their abilities or their limits. They're not wobbly like words. So Felix drives as far as she can and parks her dusty car. She puts on her rhinestone-studded, cat-eyed sunglasses and steps, believing, into the bright day.

Tufts of weedy things and a few scrappy trees partially obscure the mine entrance, but it is definitely here. She steps into the shady hole, which is just wide enough for Felix to lay down in and tall enough to jump up and down, if the mood struck her. It is so dark that Felix's other senses ramp up, bat-style. She hears the echo of her breath, smells the odor of things that haven't seen light for a long time: moldering leaves, muddy rocks. She smells her own deodorant, too faux-flowery in this world of real scents. She leans her backpack and lunch against the mine wall and feels the rough timbers shoring up the tunnel, ominous with the promise of splinters. It is so dark.

Then Felix remembers she has her sunglasses on. She takes them off and sets them next to her backpack. She blinks. It's not *that* dark.

The tunnel is pockmarked with dynamite holes as thick as a broom handle, as if she's looking at the mountain's acne-scarred cheek, the part it hasn't grown a beard of trees to cover. Shadows shift in front of her. She imagines she hears low, thick breath, but it must be her own. The mine is a Rorschach pattern, ripe for projection.

She walks further into the mouth. She takes out the small flashlight she borrowed from her car's emergency kit. But it's made to illuminate maps or punctured tire tread, not to light up a room. It makes a yellow oval in front of her, but the rest of the mine looks darker as a result, so she clicks it off. She shuffles ahead for a few more feet and then *thump*: She hits wood. Turning the flashlight back on, she scans a row of boards, nailed to the mine's support beams from floor to ceiling.

Now what? she wonders. It makes sense that the mine would be sealed. The town has its ghost; it doesn't need lawsuits. But somehow she assumed it would be open for her. She also thought there would be some kind of plaque, maybe a box of brochures. She's glad that there's not, in a way, but she's not sure what to do without some kind of guide.

She sits down and leans against the boards. The seat of her jeans is immediately wet.

What is she doing here? Lilac isn't here. Of course Lilac isn't here. Not her bones, not her presence. Eva isn't here and Anna Lisa isn't here and neither are her friends. Just Felix, and the almost-breath noise that she decides must be the hum of the mountain.

Lilac died here, she thinks. In her neighborhood at home, Felix sometimes sees curbside shrines memorializing deaths she never heard about. Mylar balloons and teddy bears for the little girl killed in a hit-and-run on the corner of Irolo and 8th Street. Poems and Virgen de Guadalupe candles and a jar of pecan cookies for the guy shot on Mariposa. Someone drew a butterfly and the Tasmanian Devil in colored chalk on the sidewalk, but they washed away the first time it rained. Felix hears about these crimes in the aggregate—she hears about *gang violence* and *drunk driving*—but the individual victims are always a block away, never anyone she's seen before.

What if she had died that night? Would her friends have built an altar in front of her apartment building, or in West Hollywood? Sleater-Kinney and Spicy Champon CDs, an issue of her magazine, a jar of buttons, framed fashion sketches, spread among organically grown flowers? Would they include a photo of her with Eva or not? Would the neighbors walk by and wonder what happened?

Lilac died here, but there's nothing to show for it, and this makes Felix feel small. What about this Cal person—why didn't he pound a wooden cross into the ground? What about Lilac's father? Everyone becomes suspicious.

There is a rumble. Felix's first thought is *cave-in!* Her second thought is that it's her stomach. She remembers her lunch and stands up, switching her flashlight back on.

This time the beam illuminates an oval of short, yellow-brown fur. She leaps back and presses her body against the other side of the tunnel. She swings her flashlight away and runs for the mouth of the cave, heart in her stomach.

Her feet pound the hard-packed dirt. This is too familiar. Again, something wants to harm her. Something bigger than both of the creatures involved, as big as fear and hunger. The too-soon reprise of the night on Cynthia Street sickens her. The melody lets her know it could wear her down: *You want to be part of something? Be a part of this worst, common thing. Fear-and-hunger.* What to do but crumple in its wake, again? But her feet are part of something bigger too, and they keep moving.

It's a short distance to the entrance, but she is out of breath by the time she hits sunlight. She stops in front of her car and remembers that her keys are in her backpack, which is in the mine, not far from the breathing, growling animal. Her first instinct is to keep running, but she doesn't want to enter a foot race with a creature who has twice as many legs as she does. Whose stomach might be the one making noise. She has to go back.

She tries to recall everything she learned when she went camping with her parents as a kid. When you see a mountain lion, you're supposed to yell and stomp. When you see a bear, crouch down and put your hands over your head and neck. Or is it the other way around? The animal was too light-colored to be a bear, she's pretty sure, but it could have been a coyote, a lost dog, a chupacabra.

She settles on a strategy of non-invasiveness. *Don't fuck with me and I won't fuck with you,* she thinks. Flashlight aimed at the side of the tunnel where her backpack is and, thankfully, where the animal isn't, Felix takes the softest steps she can into the mine. But her red Adidas sneakers still make a gentle crunch against the ground. Her backpack rests just a few feet from the half-asleep thing. There is a glistening to her right.

She crouches down, puts her hands on the backpack. Two glassy spots. Eyes. They get narrow, then large again. In the dusky perimeter of her flashlight's beam, there is a stirring of tawny fur. Holding her backpack in front of her, she creeps backward, watched.

Felix leaves her lunch as an offering. This will be the day that beasts of the Sierras discover soy salami.

It takes an eternity to reach the entrance. She hits the sun and fresh air like she's coming up from a dive. She can't resist running the remaining distance to her car, ignoring her cramping side.

She doesn't notice that her hand is shaking until she puts the key in the door. As she starts the engine, she sees a cat the size of a Vespa slink out of the tunnel and into the light. It looks around quickly, pink nose sniffing for danger, then bounds up the hillside on huge, cappuccino-colored haunches.

When she reaches the paved road, her heart stops bounding as well. The cat acted the way that Endora, Crane's girlfriend's former alley cat, did whenever someone nudged a broom in her direction. Imagine never getting to take a nap without fearing for your life.

The yawning autumn sun is low in the sky, and Felix pulls her car's visor down. Her sunglasses, she realizes, are still in the mine. They were cheap, but she liked the way they made her look. Still, she decides, they have nothing on real cat eyes.

"You saw a mountain lion? No one *ever* sees mountain lions." This is the most animated Felix has seen her aunt. "How far away did you say you were?"

"Like four feet maybe," Felix says.

"Wow. Goddamn. I mean, I've been doing search and rescue for 20 years and I've never seen one. I've seen a couple of torn-up deer carcasses that made me think that was fine by me." Anna Lisa shakes her head. "Wait till I tell the guys on the squad about this. Four feet, huh?"

"Really?" Felix bites her bottom lip to stifle her smile.

"Sure. They're so shy. More of a legend than an animal, practically. As the place gets more developed maybe there'll be more encounters—I worry about that sometimes—but for the most part they just don't want to be bothered."

"*I* just didn't want to be bothered." Felix is grinning in full now, laughing with relief. Anna Lisa's reaction makes her wonder if she was in more danger than she knew. She feels stupid, lucky, and proud.

"Shit," Anna Lisa continues, "I can't believe you just stared that thing down."

"I didn't 'stare it down,' " Felix protests. "I needed my car keys."

"Hey, when *isn't* it about survival? Maybe you've got more in you than you know." Anna Lisa hangs Felix's backpack on the hook by the door like a trophy. For the rest of the week, she calls Felix "Lion Tamer," and Felix itches to live up to it.

"Genevieve's school supposedly has the best Halloween party every year," says Crane when she calls late one Wednesday night. Usually Felix has to call her. "This year they're calling it the Terrorgasm Ball. She's going to try to get us tickets."

Felix is cross-legged on her bed, phone wedged between ear and shoulder. She feels like a teenager. The postcard is propped on a lump of blanket, the looping L facing her. She's a little tired of Genevieve, who seems to have unlimited access to all things edgy.

"If that falls through," Crane continues, "I guess we'll do the West Hollywood thing." She sighs.

"Remember last time, two years ago?" says Felix.

"Was that the year we got stuck behind the KIIS-FM booth?" Crane says.

"Yeah, and Robbie and Andrew were fighting, and the stupid DJ kept making fun of the drag queens. It's like, why is the station there then?"

" 'Cause fags love dance music."

"Mm."

"What are you doing for Halloween?" Crane asks.

"I don't know yet. Maybe nothing."

"But Halloween's your favorite holiday. It's, like, our culture. Are you still obsessing over Eva?" she demands. She says it like, *Are you still wearing body glitter?* Something Felix should be done with.

"Yeah, sort of. I'm horny, I can tell you that. But mostly there's not a lot to do here. You know what I really want to do? I want to go to a real haunted house." Felix is pacing the room now, leaning her shoulder against the window. She studies the splotchy moon and stars spilled like hole punchings on the black velvet sky.

"How are you... doing?" Crane says carefully. Her voice implies that Felix has a terminal illness. The girl who once danced at raves wearing only a glowstick is crushed by the weight of taboo.

Felix touches her ribcage. A few days ago, a doctor friend of Anna Lisa's gave her permission to remove the bandage for good. Yellow-green bruises on her pale stomach are the only remaining evidence. In a way, she feels betrayed, as if her body has moved on without her.

"I kicked a mountain lion's ass," she says.

"Huh?"

"But ultimately I felt sorry, it looked kind of ragged. All that scampering through the hills."

"Nature is crazy, girl," Crane laughs when it's clear that she won't have to play therapist. "That's why I stick to good old Koreatown. Oh, hey, before I forget, how long are you staying there again? Because Vive is graduating at the end of the semester, but she got this internship at LACMA and even though she'd rather work at MOCA, she said she'll take it if she can keep living here, 'cause the commute is so not-that-bad."

"Vive?"

"Genevieve. So would your aunt let you stay for another couple of months?"

"Thanks for missing me," Felix says.

"Honey, you know I miss you. Robbie, he cries for you every night. Neither of us are bathing till you get home."

"Shut up."

Crane laughs. "Of *course*, we miss you. But Vive wants to know, and she's cool, so, you've just gotta decide."

Felix decides she needs to find the postcard's origins. Not so she can become famous, but so her dreams will stop filling up with missing girls. Eva dancing in the mouth of the tunnel. A bonneted figure climbing the ruins of the Berlin Wall, braids swinging. She wants Lilac to stop looking like Melissa Gilbert.

She turns down lunch at Gold Nugget Pizza with Tawn, who seems slightly hurt (Tawn is hurt by the oddest things), and returns to the Visitors' Center. She has a half hour before she has to get back to work, so she gets right to the point.

"I found this postcard," Felix tells Ranger LeVoy. The ranger has ditched her blonde braids for a traffic-cone-orange pageboy. Maybe the blonde wasn't natural either. Felix describes the postcard. She could have brought it, but she didn't want it to get smudged with her backpack's 21ˢᵗ century mess: lipstick, protein bar, ballpoint pen. She wants to keep it safe.

Ranger LeVoy is immediately interested. "Well, very little is known about the Ambroses, but something like this—*if* it's the real thing— might give us some insight. Do you have it with you?" Ranger LeVoy asks eagerly.

"No, it's at home. My aunt's, I mean."

"Definitely bring it in so I can take a look at it. I'm not an expert, but I could probably gauge the era."

"It's postmarked 1899," Felix reminds her.

"I could still help. I was halfway through a Master's in Art History at U.N.L.V., but then I got married and my son sort of showed up by surprise, you know how it is."

Felix wants to say, *No, I don't.* She's impatient and she can see that Ranger LeVoy is, too.

"Maybe I'll stop by this weekend," Felix says. She was hoping Ranger LeVoy could provide her with information, but it seems like she wants the same from Felix.

"Or sooner… I could stay open late one night this week. My personal theory, and I'm not supposed to talk anything except facts on the job so keep this a little hush-hush if you don't mind, is that that little gal didn't die at all. I think she eloped. I think she and some boy headed over the mountains to Nevada to get hitched. And what you're saying about the postcard, about this Cal fellow, is right in keeping with that."

Felix wonders if this is how she seems to Anna Lisa, pressing for information to fortify her own experience. "You know, this week is pretty busy for me," Felix says. "My aunt really needs my help with some things." This is a bit of an exaggeration. Anna Lisa asked Felix to tape a TV show for her Thursday night, when she'll be a PTA meeting.

Ranger LeVoy comes around to the front of the counter, so that she is just a few feet from Felix. She is tall, broad-hipped. She smells like pine cones and hand lotion, or maybe pine cone hand lotion.

"Just don't take this too lightly," says Ranger LeVoy. Her Midwestern accent hardens at the edges. Felix feels like she's being warned not to flirt with the farmer's daughter at the barn dance. "This is our town, you know. The Historical Preservation Committee has a right to anything that contributes to the town's history. Just 'cause it's not some big city doesn't mean we don't care about it. Bring that postcard in as soon as you can."

Felix takes a step backward. Her platform sandals wobble. She wants to tell Ranger LeVoy that her "theory" sounds like a bad romance novel, that the town has been "hers" only since she ditched Vegas, apparently. But it's not like Felix has much of a claim either. So she paid 10 cents for an old postcard. Is that what ownership is? An accident?

"I'll talk to my aunt," Felix says. It sounds believable.

"Laura, Leslie, Louise," says Gary Schipp. "LaVerne. LeAnn, Lois, Lauren—well, there weren't too many Laurens in the 19th century, but you get my point."

Felix does. She is slumped in an orange plastic chair at the library. Through the window she can see a woman hanging clothes on a wire running from her trailer to a rusty swing set. Thin T-shirts, a stretched-out sundress, a pair of acid-washed jeans.

"I'll grant you," Gary continues, "it's interesting. It's incredibly, thought-provokingly fascinating. But do you know how much information is in the world? How many thousands of people sent postcards and how many thousands received them? I like Lilac Mines because it's small enough to make history seem manageable. I mean, it's my job—to record and catalog and make information available for people who, for the most part, couldn't care less. The kids at the elementary school take a field trip here once a year, and Trixie Netherby keeps the large print mystery market in business, and at least once a week I kick someone off a porn website." Gary wags his head, his pseudo-bangs shaking like flapper fringe.

"Say you did find out that Lilac Ambrose wrote that postcard," Gary says. "Say you had irrefutable proof. Then what? It would get written up in a couple of the local papers, and then the postcard would be locked behind glass at the Visitors' Center or maybe it would get a spot at one of the museums in Columbia. If you really hit the big time, a few parents would force their kids to look at it before they let them pan for gold. Felix, the ugly truth about the Information Age is that information doesn't solve anything. When people figure that out, I'm out of a job. And so what, really? I can't blame them."

Felix says something feeble like, "But *I* came in here, didn't I? *I* wanted information." Ranger LeVoy tried to take her postcard, which was bad, but Gary Schipp is trying to take her search, which is worse. She knows Ranger LeVoy's brand of desire: wanting shoes, money; for the popular kids to make room for you at their table. But Gary is at peace with futility in his rickety library, and Felix doesn't know what to do with that.

She browses the New Fiction shelf. She reads book jackets about crusading lawyers and feline detectives. About girls who find love in Paris and girls who learn about their oppressed ancestors. The blurbs are soothing. *To hell with nonfiction.* She returns to the front desk.

"One more thing before I go," she says, taking Lucas Twentyman's skinny, much-renewed book from her messenger bag. She opens it to the group photo of the miners. "You don't know any of these guys, do you?"

"How old do I look?" he says.

"You know what I mean."

His eyes gaze at the page, barely taking it in. He's seen the photo a million times. "I'm sure you already know which one Harold Ambrose is."

"Yeah."

"But," he perks up almost imperceptibly, pushing his glasses higher on his nose, "there's a book in the health section called *Mountain Air: A Health History of the Sierras.* Someone's dissertation, as you might imagine. Some Lilac Mines miners get a few pages to shine in there. If you can call lung fibrosis and blue fingernails 'shining.' "

"Yuck," Felix says. "But thanks."

That night she sits on the deck as Anna Lisa watches TV inside. She has to literally crack open the book, its pages are so stiff and unread, though already yellow. She clips a book light to the back cover, and soon a funny lime-green moth begins to romance the bulb. The night is warm, and Felix is barefoot, and if the book weren't full of dreary technical phrases, she might enjoy herself.

There aren't many pictures, but there are a few blurry reprints of obituaries from an era when people died of gruesome, poetic diseases: rubella, scarlet fever, consumption. Maybe the latter is due for a comeback. Everyone she knows is consuming and being consumed.

And so is a man named Ashley Burd. He stares up at her with light, pleading eyes. She almost doesn't recognize him in close-up. But it's him—the man she named Cal. He has the same straight nose forming a T with his flat, uncurious eyebrows. She can't tell for sure, but the grainy obituary photo looks like a crop of the larger group shot of the miners. It is the same and different. He looks weaker all by himself, even with that too-white smile.

She shivers in the warm, starlit night. She thinks of her college internship at *Variety*, where she researched and wrote obituaries for aging stars who hadn't died yet. The trade paper wanted to be ready. At the time Felix told Jia Li, "I'm actually writing about the future. How cool is that?" But all the forgotten movies and sitcom guest spots made her sad.

The caption beneath Ashley Burd's photo says, *Ashley Burd, b. 1867 Oklahoma City, d. 1898 East Beedleborough, Calif. of silicosis. Survived by wife, Clarabelle.* He is not the boy of Lilac's postcard. Here—close up and dead—he doesn't even look like a jerk. He looks like, well, a guy named Ashley. Someone unfortunate enough to live in a time where modern medicine consisted of leeches and morphine. And no matter what story the photo tells, tuberculosis got him a year before he could get Lilac.

Felix throws her head against the back of the lawn chair. Of course. Of *course* her hunch was nothing but superstition and pathology. Nevertheless, disappointment boils beneath her skin. She slams the book, inadvertently sandwiching the moth between its pages, which makes her feel even worse. Now she is helpless *and* she's a murderer of small, innocent things.

She stands up and stomps around the deck's perimeter. She'd wanted an enemy. How is she supposed to save Lilac without one? How dark the world beyond the deck is, full of animals watching and waiting to pounce. Felix opens the sliding glass door and barges into the living room, where Anna Lisa is still glued to the local news.

"Why even bother?" Felix growls. "It's just car chases and negative representations of ethnic neighborhoods."

Anna Lisa looks up, surprised. "Good evening to you, too, Lion Tamer." She adds, "I don't care to pay for cable, and I'm old and set in my ways, if you want to know. It would be pretty exciting to see *anything* about Lilac Mines on the news, honestly. Maybe instead of that 'Reno Casino of the Week' segment. Would you mind closing the door? Otherwise, mosquitoes'll get in."

Felix gives it a good slam. "Lion Tamer, my ass."

BLUES
Al: Lilac Mines, 1965-1966

"Listen to this," says Meg, with a naughty grin. She lets go of the record player's arm. The needle touches down:

> *Madame Bucks was quite deluxe,*
> *servants by the score,*
> *good ones at each door,*
> *butlers and maids galore.*
> *But one day Dan, her kitchen man,*
> *gave his notice he's through.*
> *She cried, "Oh, no, Dan, don't go—*
> *it'll grieve me if you do."*

It's an old-fashioned voice, from when Al's parents were teenagers. That Depression scratch. But she can't picture Gerald and Eudora Hill listening to this kind of music. The woman singing is clearly a Negro. Her voice is deep, etched.

"Where'd you get it?" Al asks.

"Imogen. She said when she was a girl her parents would only let her listen to gospel, and that made her love Bessie even more."

"Who's Bessie?"

"Smith," says Meg. "Singing."

> *...turnip tops, love the way he warms my chops.*
> *I can't do without my kitchen man.*
> *His jelly roll is nice and hot,*
> *never fails to hit the spot.*

Meg leans into the music, eyes closed, as if it could catch her. She's wearing a soft black sweater that sheds hairs wherever she goes. Al finds the trail of Meg comforting. They are in Meg's living room. The house is tiny, a converted miner's residence with one bedroom, and a bathroom tacked on in the back. The plumbing will freeze in a month or so, Meg warns, and the oven's pilot light swoons like a girl in a corset, but it is luxurious compared to the church, where Al has been spending less and less time. She likes to sit on the toilet and look out the window at the naked gray branches on the trees.

"Are you listening?" Meg prompts. Her cheeks glow like Saturday night, even though it's Thursday. "She's scandalous. 'His frankfurters are oh so sweet?' 'Oh how that boy can open clams?' "

Al blushes. It's hard to make out all the lyrics on the scratchy record. "I hadn't thought of it that way. I just thought she was singing about her servant."

"Well, even that would be pretty amazing. Think about it: a colored *woman* with a servant, a man who works in the kitchen."

"I didn't think about that either. But maybe the lady with the servant isn't colored. Maybe just the singer is." Servants only exist in fiction for Al. A Negro employer seems no more outlandish than a Southern belle in hoop skirts. The only people who've worked for the Hills are other Hills. "Where would she sing a song like this?" Al wonders out loud. She wants to give the lines a space to be scandalous in.

"Harlem, probably," Meg says absently. She's moving around the living room, bringing everything in her path into her dance. She picks up an abandoned feather duster and pretends to smoke it, Marlene Dietrich style. "Imogen says folks in Harlem did things 40 years ago that would *still* shock people here."

It's been almost a week since Al has seen Imogen or Jody or Sylvie or any of the people from the bar. No particular reason. But she has sensed a slight cooling. *Must be nice not to use an outhouse,* Jody said. *You can come over any time,* Al assured her, *I'm sure Meg wouldn't mind.* Meg is generous and borderless. If Meg had had a sister, she never would have divided their room with a strip of tape the way Al and Suzy did.

Al feels a fist clench inside whenever she thinks of Suzy. Or her parents. Thanksgiving is coming soon, and Al pictures them eating turkey legs wrapped in thin waffles, a family tradition from some other continent, her mother giving humble and guilt-edged thanks: *I am thankful my girls are safe, even if one of them won't talk to me.*

" 'When I eat his donuts, all I leave is the hole,' " Meg and Bessie drawl. Al tries to listen to their secret language. " 'Any time he wants to, he can use my sugar bowl.' "

A few days later, Al will encounter Bessie Smith for the second time. In the morning, Meg drops her off at the Clarkson Sawmill for her first day of work. Shallan shopped for an anniversary present for her foreman to give his wife, and he owed her a favor. She got two out of him: a job for Jody, and one for Al.

The mill consists of several large wooden buildings just north of town. Al leans out the passenger side window as Meg brakes. Below them dozens of little miners' houses occupy a sparse patch of the mountain.

"Amazing view, huh?" Al says, thinking of their night in the mine.

"The houses look like a herd of cows," Meg frowns, "who've eaten up all the grass. I gotta get to work, darling. I'm going to be late."

Al closes the car door and heads for the office. The foreman is a short, muscular man who shakes Al's hand firmly.

"Alice Hill," he says, "Shallan O'Toole spoke highly of you."

"It's Anna Lisa, actually, but, well, that's nice to hear."

"Oh, she said 'Al' and I assumed... Anyhow, you're a small girl, so I think we'll start you off as a sweeper."

Al squirms under his gaze. She's wearing a plaid flannel shirt and blue jeans and gloves with the fingers cut off.

"We've got a few ladies working at the mill now. A couple of them have been around since the War, and the younger ones... well, it's a changing world, I guess. But I won't kid you, it's a man's job, and you'll have to work like a man. Rigby Clarkson will show you around."

"Thank you, sir." Al swallows. Shallan warned her about Rig, the middle son of the Clarkson family, who has been demoted several times as a result of his drinking.

The foreman hands her off to Rig, a shaggy-haired man of indeterminable age. He's thin but potbellied. He has ruddy skin with soft-lidded, weary blue eyes.

He hands Al a broom, looks her over with blatant disgust. "You must be O'Toole's friend," he says with a huff. "My pop owns this place, so you don't want to go messing around on my watch." He leads the way with big, swaggering steps, like he has studied cowboy movies very closely.

Soon they're in a large, open room. Al sneezes. Men in work clothes and heavy boots stand around a wide trough, catching pale planks of wood as they shoot out of a gauntlet of saw blades. They inspect the planks and corral them toward one of three forks, hand-labeled "Large," "Small," and "Defective." Al holds her breath as she watches a tall man heave a two-by-four toward the "Defective" path. She can't tell what's wrong with it, and is momentarily glad that this isn't her job.

Through the haze, she scans for Shallan or Jody. They'd be dressed like the men. But she doesn't see them.

"It's way too dusty in here," says Rig. "It's tough on the eyes and lungs, but we're used to it. You might need these, though." He hands Al a pair of goggles and laughs when she puts them on. "Start in that corner over there."

Al works her way from corner to corner, mumbling apologies when she gets too close to one of the men swinging planks like baseball bats. She sneezes the whole time. When she's filled three sacks with sawdust, Rig directs her to a trash bin behind the building. The bags are light as balloons—nothing like a two-by-four—but Al's back pinches when she tries to stand up straight.

Next she sweeps what Rig calls "the log building," where the workers push downed pines through a murky stream toward spinning saw blades. She realizes this is the other side of the gauntlet, that the two buildings are attached. She's working backwards. If she kept going, she'd be in the quiet forest, where the trees are still full of birds.

"*Al,*" someone hisses. She looks up from the dusty floor and sees Shallan. Bits of red-brown hair peek out from beneath a blue knit cap.

Flakes of bark polkadot her tan work shirt. She nods like *good work, man.*

Al smiles and ducks her head. She sweeps faster. Then she spots Jody, a few paces down the line from Shallan. Jody's face is red with effort as she leans into a log the width of a car tire. Al sweeps and watches. Every few minutes, someone calls out to Jody or slaps her on the back. Al can't make out the words over the buzz and clamor of the log building. Jody is working hard, but she's a natural, it's obvious.

When Al has more or less cleared the log room of dust, she finds Rig.

"What's next?" she asks as brightly as she can.

" 'What's next?' " Rig mimics. "Lemme show you something." He leads her back to the first room that she swept. A thick layer of peach-colored sawdust has gathered like snowfall. "Keep brooming, girl," he says, and rejoins the men on the line.

What was it her mother used to mutter over a sink full of dishes about a woman's work never being done? Al shakes out her arms and legs and returns to the corner where she started.

She hopes Meg has made something wonderful for dinner. Steak, maybe. Meatloaf? Jody and Shallan were going to get beers, but Al's back hurts too much, so she is walking—slowly—to Meg's small, glowing house.

The lamp in the main room is on, but Meg isn't here.

From the bedroom, a ghost howls. That's Al's first thought. The noise is a sharp, disturbed *wahoooOOooo.* Al lunges through the doorway.

Meg does not look up. She is facedown. Her dawn-pink skirt is rumpled, her stockings lie next to her bare legs like molted snakeskin. Is she sick? A record spins on the player next to her. It's plugged in the socket that normally supports the lamp on her dresser.

This house is so haunted with dead men . . .

It's Bessie again. Another happy-and-sad tune. Al puts her hand on Meg's back, and Meg rolls over.

"What happened?" Al demands.

"What do you mean?" Meg's eye makeup runs in ghoulish rays down her cheeks.

"This." Al gestures; she's not sure to what. "I mean—"

"Maybe you should go," says Meg.

"Are you sick?"

"No."

"Were you crying?"

"So what if I was?" Meg snaps. "A girl can have a mood in her own house. I'm fine now."

"But what were you upset about?" When things go wrong for Suzy, she becomes the littlest of little sisters, collapsing into Al as if leading her in a dance. Meg moves stiffly away, and Al is left caressing the green and yellow patchwork quilt.

> *He moans when I'm sleeping, he wakes me at 2 a.m.*
> *He makes me swear I'll have no other man but him.*

"Just... sometimes I just am. Could you spend the night at the church tonight, do you think?"

"Was it work? Was Mr. Twentyman mean to you?" The knot in Al's back screams like the ghost on the record.

"No, it's nothing. It's not a *thing*."

"Is it me? Did I do something wrong?" Meg's presence in Al's life is so improbable. It stands to reason that she could slip away just as inexplicably.

Meg glares at her. "No, okay? Can we stop playing twenty questions?" Meg is curled like a snail at the corner of the bed. She turns so that she's leaning on one wall, facing the other. Away from Al.

"It's just that… my back hurts pretty bad and I don't know if I can make the walk," Al says. She kneads a square of green cloth freckled with blue flowers.

"Fine," Meg shoos her, "just go out there." She lowers her head to her knees and Al observes the delicate top vertebrae of her neck—arched and knobby, as if injured. The singing, swaying Meg is gone. Tonight Bessie frets alone: *I'm scared to see him, I'm scared to leave.* Does this song have another meaning too, again closed off to Al?

She backs out of the living room and sits down slowly on the couch. She wants to go to the church with its chorus of answers. The women there would help her. They would sit with hips touching on one of the pews, spooning burnt macaroni and cheese into their mouths. Meg's little house can look so perfect sometimes, like one you might see on a suburban block with a white fence and a sprinkler glittering the yard, but Al feels far away from everything now.

Winter inches along. Suzy mails Christmas presents from their parents. When Al tears off the brown paper and sees the duckling-yellow cardigan, trimmed with sequined flower buds, she starts to cry. Her parents have no idea who she is. She can't begin to answer the pleading letter that accompanies the package. She's relieved when the everyday numbness of January sets in.

One chilly morning in early March, Al makes her monthly, pre-arranged phone call to Suzy from the phone in Meg's kitchen. She's glad Meg is at the post office. When Al talks to Suzy, she becomes a string of tight-lipped answers, denying everything around her. It's hard enough to deny the stove, the blue-bordered ceramic dishes, the half-eaten ham on the counter. No way can she deny a living girl, her ankles wrapped around her chair in anticipation, her cigarette smoke meandering into Al's lungs.

"I can't take it here anymore," Suzy says. "Every date I go on, it's like I've been out with that boy before, even if I haven't. We already know each other too well, even if we just met that week. I dated his cousin, or he's been to the store and bought lasagna noodles from Daddy. I've got to get out. I mean it this time."

This is Suzy's usual refrain. Al is sure that one of her dates will work out. Some farm boy will transcend their shared past and look like the newest, most exotic creature Suzy has ever seen. They'll get married and present grandchildren to Gerald and Eudora like baskets of fruit.

"I have it all planned out," Suzy continues. "I'm going to go live with

Aunt Randi in Los Angeles."

Al stops slouching in the doorway and stands at attention. Would Suzy really strand their parents? Al has been counting on her to guide them gently into their old age. This is what's allowed her to stay in Lilac Mines.

"We haven't seen Auntie Randi since—must have been elementary school," says Al, stalling.

"I might as well see how spinsters are *supposed* to behave," Suzy says. But there's excitement behind her sarcasm. Al knows that excitement firsthand, and she can't bear to take it away from her sister.

Miranda Lund, their mother's older sister by ten years, lives in a tile-roofed cottage across the street from a new TV studio and a farmers' market. She took her nieces out for strawberry milkshakes and had almost no food in her ice box. Al can't remember much else about her.

"So it's settled, then?" Al asks.

The front door squeals open, then bangs shut. Meg always makes an entrance. She walks into the kitchen, a bundle of envelopes under her arm and a multiple-paged letter in her hands. She can never wait. She laughs loudly at whatever she's reading.

"What's that?" Suzy asks. She's always pressing for bits of Al's life, though she never minds returning to the subject of her own. "Is that your roommate?"

"That's her," says Al, who is supposed to be living in an all-women's boarding house, working as a secretary. Meg loves the irony of her lie; Al does not. "Listen, Suzy, I've got to go."

When she hangs up, she says, "You could be a little quieter."

Meg sits on the kitchen table. The way she leans on her right arm, thrusting her shoulder forward, looks like a dare. "I can't help it if Petra's funny."

Petra is Meg's neighbor from Kerhonkson, New York. Her family watched over Meg after her mother died, when her father was too distraught to get out of bed. Al doesn't understand why Meg puts so much stock in letters from a high school student, but she doesn't talk to her father, and she's an only child, and there are plenty of things that Al doesn't understand. There have been a few of what Al thinks of as blues episodes over the past months. Just one or two, each mysterious. And so Meg paints herself, more and more vivid, and increasingly abstract.

"Look, how would *you* feel if Petra discovered that you were sleeping with a woman? If suddenly she started picturing your life like some 10-cent paperback?" Al demands.

"Better to be a 10-cent paperback than a dictionary," Meg snaps. "And I'll have you know that she *does* know."

"You're kidding me. Meg, you could get *arrested*."

"Well, she knows most of it," Meg says. With determined casualness, she flips through the rest of the mail. "If she can halfway read between the lines, she knows." She tosses the bills on the floor. The ferocity of Meg's truth astonishes Al as much as the ease of her lies.

"But you're seven years older than her—aren't you supposed to be someone she can look up to?" Theirs is a life that cannot be translated to outsiders.

"And I suppose that couldn't possibly be me? I'm some floozy, then?" Meg is mad now, a car peeling around a hairpin curve when, a minute ago, it was purring in the driveway. She hops off the table, balls up Petra's letter and throws it at Al with surprising force. She stalks out of the room, every muscle taught.

Al remains in the kitchen, helpless again. Slowly she unfolds Petra's letter, smoothing its creases, a sort of *there, there*. It's written on plain notebook paper and decorated with ballpoint flowers. *Dear Meggie.* The handwriting is loopy and young, i's dotted with small circles. *Al sounds like the best friend ever*, Petra writes, mid-page, *Strong* and *kind, holy smokes!* Al hopes this isn't the part that made Meg laugh.

"I want to meet your sister," Meg says. She is just home from work, dusting the bedroom with nearly frightening fury. She lifts each corner of the mattress and sweeps out armfuls of crumbs. April in Lilac Mines is slushy and cold, but Meg is in her underwear. High-waisted beige panties that exaggerate the inverted heart of her backside. *You are my upside-down heart,* Al thinks.

"Why?" Al asks, though they've had this conversation several times.

"Because she's a part of you."

"We're not much alike." Suzy loves Los Angeles, according to the one postcard Al received. Aunt Randi teaches flute at Pepperdine University and will go on tour with an orchestra this summer, leaving Suzy her house with the tiled fountain and her circle of musician friends.

"You probably are alike and don't know it," Meg declares. "Come on. Let's drive down to Los Angeles. I'll be your Good Friend Meg. I'll be your Good Friend... *Michelle*. Ooh, I like that, it sounds French." She extends a dusty palm down. "Bonjour, Mademoiselle Soo-zie."

Al laughs in spite of herself. She kisses Meg's fingers and sneezes. She grabs Meg by the waist and pulls her to the bed. The feather duster clatters to the floor.

Al slips into her bedtime persona, the one that can peel away Meg's panties with one hand and reach for the dildo tucked between their pillows with the other. Meg grins up at her, dark hair Veronica Lake-ing. Al smiles back like, *I know how you like it*, tickling her with the tip of the dildo before sliding it in. It occurs to her that somewhere along the way, the look and the tickle and the slide, the flattening of Meg's thighs against the bed, became more than posturing. She really *does* know how Meg likes it, and she likes believing she is this person as much as she likes the sex itself, the actual body-parts part.

Immediately after she comes, Meg starts laughing, which she almost always does, though a few times she has started to cry. It's her who-knew-it-could-be-so-good laugh—her body's forgetting and remembering—as if she is pleasantly surprised that the world is not ending.

Meg takes the dildo from Al, draws an S-shape over the top of Al's underwear, which is white and worn ghost-thin. There is no good underwear for butches. She's heard about a law that women must wear three items of female clothing at all times in public or risk being arrested. She doesn't know if this is true, and she doesn't know how to find out. She can't very well just march into the police station and ask. The line between law and legend is ghost-thin, too.

Jody's theory on butches who let themselves be touched is this: *It's all fine and dandy till you break up. Then she goes and tells her friends exactly what you like and don't like.*

Meg's theory on butches who *don't* let themselves be touched is this: *I don't have much respect for anyone who puts acting tough ahead of feeling good. Even men aren't that stupid.*

Al wishes her bedroom life were not the crossroads of a philosophical debate. She wishes she could just be a body, that she could writhe and giggle like Meg. But her whole life is with her at any given time. It's her curse. And so she compromises: Meg can put her tongue or fingers between Al's legs, but not *that* thing.

Meg dangles the dildo by one of its pink plastic testicles. "Al, c'mon." They've been through this before.

"But it looks so real. It's creepy."

"You didn't think so when you had it up inside me," Meg says. "It's just plastic. It's a spare tire. A baby doll." Meg has retreated to sitting cross-legged on the bed. "Okay," she continues, "I want to understand. You like feeling like a guy, but you don't like feeling like a guy is fucking you?"

Al winces. Meg can be vulgar sometimes. "No... no, it's not that," Al says. Her cheeks are hot. She hates talking about sex. "I guess I like feeling like a butch. But not like a guy. I couldn't feel like a guy even if I wanted to, I don't think."

"You need to work on your imagination, Al." She knows it's true.

HAUNTED HOUSE
Felix: Lilac Mines, 2002

Tawn Twentyman lives in a mansion. It's creaky and unrestored, but it has a wide porch, French doors and gingerbread flourishes. A porthole window looks into the foyer. Ivy covers a dry stone birdbath in the front yard. It was once the mayor's house, she explains, or maybe the saloon owner's, or maybe both at different times.

Felix spends six days begging Tawn to throw a Halloween party at her perfect house. Tawn finally admits that she doesn't have enough friends to throw a proper party.

"Maybe you could get your aunt to invite some of her friends?" Tawn suggests.

"I don't know...." Felix says. She wonders if Tawn would understand her problems with her aunt. Tawn lives with her parents and grandfather, a three-generation patchwork of Washoe and Pomo and white in one house. Felix imagines them sharing recipes, passing down ancient stories.

In the end, Tawn and Felix decide to transform the front rooms into a haunted house for trick-or-treaters instead.

On the afternoon of the big night, Felix follows Tawn home, parking behind her '86 Mustang in the gravel driveway. The sky is sweatshirt gray. Tawn pushes open the heavy front door and Felix inhales a mix of dust and cat and cinnamon.

Tawn leads Felix to the dark living room, where her parents sit on the couch shouting at the TV, "Who is John Henry? What is radium? What is New Edition?" They are surrounded by what could be original furniture—dark wood saddled with velvet and strung with cobwebs. A mounted buffalo head flares its nostrils at Alex Trebek.

Tawn's mother looks nothing like her. She has a round, brick-colored face and short permed hair. Her father is thin, like Tawn, with a loosened tie dangling from his neck as if it just lassoed him by surprise.

"Don't worry, we'll get out of your way. The nursing home—that's where I work—they're having a party tonight," Mrs. Twentyman explains to Felix. "Tawny's dad and I are going to sing a couple of numbers from *Oklahoma!* and *Showboat*. They love it." She stands up and turns of the television. "Tawny, keep an eye on Gramp, okay?"

As soon as they leave, Tawn begins pushing a claw-footed coffee table toward the kitchen. "Let me get this stuff out of the way."

"No! Tawn, this stuff is great."

"But it's all just junk my mom buys at garage sales. Or that the people from the nursing home leave her in their wills. It's gross. Dead people's stuff." She gazes up at the buffalo head and shudders.

Felix sends Tawn to fetch the candy they purchased earlier in the week. She sets to work hanging black sheets (actually, they're eggplant, but the lights will be off) to make a path through the living room, dining room and out the back door. She strews appendages of borrowed mannequins and sets a mechanical hand crawling across a roll-top desk. She strategically places candles beneath a framed photo of a stoic-looking Indian.

There is noise upstairs, voices and movement. "Gramp!" Tawn's loud voice floats down the stairs.

Tawn says her grandfather is a little crazy. She thinks he's always been that way, but she can't remember for sure. Felix worries that he's had a heart attack. She pounds up the squealing staircase in her metallic blue Docs.

"...*all* of it?" Tawn is saying. She straddles a doorway. Felix peers past Tawn's shoulder and sees a wrinkled man hunched over a pile of Hershey's Miniatures wrappers.

Tawn whips her head around. "Can you believe he ate all the candy?"

The man has small dark eyes and white hair. His skin looks like a discarded paper bag, but Felix can see Tawn's cheekbones beneath the surface. He's dressed in green and white striped pajamas that make Felix feel like she should look away. She is the accidental witness to a private moment.

"I had to test it," he protests. Felix sees he's not joking, so she does not laugh, even though her dad made the same proclamation every year as he trolled for Heath bars. "For poison," he says, "for razor blades."

"Testing is one or two. Now there's no more left."

"But how am I supposed to know the next one's not the laced one?" His voice is gravelly but strong. He could narrate a documentary. "You don't know how many unsavory characters there are out there."

Felix is starting to see where Tawn gets it.

"Fine," says Tawn, "I guess I'm going to the store." She stomps down the hallway, her tangle of hair rallying behind her.

While she's gone, Felix finishes the haunted house. With the lights off, the makeshift becomes ominous. She goes back upstairs to put her costume on in Tawn's neat, sparse room.

It found her just two days ago, floating from the truck like foreign aid arriving by parachute. She doesn't know what she is supposed to be: the dress is ivory and floor-length. The sleeves are as large and round as her head. Lace fringes her elbows and plunges down the bodice, or what Felix imagines is a bodice. She knows clothing words like "capri" and "hoodie" and "shrug." This dress requires old-fashioned vocabulary, "crinoline" and "petticoat" and "brocade." Green glass beads circle the high collar, and a crumpled sash rounds the high waist. Felix buttons it up as far as she can on her own. She tries to imagine a world of ladies-in-waiting, or at least a sister always on hand with a buttonhook. Dressing as a communal art. Her upper back is naked, while her waist is more confined than it's been since she took her bandage off. She thinks of Eva hugging her from behind, that small, loved feeling.

She looks in the mirror. She could be a bride or La Llorona or just a girl with a place to go. The disguise makes her feel pretty and safe. She makes her way carefully down the hallway. The dress swishes against the carpet.

"Holy God! You!"

Felix stops. She is in front of Tawn's grandfather's room again. He is pointing at her with a jittery finger.

"I'm sorry?" says Felix. The cold air in the house grazes her bare skin.

"You're just like—you could be—"

"What? Who?"

"Oh, never mind, it was years ago and I'm an old fogy." He shakes his head. Now his voice is businesslike. "I should introduce myself properly. Luke Twentyman."

"I knew it!" says Felix. She shakes his hand. It's dry and small, but strong. "I figured Tawn must be related to the guy who wrote that book. It was you, wasn't it? *A Brief History of Lilac Mines.*"

A yellow-toothed grin peels across his face. "No one's read that old thing in ages. Used to call the library now and then to find out, but it got depressing."

"Well, I'm really interested in it," Felix hesitates, "… in the whole Lilac Ambrose thing. I didn't mean to scare you."

"Don't worry about it, it's tough to scare an old snooper like me. You just remind me of something I saw a long time ago."

"Is it the dress? I got it at the Goodwill." Luke is old, but not old enough to have gotten married in the 1890s.

"The dress and the way you walked past the door." He unwraps a surviving Mr. Goodbar and bites it with his side teeth. "Today is Halloween, right? Sit down, I've got a yarn for you."

Because he is old and because he might know things, Felix does. Ashley Burd was a dead end, but now a ribbon of hope begins to weave through Felix's stomach. She spreads the dress around her legs on the floor. The scent of brittle fabric embroiders the stronger chocolate smell.

"Let me start by saying I don't believe in ghosts," Luke begins. "That mumbo-jumbo is thick on the reservation, and that kind of backward thinking never got anyone *off* the reservation. Drives me crazy when Tawn gets all spooked in the million ways she gets spooked."

The house is quiet. Felix rubs her bare forearms and wiggles her toes. She holds her breath.

"Still," says Luke, "maybe I should qualify that. I *didn't* believe in ghosts. This was in... oh, '74? '75? Almost everyone had left town. They'd finally closed the mill, and everything else fell like dominoes. I had plans to go live with my son and his wife in Angels Camp till I could find a place around there, but he and I weren't getting along too well, and I was reluctant to leave this dive. That's how I found myself spending one last night at the Lilac Mines Hotel, even though it was closed and one of the floors had been burnt up in a fire.

"You know the place? They bulldozed it, then built one that looked just like it right over the top." *Like Berlin*, Felix thinks, recalling Eva's email. The accompanying pang is slightly less gut-wrenching than she expects. "They used photos from my collection to figure out what it was supposed to look like. It's all tarted up, and now they call it something else. Over on East Main. Lily's, that's it. 'Lily's of Lilac Bed & Breakfast.' One of those names that sounds nice to a certain kind of traveler but doesn't mean anything at all. The doll who owns it is named Becky—there's no Lily."

Luke scratches his head. His hair is thick. His brows fold over his eyelids; it seems like blinking would be tiring. Three of Felix's grandparents died before she was born, and her remaining grandmother, her mother's mother, died when she was six. Felix remembers pearl earrings, a teacup patterned with rosebuds. It's been a long time since she's seen an old person up close.

"I had a lot on my mind and I thought a good night's sleep might help. Actually, I thought a good strong drink might help, but there was nowhere to get one. Everyone had left. Everyone. So I laid down on a bed in one of the less burned-out rooms. It was May, but it was cold in that damned place. I balled myself up like a baby in a scratchy old blanket at the foot of the bed."

Felix wants him to get to the point. She wants to know where she comes in. She folds and unfolds a Krackle wrapper.

"I fell asleep easy and woke up late. Don't know what finally woke me up. You know how it is, sometimes you wake up in the middle of the story." Luke talks like an old school detective novel, but one that needs editing. Raymond Chandler by way of senior citizen. "I sat up quick, didn't know where the hell I was. Do that more and more these days, but back then I was keen. I was 50ish and thought I was ancient, thought I had sharpened my cynicism to a fine point.

"Let me tell you though, what I saw that afternoon threw me for a loop. I felt it before I saw it, really. You know how you can feel someone standing behind you? I was facing the door, but at first I didn't see anything. Then she walked by. In a dress like a cloud at sunset. Mostly I saw the dress. Snatch of brown hair. She was walking fast, like she was running late. I was still sleepy, mind you. But I got out of bed and stumbled for the doorway."

Felix sees it: the door framing the moving portrait. Luke rubs his chin.

"I stumbled for that doorway, and looked down the hall. Looked both ways. But she wasn't there. I called out, even though I didn't know her name. I called out, 'Lilac!' First girl's name that came to my mind. I rounded the corner. Not there. Looked in some other rooms. Not there."

"Do you think it was a ghost?" Felix whispers. She is a little kid at a campfire. She wants to be scared and comforted.

"Tough call," says Luke. "I'm a man of science, like I said. But I tell you, *everyone* had left town."

If this is true, Felix wonders where her aunt went during this time. But Luke seemed a little odd when he published his history book; two and a half decades haven't likely made him saner.

"Do you think it was her?" Felix presses. "You know, Lilac?"

"Not for me to say," Luke concludes. "But if I *were* to say... I'd say yes. Never saw anything like it before ...or since. But why shouldn't it be possible? We all have electric energy pulsing through us. It stands to reason that when we die—"

Downstairs the door slams. Luke puts a finger to his lips. His fingernails are pink against the dark skin of his hands. Felix nods. She hadn't even thought about the supernatural, but maybe Lilac the ghost is more real than Lilac the person.

The children of Lilac Mines are hungry for a haunted house: ghosts and bumblebees, ballerinas and vampires, thumb-sucking pumpkins, scared Spidermen, an angel who steals candy by the handful. *It's Lilac!* they whisper when a white undershirt ghost floats overhead. Felix hadn't given the haunted house any particular theme, but it takes on a local flare of its own. Tawn gets into it. Leading the shy ones by the hand. Squirting extra fake blood at the boastful ones.

In the candlelight she's a convincing witch, thin white hands dancing at the end of her billowing sleeves. Her pointed hat is wrinkled and twisted. She moves between the faux walls of the haunted house like a forest creature, like she could cast a spell.

Felix thinks Tawn is probably more interesting than anyone at the Terrorgasm Ball. She is beautiful, even, in the way that knotted tree roots are beautiful, and French manicures are not.

Between Tawn's transformation and Luke's information, Felix makes a distracted mistress of the dark. Outside, the cloudy sky darkens to a flat, starless black. The kids get bigger. They carry pillowcases instead of jack-o-lantern pails. Felix and Tawn hide behind a sheet and let them go through the maze by themselves.

"I remember them coming to the door when I was little, the big kids, after I was back from trick-or-treating," Felix remembers. "They seemed so tough. I was always afraid they'd smash my pumpkin. But they look so small now."

Through a sliver between two sheets, she watches a skinny Grim Reaper peel off his hood and look around anxiously. He steels his scythe, as if it weren't made of plastic.

"Devon?" he calls out to his friend, a short Chewbacca who is already several sheet-rooms ahead. "Devon?" His voice is higher this time.

"Maybe we should turn the lights on," Felix whispers to Tawn.

"Nah, he'll stick it out and then he'll have something to brag about," she says.

Felix elbows her. "This from the girl who's afraid of previously owned jeans."

"Shush," Tawn whisper-laughs.

A few feet away, the Grim Reaper is freaking out. "Mom?" he calls, although he didn't come in with an adult. A whimpering sound follows. Then he starts to run, tripping over the hem of his robe and swinging his scythe wildly as he crashes through the sheets.

Felix can't stand it any longer. Fuck life lessons and bragging rights. He's a little boy in a too-big costume. She stumbles toward the light switch, but the Grim Reaper thumps into her first. He's almost as tall as she is, and nearly knocks the wind out of her. For a second she stands there, flashbacking, feeling bruised and dazed. Then she wraps her arms around the boy.

"Hey," she says softly, "hey, it's okay." He's a half-grown cat, thin and flexible, clumsy with new muscle.

He hiccups and pulls away. "Shit," he says, all tough 12-year-old again. "What the fuck."

Close up, Felix can see the not-even-peach-fuzz hairs on his face. He has a round bulb of a nose and scared greenish eyes beneath his frowning brow. He is right on the cusp, half baby/half bad guy. She puts her hand on his back, his kitten spine, and guides him toward the back door.

"Chewbacca should be out there already," she smiles.

"Thanks," he mumbles, and Felix releases him into the night.

"Poor kid," sighs Tawn, fumbling with the twisted sheet. "I guess we should call it a night."

"Yeah." Felix stoops to help her. In a minute the lights will be on. In a minute Tawn will be a girl in spirit gum and a graduation robe. Grandpa Luke is probably asleep by now.

Felix tugs the sheet free from its clothesline and it falls on them with a nearly silent *fwump*.

For a second she panics, tangled in the dark. Then she feels a gentle witch hand on her waist. Tawn is warm and close. She smells like pumpkin and candle wax. Her lips taste like Hershey's Special Dark.

Tawn's hands find a place between the spiky hair at the nape of

Felix's neck and her high beaded collar. *She's a real witch*, Felix thinks as her hands search for Tawn through her robe. Felix's dress, for all its yards of cloth, binds and reveals her silhouette. Her petticoats are noisy. Tawn is whatever her body wants to be beneath her black cotton robe. Slim-hipped. Girl-bellied. Shaking a little. Her lips and hands move in strong, silent collusion. Hands on floor, lips poised above Felix's. Then, hands on Felix's face, lips at the edge of her scalp. When she puts her tongue in Felix's mouth, Felix can taste her own hair gel.

Rolling, rolling, they are a yin-yang tumbling down a hill. Finally they surface from the sea of eggplant sheets. Somehow they're beneath the banged-up oak table that holds the bowl of peeled-grape eyeballs. The half-light seems bright, now that they are night creatures.

"What's on your lip?" Tawn says finally.

Felix touches her mouth. "What do you mean?"

"That thing. Is it a scar? Or a cold sore?"

"I don't have herpes!" Felix says. Then she realizes what Tawn is referring to, what she thought she had successfully covered with lipstick every day. "It's a scar."

"From what?" Tawn, her face strewn with shadow, is somehow both innocent and scarred herself, the kind of person who might understand.

"A few weeks before I came here I went clubbing with my friends," she begins. The events flow from her imperfect mouth: the all-night parking meter, Guy Guy and Eva Guy, her purse exploding on the ground, the street sign that watched over her. It is the same story she gave the police, mostly, but now she's crouched beneath a table in a haunted house, watching Tawn's dark brown eyes crinkle at the corners. Now it's all different, as faraway as Los Angeles. It barely seems true.

"What did you do with the purse?" Tawn asks.

"Nothing. It's still in my closet at home. But I see what you mean. I probably won't carry it again."

Tawn touches the silver stud in Felix's chin, then her bottom lip, her freckles smeared with GirlPunk Long-Wearing Lip Color in Nutmeg, the tiny, raised zigzag scar apparently not. Tawn leans forward on her hands and knees and kisses Felix again, slow and light. The table forms a small cave around them. Felix wants to stay exactly here.

How do you date when there's nowhere to go? Felix thinks about Eva, how their first few dates were an elaborate, aroused game of oneupsmanship. Eva took Felix to a film festival. Felix took Eva to a fashion show. Eva took Felix to a museum of hoaxes. Felix took Eva to Miss Velma's millennium church service, where a white-haired woman with bright lipstick preached about golden pillars and Jesus in flames.

It's hard to separate a girl from her world. How would Tawn measure up in L.A.? But Lilac Mines is not L.A. It's not something Felix aspires to; more like a book she wants to read, the one assigned for class that turns out to be a page-turner. And Tawn is not a gateway to cool; she's just company. Very good company.

The next day that Felix has to work is a Tuesday. She dresses slowly, trying to quiet the okay-so-now-what chatter in her head, and skips breakfast. She wears a yellow T-shirt that says *Hermosa High History Hoe-Down '95*. She was an actual hoedown participant, which ups the shirt's conversational value ("All I remember is the Hayes-Tilden Compromise of 1877. I don't even know if that's the answer that we won or lost on.") She wears her darkest, thigh-hiding-est jeans, big silver hoop earrings, bright red Adidas. She studies her ass for a long time in the mirror. This ritual is familiar, and only by enacting it does she realize how long it's been. The early days of Eva were all about checking and double-checking her grooming. Eva was gorgeous enough to get away with not shaving her legs, but Felix believes her most beautiful self is her most controlled self.

"You have a smudge," says Tawn when Felix arrives at Goodwill. She rubs Felix's cheek with her thumb. "You really put make-up on to come to work?"

"Sure, I always wear make-up," Felix says. She means to say she's not doing anything special today, but it sounds like she won't leave the house without eyeshadow. Tawn has accented her black jeans with a man's button-down shirt. It is loose, plain white, sleeves rolled up like she's going to sit down at a typewriter. Over by the cash register, Matty is watching them.

"Oh," Tawn remembers, "I brought you something. Gramp thought you'd be interested in this. He said he's had it forever." From her back pocket, she extracts a folded piece of notebook paper, almost as yellow as Felix's shirt. She presents it to Felix, still folded, free hand behind her back, like it's a rose.

Felix opens the soft paper. On the top it says, in very light letters, *Why Alexander Hamilton Was The Best Of The Founding Father's, Not Georg Washington*. At first she wonders what Alexander Hamilton has to do with Lilac Mines or ghosts. But then she moves past content to form. The handwriting is a kid's—it hasn't found its groove yet, though all the letters are properly formed. It's shaky and so faded that it's clear Felix will never learn why Alexander Hamilton trumps George Washington. But she knows this writing: neat, slanted, eager.

"Gramp said, 'What am I going to do with it anyway? I'm an old man,' " Tawn says.

"This is Lilac's handwriting," Felix says.

"Yeah." Tawn touches the top corner of the paper where it says, *Lilac Ambrose, Grade 8*.

"Which means that she wrote the postcard," Felix says. Laughter bubbles out of her. Tawn squints and Felix explains. Tawn is less impressed than Ranger LeVoy, more cheerful than Gary Schipp. A sort of *Cool, you have fun with that*.

"Thanks for this," Felix adds, waving the paper.

"Hang on," says Tawn. She ducks behind the counter. Matty continues to stare. Tawn pulls out a wooden box carved with trees like the ones that cover the west side of town. "You could put it in here. I found it the other day, when you were off." She pauses, looking down. "I'm stupid to get involved with an employee. But that's how I am sometimes. Stupid."

Tawn sighs, resigned to her fate and hopelessly honest. Felix takes the box. It's the size of her heart. It's better than Miss Velma's kingdom of rainbows and waterfalls.

Felix puts the box in the middle of the dining room table at Anna

Lisa's house, between a crock of vegetable stew and a cooling pumpkin pie. Daylight savings time is over, and they now eat dinner against a backdrop of darkness. Autumn is always half-cozy, half-sad. Lilac Mines has real seasons, and Felix finds herself feeling delicate, as if she could be nudged toward tears at any moment.

"What is it?" Anna Lisa asks when they're halfway through their stew.

Felix finishes chewing a carrot. "The box is from Tawn Twentyman."

"Your boss."

"Mm-hmm. And the paper inside is an original school paper written by Lilac Ambrose. Her grandpa gave it to me."

"Her grand—Luke Twentyman?" Anna Lisa scoots her chair an inch closer to the table.

"You know him?"

"Not well, but—my girlfriend used to work for him. Actually."

"You're dating someone?"

"No, I mean, she *was* my girlfriend. Meg. She worked for him in the '60s. Did a little research and typing but mostly just did her best to keep the guy organized. His office looked like a crime scene in a detective movie."

Felix smiles. *Meg.* She rolls the name around in her mouth, tries to lose Meg Ryan and taste the word on its own. Bold. Quick. Red-haired?

"Tell me something else about Meg," Felix says.

"What?"

"Anything."

Anna Lisa bites her bottom lip. Felix studies her face for clues. It's creased in the expected places—not folds like Luke's, but thin, distinct lines. As if small rivers once ran there, then dried up. But she wears no make-up, and this makes her eyes look young, a secret Revlon would kill to keep. Round and brown, flecked with little gold apostrophes.

"She loved driving," Anna Lisa says finally. "She was a good driver, in a dangerous kind of way. We used to drive all through the mountains. One afternoon we drove all the way to Columbia—we didn't plan to, we just got to talking."

Felix cannot imagine her aunt sustaining a conversation all the way to the 7-Eleven. The myth of Meg doubles.

"We got there and drank sarsaparilla."

Felix nods. "I've never had sarsaparilla," she says earnestly.

"Neither had we. It was a tourist thing, even then." She gives Felix a half-smile. "I'm not *that* old, Felix."

"Oh, I know." But she has trouble with beginnings and endings sometimes. When cars were invented, did everyone stop riding horses? Did the telegraph die once telephones became common? How is it that her parents lived through segregation *and* affirmative action? How could one body contain all those contradictions?

"What was she like?" Felix asks. "Meg."

"She was... brave. Passionate. She really loved me. She had a beautiful smile."

These are the things they say on the news when someone who isn't famous dies. Honor student. Cheerleader. Beautiful smile. They don't mean anything. But as Anna Lisa tries to translate sarsaparilla and the specificity of a smile, her jaw begins to quiver. She isn't a youthful 60 now, she's an ancient girl. A stood-up prom date. It makes Felix nervous. What can she do for a 40-year-old broken heart?

"Can I show you something?" Felix jumps up, a little breathless. "Hang on."

She jogs down the hall and returns with the postcard. She'd vowed not to bring it up to anyone until she had more information. But now, with Lilac's history paper just inches from this other artifact, it seems only a matter of time before the other pieces of the puzzle shake off the dust and make a pilgrimage from the hills. Like the trick-or-treaters. Felix's desire will be enough.

"Look what I found," she says, presenting the card to her aunt. "The writing is the same."

Anna Lisa reads the postcard. "It's kind of romantic, isn't it?" she says without looking up.

"Exactly!" says Felix. "I mean, all of it. The whole mystery." Who would have thought that Anna Lisa, of all people, would be the one to understand?

"You know, there are people who say she wasn't the only one who disappeared that day."

"Really? Who?"

"Just people. You know how rumors are. I remember people saying things years ago, back when the whole thing seemed a little less like something out of a history book and a little more real, I guess. It wasn't anything specific."

"But I mean, who else disappeared?"

Anna Lisa shrugs. "A boyfriend? A friend? Some other kid from school? Her mother? Everyone has their own little theory, whatever makes sense to them."

Cal? Felix wonders.

Anna Lisa adds, "Some people think she killed herself."

Coal wanders into the room and flops at Anna Lisa's feet with a dog-sigh. Anna Lisa bends to scratch his curly ears, and Felix cuts the pie.

Later that night, Felix finds Anna Lisa in the guest room—her room. She's crouched by the short bookcase where Felix has stashed her magazines and hats. The bottom shelf is still occupied by Anna Lisa's books, titles like *TransPlants: Tropical Plants in Cool Climates.*

"Sorry, I didn't mean to snoop," says Anna Lisa when she sees Felix. "I was just looking for this."

She holds up a book with a vaguely pornographic-looking bird of paradise on the cover.

"Isn't it getting a little cold to garden?"

"No, this," says Anna Lisa. From its pages, she pulls a black and white photograph. Felix approaches slowly, as if her aunt is a mountain lion who might flee for the hills. The woman in the picture is leaning against an old, light-colored car. She has shiny hair and a beaky nose. Her outfit is so Jackie O: a tweedy, tailored jacket and narrow skirt to match. She *does* have a very nice smile. Dark lipstick. She looks toward the mountains that Felix imagines are behind the photographer, and not at the camera.

"Is this Meg?"

"Mmm," says Anna Lisa. She props the picture up next to Lilac's postcard on the dresser, and they look at it together. Felix wishes her aunt were in the photo, too.

"Hey, Anna Lisa?" Her chest is tight as a corset. "Can I... um, I was wondering if it might be okay ... if I stay here a little longer?"

Her aunt snaps her head toward Felix. Is this a bad time or the perfect time? "Why?"

Felix would not have a problem kicking Genevieve out of her apartment. She might even enjoy it. She shrugs. "I like it here. It's, you know, quiet, and people are friendly—" She's starting to sound like a newscast herself, one about the charms of small-town life, so she stops herself. "I like getting to know you, and I'm sort of maybe seeing Tawn. It's nothing yet, not really, but—"

Anna Lisa smiles knowingly. "Then it's settled. The room is yours as long as you want it."

A GIRL SPLIT IN PARTS
Al: Lilac Mines, 1966

One Saturday morning in June, Al wakes with a hangover that can only partially be attributed to Pabst at Lilac's. Equally heavy in her stomach are the words and glances she and Meg slung across the dim bedroom. She remembers "drinking" and "butch" and maybe "bitch." But she's not sure who said what—the words are a crossword puzzle she can maneuver in too many ways.

Still, the morning is crisp with possibility, and as she pads sock-footed to the porch, she wonders if the details of their life can save them. Yes, there are arguments about whether 95 cents is too much for a beer, but aren't there also pink-budded plants kissing the sides of their house, performing the glory of transformation? Aren't there Meg's old saddle shoes, the ones she announced she was exiling to yard work, sitting sweet and pigeon-toed on the bottom step? Mud freckling the bumper of Meg's car? The neighbors' orange cat glaring lazily in her direction? All of these things are part of her life, and if Al squints hard enough at them, the bigger questions disintegrate. She does not have to be a certain kind of person in a certain kind of world; she can just reach out her hand and scratch the cat between the ears.

He begins a rusty, rib-rattling purr. Then, with species-appropriate fickleness, he leaves her to go sniff something on the far side of the porch. With her own feline sluggishness, Al stands up to investigate. She's not in the mood for a dead mouse. She sees a bit of silky brown hair, but it's not a mouse.

It's a girl's braid. Tapered and innocent, except that it is in completely the wrong place. It's lying on the ground next to a bright green shrub and not on a girl's sloping shoulder. The top is secured with a rubber band out of which spiky, bluntly cut hairs extend. The bottom end is tied with a pink ribbon, which also holds a crumpled bit of paper.

Al touches her head. The braid on the ground is her color, the color of sugar pine trunks heading for the spinning saw blade. Sylvie cuts Al's hair every six weeks. She and Jody and Jean take turns in a kitchen chair like good little boys. Nevertheless, she feels as if the braid could have been sliced from her own head. The thought makes the short hairs on the back of her neck stand up, as if they are sniffing the wind for lost kin.

"Al? Darling? What're you doing out there?" Meg's voice penetrates the thin walls easily. It is like the house is talking to Al.

"Petting the cat," she calls back, surprised how calm her voice sounds.

"Scandalous!" giggles Meg. She does not come outside. Nevertheless, Meg's voice always makes her want to *do* something. It's part of what she loves about Meg. "Well, if you need me, I'm just in here writing to Petra."

Sometimes Al wonders if Petra is real. It's silly—she's seen the letters, the Kerhonkson postmark, the handwriting looping on about a junior prom dress (*No one else had silver, let me tell you!*). But Meg has a way of wielding her pen pal at just the right time. Petra is a faraway angel girl who always understands when Al does not. Al floated her theory for Meg once, in an offhand, half-kidding manner that nevertheless immediately revealed its true suspicions. Meg's face broke, as if Al had just repeated every insult Meg had ever received. As if Al were just like *them* after all.

Now Al touches the braid, gently, as if it were alive or recently dead. It inevitably belongs to someone who is one of the two. Her fingers trace its curves to the ribbon. Pink for a girl. She pulls. The slip of paper falls out. Unrolled, it reads DiKE.

The epithet's misspelling might have made it laughable, but somehow the effect is to unnerve Al even more. Whoever this threatener is, he or she is not one to research, to listen to reason. The note is written in black pen, block-lettered. The lettering is not quite stylish, but it contains no trace of doubt. Too, there is the fact that it says DiKE, not DYKES or even DiKES. She is sure, somehow, that only she has been named. Meg is the good girl who has been seduced.

Al squats, holding the paper, hands quivering. She's still in her nightshirt and someone is telling her what she is. Handing her fate to her like a fortune in a cookie. The cat slips between the rungs of the fence, and possibility slithers out of view.

Did the neighbors have anything to do with this? The Espeys are a childless couple in their 30s. Zeke Espey works at the mill and flirts with Meg. His wife, as a result, hates Meg, and both are cold to Al. It's hard to name the causes in such an intricate situation, what they know or don't know, what they're capable of and what they wouldn't waste their time on. Sometimes Meg flirts back.

"Come in, I'll make bacon... make-up bacon," calls Meg.

Al knows she should tell Meg about the braid, about the maybe-murdered girl. Meg is brave. She would run down the road in bare feet. Al should say, *Call all our friends, it's us against the world.*

Except right now it feels more like the world against us. Al feels herself shrink down to the i in DiKE. She will save her questions for later. She will not tell Meg—she wants to believe this is motivated by protectiveness of her femme, but she suspects its origins are bitter, sneaky. The product of a girl split in parts.

By August, Al is back at the church. Just over a year after arriving in Lilac Mines, she is tentatively tapping the heavy wooden doors, as nervous as when she first stepped into the bar behind Jody and Imogen.

"Can I stay here awhile?" she asks Imogen, who opens the door like a housewife expecting to hear a pitch about carpet cleaner. There's a dust rag in her hand. Clicking noises suggest the movement of curlers beneath her red headscarf. She's been leading a life behind those doors, and Al has interrupted it.

"Of course, honey. Come on in and tell me what's goin' on." Her voice is softer, slightly country.

She guides Al to a table and chairs with calico seat cushions in the kitchen. These are new—or new to the church, at least. She pours her a cup of burnt-tasting coffee, and puts a carton of milk on the table between them.

"Meg and I have been fighting. A lot."

"What about? If you don't mind my prying."

"I don't know." Al means she doesn't know what they're fighting about, but she doesn't know if she minds Imogen prying either. She wants to collapse into her soft arms, but she would need a reason, and she's not sure she has one. "Nothing? Everything? I thought it would get easier, the longer we were together, but it's not."

In her head Al sees the Ford's headlights on Meg's pale face in the mine. Bessie Smith's record tilting in circles on the phonograph. The seams of Meg's stockings. The limp ribbon on the end of the braid and the months of quiet afterward. Meg tear-stained, then happy, then tear-stained. It doesn't add up to anything she could tell anyone. She wishes she could say, *Meg snores. Meg has eyes for another butch.*

Imogen is studying Al closely. "Sounds like the honeymoon's over. I don't mean just the honeymoon between the two of you, but between you and this whole thing." She gestures abstractly. "Me and Jody, we went through that. Some time ago. Had to say to ourselves, did we really want to sneak around our whole lives? To get mean looks even from other girls in the life?"

"And did you want to? Do you?"

"Some days. But at least in a place this small you can get to know everyone one by one. Eventually most of them stop thinking, 'Jody's with that Negro,' and think, 'Jody's with Imogen.' " Her eyes angle toward the uneven wood floor in a way that is shy and tired and cynical all at once. "You stick it out 'cause you know you're not gonna find anything better. And sometimes I mean it in the best way, like what could be better? But sometimes I mean it like I'm just not cut out for an easy life."

Al adds as much milk as she can to her coffee without making the mug overflow. Now it is almost palatable. "What if I'm not cut out for a hard life?" she worries. She wants Imogen to tell her, *Yes, you are.*

"Then you'll find out, I guess."

She makes Al a bed next to Sylvie and Jean's—a pile of thin blankets that add up to something soft—and the next morning Al rides to the mill in Jody's Edsel. Even with the windows rolled down, it's unbearably hot. Dust blows in and covers the vinyl seats, sticks to their sweaty faces. When Al steps out of the car and into the burning 9 a.m. sun, she can't believe the day is just beginning.

"So, are you and Meg still together?" asks Caleb, the bartender at Lilac's. His voice strikes a note somewhere between gossip and concern.

"Yeah, we are." Al draws a squiggly line in the condensation on her beer glass. "We're just... I'm staying with Jody and the girls for awhile."

Caleb nods like he knows something that Al is too young to learn. He's wearing a navy blue turtleneck tonight and the beginnings of a mustache. Al doesn't know him well. She doesn't know if he has only two sweaters or if he considers them his uniform and wears them only on Friday and Saturday nights, or if he has hundreds of identical turtlenecks lined up in a closet.

"Meg is a gorgeous girl," Caleb says. "But she's a wild one. She burned Jean's clothes after they broke up."

"That's not true," Jody interjects. It's a Friday in September, not dark yet. They're drinking after-work beers. There are just a few butches in the bar, a couple of men, no femmes. "I thought it was true, but Imogen said no, that's just what people do to a femme when they decide her temper's too hot. They make things up."

"I heard it from Jean," Caleb says a little smugly. "Just after they broke up."

Jody leans on her elbows. There are flecks of sawdust in the light hairs on her arms. "And what makes you think some brokenhearted butch is going to tell you the truth? Jean's my buddy, I wanna make that clear, but I remember those days, before she got together with Sylvie. She was capable of anything, too. She was just quieter about it than Meg was."

It's strange hearing about this other Meg. Caleb makes her sound like a banshee, wild-eyed and match-wielding. Al tries to counter it with what she knows about Meg: the way she clenches her teeth when she's mad, the surprised giggle when Al scissors her own legs between Meg's in bed. But she hasn't seen Meg in four long days. Maybe her version is wrong as well.

Then, as if to set the record straight, Meg is suddenly there. The door to the bar lets in a small explosion of late-afternoon light. Meg is wearing the same pink and orange plaid skirt that she was wearing the first night Al saw her. For a second Al pictures them starting over, getting it right. Al will ask to buy Meg a drink. Meg will be impressed by Al's straight-backed walk, her leather wallet.

"Al, I just talked to your mother," Meg says breathlessly.

"*What?*" says Al.

"Ho boy," says Caleb.

"Your mother. She called. She said your sister gave her the number—your sister called a few minutes later to say she was sorry, but it was an emergency. Your mother said your dad had a heart attack."

Al puts her fingers on her forehead. They are beer-cold and her face feels hot. Now it is her father she tries to piece together: whenever she's pictured him over the past year, it's been at the little desk in the back room of the store, chewing on the end of his pencil as he tries to make sense of the finances. His red-brown hair mussed by his worried fingers. Somehow Al imagined he wouldn't leave that desk until she was there.

"Is he…" she whispers. It feels like something is sucking at the back of her head.

"He's not dead," Meg says, her voice a little too loud. "Sorry, I didn't mean to make it sound worse than it is. He's in the hospital." She reaches into her purse and hands Al a scrap of paper. Fresno Episcopal, where Al and Suzy were both born, is written in Meg's hard scrawl. Below that, her parents' home phone number, as if Al might have forgotten it. It's strange to see it with the area code.

Al closes her eyes and listens to what might be her own heart. Fast but functioning. Now when she pictures her father, she sees him in a hospital bed that looks like the metal-framed twin she still sometimes shares with Meg. Is this all that's left of her family? A crazy quilt of memories threaded deceitfully with details from her new life? *I need to restock*, she thinks, and it's almost literal. As if her hands would gain something from stacking chickpeas on shelves, four cans deep.

"What do I do?" Al asks. They're all staring at her.

"How would we know?" replies Caleb.

"Depends," says Jody thoughtfully. "How much do you like your pa?"

"You go home," Meg states, and Al is grateful for her decisiveness. Al slips off the barstool and into Meg's arms. Her embrace is so tight that Al can't catch her breath. "I'll loan you a dress," Meg whispers into Al's ear. "I'll take it in and shorten it tonight."

TOO YOUNG TO BE HISTORICAL
Felix: Lilac Mines, 2002

In early December Matty quits the Goodwill and moves to
Vancouver. This surprises Felix, who sort of figured that a town as small
as Lilac Mines would be static. She assumed that most people lived here
by accident, and that if they were going to leave, they would have done
so long ago.

"Bye, lezbirds. Don't forget to invite me to your big lesbo wedding,"
he says on his last day. The door dings as he steps out of the store and
into the rainy day.

Felix and Tawn are a long way from a big lesbo wedding, but they
do seem to be really and truly dating, in a teenage sort of way—not that
Felix actually dated anyone when she was a teenager. They make out
in Felix's car and have quietly reached third base in Tawn's bedroom.
Felix has learned a few unexpected things about Tawn: she's been more
or less out since high school because, she says, she's a bad liar. She has
an extensive collection of reggae CDs and dances to them with mellow,
unselfconscious grace.

After Matty's long, soggy last day, Tawn counts out the cash register
and locks the shop. They drive up North Main only to discover a road
crew jackhammering at chunks of asphalt. The detour veers west, toward
the newer part of town. The line of cars, brake lights blinking, is the first
traffic jam Felix has seen since she arrived.

"It's okay, we need to head east anyway," Tawn says. "Let's try going
down Washoe Street."

Washoe Street is a sort of shadow of East Main. The old buildings here are less restored, less like a tourist's idea of a small town and more like a small town's idea of a small town. There are hardware stores and shoe repair shops and a shooting range. Anna Lisa went there one night, and Felix was horrified.

"Your car is fucking freezing," Felix says. "No offense."

"Yeah, the fan is broken. It's actually better that it's cold out because at least this way it doesn't overheat."

"Aren't you scared of getting stuck by the side of the road? There are freaks out there who might take advantage of a cute, stranded chick. Have you looked into getting a new car? Or like, a newer car?"

"Yeah, of course I'm scared," Tawn says, glancing at her sideways. "I've looked at some ads, but anything that would be a real upgrade is too expensive. I did meet this girl with a year-old Beetle, though," she smiles.

Felix puts her hand on the back of Tawn's warm, slender neck. Tawn jumps. The car zigzags.

"Oh my *God*, your hands are cold," says Tawn when she's regained control of the wheel.

"Let's stop there," Felix says, pointing to a low wooden building that says Nora's Unisex Salon on one side and Coffee - Cold Beer - Ammo on the other. "Let's get some coffee."

"I hate coffee," Tawn says. "It doesn't taste like something you're actually supposed to *drink*."

"We can just warm our hands on the cups," she promises. "And pick up some bullets."

The store is small and dark, crowded with dusty displays. The stringy-haired woman slouched on a stool behind the counter glares at them. Felix wonders if it's obvious they're a couple. She wonders if they are a couple.

She decides to be friendly. "Afternoon. Hey, um, how old is this building?"

The woman looks Felix up and down with small blue eyes the color of swimming pools. She takes in the rainbow of plastic clips twisting

Felix's spiky hair, the bomber jacket, the pink wool pants.

"You're not from the Historical Society, are you?"

"Huh? No."

"Good, 'cause they're always snooping around here. Guess they know how old this place is by now, though. They want to take it. Commies."

"Why do they want to take it?" Felix asks. Tawn is investigating the store's lip balm selection, conveniently located next to a dangerous-looking—but powerful—space heater.

"Used to be the post office and the newspaper office. Back in olden times. They want to put some stupid plaque up that says '319 Washoe Street used to be the post office and newspaper office in 18-hundred-and-such-and-such.' Tell me, where're people gonna get their coffee and beer then?"

"And ammo," Felix says, then clamps her mouth shut. Tawn giggles and studies a tube of Blistex intensely.

Three-nineteen Washoe Street. Why does that sound familiar? Her reading about the town has centered on the mine. One book mentioned a bank robbery, and another recalled a popular update of *Romeo and Juliet* at the Silver Bird Playhouse, but there's been nothing about a post office or newspaper office—and why would there be?

Then she sees the number written out in her mind—319, with a flat top on the 3, and a little flag on the 1. A soft-bottomed W.

"That's the address on the postcard," she says aloud. She's giddy with the information, and embarrassed that she hadn't even thought about where the postcard was *sent*. Maybe Cal is just around the corner.

Tawn looks up. "Yeah, of course it is. It's the *post office*. They didn't have mailmen in a place like this, way back then. Even now, a lot of people farther up in the mountains come into town to pick their mail up."

"Oh. Right. Duh," Felix says. "I'm such a city girl. And she... you," she looks at the beady-eyed clerk, "just said it was the post office."

"Are you going to buy something?" asks the clerk. A cigarette smolders in an ashtray next to her.

There are two metal canisters of coffee next to a rack of heat-lamp-haloed pretzels, and Felix fills a styrofoam cup. Tawn buys a hot chocolate, and they sit down on the patio furniture that is the store's dining area.

"I really want to find out what happened to Lilac," Felix sighs. "I know it's stupid and impossible, but it's like, I would just be so happy if I knew. It would feel so good to have a solid answer. Nothing else does."

Tawn stabs at her drink with a skinny red straw. "This is definitely the powdered stuff." She leans in. "That woman is watching us. Doesn't she know we're too young to be historical?"

Felix adds, "When I said nothing is solid, I didn't mean—I'm not saying we're not. I'm not saying we *are*. I mean, I'm not one of those U-Haul lesbians, I just—"

Tawn lowers her voice. "U-Haul lesbians?"

"You know, the joke—what do dykes bring on the second date?"

"Oh. Because they can't afford movers?"

"No, because they shack up right away. You haven't heard that one before?"

"Oh, I get it," says Tawn. "You know, it's not like there's some big—I don't know—lesbian joke conference in Lilac Mines."

Felix laughs. "Yeah, I picked that one up at the lesbian joke conference in L.A. The tenth annual."

They're quiet for a minute. The clerk goes to the freezer case and fusses with the bottles of beer and soda.

"Um, there's something I wanted to talk to you about," Tawn says. Felix thinks, *This is it, this is where she lays out the future.* Felix feels strangely calm. Like she might be ready for this.

"I'm going to be hiring someone to fill in for Matty pretty soon," Tawn says, "and I think it would be a good idea not to mention that we're, you know, seeing each other."

"Okay..." Felix lets it sink in. Tawn was talking work-future. "Right. Well, that seems fair."

But as her coffee burns her tongue and Tawn watches the parking lot, Felix starts to think about the reality. She will have to go into the Goodwill four mornings a week and not touch Tawn's arm and not call her "honey." Not that she *does* call her "honey," but suddenly she wants to. What if whoever Tawn hires asks if Felix is dating someone? A few months ago, when she was still jittery from the attack, she might have found forced silence shamefully appealing. But now she's ricocheted to the opposite end of the out-ness spectrum.

"I thought you said you were a bad liar," Felix says.

"I am. But we have to be professional. I don't think we really have a choice."

"Sure we do. We could be pioneers. We could really make a statement."

"A statement about what? I'm not saying we can't be gay—it's not the Salvation Army—but I wouldn't like it if, like, you and Matty were dating. I don't want to be a hypocrite or a bad example to the new person."

"I just believe in trying new things."

"Felix, this is my *job*. I have to talk to people from corporate and stuff. I can't just screw around. So to speak." She half-smiles, but her dark eyebrows are still clenched with worry.

Felix's first thought is that Eva would have put boundary-breaking principles above corporate principles any day. Of course, it's broken boundaries and a sizeable savings account that are sending Eva on her European tour. Felix's second thought is that this must be how her aunt felt. Back in the day. Or maybe today.

"I get it," Felix says slowly.

"I'm not really sure you do, actually," Tawn says. "If I ever want to get my own apartment, I have to stick it out at the Goodwill. My life isn't like yours—it's not some big, fun closet where I wake up and say, 'Hmm, what am I going to wear today?' "

"Maybe you don't get *me*. I'm trying to be political here," Felix says. She's hurt. Doesn't activism mean speaking your truth and all that? So why does her truth feel alternately shallow and impossibly, murkily deep in Lilac Mines? She takes a slow breath. "I mean, I *get* it, okay. I'm just not looking forward to going into work and acting like I wasn't at your house all night."

"You don't have to *be* at my house all night if you don't want to,"

Tawn says icily. "You're only here for another few weeks anyway. You'll last as long as a pair of designer jeans at the Goodwill. I know you're just slumming."

"Tawn! I am not fuckin' slumming! Do you know how many local history books I've read since I got here? I'm trying to figure out what actually *happened* to Lilac Ambrose. Who hurt her. Lilac the person, not the mascot. Have you even read your grandfather's own book?"

Tawn wraps her arms around herself. Her eyes are huge and liquid. "If you're so into history, maybe you should realize that it's still real for some of us. The old, homophobic days are *now*."

Felix doesn't mean to touch the scar on her lip, to be so cheap and obvious, but her fingers gravitate to the white bump of skin. "Yeah, I know that, thanks."

"Sorry," Tawn says in a low voice. "But, well, there's still a difference between one really bad day and every day. I just feel like sometimes you don't even notice what's around you."

"Whatever," Felix sighs.

Tawn is shivering and looking hard at the parking lot. "Hey, is that your aunt?"

"Where?"

Tawn points. Felix sees the poodle in the truck bed, then Anna Lisa walking toward Nora's Unisex Salon. She's bundled in a shapeless blue jacket, as utilitarian as a unisex hair salon. Her hair does look a little shaggy.

Felix dumps the rest of her coffee and introduces Tawn to Anna Lisa on the freezing boardwalk that connects the store and the hair salon. It's strange to see them together, since she started working at the Goodwill partly to get away from Anna Lisa. *I could put my hand on Tawn's back,* Felix thinks. *I could hold her hand while I introduce her, show Aunt Anna Lisa how it's done.* But she doesn't feel like touching Tawn right now. She feels like letting her shiver.

"Nice to meet you," Anna Lisa says with a nod.

"You too," Tawn nods back, still clutching her hot chocolate.

"I was going to get a haircut," Anna Lisa says.

156

"Is this a good place?" Tawn asks politely.

"The only other place I've gone is A La Carte Nails, which does hair too now, but it's not open Mondays and it's so… pink."

Tawn laughs and Felix hates them both.

"I was about to leave," Tawn says. "Felix, why don't you get a ride home with your aunt?" She turns, with a flip of her rain-frizzed hair, and walks across the parking lot.

And so Felix finds herself in the waiting area of Nora's with a year-old issue of *Good Housekeeping*, thinking about how little the magazine has to do with housekeeping, trying not to think about Tawn.

Nora Banister emerges, aproned, scissors in hand. She has a manic blonde perm and bright pink lips (raspberry? Pepto-Bismol?). Felix's aunt sits in what looks like an old dental chair, a piece of furniture that might be found in a particularly creative BDSM club.

"The usual?" Nora asks.

"Same old, same old," smiles Anna Lisa. Apparently Nora's Unisex Salon doesn't shampoo. Nora examines Anna Lisa's dry hair with her fingers, and places her hands on Anna Lisa's shoulders when she talks. Felix watches them, thinking, *This is what it would look like if Anna Lisa had a girlfriend.*

Felix grows bored with an article about "Jeans For *Every* Body." How was it she used to spend every day writing this shit?

She stands up and walks around the salon. In addition to several hanging plants, there is a large wood and metal contraption in the corner of the waiting area. It's an architecture of keys and rollers, with one big flat area. It seems to fit with the old dental chair and the peeling windows, but she can't imagine what it has to do with the beauty biz.

"What's this?" she calls to Nora.

"Old printing press," Nora says, continuing to snip. "From back when this was a newspaper office. It's been here since we opened, and I haven't gotten rid of it 'cause I think it's kind of cool. I keep meaning to paint it, though, and put some plants on it."

Felix leans in. Ancient, inky fingerprints smudge the levers and even the legs of the press. Hands fed the news into the machine, following the same trails day after day. One day, she imagines, they arranged the letters to say LILAC AMBROSE LOST. Or (is this how printing presses work?) TSOL ESORBMA CALIL. The word HOGAN is scratched into the metal edge of the press, and Felix's mind wanders to that sitcom, *The Hogan Family.*

The address of the newspaper office/salon is also 319 Washoe Street. What if, Felix wonders, the postcard was sent here, and not to the post office? It's not like it's a letter to the editor, but what if Cal worked for the newspaper?

"Any idiots out there this season?" Nora asks Anna Lisa.

"Not yet, but it's only a matter of time. There are always people who think hiking in the off-season is some well-kept secret. They don't stop to realize there's a reason that most people don't head up into the mountains when it might snow any minute." Anna Lisa doesn't turn her head but calls to Felix, "Nora's husband TJ does search and rescue with me."

Nora combs and scissors, her acrylic nails clicking. If she lived in L.A., Felix thinks, she'd have layered hair, ironed straight. She'd wear velour sweatsuits. Bits of brown hair fall on Anna Lisa's cloth bib like snowflakes.

"We've known your aunt forever," Nora says cheerfully. "Me and TJ. She was at our wedding, and just last week she did a lice check on our little girl's class. I still can't believe Charlotte had lice." She laughs heartily. "How embarrassing, a hairdresser's daughter with lice."

But she doesn't seem embarrassed. Plastic hearts swing from her earlobes as she laughs.

"How long have you lived here?" Felix asks. She still wants to find old-timers; Nora Banister doesn't look older than 40, but, well, she said she's known Anna Lisa forever.

"Let's see, TJ and I moved here from San Diego just after he got out of the Marines, and before I had Dillon, so... 18 years? Lilac Mines was really just starting up again at that point... right, Anna Lisa?"

"Yep," Anna Lisa agrees, still not moving her head.

"What do you mean?" Felix is confused. "I thought it stopped being a ghost town in, like, the '40s."

"Oh no, no," says Nora, shaking her curly head. "Well, it did—there was a saw mill and such here during World War II and into the '50s and '60s—but by the mid-'70s *no one* was here. Ask around. You won't meet anyone who's lived here longer than 20 years."

Anna Lisa stares straight ahead.

Felix thinks about the people she's met, oldish people with history. Gary Schipp and Luke Twentyman and the haggard woman next door. Not that she's asked most of them what they were doing in the '70s and '80s. People carry their histories like luggage, and you try to decipher whether it's Louis Vuitton or JanSport or a stickered steamer trunk. Busy strangers. Didn't Luke say something about everyone leaving?

"Well, a few people lived here, off and on," says Anna Lisa. "But hardly anyone."

Nora continues, "In the '80s, when real estate in the cities started to skyrocket, people started moving back here in big numbers. It was one place normal folks could still buy a house with a yard bigger than a postage stamp." Nora plugs an electric shaver into a nearby outlet and expertly mows the nape of Anna Lisa's neck. "We're a double ghost town," Nora says over the buzz. "Even if there was nothing exciting like a lost girl in a mine to kick off the second round." She turns off the shaver and steps between Anna Lisa and the mirror to appraise her work. She snips above Anna Lisa's right ear and says, "There. Looking good."

Then Nora whirls around to face Felix. "Hey, I've got an idea. Let me cut your hair, too. It's looking pretty overgrown." She is so enthusiastic, in her tight flowered dress, waving her eager scissors, that Felix doesn't have time to feel insulted. Her head is still reeling with the news: while she was searching for what happened a century ago, she didn't bother to notice what happened 30 years ago. Felix finds herself easing into the kinky chair, which is surprisingly comfortable. Anna Lisa smiles her encouragement. Her hair is short and neat.

"Just a trim," Felix says. She removes the plastic clips from her hair one by one and sprinkles them on the counter. A few strands of coarse brown hair come with them. "Just an inch or two," she says again. If she were home, she wouldn't mind a good chop, but she wants to minimize any potential damage.

She closes her eyes as Nora cuts. There's something slightly medical about the process, and she thinks of her night in the hospital. The hum and click of alien instruments, being at the mercy of hands that might be good or bad. She forces her thoughts elsewhere.

Where was her aunt during the '70s? Maybe she did have a fabulous queer life, maybe those were her glory years. Maybe she went to a big city and met a nice girl. Or maybe Meg came with her. Maybe they lived in a skinny Victorian in the Castro.

Nora's nails catch on the small silver hoop at the crest of Felix's left ear. "Ow!"

"Sorry." But Nora doesn't sound too worried.

Eventually Felix relaxes into the rhythm of the scissors. Her dry hair is so light. She's awed by how easily her hair gives in. Gives up. Now it's on her head, now it's on her shoulders, now it's in a dustpan. It doesn't fight for its place, it just adapts. The difference between dead and alive left to the squeezing of metal handles.

She can't bring herself to watch the mirror, so she slides her gaze over to the parking lot, and beyond that to the cold brown strip of town. There are no dewy trees here to evoke Christmas, just a general gloom. What still surprises her about this part of town is that she never would have guessed there used to be trees here. When she was an obedient Hermosa High Ecology Club member contemplating Depleted Rainforests, she visualized fields of stumps, perhaps a gangly, confused monkey here and there. But the clear-cut portion of Lilac Mines looks as if it always was a stripped field disguised as destiny.

"So... what do you think?" Nora wants to know.

Felix turns toward the mirror. Her hair is short and neat. What she usually spikes up is now flattened down. Nora stands over one shoulder, pink-faced and expectant. Anna Lisa stands over the other, looking exactly like Felix.

It's no longer just a family resemblance. Anna Lisa looks like one of those computerized images of kidnapped children, aged but not updated. Two round faces, one lined but still chubby-cheeked. Two showers of freckles. Two ready-for-the-big-softball game haircuts.

"Wow, you all look just alike!" Nora exclaims. "I didn't see it when you came in here, but wow. If you went to the same salon all the time, you'd be twins."

Felix purses her lips and tastes her scar. She has an overwhelming urge to slather her hair with gel. Would it be rude to ask what sorts of styling products Nora has on hand? Anna Lisa makes her uneasy, looking back at Felix with Felix's face. *If we had the same salon,* Felix repeats in her head.

Anna Lisa, for her part, has a strange smile on her face.

THE EFFECTS OF OATMEAL COOKIES
Al: Fresno, 1966

It was not a heart attack. By the time Al learns this, she's home already, standing in the kitchen of the old farmhouse. Her mother has put up new curtains—printed with apples and corn and other things that don't grow in California—but everything else is the same. The smell of Lemon Pledge, the clay ashtrays Al and Suzy made in school.

"It's congestive heart failure," Eudora Hill tells her daughters. "Which can cause heart attacks, but didn't, technically, in your father's case."

Suzy has come home, too. She loves Los Angeles, is tan and nearly blonde, has befriended the students Aunt Randi teaches flute to at Pepperdine. The bored and panicked girl Al heard on the phone is gone; she's back to being a streak of forward motion. Al feels almost shy.

"Oh, thank God," Suzy says.

"Yes, I think we should thank God," agrees their mother. "Dr. Shannon says he still needs to take it easy until his body adapts to the medication and we figure out just how much work he can handle. We've hired a nice young man to help out at the store. Terry Kristalovich— he manages the office supply store across the street and helps out with restocking after he closes up shop for the day. You have to admire that sort of enterprise in a young person."

Is it Anna Lisa's imagination, or is her mother looking at her pointedly? Eudora Hill has blue eyes that match the flowers on her

CorningWare bowls. Neither of her daughters inherited them. She's taller than both girls too, sturdy despite her fragile housedress. Her nut-brown hair is marbled with more gray than Al remembered.

"I'm so anxious for Daddy to come home. Let's make him a big sign or something," Suzy says. She bends down and pats Al's suitcase as if it were a dog. "Aw, the old suitcase. I remember. Looks like it's been through a lot, Anna Lisa."

"It has," Al says quietly. So far her mother and sister have done most of the talking. It's easier this way. Meg dropped Al off early this morning. Al kissed her on the cheek and said, "You'll wait for me, right?" She immediately hated herself for sounding so insecure. Eudora wanted to know why Al didn't invite her roommate in for coffee and cookies. She was cheerful, glad, apparently, that her mysterious daughter was not shacked up with some man.

Suzy had defended her: "Golly, Mother, Anna Lisa's worried about Daddy. She doesn't want to make small talk over cookies." Al wondered what Suzy had guessed.

Now Eudora scoops up the suitcase and carries it upstairs, daughters trailing behind. Before Al can stop her, she has tossed it on Al's old bed, unclasped it and removed two neat stacks of folded clothing.

"Let's get you settled," she says.

Then Eudora sees the men's shirts and slacks. Al could probably get away with wearing them one at a time, but they implicate her in the aggregate. Right now she's wearing a button-down shirt with the sandstone-colored skirt that Meg hemmed for her. It's a safe costume, but her bare calves make her feel more vulnerable than ever.

Her mother holds up a pair black pants, the ones she bought with Jody and Imogen. The cuffs are frayed now, but that's not what concerns Eudora. "Anna Lisa, I thought you worked as a secretary. Don't tell me this is what you wear to *work*."

"It's not," Al says truthfully. She wears blue jeans and heavy tan boots. This is what she wears to Lilac's.

"Then what...?" Her mother's eyes beg her for a story.

She didn't really think she could come home without explaining anything, did she? Nevertheless, she's caught off guard.

"It gets cold in the mountains," she explains. This is also true.

"But honey, these look like *men's* clothes. And it's 90 degrees here."

Al feels every bit of the heat. Her cotton shirt is damp against her back and armpits. The bedroom where she slept every night for 19 years seems to have shrunk.

"I—" Al begins. What would happen if she told the truth? She looks at her mother for a clue. Eudora's face is pulled out of shape, like a wad of Silly Putty pressed against the comics page and stretched by her sick husband, her mysterious older daughter. Al remembers playing with Silly Putty as a kid, how the picture would snap in half if she pulled too fast, or collapse into a limp string if she pulled too hard.

"I work for this old man," Al says a little too quickly. "His name is Luke Twentyman. He's a historian, and he's researching some of the old mines in the area, including this one where a girl died back at the turn of the century. Sometimes we have to go down in the mines. It's cold and slippery, and it would be dangerous to wear a skirt or high heels."

Suzy's expression is intrigued but wary. Her green-gold eyes narrow. "You never told me that."

"Well, she never told *me* anything at all," Eudora says, taking a step closer to her younger daughter. Al pictures them staying up late, talking about her over tea. "A girl died there? Is it safe for you to be down there? Aren't mines always caving in?"

"We don't go that far," Al assures her. "And Luke, well, he knows everything there is to know about the area." She takes a breath, and inches toward neutral territory. "There are rumors that the girl's ghost still haunts the mines, though."

"Yeah?" Suzy sits down on the bed, folding her legs neatly beneath her fern-print skirt. She settles in for a story.

Eudora puts down the black pants. "Ghosts—I hope you know better than that." But she's listening, too. And so, in the middle of the sun-bleached room, Al tells them what she knows about Lilac Ambrose, and a few things she doesn't. She embroiders the story with eerie details from the safe, dead past, and silently thanks Lilac for saving her.

Gerald Hill has lost weight and gained wrinkles. But his hair and mustache maintain their color and wiry texture, and he plunges back into the store the minute he can, humming among the dried beans sandbagged around him like a fortress. Al and Suzy help out, punching orders into the cash register and tossing out blemished fruit. No one minds that Al wears slacks as long as she wears her maroon Hill Food & Supply apron, as if one balances the other. Summer crystallizes into autumn. Al's hips and belly begin to show the effects of her mother's oatmeal cookies. Her hair brushes her chin now and falls in front of her eyes.

"When are you coming home?" Meg wants to know. The connection is as bad as it usually is and her strong, deep voice is unnaturally quiet.

"They need me here at home," Al protests. The two homes. Tonight she's on a pay phone on Fulton Street, the cold air nipping at her elbows.

"It's been two months," Meg pleads. She is so far away.

Al's skin feels ready to crack open from the cold. Her warm insides will slither along the ground, then melt into it. "I know, I miss you something fierce."

"I'm not Edith," Meg says suddenly.

"What do you mean?"

"Before Shallan worked at the mill, she drove a truck for her uncle's company in Nevada City. She had to drive up over the mountains just to get to the place she was supposed to start driving from. Then she headed up into Oregon, back east as far as Ohio. Edith saw her once every two months, maybe. And she waited and waited. She was such a good little femme." Meg's voice is tight, bordering on a hiss. "She stitched her a pillow, for God's sake."

Al opens her mouth, but only a puff of steam comes out. A little ghost that hovers in front of her face and disappears.

"I'm not Edith," Meg says.

Al goes to Hill Food & Supply the next morning puffy-eyed, her limbs big and clumsy. She stayed awake most of the night listening to the blood rushing past her ears. She has to get back to Lilac Mines. *Today*

I'll tell them, she promises herself. Initially, she assured her family that her boss had granted her an unlimited leave of absence, and they bought it without question. Maybe she can say that Luke needs her help with a special research project. Will they buy that she has a unique skill of some sort? The burden of proof will undoubtedly be higher when explaining why she needs to leave than why she's able to stay.

She's glad to see Terry Kristalovich behind the counter when she enters the store, the bell dinging behind her. Usually, he comes in the evenings and Al nods at him as the guard changes. He's a skinny man who always wears pressed slacks and a tie. *Such a strong work ethic,* her mother says, *and handsome, too.* He has dark curly hair, and black stubble peeks from his pale chin when he arrives at the store each night.

But on this bright, cold morning, Terry's face is smooth. Al sees it for the first time, angular and almost feminine in its white translucence.

"Hello, Anna Lisa," he says. He takes his time with her name, making in two separate words, as far from Al as one can get.

"Hi, Terry," she croaks.

"Late night?" he asks, concerned, not teasing.

"I didn't sleep so well."

"Oh, I thought maybe you were out on a date."

"Oh, no."

"Do you—if you're not too tired—do you want to give me a hand with this?" He holds up a flat cardboard box.

"Sure, what is it?" Al flings her house keys under the counter. She's wearing a light yellow blouse with a round Peter Pan collar, but she will not carry a purse.

"It's the new promotion from Miller Brewing Company." He slides a box cutter along the edge of the box with expert grace and extracts a pair of cardboard legs. They are nearly bare, except for a sliver of red skirt at the top and a pair of tall black pumps at the bottom. Two round white thighs above muscular calves. With a pang, Al thinks that they look like Meg. Half of Meg.

Terry reaches into the box and pulls out the top half of the woman, who (to Al's relief and disappointment) looks nothing like Meg. She is yellow-haired, smiling too big, holding a glistening mug as if it's an exotic but dangerous animal. The way Johnny Carson holds beady-eyed falcons.

Terry blushes. "Do you think it's too risqué? I wouldn't want to upset your father. I ordered it out of the catalog, but, well, it didn't say her dress would be so short."

"My father won't mind. Anything that will bring more customers. But I don't know about my mother. She thinks girls today get themselves in trouble."

"Maybe we shouldn't put it up then. It's her store, too."

"No," Al says. She's not sure what she thinks—whether girls get themselves in trouble or trouble finds girls, whether she likes the legs or hates the beer girl's phony smile—but she knows she wants to erect the flat statue. "The store could use a boost. My mother will understand, eventually."

Terry holds the halves together while Anna Lisa fumbles with the cardboard tabs. She secures the girl with masking tape. Terry watches her over his arching nose. He smells like erasers.

"What about your office supply store?" Al asks. "Who's running it?"

"Nancy-Jane Sammartino, my shop girl. I try to be there as much as I can, but there was so much to do *here* this..."

"Nancy-Jane?" Al interrupts. "Nancy-Jane Keeler? I went to high school with her. If she married..."

"Walter Sammartino," Terry finishes. "That's her husband."

"Wally, right." Al doesn't know why this should feel like a betrayal. She knows most of the girls from school are married by now. She only had one class with Nancy-Jane. But she's one more person who has led a real life while Al was off in the mountains, accumulating nothing that she can utter a word of.

"They're a great couple, really nice people," Terry says wholeheartedly. He positions the Miller girl in the window, so that they can only see her brown silhouette. It's as if she's walking away from them, off toward Oktoberfest. "Hey, I know! We should all have dinner. Since you know them."

"Well, not really. Just barely..."

"They invite me over quite frequently. Sometimes I go, but, you know, I always imagine I'm imposing a little, a lonely bachelor in need of a home-cooked meal. But this way it would be more like—a gathering of friends."

Al changes the subject. "Why do you work so hard? If you don't mind my asking. I mean, those are long hours. Your store and then our store."

"Planning for the future," Terry says, smoothing his paisley tie. For a moment he looks like a bright young politician; then he slumps a little. "I hope I'll have a wife one day, children, all those things that everyone wants. But they're not easy—not for everybody."

Al holds her breath. What does he know? What does he feel?

"When I was a baby, during the Depression, my mother used to bathe me in the sink with soap chips she'd saved," he says. "She said I chased them all around, tried to eat them like they were candy. She said, 'You loved order. You loved things to be clean even back then.' Of course, I don't remember it. Parents always save that one symbolic story about you."

Al wonders what story her parents would tell about her, whether it would giver her a clue as to who she's supposed to be now.

"She said I'd have to work extra hard. That, being Jewish, people would try to find things to hold against me. I don't know if that's completely true—maybe things were harder for her when she came over from Russia—but I do work hard. Just in case. And that's why I admire your father, Anna Lisa. He works so hard, and keeps things orderly. Look around, you can see how much pride he takes in this store." Terry pauses. "I'm sure I don't have to tell *you* that."

Gerald Hill has always been inseparable from the store: Daddy weeding green beans, Daddy mopping up broken eggs, Daddy calling gentle instructions to the man backing his truck of frozen dinners up to the rear door. It's been strange seeing him pad around the house in slippers. Al looks around. She tries to see the store the way a stranger might, not broken down into details. It's small but thorough, with a one-door freezer case, a colorful produce section, aisles of dried and canned goods, an aisle of what Al supposes are the "supplies": pencils, rubber balls, aspirin, instant coffee, sanitary napkins. The selection has grown over the years. Al remembers when her father installed the freezer case. It was the first time she heard swear words. The walls are clean and cream-colored. The store sponsors its share of Little League teams, but Gerald doesn't put their pictures up. He says it's bragging, it's clutter. A wooden ceiling fan ensures that there is always a gentle, rhythmic breeze blowing.

The store is like her father: neat, quiet, complete. A monument to diligent work. Some people might think it was the epitome of ordinary, but Al appreciates that Terry is not one of them. She sees the satisfaction in his dark eyes, as if life is just a matter of stocking the shelves, can by can. She wonders what else she hasn't seen.

COLUMBIA'S THRIVING LITERARY SCENE
Felix: Lilac Mines, 2002

Felix's brain bounces around in her newly shorn head as Anna Lisa's truck bumps down Washoe Street. Cal, the post office, the Hogans, Tawn, Matty, whether she'll be expected to leave her 12-hole Docs at home now, her depressing hair.

They drive in silence until Anna Lisa makes a sudden left. They're in the parking lot of a dingy strip mall. Gold Nugget Pizza is on one end, the Goldrush Tavern is on the other.

"What are we doing?"

"Want a drink?" Anna Lisa asks. "I haven't been to this place in years."

"Um… okay."

The smell hits her the minute they walk in. Stale beer, sticky floors. This is the first bar she's been in since Sourpuss.

She feels like a neon sign with her pink wool pants, yellow-striped sweater, and terrible haircut. The confusion of the night on Cynthia Street comes rushing back, the sense that she should apologize for something or fight back, and that she's unprepared to do either. She puts a hand on the coat tree near the door to steady herself.

"Um, Anna Lisa?" Her voice is a whisper. "I'm in more of a coffee mood, I think. There's a cappuccino place at the other end of this strip mall, isn't there?"

"Well, I could use a beer, honestly," Anna Lisa says. "I could meet you down there."

"No! I'll be fine here." Her aunt's solution is always to go their separate ways. Suddenly, as much as Felix doesn't want to be in the bar, she doesn't want to be alone.

The bar has a low tin ceiling and several ornate ceiling fans that suggest the building is older than its dirty white stucco facade. There's a balding pool table, some beat-up furniture, and a wall poster of a girl in a high-cut yellow bikini.

Anna Lisa orders a Bud. Felix asks for a Diet Coke. The bartender is a vaguely pear-shaped man in a fringed vest that Felix supposes is meant to be Western, not Village People. When he hands Felix her soda, she holds it close and lets the fizz pop in her face. She takes a long sip, hoping the faux sugar will overpower the alcohol in the room.

"It'll grow out," Anna Lisa says, half concerned, half annoyed.

"It's not the fucking haircut," Felix says too loudly. The only other people in the bar—a man and a woman in their late 60s—look up. The woman pulls a large straw bag from the back of her chair to her lap, as if Felix had just announced plans to rob this joint.

"Tawn thinks we shouldn't be girlfriends at work," Felix says more quietly. "I don't even know if we're girlfriends *outside* of work, but it's like, as soon as she said that, I wanted to be super-out at work." She sighs, "I guess I'm just contrary."

"Maybe you just *like* her," Anna Lisa says. "I bet you'd do things for her you never thought you'd be capable of. Just don't wait too long to do them. Don't be so hung up on whoever you think you are that she's long gone by the time you come to your senses."

"Um, okay…." Felix says. She's not sure what her aunt is talking about, exactly, but her words are warm and sad. Anna Lisa hasn't removed the hood of her blue all-weather jacket, even though she presumably likes her haircut. She looks like a turtle, slow and wise.

As they drink and talk, Felix's stomach begins to settle down. The heating system pings a comforting rhythm, and the smell of rain outside overpowers the manmade residue of the bar.

"Why do you think it's called the Goldrush Tavern?" Felix muses.

"This is silver country, right?"

"I guess because there was never a silver rush," Anna Lisa says. "Silver just sort of plodded along next to gold. They're often found in the same mine, you know."

"Silver's the boring sister."

"This place used to be called Lilac's. I came here with Meg." Anna Lisa caresses the handle of her beer mug.

Felix sits up straight on her stool. "Really? Was it a gay bar? I can't believe there was a gay bar in Lilac Mines."

She looks around again. The details of the bar take on a new tint. Now she sees the ghosts of butches and femmes (that's how they did it then, right?) twirling the pool sticks that lean against the wall.

Anna Lisa nods. "There was. There was a jukebox over there—my friend Jody used to always play "Fun, Fun, Fun" and Meg would say, 'Doesn't she know that there were thousands of songs written before the Beach Boys were even born?' You'd think she was 50 years old." She pauses. "It's so strange to say that. I mean, I'm almost 60 now."

"What happened?" Felix asks. "Why did you break up?" Her aunt seems sadder about Meg than Felix is about Eva. Her skin looks so delicate.

"We broke up because I gave up," Anna Lisa says. She picks up her mug and it shakes in her hand. Felix hopes she doesn't start crying. She wouldn't know what to do. But she sees that Anna Lisa wouldn't know what to do either—that being weak and femme and gushing about her problems is the scariest thing in the world to her. Whatever happened between Anna Lisa and Meg, it's clear Felix's aunt blames herself.

"One time," Anna Lisa continues, "we spent the whole night in one of the caves, one of the entrances to the mine."

"The one I visited? With the mountain lion?"

"No, no, that's the one all the kids go to." This makes Felix feel small and ordinary. "A smaller one. Farther up the same dirt road. Maybe seven or eight miles. Last time I was there, there was an old rusted-out Chevy up there, so I guess someone else was there, at some point.

"Meg and I stayed there all night," she says again. "And I thought

we were so brave. I thought I could stop anyone who hurt her or me…
or anyone."

Maybe Felix went searching in the wrong place. Maybe Lilac
disappeared near this other mine entrance. Felix wants to drive there
right now.

Anna Lisa gulps a mouthful of beer and air. Her eyes trace the
edge of the tin ceiling. It's like she's looking for a rope to grab a hold
of and climb out of the past. "And this street, it used to be called Calla
Boulevard. I don't know why they changed it."

"They?"

"I guess I don't know who 'they' are," Anna Lisa laughs. Her face
has recovered, but her eyes stay behind.

Felix thinks, *Cal, Calla, California*, the words bubbly as her drink
inside her. "I wish that was my job. Wouldn't that be a great job, to be the
person who figures out who 'they' are? All the theys in the world. Like,
somewhere out there, there's a *they* who knows what happened to Lilac
Ambrose."

"Meg always thought she killed herself," Anna Lisa says. "That
seemed like the most logical explanation to her."

Felix hasn't thought of this. The bartender refills Anna Lisa's glass
and asks Felix, " 'Nother Diet Coke?"

Felix nods at the bartender, then turns to her aunt, "I guess we'll
never know."

"You could find out *more*, though," Anna Lisa says. "More is better
than nothing, better than just-a-little. You work part time, you've got a
car. The world is yours, kiddo."

"I know it is," Felix replies. She stares into her brown soda sea.

"You make it sound like that's a bad thing," Anna Lisa says.

The world is Felix's with a morning that's cold but sunny. The
mailbox at the end of Juliet Street opens its blue mouth and swallows
her F.I.T. application. Simple as that. Color copies of her sketches—a
bondagesque ball gown, some punk pants, a pair of gravity-defying
shoes—are now on their way to New York. The mailbox clangs shut and

Felix feels satisfied. Her fate is now in the hands of smart, well-dressed city dwellers.

In her car, she flips through the local radio channels. There is a lot of static, but she surprisingly finds a station she likes. A mix of lonely folk music and blues and pared-down country. Who knew?

How come I'm blue as can be?
How come I need sympathy?

The woman's voice is deep and scratchy and mournful. Driving toward Columbia, Felix feels like she's following the music, like if she keeps listening she'll make it through the trees to a small warm place that produces these sad, perfect sounds.

Did you ever wake up on a frosty morning
and discover a good man gone?

Felix thinks of Lilac and Cal. It wouldn't have been a frosty morning, but maybe Cal left. Maybe Cal was a good man, and maybe he wasn't. She hopes the answer awaits her at the Columbia library, and that Anna Lisa will notice that she's trying. *You said the world was mine, and I listened,* Felix thinks.

When you lose a man you love,
a gal is good as dead.

The DJ breaks in, "That was Bessie Smith with 'Frosty Mornin' Blues,' a nice song for a frosty morning, I think. Up next, Dar Will—" The station fades out, leaving Felix with the hum of her engine.

Columbia looks much like Lilac Mines—turn-of-the-century buildings with false fronts, Victorian aspirations modified to meet boomtown necessities—but it's busier, and the kitsch is stifling. One block has *three* stores selling bonnets, the kind that streamed behind tomboy Laura Ingalls as she ran across the prairie. Felix went through a *Little House* phase, too. She wouldn't wear anything but dresses, with three or four skirts as "petticoats" underneath.

As she drives down Main Street—another Main Street—signs urge her to PAN FOR REAL GOLD! A man in a cowboy hat and holster passes out flyers in front of a restaurant advertising bison burgers. Felix is pretty sure that the buffalo roam in Wyoming, not California.

The library, a small brick building with a weed-plagued parking lot, is on Jackson Street, a less spectacular avenue, one meant for townies. Felix approaches the circulation desk, but a woman and a little girl barge through the door and shove in front of her.

"Excuse me," the woman demands. Her expertly highlighted red hair makes a gentle nest for her Gucci sunglasses. "Do you have a restroom?"

"I have to peeeee!" whines the girl at her side. She is maybe six or seven, with naturally mousy hair.

The librarian rolls her eyes. "Over there." She gestures with her head.

The woman and her daughter charge toward the back of the library. The girl starts to grab a book off one of the lower shelves and the woman snaps, "Carly! I thought you had to potty! Besides, these books are covered with germs."

"Thanks for your interest in Columbia's thriving literary scene, please come again," the librarian mutters to her keyboard.

She appears to be a few years older than Felix. The sign on her desk says Henrietta Keyes. She has shiny, blue-black hair that falls at a perfect slant below her chin. She wears black cat-eye glasses with rhinestones in the corners of the frames, and a little black cardigan sweater. She looks exactly like a Silver Lake fashion designer (or writer or musician or neo-burlesque dancer) who is trying to look like a librarian.

The image confuses Felix for a minute. Then it makes her grin.

Henrietta looks up. "Can I help you?" she asks wearily. She takes in Felix's tight red T-shirt and elbow-high knit gloves, her furiously gelled hair. *She thinks I'm a tourist,* Felix thinks, *and that I'm going to ask about the bathroom, too.* The thought repels her. Does that mean she's a townie now?

"I wanted to look up some old issues of the *East Beedleborough Examiner*," Felix says.

"Seriously? Wow. It's all here, on microfiche. Do you know how to use a microfiche machine?"

"It's been a while," Felix admits. College research paper assignments always required at least one newspaper source. Felix would jot down a fact or two, just enough so that she could cite the paper in a footnote, and then escape to airier parts of campus.

Henrietta blows dust off the lone microfiche machine and switches it on. It emits an eerie green glow. She removes what looks like a shoebox from a tall brown file cabinet, extracts a smaller box. "All this stuff used to be at the Calaveras County branch in San Andreas," Henrietta explains. "But because of budget cuts, they had to give half their space over to adult day care. None of the other Calaveras branches had any spare room, so now it's here, in Tuolumne County, and who's going to find it? Well, I guess you did. Anyway..." She thrusts the box at Felix. "All the secrets of the past, at your fingertips," she says, somehow sarcastic and excited at the same time.

She bites one of her burgundy lips and says, "Mind if I ask what you're looking up? We're not supposed to be nosy, but... well, it's pretty much my nature."

Felix is slowly learning that it pays to be nosy.

"Some stuff about Lilac Ambrose."

"Who's that?"

"Oh, I thought everyone out here had heard of her. The girl who got lost in Lilac Mines, who they named the town after?" Maybe Gary Schipp is right—no one cares about something that happened a century ago.

"Sure, right," nods Henrietta. "The girl who babysat me when I was little, Marisol, used to tell me stories, scared the shit out of me. She always just called her 'The Ghost of Lilac Mines.' She said she roamed the town, crying out for her lost children. When I went to college and took a folklore class, I realized that Marisol had just ripped off La Llorona."

"Well, the real Lilac Ambrose was only 16 when she disappeared,"

Felix says. "I doubt she had any children."

Henrietta shrugs. "Maybe she got knocked up."

"I'll let you know what I find out," Felix says as Henrietta heads back toward the circulation desk. She's wearing fishnets and thick-heeled mary janes. "Thanks, Henrietta."

Henrietta stops and laughs. "Oh—no, Henrietta's the other librarian I'm subbing for today. I'm Brittany."

The name "Brittany" doesn't collapse the divide between hip and lame, retro and kitsch, quite so well as "Henrietta" but Felix will take it.

Lilac Ambrose disappeared on August 24, 1899, four months before the new century (exactly 49 years before Felix's mother was born). According to the first slide, Calaveras County was in the middle of a record heat wave. Felix sifts through stories about a mule shortage, a pie bake-off, a mayoral race. Everything seems touched by sepia fairydust, ripe with the possibility of clues. At the same time, there's just so much of it, and she doesn't know where to focus her attention. She keeps waiting for the camera to pan in on the thing she's supposed to learn. But this isn't a movie, it's microfiche, and the slide slips in and out of focus beneath the light. Every time she twists the knob, she seems to make it worse.

When she gets to August 25, she finds an article she's already read bits of in Luke's book. MINER'S DAUGHTER MISSING. Poor girl didn't even get her name in the headline. Felix plods through the familiar facts. She learns a few new things. Lilac was said to have a lovely singing voice. Everyone agreed that her father doted on her. Finally Felix gets to something concrete: "Miss Ambrose was last seen near a home on Moon Avenue near the Church in the late afternoon. Passersby recalled her poplin dress and brown, plaited hair."

Moon Avenue, Moon Avenue. Felix thinks she remembers passing it with Tawn, a skinny, particularly shabby road that ran north-south. Somewhere between Washoe Street and the endless chaparral. Is it within walking distance of the other mine entrance? Riding distance? But the article doesn't say anything about a horse. Or a mule.

There are more articles, printed over the next few weeks, providing updates on the search. Blurry photos of men in hats and an occasional woman in, natch, a bonnet, gathered around a hole in the mountain. Twenty men and ten mules looking for her, says one article. Then 15 men, then nine, eventually just her father. After that the articles stop. There's a story about the mine closing a few years later. It wasn't out of reverence for Lilac, though some people said the mine was cursed—the silver was simply gone. A year later, the newspaper was, too. And a few years after that, the town was empty.

Felix returns to the August 25th issue. Out of habit, Felix's eyes wander to the masthead. When she was an intern, she was always looking at the magazine's masthead to make sure that the New York intern hadn't been promoted to contributing writer before she was. Now she sees the Washoe Street address of Nora's Unisex Salon. Below it, the names of the *Examiner* staff:

> Danis Hogan - Editor In Chief
> Danis Hogan, Jr. - Deputy Editor, Senior Reporter
> Barrett Lyman - Reporter
> Olive Hogan - Printer
> Calla Hogan - Assistant Printer

The last name is in tiny, smudgy type, but it screams like a war headline. North and South Main used to be called Calla Boulevard, Anna Lisa had mentioned. Why would the town name a street after the assistant printer at the newspaper? Did she do something heroic? If her family ran the paper, surely they'd report it if she did.

Felix sits on the edge of her chair and slides sheet after sheet of microfiche under the magnifier, dates both before and after August 24th. But there are no headlines about Calla Hogan. She didn't win a pie bake-off, and she definitely didn't rescue Lilac Ambrose from the mine.

Felix pauses at September 11, 1899. It's weird, how September 11th was just September 11th back then, not *September 11th*. It was the day that something called *Good-Bye, My Lady* opened at the Silver Bird Theater, and another day that no one found Lilac Ambrose. Felix locates the masthead, hoping to find that Calla Hogan has been promoted to reporter. *Kick that Barrett Lyman's ass, girl,* she thinks.

But Calla isn't there at all. Felix works backward. September 10th, not there. September 9th, not there. The last day that her name appears on the masthead is August 26th. She left the paper just after Lilac left forever.

Just in case the babysitter sprinkled some truth in with her stories, Felix asks Henrietta/Brittany if she knows anything about Calla Hogan's semi-simultaneous, seemingly silent disappearance. She doesn't, but she does produce a city social register from 1899. Felix scrolls the brittle book of names, addresses and professions. For the most part, only the men's professions ("miner," "miner," "doctor," "newspaperman," "miner") are listed. The few women who aren't wives have titles like "teacher" and "widow."

Felix scans the pages for Moon Avenue addresses. Who was Lilac visiting that day? The register is listed alphabetically by name, not address, and there is no index. Painstakingly, she copies:

G. Burke, 139 Moon Ave.
Mr. & Mrs. John Crabb, 490 Moon Ave.
Mr. & Mrs. Theodore Downs, 211 Moon Ave.
T.E. Duncan, 232 Moon Ave.
Mr. & Mrs. Kelly Gundersen, 363 Moon Ave.

When she discovers "Mr. & Mrs. Danis Hogan, 423 Moon Ave.," her heart cartwheels in her chest. Barrett Lyman lives down the street at 501. She underlines his name and draws two asterisks next to it.

She sticks it out through "Beale Winston, 370 Moon Ave." She thanks Henrietta/Brittany, who is reading *Maus* with her feet up on the circulation desk, and leaves the library. Felix's skin tingles with excitement as she steps into the bright outdoors. The day has gotten windy, and the gap of arm between her T-shirt and tall gloves is punctuated with goosebumps.

She stops at Lyle's Olde-Fashioned Soda Fountain at the corner of Main and Fulton Streets. The store is spacious, the walls lined with a rainbow of candy: licorice, gumdrops, tiny wax soda bottles, peppermint sticks like barbershop poles, pastel taffy. All the stuff that makes for a great display but tastes kind of nasty. She likes the smell, though: dust and wood polish and sugar.

"What can I getcha?" asks the old man behind the counter. He reminds Felix of the greeter in that Wal-Mart commercial, the feeble, sad man who made Felix never want to go to a Wal-Mart.

Felix studies the menu, a miniature marquee above the counter. "A sarsaparilla, please."

Is this the place Anna Lisa and Meg came, after they drove and drove? Did they share a glass with two red-and-white straws? They couldn't have, she realizes, it might have gotten them arrested.

Felix sits at a table near the window, where she watches a horse and buggy carry tourists past her car. Sarsaparilla is surprisingly earthy, somewhere between root beer and Dr. Pepper and a-long-time-ago. It tastes the way the store smells. She takes her sketchbook out of her bag, flips past a line drawing of a Tawn-esque girl in retro lingerie, and writes:

> Moon Avenue near church—close to mine entrance #2?
> Calla Hogan—asst. printer till 8/26/05, then ??
> Calla Blvd.?
> Lilac: liked singing

That's it, really. She does not have new information, she has a new mystery. All she can come up with are detective-show plotlines: Barrett Lyman was a serial killer who stashed young women's bodies in the mine; or Lilac was pregnant with Barrett Lyman's baby and got chased out of town.

She slouches in the wrought-iron chair. The red sun rests in a hammock of mountainscape, as if it too is contemplating invisibility. Felix wonders what Tawn is doing. She looks at her cell phone, but there are no messages.

SORRY BUTCH
Al: Fresno, 1966

"You know you're not supposed to lift heavy things," Al scolds. Gerald Hill's face is as red as the crate of tomatoes he's carrying. Al, who was sitting behind the cash register writing to Meg in very tiny letters on the back of a paper napkin, saw him struggling and ran over, placing her arms beneath her father's. His are wirier than she remembers. She swallows her surprise.

He sighs. "A girl shouldn't lift things for her father. It's just not right." But he lets Al carry the tomatoes to the produce section. "I have to admit, though, I don't know what I would have done without your help these past few months."

Al arranges the tomatoes in staggered rows. She hates being reminded that it's been months.

"You have a knack for this, you know," Gerald says. "Everything is stocked and put away. The back office is neater than it's ever been. That secretarial training has paid off."

"I just try to finish what I start is all," Al says, wiping a blob of tomato pulp on her apron. She feels her own face reddening as a result of her continuing lie, yes, but also something like pride. Everything here is so comfortable. To be a good clerk, all she has to do is imitate her father. To be a good girlfriend—well, she has no idea.

"But you seem a little down sometimes," Gerald says gently, ducking his head to look Al in the eye. He wrings a corner of his apron. He's not used to counseling his daughters. "Am I right?"

"Well, I'm worried about you." This is true. His arms are so thin. His copper hair is thin, too. The father she always assumed could save her from an H-bomb can now be defeated by a few pounds of tomatoes.

"Oh, no need to worry." He puts his arm around her shoulders in a gesture of forced jolliness. "I'll be fine. I'm not the young man I used to be, but if I were, how could I have such a beautiful, grown-up daughter?"

"*Dad.*"

"I'm serious. You're almost 21 years old. In fact, I think it's time you took more responsibility around here. I think you're ready for it. How would you like to help me out with the books at the end of the month?"

He looks so excited, like he's giving her a gift. She cannot tell him she doesn't plan to be here at the end of the month.

"You have a good mind," he continues. "You know how to look around and say, 'What needs to be done here?' That's a priceless skill in this line of work. You're trustworthy, you're a real helper. You could be a great... oh, a teacher or a nurse."

He beams, and it makes Al want to be a teacher or a nurse. She returns to the counter, where she rolls her letter into a gumball-sized wad and puts it in her pocket.

That night the Hills have a good, heavy dinner. Rice and chicken smothered in cream of mushroom soup, green beans with Durkee onions, buttery biscuits. The food is a lullaby, making Al never want to leave this table.

It's early December, and the living room windowsill is already lined with a row of vigilant Santa Clauses. Suzy pushes a sliver of chicken around her plate, the beads of her bracelet clicking when she moves.

"I... I think I'd like to go back to L.A.," she murmurs. All other noises stop.

"But that was only supposed to be for a little while," her mother replies. Eudora's hair is pulled back in a bun, making her face look more heart-shaped. Like her daughters, she has a trail of freckles marching over cheeks and nose. But hers are pale and peachy, like footprints about to be washed away by rain.

"I know, but I *like* L.A.," Suzy says stubbornly. Words fail to describe what the city is to her, Al can tell. And Al doesn't know what Los Angeles is to Suzy any more than Suzy knows what Lilac Mines is to Al. But there's something in the way she calls it L.A. now, not Los Angeles. The lilt of a local.

"I'm 19, you know," Suzy continues. "A lot of girls my age are married or in college, or they have jobs."

"You've been working at the store," Gerald reminds her. He always sits up straight at the table, knife and fork propped in anticipation.

"Sure, but I've been working in L.A., too."

"For your aunt," Eudora adds.

"No... lately at a hot dog stand in Santa Monica. On the beach." Suzy plays with her bracelet, stretching the elastic and rolling the pink faux pearls between her fingers. "It's slow in winter, so they didn't mind me taking off for a while. They said I could start up again when I got back. But there's also... there's also this man I've been going with."

"A *man?*" says Eudora. Al knows her mother means "not a boy?" but she hears "not a woman?"

"His name is Peter Weems. He's a student at Pepperdine, he's going to be an English professor someday. It's not serious yet. I'm just saying a girl needs to be loyal to her boyfriend."

Their parents have lots of questions about this Peter Weems. But they seem to agree with Suzy: a girl has to think of her future. Suzy won't be the one to help her parents into their old age. She is called by a city so big it can be known by initials, by a man with his own house in Santa Monica.

Later, Al helps her mother with the dishes, dinner heavy in her stomach. "Suzy causes me so much heartache," Eudora sighs, elbow-deep in water that would burn Al on contact. "This Peter sounds like a solid young man, but you never know. And I worry when you girls are so far away. I suppose that's a mother's job, though."

"What about seeing the world?" Al protests. "I mean, it can be... educational... to be far away. People go to other countries, they..."

"Oh, of course," Eudora agrees, "of course." She blasts the soapsuds off a plate. "But then they come home. That's how the world works." She turns to her oldest daughter, and Al wants to melt into her sureness. "I'm glad that at least *you* have a good head on your shoulders. I probably don't tell you that enough, but I want you to know. I think you're a smart, sensible girl, and I don't take it for granted. Even if I do pick on your hair and your clothes, it's been good having you home."

That night Al puts on one of her men's button-down shirts. She needs men's clothes for strength right now. She pulls a brown wool sweater over it, and puts on her winter coat. She needs warmth, she needs layers of protection. She tells her parents she's going to Nancy-Jane's house. *Again?* they say. In truth, she's only seen Nancy-Jane once, with Terry, but she is Al's new fake best friend. The fake part reminds Al that she has no real friends here.

She walks halfway across town to get the blood flowing in her frozen veins. By the time she gets to the pay phone in front of Lola Felix's Beauty Shoppe, she's shaking so hard she has to hold the receiver with both hands.

"Hello?" says Meg.

"Meg?" Al says. It's barely a squeak.

"*Hello?*" She sounds impatient.

"Meg! It's me."

"Oh, sorry, you're so quiet."

"How are you?"

Meg laughs sharply. "Um, fine. I don't know. How can I answer that question, Al?" It feels good to be called Al, even though it would feel better to be called Darling. "Sometimes I'm fine, sometimes I'm not. That's life. It's hard to sum up."

"I know..."

"Jean and Sylvie broke up," Meg says. She's quiet for a minute. "Jean and I have been talking, finally. I mean, really talking. At Lilac's," she clarifies.

"Oh," says Al. She watches her reflection in Lola Felix's window. A shaggy-haired, boyish girl superimposed over a landscape of barber's chairs and photos of movie stars with perfect curls.

"Are you trying to make me jealous?" Al hears herself say.

"Probably." Al imagines Meg twirling her ponytail. Then she imagines her sitting down on the edge of the bed, in that hard, resolute way she sometimes does. She realizes she can't remember the color of Meg's bedspread.

"I want to come home. To my real home, with you. I really do, but, well Suzy's leaving soon to go back to Los Angeles and…"

"Do you? Because you could. You left once. You could do it again."

"It's not that easy," Al protests. "My family needs me."

"*I* need you, stupid." Meg's voice cracks. Even so quiet, even over the distance, it's unbearable. Al holds her breath. "I'm not going to beg you," Meg says finally.

Is the quilt blue? Maybe a couple of the patches, but that's not the predominant color. Al wants to summon that world, the feeling of watching Jody and Imogen dance, the hard work of the mill, the curve of Meg's hips. But all she can see is herself, lamp-lit, half-formed beneath the red FELIX'S arcing across the glass.

Fine, she thinks. If she can't summon it, she will make it go away. This limbo is too much. She'll fold Lilac Mines into a little black ball, like the unsent letter in her pocket.

"Fine," Al stutters, "m-m-m aybe… maybe…" Maybe she can get on a bus. She'll run to the bus station and sleep on one of the hard benches until it opens in the morning.

"Just say it, Al," whispers Meg. And because Al has to say what Meg thinks she's going to say, and what her family—if they knew—would want her to say, she says it.

"Maybe I should stay here. Maybe we should… call it off." Her words are blurry. Her nose is running.

"That's what I thought. You are a sorry butch, Al." Meg is sobbing and coughing. "I love you, but I can't have all the courage for both of us."

Al is crying too, but she makes no noise. She's always been this way, a tears-on-pillow crier. As a child, when she would emerge from her bedroom after what she thought was a tantrum, people would look up and say, *Oh, where were you?*

Where am I? Al wonders now.

There is a long silence. Finally Meg says, "Good-bye."

And Al tries to say, "Good-bye," but it's just her lips moving in the window.

THE IDIOT OF 2002
Felix: Lilac Mines, 2002

It's after 9 p.m. by the time Felix gets back to Lilac Mines. Instead of heading north toward Juliet Street, she makes an abrupt right on Washoe Street, feeling a pang as she passes Coffee - Cold Beer - Ammo and Nora's Unisex Salon. She dials Anna Lisa's number to tell her she's going to run an errand before returning, but her cell phone is devoid of signal bars. Service in the mountains sucks.

Washoe Street meanders past a row of semi-restored houses and a small cinderblock church. Is this the church mentioned in the article? From what she can see in the glow of the streetlights, the architecture is '70s: modern and brave when new but quickly fades to drab.

Nevertheless, Moon Avenue is the next cross-street. Most of the "houses" here are trailers with sagging awnings and astroturf lawns. Felix looks for numbers. The lots have been divided up, but 423 (the Hogans' house) is still standing, more or less. It appears to be a small house in the process of being eaten by a large house. A second story and a garage bloom out of the old house beneath. The total is painted yield-sign yellow in a determined attempt to foster unity.

Felix parks her car by the side of the road and gets out. She looks around carefully, checking for suspicious shadows beneath other parked cars. There is no sidewalk. The wind blows furiously. Just walking into it makes her feel courageous.

The house is dark. She makes a U around the front and sides of the building, taking in the ragged scars where past has been stitched to present: the wood-framed downstairs windows and tin ones upstairs, wood shingles versus shake, green-patinaed doorknob versus Qwikset.

Calla lived here, she thinks. Her brand new ghost. She has decided Calla was the Hogans' daughter, young enough to be a fairytale heroine, although of course she could have been a sister, a maiden aunt.

She makes her way toward 501, Barrett Lyman's house. She finds another diaspora: 501-1/4, 501-1/2, 501-3/4. Airstream and Bounder and Winnebago. For some reason she's happy that Calla's house has survived and Barrett's hasn't, as if this is a small triumph for feminism.

The street is steep. She's just a few blocks from the eastern edge of town, which means the second mine entrance is nearby. She charges up the street, hardly noticing the cold. When she reaches the top spindle of Moon Avenue—which feels like the moon, bald and icy—she decides she needs a flashlight. After a quick trip to her car, it's back to the edge. The road tapers off and she's in the nighttime wilderness.

The trail is easy enough to follow, even in the dark. It's just a few feet across, a pebbled scar running across a ruddy skin of dried weeds and shrubs. It has to lead to the mine eventually. Where else is there to go?

Here, on the moon, the bad movie plot lines that plagued her at the soda fountain begin to fall away. What if Lilac is nothing like a *Law &* *Order* victim? What if she's like Felix, or Anna Lisa? Felix thinks about what she wants for Lilac—truth and redemption, yes, but she also wants, in a strange way, to be friends with her.

The path curves around scrawny trees and bumps in the mountain. Felix can't see much past her flashlight's beam. She is surprised to come upon a pile of wood. She is even more surprised to discover that the pile is a house. A fallen door and cracked windows float on the splintery beams like a carrot and a coal-smile in a puddle of snowman. The wind whistles over the rubble.

She sits on a miniature pile that might have been a chair, once. She is fairly sure it's too cold for snakes tonight, but she's less confident about spiders. She covers the rips in her jeans with her freezing hands. Sitting in the deconstructed house, she wonders if Lilac traveled this same path on her way to the mine. Did she stop here? With someone? Barrett Lyman is the obvious choice, with his house perched scandalously at the edge of Moon Avenue, but Felix craves the not-obvious.

There's a cracked bottle at her feet. Felix picks it up and examines it beneath her flashlight. It's sun-purpled like the ones in Anna Lisa's window. Did Anna Lisa walk through these ruins too, salvaging artifacts? It's some kind of soda bottle, Felix guesses, but she doesn't know whether it belongs to Lilac's era or her aunt's. With her car key, Felix hollows out the dirt-choked neck of the bottle and tucks it beneath her jacket. Maybe she can make it into a gift for Anna Lisa—a funky lamp or something.

Lilac, did you drink sarsaparilla from a glass bottle? she asks the star-salted sky. Then, to her surprise, an image appears in her mind like a treasure map unfurling: two girls, one with long brown braids, one older and blonde, making their way up the mountain. Two hands hold capped soda bottles that sweat in the record heat. Their free hands hold each other.

That's it: Lilac and Calla. The words themselves belong together, five letters, la-la syllables like a Christmas carol. The girls knew this. They heard the truth in their names, whispered like a secret code, passed from Lilac's salty tongue to Calla's sweet one. But it was 1899 and no one else spoke their language. They went looking for a country that did, in the hot, delirious hills, in the cool refuge of the mine.

And when they didn't come back, the town went looking for them. The Hogans, who ran the newspaper, published a story about just one lost girl. History would condemn Lilac to loneliness. Their ink-stained daughter would fade to lemon juice on paper. Some of the townspeople would try to remember Calla, naming the city's biggest street after her. But the Hogans pushed down everything they could push down, their shame and their sadness, until people weren't sure whether Calla was the name of Lilac's lover or the type of lilies that filled her empty coffin.

It's too cold to sit for long, so she gets up and keeps walking. The wind dies down as she makes her way up the mountain, but the night has lost all of its heat-memory, as if daytime is a myth. She aims her flashlight at her watch and is surprised to see it's almost midnight. Shit. Anna Lisa will be worried. She'll have to turn back and save the mine for another day.

She's retraced a good stretch of the trail when it occurs to her that Anna Lisa might *not* be worried; she might have gone to bed hours ago after enjoying a quiet night without her annoying niece. Felix has walked another half-mile (mile? two miles?) when it occurs to her that the collapsed house is nowhere in sight. She should have passed it 20 minutes ago. Thirty? Time seems as frozen and jagged as the air.

Her heart begins a small, nervous flutter. Is she lost? She hasn't strayed from the trail, but the only other explanation is that the house was a ghost-house, performing its ghost-house show for a weary traveler, then retreating to the shadows.

I'll just travel downward, Felix thinks. *If I head down the mountain, I'll end up on Moon Avenue, or at least close.* She abandons the winding path for a direct, downward tromp through the chaparral. Almost immediately, this seems like a stupid idea. Twigs nip through the holes in her jeans, and she's pretty sure that being away from the main trail will make her harder to find, if it comes to that. What did Anna Lisa say? Every year some idiot thinks he can go hiking in the off-season, that it's some well-kept secret. Felix wishes she'd paid closer attention to her aunt. She doesn't want to be the idiot of 2002.

It's 1:13 a.m. Now the night is so still that Felix feels like she's dropped off the Earth and out of time. There is no atmosphere on the moon. She curses her flashlight's myopia. It illuminates manhole-sized circles or narrow beams quite nicely, but it doesn't do anything about the big picture. Her downhill strategy isn't working. She may be angling east, when she wants to head southwest. But when she shines her flashlight in the direction she thinks is southwest, she can't see anything different. No buildings, no lights. *Don't panic,* she tells herself.

There is a store in West Hollywood by that name, Don't Panic. It sells things like rainbow paperweights and Billy: the Out and Proud Gay Doll. The concept seems absurd now, as if the biggest problem gay people face is a lack of pride-related tchochkes.

She jogs in place, trying to keep warm without getting more lost. Her fingers are numb inside her pockets. She pulls her T-shirt over the bottom half of her face, but that leaves her belly bare. Her bomber jacket only warms the parts it covers, which aren't many. She blows on her hands and rubs them together. Something cold hits her momentarily-warm skin. It is small and light. Snow.

And soon it is snowing, not just the noun but a powerful verb, something the whole sly sky is doing. It accumulates on her shoulders like dandruff. It makes little crunching noises beneath her boots. She pictures it covering her, suffocating, as she becomes the casualty of a perfect Christmas card.

She needs to find shelter, but there's nothing bigger than a scrub oak in this part of town. She has two choices: 1) keep looking for her snow-blue New Beetle, with its heater and defroster and the granola bar she's pretty sure she left in the glove compartment; or 2) find the only other safe spot out here.

But how to find a dark hole in the dark? The mine entrance, the *other* one, the one where Lilac vanished and Anna Lisa blossomed, has to be nearby. Finding it seems impossible. At the same time, it seems like Felix's only chance. So she heads uphill. If nothing else, she will try to keep moving until morning. She can't feel her feet—they are just two empty boots she watches with removed interest as they hit the ground, one-two, one-two, 20, 100, 1,000, up the steep incline. She tries to think warm thoughts as her eyes follow her flashlight's wimpy revelations. Fires in fireplaces. Just-baked pie. Tabasco sauce. Koreatown in August. Lilac Mines in August. The scared, sweaty grip that unites Lilac and Calla. Flat tires.

Flat tires? Her flashlight frames a deflated tire clinging to a rusty wheel. Strewn over a span of 50 feet or so, her flashlight has found a steering wheel. A seat that is a skeleton of springs. Something that looks like a canteen but is probably a muffler. It looks like the whole car is here, except for the actual body, the skin that held it together.

Felix forgets about her own car and puts the pieces together. Anna Lisa said there was a rotted car near the second mine entrance. She swings her flashlight upward and starts jabbing the light madly at various spots on the mountain. Chaparral. Chaparral. Nothing. It is the exact nothing she's been looking for, the dark space that will protect her. She runs toward it on her frozen feet, tripping twice.

Mountain lions be damned, she thinks as she pries off a loose board with her numb fingers. One of her fingernails bends backward in the process, but she doesn't even feel it. Don't mountain lions hibernate in the winter anyway? Or is that bears?

She climbs inside. It's not warm, but it's out of the snowfall, and if the wind kicks up again, it won't cut through to her bones. She looks at her watch. 3:27 a.m., a few hours until sunrise. For the first time in hours, her shoulders unclench.

"Lilac, you saved me," she whispers into the dark cave. But that's not quite right. "And Calla," she adds, "I have to give you credit, too."

She curls into a soybean shape, thinking of sleep, but the cold and the hard ground make her side hurt. Maybe she should do some stretches. She hasn't been to a gym since she left L.A. Her body feels old and stiff, and, since the night it proved its uselessness, she's done her best to ignore it. All the kickboxing classes in the world aren't going to help her fight off the gangs of Cynthia Street. She does a creaky downward-facing dog, a few jazz pliés. Then she leans into one of the worn-smooth wooden beams that hold up the mountain and stretches her calves.

Her fingers touch grooves in the wood. Almost like... letters? She picks up her flashlight, but this time, when she clicks the switch, nothing happens. *Shit shit shit,* she thinks. Now she is really, truly stranded. Now she is officially waiting for someone to rescue her. She doubts there are 20 people in Lilac Mines willing to look for *her.* She despises feeling so lost and pathetic and hungry.

Felix forces herself to focus on the carvings. She's worried that they're worm tracks, that the mountain might collapse if its weak skeleton gives way. But the half-centimeter-wide lines in the wood are too straight— some of them, at least—to be the meandering work of worms or insects. She Brailles them out, pretending she's post-scarlet fever Mary Ingalls. They're definitely manmade, definitely letters. The first one, she's pretty sure, is an L. She thinks of her postcard and is struck by a tiny bolt of excitement. The next letter is a vertical line sandwiched between two horizontal lines. An I.

Her fingers speed up, anxious to get to the last page. *Be objective*, she tells herself. *Don't read 'Calla' if it's not there.* But, while some of the letters are jagged and indecipherable, there's definitely a C followed by a roundish letter that could be a lowercase A. *They were here and they left me a message.* They are inviting Felix into their secret language, turning it over to her like a sacred sword endowed with ancestor spirits. Tears cut warm paths across her nearly numb face. She wills herself to return to her stretches, to do a few pushups on the black ground, and wait for the light.

When she can see her watch again, it says 5:47. Blades of dusty gold light are filtering through the boards covering the mine entrance. As soon as it's light enough to read by, she checks on her 100-year-old girl graffiti.

LET'S GeT OUt oF Here. A + M Forever

Her I is an E. Her C and A are a G and E. A and M are not Lilac and Calla. Felix wilts, as if this is proof that she won't be found. Her ancestor spirits won't fly her out of this place. She'll just rot like Lilac did, like Calla did or did not. She thinks of Gary Schipp, riffing on the letter L. Andrew plus Michelle. Aaron plus Mandy. Alison plus Mike. Ann plus Myron. Al plus Megan.

Or... is it possible?... Anna Lisa plus Meg?

This time, instead of a single scrap of ancient evidence, she has two pieces of 40-year-old evidence. Hell, she'll take that. She knows, she *knows* now. She had pictured it like a slumber party, but now she knows: her aunt and Meg had sex in here.

And that's who has saved her. Not Lilac or Calla, but her own sweet, boring aunt. Felix has come to think of Anna Lisa as something of an anti-role model, the person to watch if you want to see where a life of silence will get you. But there's more. Anna Lisa was once a young woman with her hand in someone's pants, deep in the middle of nowhere. She might not be the warrior Felix wanted her to be, but she might know something about survival.

The morning is covered in unbroken snow. Without any trees, Felix feels like she is standing on the train of a giant wedding dress. But she can't see any buildings, and she certainly can't find a trail. Maybe winter is beautiful precisely because it is dangerous. She kicks the snow off a rusty lump of engine outside the mine and sits down. The sun is a pearl earring in the blamelessly blue sky.

She waits. Anna Lisa must be looking for her. Right? But maybe she thinks Felix spent the night at Tawn's and then went to work. She hasn't always been forthcoming about her plans. It could be another eight hours before anyone is sure she's missing. By then it will be dark again. Felix's chest clenches at the thought of another night in the mine. Her mouth is pasty and waves of acid crash in her stomach. Her muscles feel anything but muscular. She won't be doing any pushups tonight. Even if she knew which direction to walk in, she's not sure how far she'd get.

She alters between panic and boredom as the earring moves across the sky and the snow shrinks into the shadows. A small brown rabbit hops by, leaving lucky footprints in the mud. It's a jackrabbit—she saw a stuffed one in the Visitors Center. Despite its name, it's actually a hare, the plaque said. Its legs are so muscular that if it kicks while being held, it can break its own spine. It seems strange that nature would design something so strong and delicate at the same time.

The sky brightens, then dims again, to an indecisive blue-pink. Her thoughts are divided between death and bean burritos when she hears hooves. Horseback riders! She turns in the direction of the sound. There is Anna Lisa, looking down from a tall silvery mule.

"You came *here*?!" is the first thing her aunt says. Felix can't tell if it's a question or not. Anna Lisa is wearing an orange, roadwork-style vest, mud-caked boots, and a frown.

"*You* came here!" Felix echoes. She's not sure if she's talking about right now or 40 years ago, when Anna Lisa came here with Meg. Anna Lisa climbs down from the mule, and Felix falls into her aunt's stiff frame, no larger than her own. She hangs on as tears pool on the crinkly vest.

Anna Lisa jerks away. "I thought, 'Well, she's an adult. She doesn't have a curfew. She doesn't owe me anything.' I thought maybe you met someone in Columbia, or went over to Tawn's. I don't know."

Anna Lisa opens one of the mule's saddlebags and takes out a wooly green blanket. She's all business as she wraps it around Felix's shoulders. Felix is suddenly sixteen, about to get grounded for worrying her parents. "I would have called you. I tried to call you, but my cell wasn't getting any reception and I thought I was just going to be gone a minute. I found out some stuff about Lilac and this other girl, Calla Hogan. I think they—"

"You thought you could go storming through the mountains and come up with some bones? A treasure chest? In a minute?" Anna Lisa huffs incredulously, even as she hands Felix a water bottle.

"I know," Felix says, now sobbing in full. "I'm such a city girl. I wish I had your skills. I can't do shit out here."

Anna Lisa doesn't look at her. She just says, "Let's get out of here. It's supposed to snow again today."

She helps Felix onto the mule's back and walks in front, carrying the reins. It's one of Ernie's, she says. He does search-and-rescue, too. "But you're not an official search-and-rescue case. You've gotta be gone 48 hours before they call in the team."

"God, I feel so stupid," Felix calls down. "I couldn't even get *lost* right."

"Be glad," Anna Lisa says. Felix watches the back of her head as she marches down the trail, which has suddenly manifested, a two-foot-wide snake of damp dirt and flattened grass.

The path hugs a steep bank. They round a corner, and Felix is shocked to see rows of houses and trailers in the distance.

"It was here this whole time?" Felix says. "I can't believe I lost it."

Anna Lisa doesn't look back. "You came pretty far."

After a while, Felix's legs begin to chafe. The parts of her inner thighs that are covered by her torn jeans are okay, but her long johns don't hold up. Anna Lisa helps her off the mule, who seems indifferent about the whole thing. He twitches his ears and blinks his long-lashed eyelids, as if to say, *Another day, another lost girl.* Felix remembers what Ernie said about the mules in the mine, and wonders if this particular animal had ancestors who perished in the tunnels.

Now she walks shoulder to shoulder with Anna Lisa. She's gotten a bit of a second wind. She tries to match her aunt's short-legged stride. As much as she hates their twin haircuts, she thinks she would like to have Anna Lisa's sturdy, flat-shoed walk. The day has become almost spring-warm, so she throws her jacket over the mule's wide back. Sweat begins to prickle in her armpits and at the back of her neck. They keep going.

"You should have come straight home," Anna Lisa says finally.

"I know, I—"

"You don't really understand that this is real, do you?" Her tone is bitter and judgmental.

"I do, now," Felix promises. All of this. How can she make her aunt believe her?

"Hmph."

Felix stops abruptly, her feet skidding slightly in the mud. "How would you know *what* I know? You've pretty much ignored me since the day I got here."

"I've cooked for you, I offered to get you a job at the school. I don't know what you want from me. You seemed pretty content poking around in the library, in mineshafts. You seemed to be enjoying your little field trip."

Felix stares at her aunt. "You can't imagine that there *might* be anything else I'd need from you?"

A cloud creeps across the sky above them. Seconds go by.

"Well." Anna Lisa rubs the mule's nose nervously. "I know Suzy wanted me to step in for her, to be the lesbian fairy godmother you never had. Who the hell knows why she thought I'd be qualified."

Felix doesn't want to admit that her own hopes were as ridiculous as her mother's. "I know you're not out and all. I don't care, anymore. I want to hear all of it."

"All of *what?*"

"Everything!" The sky has turned a dark red-purple, and now it finally opens up. Fat warm droplets land on their shoulders like blood breaking through a bruise. "Everything from... before."

"What makes you think I have anything to tell?" Anna Lisa retorts.

Felix studies her profile, the hard jaw beneath the soft skin.

Lightning zags across the sky, a white, stinging cut. Felix opens her mouth to speak. Thunder chases the lightning, trampling over her words. The mule does a nervous dance step behind them.

"That's close by. We shouldn't be walking in this weather," Anna Lisa says, studying the sky. "We should wait it out." Her voice is even and confident now. As long as she can talk about weather or baking or nursing, she's fine.

"But where?"

Anna Lisa points to a shack 50 feet or so from the trail. Felix must have passed it last night, but it's unfamiliar to her. She could have been shining her flashlight in the other direction at that moment. The weight of this arbitrariness presses down on her.

"But what if lightning hits the house?" Felix asks as Anna Lisa pries open the door.

"Lighting rod." Anna Lisa points. Sure enough, a thin shaft of metal is fixed to the roof, pointing at the sky.

"Wow," says Felix. "I thought they only had those on the East Coast."

"They're pretty rare out here," Anna Lisa agrees. "But I guess when the trees came down, whoever lived here had to own up to being the tallest thing around."

She guides the mule through the door. He stands in the middle of the shack, swishing his tail, as if he hangs out in houses all the time. Felix wonders where the phrase "stubborn as a mule" came from; this one seems amenable to everything.

"What's his name?" Felix asks. She and her aunt sit on a wobbly bench that has fallen partway through the wood floor.

"Lilac. Ernie thought he was a girl when he bought him."

"Oh." So this is Lilac. Felix doesn't want to think about that name right now.

There's nothing to do but sit side by side, watching the mule like a TV set as the rain gushes through the soccer ball-sized holes in the roof.

"I don't know why I've been so obsessed with Lilac," Felix begins slowly. "Not you," she clarifies to the mule. "I mean, she's gone, right? Whatever the truth is about her, it's lost. So why bother?"

"Words to live by." Anna Lisa echoes, "Why bother?" She studies her gloved hands, clenched together in her lap, for a long time. "Suzy's going to kill me. I don't know what she thought I'd do for you, but losing you in an abandoned mine shaft probably wasn't high on her list."

"Anna Lisa," Felix pleads. "What did I do? Other than act a little… I don't know, impatient?… sometimes. I don't get it."

Anna Lisa looks at her so hard Felix thinks she'll melt. "Did it ever occur to you that I might be envious? You have everything handed to you, the whole damn world. And what do you do? You turn against the butches and femmes, you say you hate the 'labels' that we came up with—well, we invented them because before that there were only epithets. You go to rave parties…"

"Wait, what are you talking about? Do you mean me personally or my whole generation?" She thinks about her Women's Studies class. Is Anna Lisa right about Felix's generation, or is she lumping two or three eras together? Wasn't the whole butch/femme thing reclaimed in the '80s? The textbook didn't go past the early '90s, so Felix is not sure what movement she's supposed to claim.

"You *are* your generation," Anna Lisa seethes, lips tight. "You might think you're an individual, but you're just pushed along on the current. We all are."

Felix is shaking. The Sunset guys shoved her into the past, into wondering what it really meant to be gay, and now Anna Lisa has just shoved her back, a we-don't-want-your-kind-here-either.

She wants to run out of the ruined cabin and into the rain. But she has nowhere else to go.

"When I was atta—… When those guys came at me—" her throat feels like it's full of splinters "—I didn't know where to *put* it. Does that make any sense? And when Eva took off, I didn't know what to do with that either. It was, like, I looked around and all the stuff that I thought would make me feel better didn't do anything at all. I figured you would at least have some… context."

"You think a lifetime of taking shit from people makes you stronger?" Now Anna Lisa rubs her hands furiously against her jeans. "That would be nice, wouldn't it?"

"But doesn't it make you at least, you know... um, wise?" Felix whispers.

"Maybe that's the consolation prize. I get to sit home with my dog and be wise. Look, the thing about bad things that happen is, they are *bad*. If they were all blessings in disguise, CEOs would sign up to sit in the back of the bus."

"What bad things, exactly?" Felix ventures.

"Look, I'm not complaining, I'm not saying my life was so hard. It's just that, some of that context you want? I wasn't even *there* for it."

Felix craves the mosaic of her aunt's life as deeply as she craved Lilac, a day and a lifetime ago. She shivers and hugs herself. She feels a lump against her side. Remembering, she pulls the purple glass bottle from her jacket.

"I found this," she explains. "Last night. I thought you could put it with the others in the living room. I like them, the way the sun hits them in the morning. I don't think I ever told you that."

Anna Lisa takes the broken bottle from Felix. She runs a finger over one of its jagged edges, pressing down so hard Felix worries she'll cut right through her glove. She glances at Felix, then back at the bottle. A drop of water splashes through the roof and onto the glass, polishing a small spot on the murky surface.

"Thanks," Anna Lisa says. Then: "I don't know where to start." There is surrender in her voice, along with fear and gratitude and endless shards of broken glass.

"Start here," Felix offers. "Lilac Mines. What about all those years that the town was empty? What happened then?"

"You really want to know?" Anna Lisa asks. It's a challenge, but she also seems genuinely incredulous that Felix would want to hear this story.

"Yes."

"Fine, okay. Well," Anna Lisa clears her throat, takes a deep breath,

"I wasn't here for all of it, you know. There's a lot I just heard, and a lot I probably missed entirely."

"Stop qualifying, just tell me what happened."

"You're so impatient…. Okay. Well, it started in Fresno, actually…"

"Fresno?"

"It always starts somewhere else," Anna Lisa says. The rain pounds a steady beat as she talks.

BROKEN VASES
Meg: Lilac Mines / Fresno, 1967

Meg shows Jean the invitation written on pale green paper, tied with
a pink seersucker ribbon.

Mrs. Gerald Hill
and
Ms. Irena Kristalovich
Request your Presence at
A Bridal Shower
for
Anna Lisa Hill
on
October 3, 1967

Jean studies the card in the dim light of Lilac's. "Who's Anna Lisa
Hill?" She sips her beer and studies Meg with cool blue eyes. Even though
they were together for almost a year, Jean consistently looks at Meg with
poorly veiled surprise.

"Jean! Anna Lisa is *Al.*"

"Al's getting married?!" Jean laughs. "She wasn't a very good butch,
but she sure as hell wasn't straight."

"Don't rag on Al just because you're jealous," admonishes Meg. "But
yes, she's getting married. Her little sister called one day out of the blue.
She said she knew I was one of Al's oldest friends—well, she said 'one of
Anna Lisa's oldest friends'—and that she and her mother were throwing

her a surprise wedding shower, and could she get my address so she could send me a proper invitation."

"A proper invitation," Jean huffs. "You're not going to *go*, are you?"

When Meg says, "Of course I am," Jean cringes. It would never occur to Meg *not* to do things. Also, she's in the process of winning Jean back, and a little competition—even from an engaged woman—couldn't hurt. It's Saturday night at Lilac's, in the middle of Indian summer. The ceiling fan blows Meg's dark hair into a wild mess, but Jean's short, waxed cut stands at attention. Meg is on her second martini. She's enjoying the selective flashbacks that roll through her mind: Jean standing straight and courtly behind a bouquet of purple-black flowers, Jean pressing her against the headboard as she unbuttoned Meg's blouse. Elsewhere in the bar, Sylvie—Jean's more recent ex—is surrounded by a fortress of femmes.

"I don't get it," Jean says. "Why are you still hung up on Al?"

"Well, that seems like a perfectly useless question. Why is anyone hung up on anyone?" But Meg twists back and forth on her barstool, watching her hound's-tooth pumps as she swings her feet. What *is* it about Al? When she came to Lilac Mines, when they met in the alley behind this bar, Meg was astonished by the newness of her skin: her Tom Sawyer freckles and tiny pores. But Meg is always attracted to newness, and Al is The Past. Meg says slowly, "I liked how she looked at me."

"You're a sexy woman, Meg." Jean smiles with half her mouth, relieving the perpetual sorrow of her sloping eyebrows.

"No, I mean, she always had this look like, 'Where are we going next?' Like she knew it would be somewhere good. She didn't act like I was going to fuck up her life."

"Are you saying that I…?"

"I'm saying that I have to find out who she's marrying. I'm curious."

Fresno is flat, the highway flanked by orange trees standing in straight rows like good soldiers. The landscape makes Meg think of Al's face, the flat plane of her cheeks, the way any hint of drama made her cringe.

She's angry. She's not going to this shower to entice Al, even though she's wearing her low-cut red sweater. Meg's going to show Al what she's missing. She steps harder on the gas.

The Hills live in a big, square farmhouse. Every inch has been freshly painted white. Curtains in gingham and vegetable prints wave from open windows. A neat parade of old-but-clean cars line the road leading up to the house. Meg savors the details: this is the life Al wouldn't show her, even for an afternoon.

A middle-aged woman with wiry gray hair peeking out of a pink scarf opens the door. Her gaze wanders over Meg's cleavage, her flowered mini-skirt, her tall brown boots.

"Mrs. Hill?" Meg says, extending her hand.

"No, no, I am Irena Kristalovich," the woman corrects. She has a slight accent from somewhere in Europe. The fiancé's mother. Meg tries to imagine what a younger, male version of her would look like.

"You are?" Mrs. Kristalovich prompts.

"Meg Almond, a friend of Anna Lisa's." Meg practiced saying "Anna Lisa" in the car. She will be so smooth, Al will see.

"Come in, Meg. We have just started some silly game." Mrs. Kristalovich shrugs and rolls her eyes. Meg decides she likes her.

Laughter flutters down the hallway. They round a corner and enter the parlor. Women of various ages, dressed in pink and aqua and duckling-yellow, ring the room. At the center of the pastel frame is Al.

Her hair is long, falling in loose brown waves around her face. She's wearing a black V-neck blouse and green wide-legged slacks. In the moment Meg's mind takes this snapshot, Al does not look like a butch contorting to fit the normal world. She looks like a Regular Girl at a nice Sunday afternoon party. The normal world is *her* world.

Then Al looks up. The brown eyes Meg knew so well blink, and blink again. Recognition takes hold, and for a fraction of a second, Al looks happy to see her. A body recognizing another body, one that used to echo its curves as they spooned beneath Meg's patchwork quilt.

But then it's gone, replaced by fear. Al opens her thin, freckled lips slightly. She searches Meg's face, and Meg knows what her lips aren't saying: *Are you here to expose me? Is this your revenge?* It is not anything so simple, but Meg lingers in her new position of power. Let Al squirm.

Meg introduces herself to the ring of expectant faces. The girl who is Suzy is slim and stylish in a short dress and yellow tights. She smiles from beneath a row of gold-brown bangs.

"We're playing 'Who Knows Anna Lisa Best?' " she explains. "Only Mother and I don't get to play, of course, since it wouldn't be fair. We already know her too well. The question I just asked—nobody's answered yet—is 'When did Anna Lisa have her first drink?' "

"Oh, you're bad!" says a dark-haired girl in a pink pantsuit.

"Do you know, Nancy-Jane?" Suzy asks, and the girl shakes her head.

Al looks at her knees. Meg arranges herself on an ottoman between an auntish-looking woman and a red-haired girl with a wide headband. The room is quiet.

"Come on, one of us must have been there," Suzy prompts. "I know my sister's good, but she's not *that* good." A chorus of relieved laughter relaxes the circle of women momentarily.

"Now that I think about it, I do remember," Meg hears herself saying in a loud, bright voice. "Yes, that's it—it was Anna Lisa's 20th birthday, and our friend Jody brought some champagne to our little house to celebrate. Anna Lisa and I were roommates, you know. Anyhow, Jody brought a bottle of French champagne she'd been saving for a special occasion. We were all quite excited about it, naturally, but we realized we didn't have any glasses, not even one plain old wine glass, let alone a champagne flute. So there we were, drinking French champagne out of juice glasses!"

The ladies laugh enthusiastically. The story is tame and silly and specific, just what they were hoping for. It's so easy. People's faces are etched with longing, telling you the stories they want to hear without saying a word. Al shoots Meg a sheepish and grateful glance.

Suzy throws out the next question: "Who's the first boy Anna Lisa ever kissed?"

"Suzy, good grief, can't we just eat lunch now?" Al moans.

"Nope. Come on, girls, who is it?"

"The first boy?" Meg repeats. She sits with her back straight and her hands on her knees. She blinks her long false eyelashes.

Again, no one can come up with an answer. Finally the girl with the headband says, "Um, was it what's-his-name... Kevin Zacky?"

"No, Marla, that was me," Suzy hisses. This time the round of laughter is nervous.

"His name was Caleb," Meg volunteers when the hush that follows becomes unbearable. "It was very tame, just a little peck, but you know how shy Anna Lisa is. And Caleb, he could barely *talk* to girls."

"Did you girls go to college together?" asks the aunt.

"Practically," Meg says with a wave.

"Okay," Suzy says, "here's an easy one. What's Anna Lisa's favorite dessert?"

Al seems to relax a bit, but no one has a quick reply.

"German chocolate cake?" Nancy-Jane says hesitantly.

"Apple pie?" says a woman on the other side of the room.

"No, pumpkin pie!"

"Peppermint ice cream?"

The women are as sticky-sweet as the desserts they're naming. Meg feels like a sour lemon next to them. Like a chili pepper. Like tea so hot it burns your tongue.

"I do like all those things," Al says amiably. She defers to her mother and sister, the judges.

"But butterscotch pudding is your favorite. Right, sweetheart?" Mrs. Hill says.

Meg doesn't have a story ready this time. She doesn't have a truth to cover up. She has no idea what Anna Lisa's favorite dessert is.

"Actually, I mean, my most *favorite* dessert is strawberry ice cream," Al says. Her face writhes, as if she has done something terrible to these women by liking strawberry ice cream over the desserts on their menus. Meg fidgets on the ottoman. She wants to be back on the road, driving through fields that smell like onions, pungent and harsh.

The group breaks into smaller circles when lunch is served. The ladies cluster in the backyard with plates of tea sandwiches and Swedish meatballs. Meg has trouble balancing her glass of too-sweet lemonade and the delicate china plate that holds her food. She feels oafish and unfeminine. All the ladies smile politely and walk past her. Her red sweater is hot and prickly beneath the early October sun. Give her a dark bar and a leering butch any day.

Al approaches her, green pants brushing the green grass as she walks. Meg doesn't know how to act around this new girlish Al.

"What are you doing here?" Al asks. It doesn't even sound mean the way she says it, just scared. Meg wants something to push against. So she pushes first.

"Suzy invited me. What, you didn't want me to see you prancing around with the Fresno Knitting Club?"

"They're just relatives, my mom's family. Most of the younger ones are Suzy's friends. Some of them drove up here from L.A. with her for the weekend. I hadn't even met them before."

"What's he like, Al? I bet he lives in a really nice house that no one ever throws things at."

"Don't call me—"

"Is he the first boy you ever kissed? Is he a good kisser?" Meg's voice is rising.

"What are you trying to do?" Al hisses miserably.

Meg doesn't know how to stop herself, "Do you like getting fucked with a dick *now*?"

"God, Meg, my mother is ten feet away, can you be a little quieter?" She looks so desperate, curling up in a ball at the first sign of conflict. "Can we go somewhere and talk?"

Meg stalks over to the card table and slams down her plate and glass. Lemonade sloshes onto a tray of shortbread cookies. She can feel people staring, although she doubts any of them actually heard the exchange between her and Al.

She returns to Al. "Fine, let's go talk."

But Mrs. Hill reaches them before they can escape, carrying a pitcher of pink punch. "Meg, you're the one who drove Anna Lisa home after her father's heart trouble, isn't that right?"

The word "home" pinches the back of Meg's neck. "That's right." She tries to smile, but she just bares her teeth.

"I can't thank you enough for that." Mrs. Hill puts both hands on Meg's forearm. Her fingers are cool and dry and comforting. She has short nails and thin blue veins that push against her skin. Meg wonders if this is what her own mother's hands would feel like if she were still alive, strong and delicate at the same time.

"A girl needs good friends like that," Mrs. Hill continues. The corners of her eyes—pale blue but the same round shape as Al's—crinkle as she studies Meg. "And it's been so nice having her home. Would you like some punch, dear? I can get you a glass."

Meg feels tears well up. Shit. How is she supposed to deprive Al of this kind woman who only wants to feed people? Just for a minute, she wants to put on a sundress and curl up in a patch of light in a backyard that is not blanketed in pine needles.

Suzy announces that it's time to open presents. Meg and Al don't find a place to be alone, or a time. *Figures*, Meg thinks.

Everyone gives Al vases. An aunt gives her a pearly ceramic vase. An older aunt gives her a showy crystal vase big enough to hold sunflowers. The redhead named Marla gives her a cobalt blue vase, and everyone exclaims that cobalt is *the* color this season. When Al opens her fourth vase, a cloudy glass bud vase, Mrs. Hill assures her daughter, "Don't worry, you can never have too many vases…"

"Because you can never have too many flowers!" chorus the ladies. They all laugh and nod. *Did they rehearse this?* Meg wonders. *Is this a common phrase in Fresno?* Al, at least, looks slightly unnerved.

"Thank you, it's so thoughtful," Al says again.

Then she takes Meg's gift from the pile. Meg is already regretting her present. It made sense at the time, seemed deep and right, but she failed to see it in a larger context. Al removes the bright red tissue paper and tosses it gently on the pile of white wrappings at her feet. She turns the gift around in her hands. It is a mason jar, full of broken bits of glass in various shades of purple. Lavender and lilac and dark purple-blue. Shards and bottlenecks. Broken vases, maybe. Meg has been collecting them since she came to Lilac Mines. She takes long walks through the sun-scorched hills, and they wink at her in the treeless light. They remind her of butterflies, how they can turn from one thing into another.

"What is it, exactly?" says one of Suzy's friends politely.

That's the problem, of course. It isn't anything. It doesn't *do* anything, it doesn't even hold flowers. Meg feels heavy and useless, too, beneath the ladies' cheerful gaze. "It's, um, just a decoration, I guess," Meg mumbles. Her ears are hot. She's sweating fiercely. She can't even come up with a good story this time. She hates them all. More silence. What was Meg thinking? That she could come here, present Al with a jar of broken glass, and whisk her back to Lilac Mines, all while making small talk with the knitting club?

Finally, the girl named Nancy-Jane says brightly, "Oh, like arts and crafts?"

"Well, um…" Meg begins. But then she quickly agrees, "Right, yes, like arts and crafts."

Mrs. Hill announces a little too loudly, "Well, I think that's *lovely*, Meg. That's how we used to do it, back when I was a girl. We all gave each other handmade gifts, every holiday. It's nice to see a young lady who understands tradition."

Meg nods. Maybe she doesn't hate Mrs. Hill. Al looks like she's going to cry. Meg will hate her if she cries because Meg feels like crying herself. "Thank you," Al whispers. "I'll keep it."

As soon as the last curl of ribbon hits the floor, Meg says, "I have to go."

"You have a long drive ahead of you," Mrs. Hill nods. "Back to… where is it, dear?"

"Lilac Mines."

"I'll walk Meg to her car," Al tells her mother.

"But sweetheart, your guests…" They're standing at the edge of the parlor. The women are clustering again. It must be something in their genes. Even most of the bar femmes do this.

"I'll be right back, Mother," Al says impatiently.

They walk down the gravel road toward Meg's old Ford. There's a breeze, finally, although it is not cool. The big egg-yolk sun looks exhausted as it sinks into the flat horizon.

"I never wanted to be normal, you know," Meg says off-handedly into the hot wind. She doesn't look at Al. "Not even when I was little. Not even when my mother was alive. I was always running away, just to run away. I never wanted to go to tea parties."

"I know," Al sighs, "it's what I always liked about you."

"But," Meg adds, "it would have been nice to be asked." When she was around Al, at the beginning, she felt like she was being invited to a hundred tea parties. Everything's quiet. Here is Meg's car that will not take them to the mine tonight, that will not bathe them in dusty yellow light while they devour each other's bodies.

"Why are you doing this?" Meg says finally. She is not afraid of being hurt. She is not afraid of knowing. Al squirms, but Meg can give herself over to the ache. She wants to put a shard of purple glass in Al's hands and hold out her pale white wrists. *Just do it,* she silently dares Al. *Just cut through my veins.* Out of the corner of her eye, Meg sees someone running toward them. Soon the figure turns into Suzy, her gold hair floating behind her as her boots pound the gravel.

"Meg! You forgot your party favor!" She thrusts a small flowerpot into Meg's hands. It contains tiny, perfect pink roses. She knows it will die—she has no patience for the slow, finicky lifecycle of plants—but she thanks Suzy politely.

"Goodbye, Meg," says Al steadily, eyeing Suzy, "I'm glad you came." She kisses Meg lightly on the cheek, and Meg can feel her lips quivering.

Meg keeps her foot on the gas the whole way back, narrowly missing a late-grazing deer. She pulls into Lilac's and orders a shot of whiskey. She likes the way the alcohol sizzles through her body like a threat. It's a Sunday night, and the bar is sparsely populated.

"Rough day?" Caleb asks when she orders a second shot.

"Just let Jean know that I saw Al and she kissed me," Meg says with a half-smile. She spent much of her drive reminding herself of her original plan. If Al didn't know what she was missing, she would make sure Jean sure did.

Caleb narrows his ale-colored eyes. "Is this one of your games, Meg, honey? Because Jean is back with Miz Sylvie. You knew that, right?"

"Shit, Caleb, you're kidding me, right? They've been broken up for a year."

"Well, they were in here last night, slow dancing and necking like the world was ending. And you know Sylvie, she doesn't do that sort of thing with a butch who's not her steady."

"Goddamn... She didn't say anything to me." Meg lights her cigarette and offers her open box to Caleb, who takes one and lights it off Meg's. "Honestly, it was months."

"I guess there's always hope," Caleb says absently, wiping down the bar.

"Bullshit," says Meg.

The wedding is in December, that's what someone at the shower said. Winter comes but no invitation arrives.

HALLUCINOGENIC QUALITIES
Petra: New York City / Lilac Mines, 1970

The letter is wrinkled from so many readings, and smells faintly of vanilla. Meg's sprawling handwriting plainly states, *You'll be done with school soon. Why don't you come visit me?* This invitation has kept Petra going for months, through bitter meetings and irksome finals and her parents' well-meaning graduation party.

The only good thing about Kerhonkson, New York, Petra Blumenschein decides on her way back to the city, is their family's long gravel driveway. The sort of driveway where (after your parents give you a generous graduation check and demand to know when you're applying to PhD programs) you can paint your '65 Thunderbird purple.

"But that car's a beaut," Meg's father had protested, "and only five years old!" Petra always nodded politely at his nosy neighbor comments. His wife had left the earth and his daughter had left town, and Petra could smell his sadness of burnt coffee and clothes retrieved from the hamper. It made her want to tell him, *I know where your daughter is. She's in a place with black mountains and gold-pink sunsets.*

"It's more beautiful this way," Petra grinned, but didn't expect him to understand.

With the windows down, her wavy blonde hair whips in the wind and cool air rushes over her bare arms, but she's not fooled. The city is about to begin another hot, writhing summer. For four years now, she's joined her fellow NYU students in protesting the war, racism, pollution, and patriarchy. They've screamed all day and smoked all night. Now New York announces itself once again, a charcoal silhouette on the horizon beyond the matte-purple nose of her car.

Lately she's gotten tired of championing everyone else's cause. Even her women's group, Women for Equality on Earth (a.k.a. WEE), has fragmented like a building going co-op. Most of the girls are focused on legalizing abortion, and Petra just can't get into it. Ever since she abandoned sleeping with guys, she hasn't had to worry about that. When she pulls into Soho, it's almost dark. By the time she finds a parking place and walks up the five flights of stairs to her apartment, the WEE meeting is over. Only those too zealous or too stoned to go home remain. And Francine, of course.

"Where were you?" Francine greets her at the door. "You said you'd be back by six at the latest."

"I had to wait for my car to dry. Fran, it's so cool. I wish you could see it from the window. I painted it purple. I'm gonna call it The Lavender Menace. Get it? Then we can run over those..."

"Sshhh," hisses Francine, "some of them are still here." Her lips are pursed, a tight asterisk.

Petra sighs, "So no kiss?" She steps inside and tosses her big cloth satchel on the bed.

The two remaining WEE women, a reformed sorority girl and a jaded communist, shoot sharp looks in her direction. Petra glares back. This is her apartment... well, hers and Francine's and their Greek subletter's.

"Is that a letter from the girl you grew up with?" Francine asks, all friendly-cuddly, the fringe on her blouse tickling Petra's bare shoulders. Petra smiles at the person she first encountered six months ago, back when they were breaking up with their male chauvinist boyfriends, back when they discovered each other's soft girl-skin.

"She wants me to visit her," Petra replies. "I'm going to do better than that. I'm going to *move* out there, to California. And you can come with me."

Francine takes her arm from Petra's shoulders and rakes her fingers through her wild brown hair, frowning.

"Come *on*," Petra presses. "It will be fun."

"I don't know," Francine says reluctantly. "There's really so much going on here."

"That's the problem. Too much has already happened. We can't have a meeting without arguing about some theory from some other meeting. I need to be out west, Fran, where the air doesn't turn your lungs black." Petra perches on the window ledge by the fire escape. "I'm smart, Fran. I know that's blasphemy in WEE, saying you're actually good at something and not just a worker bee for the movement, but it's true. And I'm sick of them not listening to us because we want 'too much, too fast.' They call it strategy, but it's just another way of calling us queer."

Francine is glued to the bed. Her round face is shadowy, anguished. "Let me think about it," she says softly. "Let me think about it. Give me some time."

Petra leaves the next morning. She wakes up sweating, wearing the summer humidity like a too-small shirt, and she can't take it one second longer. She kisses Francine's sleeping face. Fran's peanut butter-brown hair is fanned out on the pillow like sunrays. Her mouth is slack, a sort of stoned smile. Francine is so beautiful when she's relaxed. Petra will try to remember her like this.

Surprisingly, the Greek subletter wants to come along. Agapi has attended a handful of WEE meetings and is now nominally a feminist. *She's just in it for the pot and free food,* Francine had said. But that seems cynical, especially when Petra watches Agapi rope her suitcase to the roof of the Lavender Menace. She's a thick-trunked girl with wiry copper-black hair that's always hovering dangerously close to her lit cigarette. She is happy to pump when they gas up at the Esso station on Broadway. When they pass the shoe repair shop where she works, Agapi waves to the dark window and shouts, "Fuck with you, Mr. Theophilus."

They reach Pennsylvania by lunchtime, Cleveland by nightfall. Petra is glad to have a travel partner, even if it's not Francine. The dingy motel where they're staying would make her nervous on her own, despite the six judo lessons she took in an East Village basement last year.

"You have a girl in the Lilac Town?" Agapi asks. She's stretched out on the bed in her white cotton underwear. Her blouse is open, revealing an equally no-nonsense bra and olive-colored breasts as big as grapefruits. Agapi is definitely a go-with-the-flow kind of girl.

Petra says, "Lilac Mines. I don't 'have a girl' there, but yeah, I know someone. Meg. She grew up across the street from me in Kerhonkson. After her mom died when she was 10, she spent a ton of time at our place. She was kind of like my big sister. She moved to Santa Clara, which is kind of near San Francisco, I think, for college, and wrote me letters. I was just a kid and I thought they were about the neatest thing in the world. Then when *I* went to college and wrote to her—she was probably the only person from Kerhonkson who didn't think I'd gone off the deep end." Petra laughs.

Petra slips off her flowered nightgown. She's not about to be out-nuded. "I went back and reread some of her old letters and it was all there—stuff about the women she was with. How she got kicked out of Santa Clara University for an 'indiscretion' in the dorms. I thought that meant her room was a mess," she laughs. "It's so trippy, looking back from an enlightened perspective."

The woman who opens the door of the shabby wooden cottage looks like a secretary. She's wearing a yellow polyester dress and high heels. Her sculpted brown hair is clearly the product of curlers. She is a catalog of oppressive beauty regimens. They've arrived in Lilac Mines on a Friday afternoon after two and a half weeks on the road. Petra's stomach is doing flip-flops. She's not sure if it's from the mountain roads or the anticipation.

"Meg?" It comes out as a squeal.

"Petra! God, you're a full-grown woman!" Meg pulls her in for a bone-squeezing hug. Then she stands back and takes in Petra's patched bellbottoms, Madras plaid shirt, and tangled blonde hair.

Over the last few years, Petra has reconstructed Meg in her mind, from the teenager who told her ghost stories about the abandoned cattle barn on Abel Drive while braiding her hair, to a frontier-living rebel. But the woman in front of her looks like a nice lady enjoying small-town life. Petra prays to goddess that she hasn't come all this way for nothing. Meg shakes Agapi's hand and helps them with their suitcases. She gestures for them to sit down on the sagging couch and brings them tea in mismatched cups.

"I didn't know you'd be bringing a friend," Meg says. "I don't have room for you both, but I have some friends you might be able to stay with. They live in an old church not too far from here. Well, it's not a church anymore…"

"Right on!" Petra enthuses. A big, abandoned building is exactly what she needs. She will paint her perfect world on the walls.

"But it's freezing in the winter, and no one has their own bedroom," explains Meg, puzzled.

"Rooms just keep people apart," says Petra. "They're meant to divide people."

"What is it you girls want to do here, exactly?" Meg asks.

"New York has too much negative energy," Petra says. " I just have this sense that things could be perfect out here. We could build a whole new society."

"A whole new society?" repeats Meg. "Um, you know this town is basically two bars, one hotel, and a post office, right?"

Petra nods. "Room to grow."

"Petra's mama and papa give her a big chunk of money," Agapi adds.

"Just enough to get started," Petra says quickly. For former communists, Dr. and Dr. Blumenschein earn good money; and because they are still semi-communists, they are generous about sharing it.

"I am bored," Agapi announces. "Before the new society, let's go out, no?"

"I could take you to Lilac's," Meg offers. "It's the gay bar. *Officially*, this town only has one bar, Lou's." She smiles, revealing big teeth with a small gap in front. "I'll make dinner while you change."

"What do you mean?" Petra looks down at her rumpled shirt and jeans. She sewed the patches—a turtle and a duck—on the pockets herself.

"I just figured you'd want to dress up a bit. I can loan you some clothes if you don't want to unpack yet. Agapi, I bet Sunny—she's my butch—has a jacket that would fit you. Anything she's left in my closet is yours."

Meg's face radiates warmth, and Petra almost wants to return the favor, to say *Yes, we'll wear your dresses and suits.*

"Why you say I'm butch?" Agapi doesn't sound offended, but stares with her round, dark eyes.

"Oh... well, I guess I don't know," muses Meg.

"It's just that we don't believe in gender roles," Petra says politely. She likes the way it sounds, as if this is one of the rules of their collective. She feels it forming inside all of them, a bead, an idea, a baby.

"Suit yourself. Or don't," Meg laughs.

And so, after a dinner of beans and crunchy rice, they pile into Meg's car, an ancient Ford that makes a troubling noise whenever Meg brakes, which she does suddenly whenever a stop sign pops out of the twilight. As if the town she's lived in for a decade is full of surprises.

Calla Boulevard is so steep that Petra's nails make half-moons in her palms as she grips the door handle. Quaint but ragged buildings line the street. Petra's first thought when they enter the smoky, dilapidated bar is that they must have walked into Lou's by accident. Or maybe back in time, to the '50s or junior high school: men on one side, women on the other. But most of the men are women, of course. Dressed with precision in crisp shirts and ties, as if in defiance of the bar's chipped glasses and weak yellow light.

This is not her whole new world. But it is definitely a *world*: it is Friday night and the bar is packed with gay men and lesbians basking in its Friday night-ness, safe in the rhythms of the bar. There are more people here than on Main Street when Petra and her friend drove into town.

"It's so crowded," Petra whispers to Meg. "How...?"

"I don't know how," laughs Meg. "A million reasons, probably. Not enough men to work at the mill? The town's named after a girl? Who knows? That's just Lilac Mines for you."

Agapi walks up to the bar and orders a beer. Meg waves to a white woman in a suit and a black woman with relaxed hair that doesn't look very relaxed.

A man leaning on the jukebox, glowing in the reflected neon, looks the newcomers up and down. "Ooh, hippies," he purrs to the femme standing next to him. She chews her gum in agreement.

There are four other lesbians living in the church: Imogen and Jody—the black and white couple from the bar—and Jean and Sylvie, also frustratingly butch/femme. Sylvie is so quiet, Gapi says, that she wants to strangle the girl with her own omnipresent needle and thread. But Petra convinces her that Sylvie just needs enlightening. Meg comes to visit, but not as much as Petra would like. She spends a lot of time in San Andreas with Sunny.

By September, when Petra's parents would like her to be starting graduate school, she has wooed another WEE exile from New York. Marilyn Joice, who has an IQ of 162 and glasses that cover a third of her classically beautiful face, helps Petra and Agapi string beads over the doorway of the church kitchen. They also draft a manifesto and install a new toilet.

"Wouldn't it be more natural to use the outhouse?" asks Petra. There is nothing about revolutionary plumbing in the manifesto, but maybe there should be.

"I'm not sure, I think sewage has to be treated," says Marilyn. "It might be *worse* for the environment."

"When I am on the rag, I'm not crapping in shack," says Gapi, and that settles it.

They've replaced the dangerous-looking wood-burning stove with a gas heater. They've planted a vegetable garden that has yielded two delicious tomatoes and a handful of stunted zucchini.

In October, Petra suggests a séance. The women have been bickering, and she thinks a good pagan ritual would bring them together.

"I have a theory that it's Lilac Ambrose's spirit—that that's why there are so many lesbians in such a small town," Petra tells Marilyn.

Marilyn is skeptical. She's sitting on one of the church pews, and even though she's wearing a flowered halter-top and jeans and Mexican sandals, she looks almost prim. "So you're saying the little girl who got lost in the mine was a lesbian? They didn't even *have* lesbians in the 1800s. Women were considered their husbands' property. They..."

"Don't be so literal, Marilyn," Petra says. "I'm just saying that Lilac is a spirit of female-ness. And that kind of... *radiates*."

"Petra, you are trip," says Gapi, coming in from the kitchen. It's late afternoon and chilly outside, but the church is still warm from the sun. The stained glass Virgin Mary casts a long shadow over the women's beds: her blue robe rippling over Gapi's sleeping bag, her halo turning Sylvie's white sheets golden, the baby Jesus resting on Petra's pillow.

"I love séance, man," Gapi concludes.

"*Woman*," corrects Petra.

Marilyn has a college friend who sends some Afghani pot that allegedly possesses near hallucinogenic qualities. Petra and Imogen light candles and lay out an old army blanket in the mouth of a mine entrance. Not the main one, which Imogen says is frequented by high school kids and sheriffs with roving flashlights, but a smaller, more hidden entrance further up the mountain.

"This is so spooky," breathes Petra. "Or at least it will be when it gets dark." The sun is low and orange, giving the scrub oaks and manzanita a shadowy, burnt look.

"This is the best part of town," Imogen agrees. "Sometimes I come up here to sit and think. It gets real quiet, and you feel like if you listen hard enough, the mountain will just tell you what to do."

Petra likes Imogen. She's more relaxed than Jody or Jean or Sylvie. Petra loaned her *The Feminine Mystique* and Imogen stayed up all night reading, curlers in her hair and flashlight in her hand. Tonight she wears light blue polyester pants and a striped, boat-neck shirt. She is thin with wide, graceful hips.

"Who all is coming tonight?" Imogen asks, taking a beer from the cooler in the Lavender Menace's trunk.

"Well, Gapi and Marilyn, of course. Three of Marilyn's friends from Berkeley are driving out. Don't worry, they're like us. Meg said she might come with Sunny from San Andreas. And we invited Jean and Sylvie, but Jean seemed a little... skeptical, and Sylvie seemed a little freaked out about the whole ghost thing."

"Good old Sylvie," laughs Imogen. "You just gotta give 'em time. That's a pretty good group, though."

Not long after the sun goes down, Petra spots a pair of headlights bobbing up the hill, followed by another, closer-set pair. The first car opens and five girls in beads and fringe and pink and orange and red bounce out like clowns. Gapi and Marilyn and three women Marilyn knows from the days before she transferred to NYU. Essie and Emily are a couple, plump arms and wavy brown hair draped over each other as if they are trees planted inches apart. Linda is a short girl with short, dirty-blonde hair who flutters around Gapi like a moth all night.

Sylvie opens the door of the second car gingerly, and peers out at the group from behind a curtain of limp hair. Jean jumps out of the driver's side and extends her arm for Sylvie, who is wearing brown pumps on her small feet. Meg arrives late, on the back of a motorcycle driven by a leather-clad butch who introduces herself as Sunny. She lives up to her name, helping herself to beer and joking around with Jody, who comes as soon as she gets off work. Petra hopes Meg will hit it off with Marilyn or maybe Linda, anything to lure her away from these stifling, archaic roles. Petra thinks of Meg as her older sister, and big sisters are supposed to do things first, not linger in the past.

The night is moonless, and Petra thinks about all the shrubs, rocks, and other things sitting in the dark, watching them with night-creature eyes.

"Who want to get high?" Gapi asks, waving her bag of tightly rolled joints.

"Gapi, you're the coolest," says Linda, reaching her arm around Gapi's waist and putting her head to Gapi's huge breasts.

"I'll try it," Meg says. She already smells like alcohol, warm and alive.

Petra cups her hands to block out the breeze as Gapi strikes a match, and takes the first hit. And the second, eleventh, and twenty-second as each joints makes its rounds. She loves the moist, scratchy feeling in her lungs. She loves how everything becomes a good idea. She loves Imogen's long black eyelashes.

"Let's get started," Petra says. "I can feel something in the air and I don't want to lose it." She also wants to give the women something to focus on rather than each other's miles-apart clothes and mannerisms. They duck into the mineshaft and form a circle on the blanket. Candles flicker from little pockets in the rough rock walls.

Petra crosses her legs and clears her throat. The women follow. She feels their bright eyes on her. Waiting, giving her power. A swirl of cold wind moves through the cave and sweeps out again. Petra takes the hands on either side of her—Imogen's rough brown hand and Gapi's short-nailed olive hand. Imogen gives her an encouraging squeeze. A candle winks, or maybe an eye. For the first time since being with Francine, Petra feels something deep, ancient.

"Spirits," she says in her strongest voice, "we are the women of Lilac Mines. We are calling you on this sacred night, All Hallows Eve. We are humble, Spirits. We want to learn from your wisdom. Reveal yourselves, or your*self* if there is only one of you."

Petra checked out a book called *The Dark Arts Through the Ages* from the tiny library next to the post office. The librarian, who looked as if she might practice the dark arts herself, glared as she stamped the card. Petra read a few chapters, but it was unnerving to open the book in a church after dark, so she hopes the spirits will guide her in proper séance etiquette.

"Will you pass me a beer?" someone whispers.

"Lilac, is that you?" giggles someone else.

"Shh!" hisses Marilyn.

Petra decides to get to the point. "Lilac Ambrose, we, the women of the town of your namesake are calling you."

Of the, of the, of the. She likes the chain, how the world contains them like a big Russian nesting doll. The wind plays the crannies of the cave like a harp. Petra's eyes are squeezed shut, and she can hear the wind play her body, too, plink-plinking her heart and strumming her ribs.

"I can hear her!" someone exclaims. Petra snaps her eyes open. It's Sylvie, of all people, her mouth an O like a cave.

"They're planting ideas in your head," Jean grumbles, or maybe she just thinks it. Petra might be able to hear thoughts right now.

"No, ssshhh, I heard her, I swear." Sylvie lets go of Essie's (or maybe Emily's) hand and grips Jean with both hands. "She said... well, it was this long, low noise, like *ohhh*. But I think she was saying *love*. She wants us all to love each other." She looks around with green, green eyes. Petra wants to cross the circle and touch her.

Petra stands up, swaying a little. She walks outside the circle, past Gapi and Linda and Emily (or maybe Essie). She reaches the Lavender Menace parked inches from the mine entrance, and its long purple cat nose and chrome grill smile at her. Then she looks up at the windshield. Lilac is there, in the passenger seat, staring straight at her. She is a hardy-looking girl in a calico dress. She has thick, banana-blonde hair that falls in waves over the mutton-sleeves of her dress, and wide-set, light brown eyes. She puts her feet on the dashboard and smiles. She looks like the kind of girl to raise six kids and live to 80, not get lost in a mine at 15.

I will sit next to her, Petra decides, *I'll just ask her, once and for all.* She opens the driver-side door, but as soon as she's in, Lilac is gone.

"Lilac! Lila-la-la-la-la." Petra lies on her stomach across the glove box and tries to peer under the car, where there is only night. The Lavender Menace is floating. When she sits up in the driver's seat, her head swirls. Meg and Imogen stand in front of her. Their bodies merge together, into one coffee-and-cream-and-curves femme, then pull apart again.

"You okay?" Imogen asks.

"Yeah, yeah. I saw her. Then she disappeared. Got pulled under the car, actually. I think she's trying to say... I think she was murdered. Someone mowed her down and threw her body in the mine. She just wanted to live this long, great, fun life, and outside forces—patriarchal forces—wouldn't let her."

"This is too much." Meg puts her fingers on her temples.

"No, I'm serious, I saw her. She was wearing one of those old-fashioned dresses and she had blonde hair… well, she looked a little like me, actually."

"No, I mean *this* is too much." Meg waves to the flickering mine and the broken circle of women, all waiting. "I can't be here. This place is just too… Al and I came here…"

Sunny is behind her now, hands on Meg's shoulders. "Good lord, not again. She left you, what, five years ago? Don't be such a drama queen."

Meg yanks herself away from Sunny's grip. "Fuck you." She reaches in the pocket of Sunny's leather jacket and pulls out a silver jingle of keys. She gives the bike a few kicks as Sunny moves from shock to annoyance to calculated nonchalance.

"Meg, come on, stay," Petra protests. She touches the sleeve of Meg's green sweater, and Meg shakes her away. "We need you." Petra hovers in the sky above them. From that height, she and Meg are little girls in play clothes. Meg with her curled ponytail and drama-plagued Barbie dolls, Petra dancing around her, thrilled that this important older girl wants to spend time with her, wants to tell her why the girls in her own grade are ugly witches. Meg takes off down the mountain, and Petra thinks she can see something filmy and blonde following her. Lilac or Little Petra.

"That girl should not be driving," Imogen says seriously. "She shouldn't even drive when she's sober. Jody, you better follow her in the car."

"I know," Jody says, extracting herself from the circle.

"No, no, it's okay," Petra assures them. She puts her hands on Imogen's worried face. Her hands look like pink stars. They could all be friends if they're quiet and listen. She's sure of it. The bead inside her head rolls into her throat, cold on her tongue, out her mouth and into the world. Everyone has one bead and together they form a necklace. "She's fine. Lilac is watching over her, I saw her."

"No offense, Petra, but Meg needs more than a ghost to help her out.

That girl's got enough ghosts," Jody says, climbing into her Edsel.

"But the world is a necklace," Petra explains.

"You are high, woman," Imogen says.

Petra wakes up to the mine's rock ceiling. For a minute she thinks that it's the floor of the mine, and that she is Lilac, dead and floating above it. Then she sits up and looks around. Emily and Essie are a knot of sleep beside her. Linda and Gapi and Marilyn are wrapped in the army blanket. Gapi is snoring. Jody and Imogen are in Jody's Edsel. When Petra stands up she can see Sylvie and Jean curled in the back seat.

The morning is thin and golden. Petra stretches to release a kink in her shoulder blade. There's gravel stuck to her cheek. Her paisley blouse is twisted around her torso. Then she remembers: Lilac. She definitely saw her. Except she also smoked more and stronger pot than ever before. Shit.

"Petra?" Marilyn sits up, pulling a strand of wooden beads from her tangled hair. "What's that smell?" She wiggles her small bunny nose.

Petra's face feels frozen, but she sniffs. "Bacon, I think. What....?"

She and Marilyn walk around the corner, where the mountain retreats like regret after the jut of the mine. There is Meg, prim and fresh in a wool wraparound skirt, white blouse, and meticulously applied red lipstick, kneeling beside a camping stove. She flips strips of bacon and smiles as if this is June Cleaver's kitchen, not the side of a mountain. Her eyes are bloodshot, but a thick line of black eyeliner provides sufficient distraction.

"You came back!" Petra exclaims. She can't wait to tell Meg about Lilac, how she's watching over all of them.

"Sunny broke up with me," Meg says matter-of-factly. "Jody followed us and I caught a ride back with her." She chases a stubborn strip of bacon around the grill with her metal spatula.

"Oh, Meg, wow. Like, who was Sunny anyway to tell you how you should feel about Al?"

"She said I was too hung up, but she was just itching to break things off. I've known for weeks." She shrugs. "It's fine. I'm over it. There are other butches in the sea."

"You know what your problem is, Meggie? You keep waiting for a butch to save you." Petra looks at Marilyn, who nods in agreement. "No man will save you, and no one woman will save you. Especially not one who barely knows she's a woman. But *women*—plural—we could. Come live with us at the church, you'd see." She's asked before, but maybe now Meg will understand.

Meg stands up, puts her spatula hand on her hip. "I really don't need you to tell me what my problem is. You don't have the faintest idea what my problem is."

Marilyn looks uncomfortable. She's a theorist, not a front-lines woman. Petra counters, "If anyone knows, it's me." History is her trump card. She's seen Meg beg and brownnose and turn cartwheels in the snow, all the things she'd never do now.

The women are clustering, lured by bacon and conflict. Jean grabs a strip straight from the grill. It doesn't seem to burn her fingers. "Why don't you back off, Petra?" she challenges.

"Meg doesn't need her ex-girlfriend to defend her," Petra says, arms are crossed in front of her, hardly the welcoming embrace of feminism. She takes a deep breath and tries again. "Meg, come on, just stay with us at the church for a little while. It will be fun, like a slumber party." She turns to face the women who've gathered behind her. "You *all* should. Seriously—you said rent was getting high in Berkeley, right? All of you," she looks at Essie and Emily, who are holding hands and looking at each other, "all of you should go home, pack, and come right back. Think about it: no men; no women who, uh, support patriarchy; and no rent. The church is big. You could just pull up a mattress. And then we'll have enough people to really enact change. We'd be a real women's colony."

"Are you serious?" squeals Linda. Gapi looks nervous. "Wow, I don't know what to say. I mean, God, *yes*, of course."

Essie (or Emily) doesn't take her eyes off her girlfriend. "We could do that, right, babe? I know you're more of a homebody than I am, but remember what you said after the last rally, after we made all those signs and then Mark Lannan took credit for everything? This could be our big chance."

Emily (or Essie) nods. "Let's not think about it. Let's just follow our intuition, babe."

Petra lunges at all three with open arms, and she can feel their muscles relax into her hug, the way people always do when she touches them. She loves their squirming girl-energy. She laughs into the tangle of arms and breasts and beads and hair. Their voices ring through the mountains like church bells. The rest of the women gather around the camping stove. Jody rubs her eyes and tries unsuccessfully to pull the wrinkles from her blue work shirt.

Meg points the spatula. "Petra, last I checked, it wasn't your church to give away."

"It's not anyone's," Petra replies. "It's like the American Indians— they knew no one could own the land."

Jean steps in, her eyes the color of a brewing storm. "But you've lived there less than four months, and we've been there for years. I'm really tired of you and your hippie friends drinking my beer and telling my girl she's 'oppressed' and deciding that we have to rotate chores even though you don't even know where to find the dump when it's your turn to take the garbage there."

Meg glares at Petra from beneath her false eyelashes. "I like keeping to myself. It's nice, you should try it some time."

"Maybe we should let Jody and Imogen decide," Sylvie whispers. "They've lived there the longest."

Jody smacks her own cheeks to wake up. "Uh. Well. It would be pretty crowded with ten people."

"Jo, we could do it," Imogen urges. "There's plenty of floor space and we could all chip in for expenses. With more people we could replace that broken window."

"I don't know," says Jody.

"Come on," Petra says, looking at Imogen. Her waxed hairdo has survived the night, although it seems to have shifted a few inches to the right.

"Jesus, Jody..." Jean looks at her fellow butch.

"We've always taken in anyone who needs help," Imogen says. "I don't see why Petra's friends would be different."

"My girl has a point," Jody says, looking at Jean.

"Maybe there's some kind of compromise..." Imogen offers.

But Petra doesn't want to compromise. She doesn't want to be part of a halfhearted movement, a halfway-there generation. Apparently Jean doesn't want to compromise either. She grabs Sylvie's wrist. "Fine. I'll make it easy. Sylvie and I are out of there. We're too old to be living like freaks in a communist commune anyway."

"That's redundant: 'communist commune,' " says Marilyn, blinking from behind her glasses.

"That," says Jean, "is exactly why we're moving out. We don't need *correcting*, you little co-ed bitch." She pulls Sylvie toward the cluster of cars. Meg follows them with long strides, muscular calves flashing beneath her skirt. Soon she passes Jean and Sylvie.

"But Sylvie, remember Lilac and love?" Petra calls.

Jody runs after them.

"Don't run after them, Jo," Imogen calls. "If they're gonna be like that..."

Jody looks over her shoulder. "Don't tell me what to do!"

This is how it has to be, Petra realizes. The old retreating and becoming whatever it will become. New bright food setting the table. There's no place for Jean or even an enlightened Sylvie in Petra's perfect world. Maybe not even for Meg. This makes her sad, but it feels non-negotiable.

Lilac, what happened? she asks, looking up at the clear early November sky. When she had a boyfriend, doing drugs with him made sex better, more significant. But she doesn't like that she cannot extract beaming, sacrificed Lilac from marijuana loopiness and the mine-deep division of her friends.

A REGULAR FESTIVAL
Imogen: Lilac Mines, 1971

They have a week to make the world, and when Imogen looks at Petra, she thinks they just might do it. Petra is standing on a wobbly ladder, stringing Christmas tree lights around the rafters of the church.

"But it's our *house*," Jody keeps saying. "If this festival is going to be big, I don't want everyone traipsing through with their muddy feet."

"The personal is political," Petra keeps saying.

This will be the first (*First Annual*, Petra says in capital letters) Lilac Mines Festival, organized by the Lilac Womyn's Colony. There is a carved wooden sign over the church identifying the latter, and a spray-painted bed sheet announcing the former. Imogen was worried that the Colony sign might attract unwanted attention, but it seems to have had the opposite effect. When they were just squatters, they periodically had to shoo away other would-be squatters—hitchhikers and campers. Now that they are a real place with a name, people grant them space. Whether it's out of respect or scorn, Imogen can't tell. Her boss, Dr. Tracy, said, *So you're living in that Women's Club?* Imogen nodded nervously. She'd worked for him for years, and he'd never asked anything personal, other than what her favorite sexual position was. *Well*, he snorted, *I guess that explains why you're such a tight little wench.*

Petra owns the church. She had enough money to make the down payment, and her father helped her with the paperwork. There was a heated discussion about whether the women wanted to perpetuate such a patriarchal capitalist system as the buying and selling of property, about

229

whether Petra would assume more than her fair share of power as a result. But the truth is that they all sleep easier knowing that the sheriff can't kick them out, and Petra sort of runs things anyway, although Imogen and Jody, 32 and 33 respectively, are regarded as wise old matriarchs.

"Jody, switch on that light," Petra instructs. It's a blue-pink April afternoon, the air hesitantly warm. The tiny bulbs make soft circles of light—red and yellow and green—on Petra's white dress. Her wavy blonde hair is pulled into a low ponytail, and her round cheeks are pink as always. She has a Heidi-like innocence that fascinates Imogen, as if she were raised in a field of flowers and kissed each winter by soft, clean snow.

"Oh, you know what we need?" Petra says, climbing down from the ladder. She grips Imogen's shoulder for support. "Paper lanterns! I was reading one of those horrible, oppressive ladies' magazines the other day, and in between all the articles about making nice dinners, there was a story about how to throw an oriental tea party. And there were the most beautiful Chinese lanterns. Or Japanese, maybe. Wouldn't they be gorgeous in here?"

"Japanese," says Imogen. "My neighbors had one when I was a kid. But where would we get them?"

"What's so terrible about making a nice dinner?" Jody wants to know. She coils the remaining lights and wrestles them back into their box.

"What's *not* terrible about it?" Petra laughs. "*I* don't want to do it, do you?"

"Well, I guess not, but..."

Lately, Jody has acquired a subtle awkwardness. Imogen can't quite place it. It's as if Jody just woke up and noticed—really noticed—her own big body, which used to move like a tree in the wind, solid and slow and tall. Now she's skittish, easily offended. Imogen will come to recognize this certain brand of fear on the faces of men and white people when they see that gender and race are not facts after all. But the first place she sees it is behind Jody's freckles; she seems confused and vaguely betrayed.

On their way to May Company, where Petra is sure they'll find paper lanterns, they pick up Meg, who is recovering from her second breakup with Kay. All of her recent butches have been deep-voiced, fond of all things motorized, and in unmitigated awe of Meg. It's hard for Imogen to understand devastation over such indistinguishable women. But Meg's face makes her believe. The lines of disappointment thread across her forehead, deepening with each new, predictable blow. Each time Jody whispers to Imogen, *We've got to make sure she doesn't stay cooped up in her house.* Not that she would, but for the sake of the family, Imogen makes sure. Meg, their unruly teenage daughter.

May Company has table lamps with fat bottoms and brocade shades. Tall brass floor lamps. Faux Tiffany lamps that make an unsatisfying thump when Imogen raps on their plastic shades. But no Oriental paper lanterns. Meg does seem cheered by the hunt. She models an olive-green velvet shade. "Shall I wear this to the festival? I think the fringe will keep the sun out of my eyes nicely."

Petra giggles and grabs a wicker shade for her own head. "How about this one?"

Meg poo-poos it with a flick of her hand. "Wicker was last season." She's kidding, but there's a flicker of genuine hurt on Petra's face. It's the look Imogen's little sister used to get when Imogen's dolls were mean to Lynette's. Imogen saves this moment, puts it in her pocket for all the times Petra is bossy and over-confident.

She spots a clerk folding tablecloths on her knees. "Excuse me. I'm looking for this certain kind of lamp. It sort of looks like a white paper globe?"

"A lamp made out of paper?" The clerk can't be older than 17. She's wearing a short plaid dress over jeans, and her straight black hair is in two long pigtails, like Marcia Brady in negative.

"It's Japanese."

"Sounds neat." The clerk nods, keeping the beat to the gum she is chewing. "But we don't have anything like that here. Lilac Mines isn't very exotic, in case you haven't noticed."

Imogen can hear Meg and Petra laughing and talking in the lampshade aisle. They fight all the time, but Petra worships Meg too much to stay away, and grudges require an even keel Meg isn't capable of.

"Yeah, I've noticed," Imogen says. "Do you know where we could find them?"

"Nuh-uh. I mean, like, San Francisco maybe."

"Well, thanks anyway. Hey, my friends and I are putting together, like, a big party. If I give you a poster, can you put it up in the store?" Imogen opens her big canvas bag and unrolls one of the posters. They used the letterpress in the old abandoned newspaper office, which is easy to break into if you slip through the door that connects it to the post office. Essie, who was an art major, made a linoleum block of a woman wrapped in vines. She said it was a goddess, but Imogen thought it looked like Eve. The vines curl above her head and spell out "1st Annual Lilac Mines Festival." The last part of "Festival" is slightly crowded.

"Neat," says the clerk, looking at Eve in her stylized fig leaf. "Is it, um, a nudist festival or something?" Imogen can tell from the girl's face that she half wants it to be.

"No, but there's gonna be poetry and music and crafts, things like that."

"Oh." She grabs a roll of tape from behind the counter and presses the poster to the window, so that it faces Calla Boulevard.

"Hey, you can't do that," thunders a man's voice. Imogen and the clerk whip around to see a man with very little neck and a badge that says *Manager*. "I don't care whose puppy is lost, you can't put anything in the window without clearing it with corporate."

The clerk gathers herself. She opens her mouth and then closes it. Imogen watches her wrestle with a Marcia Brady sort of decision: be good or be groovy. "Come on, Mr. Jones," the girl says. "It's just a regular festival. There's going to be music and, um, poetry—"

But suddenly the manager's attention is diverted. "What in tarnation? Hey! You!" He turns to the aisle behind them, where Meg is doing a Charlie Chaplin walk with a shade-less floor lamp as her cane. Petra sits cross-legged on the floor, cracking up, her laughter more dramatic than Meg's halfhearted impression. *Can't take these kids anywhere,* Imogen thinks.

"Sorry, sir." Petra purses her lips and blinks her denim-blue eyes at Mr. Jones.

But Meg looks genuinely annoyed at the interruption. "Hey, we're just shopping for a lamp."

"Right." Mr. Jones crosses his arms over his big belly.

"We can use our new lamp however we want," Meg protests, ready to go to battle for this bit of theater.

"You're telling me you're going to buy that? You hippies never made an honest dollar in your life."

As if they all share one life. As if Meg, in her knee-length polyester skirt and patent leather pumps, is a hippie. The straight folk of Lilac Mines don't know the difference between hippies, lesbians, and lesbian feminists. Imogen can't blame them, she's still learning the nuances herself. Sometimes their ignorance works in the Colony's favor: they're seen as wild girls-who-will-never-find-a-man if they keep this up. Imogen studies Mr. Jones in his short-sleeved shirt and crooked tie. Are they are both more and less dangerous than he thinks?

Meg glares at Mr. Jones. She sees a fire that no one else sees, and she's ready to walk into it headfirst. "You want fucking honest?" she demands. She grabs Petra by the lacy collar of her dress and pulls the bewildered girl toward her. She plants a long, hard kiss on Petra's lips.

Imogen is as paralyzed as the clerk and the manager. They are like a photo from the future. Something is horribly wrong yet makes perfect sense. Two girls in dresses. Two shades of long hair mingling on close-pressed shoulders. A flash of something like envy pulses through Imogen's body. Petra moves her arms like she's trying to find the beat of a bizarre new song. Imogen wants to hear it, too. She opens her mouth. To sing. To kiss. What comes out is, "*Meg*. Stop it!"

"I'm going to call the police right now," growls Mr. Jones. "I've had enough of you hippies thinking you own this town."

The kiss breaks, and Petra, her face flushed, begins furiously pushing her hair behind her ears, which is what she does when she's trying to make sense of something quickly. Meg just stands there defiantly, high-heeled feet wide apart on the durable carpet. Imogen knows she's still the voice of reason here, and she hates it. "C'mon, Meg, we gotta go."

"We don't have to go anywhere." Meg looks at Mr. Jones with dead brown eyes. "Call the cops, I don't care."

"I care," Imogen says. She grabs Meg's hand, and although Meg is strong, her shoes slide on the floor. "You want to ruin it for everybody?" Imogen pulls Meg through the linens aisle and out the door.

When they are sealed in Jody's Edsel, Petra turns ecstatic. "That was so amazing! I knew you had it in you!" She leans forward from the back seat, a flower in time-lapse bloom.

Meg attempts to roll down the passenger side window, but it sticks after three inches. "I don't like being told what to do," she says simply.

"Right on!" Petra cheers. "We should all stick it to the man like that. Seriously, we could organize a protest. We could gather up all the lesbians in Lilac Mines and we could go back to the store and all start kissing each other. If there are enough of us, they can't do anything."

"Pet," Imogen says patiently, "most of the lesbians in Lilac Mines are happy if they can just *shop* at May Company without getting harassed. They're not gonna draw attention to themselves on purpose."

They're on Meg's block of Gemini Street now. "You organize it," Meg says. "And call me if any handsome butches show up."

Petra wilts in the back seat. "Fine, don't be a feminist. It's your loss."

And what Petra does not see is that Meg already is a feminist. Petra sees curled hair and pressed clothing and assumes the past, when in fact Meg is outside of time. Her saving grace and her downfall.

"Your stop, girl," Imogen says, pulling up in front of Meg's small brown house. Meg waves goodbye and Petra climbs into the front seat.

Like a rock tumbling down the mountain, or gossip moving through a school, an invisible energy draws people to the church from Lilac Mines and Beedleborough and even Columbia. They look at the painted bed sheet. At the table of necklaces Linda and her cousin made, sparkling in the sun. At Emily pressing the pedal on the pottery wheel with her foot to the rhythm of Essie's folk guitar. The people smile or wrinkle their noses. But either way, they believe it. This is what amazes Imogen. They just take it all in like it's real, like it always was, like the colony is as much a part of town as Lou's Bar, which has a sticky floor and slow service, but is where you go nonetheless.

At three points during the day they'll rotate jobs, because that way they'll all learn a variety of skills and no one will have exclusive power over any given domain. Emily is the only one who knows how to use a pottery wheel, though—the other women have tried, but they've only created imploded lumps of wet clay—so Linda and Marilyn will teach festival-goers how to make pinch pots on their ceramics shifts.

From her shift at the baked goods table, Imogen has a perfect view of Petra and Massassi, the dance teacher Petra has imported from Oakland. She is taller even than Petra, with golden brown skin and square shoulders. She wears pounds and pounds of beads—wood and bone and coral—but dances as if they weigh nothing. Massassi has agreed to teach an Umfundalai dance at the festival in exchange for a $25 check made out to the Oakland Dance Revolution. So she dances, now, with a circle of white people. Most are spastic or painfully inhibited, but Petra—in homemade turban and tube top—holds her own. She raises her elbows and moves her ribcage to the beat Gapi is slapping out on a set of bongo drums. And she looks good. Flat bellybutton looking this way and that. Strands of blonde hair escaping her turban, turban loosening. Every part in motion. She is no Massassi, who is as bored and graceful as a waking cat, but she is very much a Petra.

A teenage boy with curly hair erupting from beneath his baseball cap points to a plate of brownies. "Are these... you know..."

"Twenty-five cents each," Imogen says. She keeps her eyes on Petra.

"Yeah, but are they..." He lowers his voice. "I mean, are there any *special ingredients?*"

"Oh. Those will cost you a buck, and you'll have to ask Agapi. She's the woman on the drums over there. But wait till she's done."

Imogen hands out oatmeal cookies and carob-chip muffins, and watches and watches. There are people who bend under the weight of the world, she thinks, like timid Al seemed to, and people who wrestle it, like Meg. Then there are people like Petra, who bend the world to them. Petra dances over to the baked goods table. "Can you believe this?" she bubbles. "People love it!"

"I know."

"Can I have a sip of your iced tea?" Petra nods toward the half-full Emily-made mug at the edge of the table.

" 'Course." Imogen hands it to her, and Petra gulps. "But you know you could get a whole glass from Marilyn at the beverage table."

Petra smiles with small straight teeth. She had braces as a child. "I know." She goes back to her dance.

The drums are not hard to play. The key, Imogen discovers during her dance rotation, is to let her hands lead. Skin bouncing off skin, sweating beneath the late afternoon sun. Massassi doing her thing inches from Imogen and a world away.

"This is wonderful, just wonderful," gushes a white woman who is already wearing one of the Lilac Mines Festival '71 T-shirts that Emily silk-screened. "My husband, he said this was a bunch of nonsense, but I kept telling him, 'Carl, it's good to know how other people live.' "

Imogen's final shift is at the tie-dyeing station. She shows the festival-goers how to bind T-shirts and cotton skirts and even a canvas hat with twine, and submerge them in buckets of dye. Red and green and eggplant purple. When they unfurl the wadded items, there are white lines snaking through the newly red or green or purple clothes. The grin and shake their heads at the results. Who knew that *their* boring old work shirts could be so transformed? Perhaps anything is possible. They clap their red and green and purple hands. Imogen feels a hand on her shoulder.

It's Jody, who has been grilling hamburgers in the church kitchen. She points toward Petra, who has resumed her place dancing beside Massassi. "What a goofball."

"Oh, come on, you gotta admit she's good," Imogen laughs. "She's got her own goofball rhythm."

Jody hugs Imogen from behind, putting her hand on Imogen's

stomach. She has never done this outside of home or Lilac's. Two young girls with their arms in the buckets look up at them. Imogen feels the weight of Jody's large palm, smells the hamburger grease. The girls blink and go back to their inky ponds.

This can happen, Imogen thinks. The sun is bright above them, the air is new and piney, as if spring is not a season but a revolution.

The gesture ends after a few seconds, and Jody slips one of the dry shirts—pale green with a trail of white spiraling out from the left shoulder—over her head. Imogen looks at her butch. She knows where they fall, she and Jody. They are the ones who stay.

THE INTEGUMENTARY SYSTEM
Anna Lisa: Fresno, 1971

The cradle is perfect. The dark red wood is worn so smooth that the cradle seems to promise a splinterless life. A soft, cream-colored blanket is folded inside.

"My mother knitted it," Terry explains. He holds the cradle in his arm, as if it's the baby itself. "She thought it would be bad luck to give it to me empty. Can you believe I fit in here once? And my dad before me? And that this is made from a tree that grew in a Russian forest somewhere?"

He sets it down in the spare room he insisted on painting pale yellow. For Terry it's always been a matter of when, not if. In theory Anna Lisa feels the same. But she is 25 now, Terry 31, and she can't bring herself to stop taking her small pastel pills every day after breakfast. Lately, Terry seems to have adopted a strategy of material evidence. If they have a yellow room and an heirloom cradle and the tricycle that the Sammartinos' son recently outgrew, soon they'll have to have a baby to occupy the place they've created.

Terry sits down on the guest bed—Anna Lisa's twin bed, imported from her parents' house—and admires the cradle. It's a pink Sunday in June, the kind that could grow a baby all on its own. Through the open window, with its sighing white curtains, Anna Lisa can see her flower and vegetable garden in the backyard. It's bursting with delphiniums and purple, lion-headed flowers called Lilac Time Dahlias. It turns out she has a bright green thumb. She half expects to see an infant crawl out of the cabbages.

Terry gestures for her to join him. "Come, look. Doesn't it just all make perfect sense?"

She sits down next to him, but doesn't touch him. "I know you're anxious, but I can't pretend I'm ready when I'm not."

"You're 25! If not now, when? I'm just being practical."

Which is of course part of the problem: Terry is practical and the wisps of thoughts that float through Anna Lisa's head are not. She can't tell him: *I'm a butch, I'm not getting pregnant.* "Maybe I should babysit Wally Jr. more. You know, to get used to it."

Terry unbuttons his wide-collared brown shirt and folds it neatly. He has the beginning of a belly beneath his undershirt, which Anna Lisa supposes most wives would find charming. But his body is always waiting for her, or disappointed in her, or reminding her how things are supposed to be. "Annie, I don't think being a mother is something you 'get used to.' It's what we're born to do, it's nature."

What's the reason? Anna Lisa asks herself sternly. She likes children. She loves building block towers with Wally Jr., then smashing them with a vigor that is frowned upon in adult circles. She loves Terry. Or at least, she is linked to him in a way that cannot be separated from love. And she wouldn't mind giving up her part-time job at The Quill Pen. She's gotten enough paper cuts to last a lifetime. So… what?

"I wish you'd talk to me more about things," he says. His embrace clamps her arms at her sides. "Sometimes it's like you're only half here."

"That's just how I am. I just don't have a lot to talk about," Anna Lisa protests. Her thoughts grow inward, like roots in a potted plant.

"That's not true. I see you, Annie. You're beautiful and brilliant and interesting and mysterious. Or at least, that's how I've always thought of you. But maybe it's just that you're not that interested in me. Maybe you're always dreaming about being somewhere else." His voice grows small and nervous. "Or with another man?"

"Don't be crazy. I couldn't be with anyone else. I can't even imagine it." And this is true. She thinks about Meg all the time, but those feelings are ancient and historical, not the kind that might be linked to action.

"Promise?" Terry turns to face her. Anna Lisa shakes out her arms, and he rubs her thighs through her jeans. Soon he is unzipping them, peeling off her blue paisley blouse. It's been a while since they've had sex, longer since they've undressed each other.

Even though Anna Lisa is on the pill, Terry always makes love like he's trying to produce a baby, industrious and cheerful if not quite passionate. His thrusts are rhythmic, as if the inside of Anna Lisa is not a cave to be explored but a closet to be swept. It's reassuring, in a way, as if they're both concluding, *No mystery here, just some shirts to fold!* She tries not to be one of those I-Have-A-Headache wives. She can't give him her mind or her past, so her body is a consolation prize.

"Thank you," he says when he rolls off of her. "That was nice."

Afterward, Terry watches TV in the family room, and Anna Lisa begins dinner in the connected kitchen. It seems the hard part of the day has passed. She moves lightly from fridge to cupboards to stove.

"I'm trying a new recipe," she calls to Terry. "This casserole with brown rice and cheese and artichoke hearts."

"Brown rice and what?" he asks over the sound of a sports game.

"Artichoke hearts."

"Sounds strange."

"Well, it's new. We'll see."

They eat off trays in the family room, the evening news unfurling in front of them. They bought the color television a few weeks ago. Now olive-green planes soar over Crayola-green jungles and light Halloween-orange fires. Then the whole scene is eclipsed by thick black smoke, somehow different than the black of their black-and-white TV.

"What a thing to see in color," Anna Lisa sighs.

"I don't know what to wish for anymore," Terry says. "For America to do more, or do less."

She touches the blue veins on his hand. It comforts her to know that Terry is capable of something other than complete self-assurance when it comes to his own desires.

The story switches. A young woman news reporter with a bright red beehive stands against a crowd of men. "I'm here in San Francisco where local homosexuals are marching up Folsom Street in observance of what they call 'Christopher Street Liberation Day,' " she says. "They say that they're here to prove there's nothing wrong with homosexuality. But as you'll see, some are nearly naked, and some are even dressed as women. A theatrical group calling themselves the Cockettes 'mooned' our cameraman." She looks nervous, like she's not sure whether this is a funny human interest story or the next Kent State. The men are a parade of color in yellow feathered headdresses and pink feather boas, tight blue jeans and tanned hairy chests. Signs painted with red letters: COME OUT!; GAY LIBERATION NOW!; RED, WHITE, BLUE & LAVENDER. The day is golden around them.

San Francisco is so far away. Anna Lisa looks down at her dinner. She thought she was being adventurous, going to the Safeway instead of her parents' store for artichoke hearts. Writing names in increasingly calligraphic handwriting on scraps of paper, then stowing them in strange, secret places. She knows why she doesn't want to have a baby: she can't bring a child into a world she doesn't know how to fully participate in. How can she tell it *Do your best, be your best* when she has no idea how to do it herself? She would doom her son or daughter to mediocrity. That would be her legacy.

"Can you believe it?" Terry remarks. "A parade of homosexuals?!"

Anna Lisa feels her face and neck turn as red as the letters on the signs. "It makes them happy," she whispers. "It seems to."

"Say it's true what the homosexuals say, that they were born that way," Terry says in his his which-councilman-should-we-vote-for voice, "that still doesn't make it something to be *proud* of. You can only be proud of something you've worked for. Worked at. A business or a house. Or a child you've raised."

There was a time when Anna Lisa believed that Terry saved her from something desperate, being a lesbian or an old maid. Lately she's been wondering if he's keeping her from something. It's a tiny, bitter voice inside her, and quickly stifled by the thick chords of their life. She's in deep. There are her parents: her father's condition is steady but demanding, while her mother's arthritis is unpredictable though often undetectable. There is this house and its papers showing both their names. There is the store and more papers with both their names. It was a big gesture from Terry: these are your envelopes, too, your three-ring binders, your plastic sheet covers, your No. 2 pencils. There are the Sammartinos and the Carys and the Jensens. There is bowling on Saturdays and church on Sundays.

And, of course, there is Terry himself. Anna Lisa cannot break his heart, so she lets her own grow so small and hard that it, too, is unbreakable, a miniature bowling ball.

Looking around the classroom, Anna Lisa is acutely aware of her age. Most of these kids were born in the '50s. Their shaggy hair and lazily draped clothing, though, emits a long stoned cackle at that decade. A girl in a plaid vest and clashing pants sits cross-legged on the desk next to her. She hands Anna Lisa a bright yellow flyer. "The Women's Collective is having a meeting tomorrow afternoon."

Anna Lisa holds the flyer gingerly, as if leaving fingerprints might implicate her. "What do you do there?"

"Oh, you know, CR, talk about books, that sort of thing." She pushes a strand of dark hair behind her ear.

"CR?"

"Consciousness-raising. If you have to ask, your consciousness probably needs to be raised."

The prospect sounds frightening to Anna Lisa. This girl, with her shiny face and bold clothing, doesn't seem like she has anything to hide. Even her subconscious is probably a straight clean wishing well.

"Thanks for the invitation," Anna Lisa says. She folds the flyer and slips it into the index pages of her new textbook. She wants to go to the meeting, she wants to soak up youth and femaleness until her consciousness rises so high it spills out her ears. And the intensity of her desire is precisely why she can't go. She reminds herself that she's at Cal State Fresno to become a nurse, not to join clubs.

The girl picks up on Anna Lisa's wariness. "It's not like we burn our bras or go lesbian or anything."

Anna Lisa nods and looks down at her book. It is September. In July, she missed her period. She didn't tell Terry. She waited with dread for her body to do something definitive. While she waited she made a list:

Anita
Sonja
Maribeth
Julie
Christine
Stacey
Daphne
Violet

Little scraps from TV, names signed to checks. She gathers them everywhere. Always girls' names. Then, in August, blood came like rain in the dry summer, and Anna Lisa was as grateful as cracked earth. Her body was just playing tricks on her, daring her to make a decision. She tore up the list of names, although she's made others since, and then torn them up, too. If she did not want children with Terry, she needed to do something. And her life seemed to be hinting that she *could* do something. Maybe not *anything*, but something.

Cal State Fresno had just started its nursing program, and allowed Anna Lisa to apply over the summer for admission to the first fall class. She feels strange sitting at a classroom desk again. Her butt takes up more of the seat than it did in high school. DONNY '67 is carved into the Formica surface. She conjugates in her head: Donny, Donald, Don, Dawn, Donna.

Anna Lisa is grateful to see an older woman enter the room. Dressed in a tweed skirt and ruffled blouse, with a red scarf knotted at her starting-to-wrinkle neck, her neat straw-colored curls are beginning to gray. Anna Lisa half hopes the woman will sit at the empty desk to her left, half prays that she won't. She's not sure if she would be young in contrast, or old by association.

But the woman walks straight to the front of the classroom. She takes her place behind the wooden podium, and clears her throat. Slowly, the buzzing kids quiet down. "Hello, welcome to Anatomy 64. I'm Professor Rettig. We'll be learning many interesting things this semester—the human body is a fascinating machine. I trust that you've all purchased the textbook for this class, *Introduction to Human Biology*? You'll be able to use it in Nursing 10 as well, so don't let the price panic you too much."

Anna Lisa takes her book out of her bag and puts it on top of DONNY '67. She can't believe the professor is a woman. It makes the class feel more like high school, which is both comforting and disappointing. She's immediately intrigued by this Professor Rettig... A. Rettig, it said in the schedule of classes. Her own Aunt Randi taught at Pepperdine before retiring last year, but that was music, not science, and she wasn't a full professor. (Suzy is still in L.A. She works for a company that manufactures party supplies. Anna Lisa pictures her in a warehouse surrounded by balloons and streamers and paper hats. It seems about right.) All of Anna Lisa's own jobs have been out of necessity, and haven't demanded any skills she couldn't learn on the job.

Professor Rettig unrolls a screen above the blackboard. On it there are two transparent figures, one male and one female. Anna Lisa feels slightly bashful. A woman up there with those exposed bodies—it seems too intimate. But she supposes she'll have to get used to these things if she's going to be a nurse. There are so many things she's afraid of, but she doesn't mind blood or dirt or standing up for a long time. She thinks she can do it.

"Who can tell me what the biggest organ in the body is?" Professor Rettig asks.

"The liver," a boy in the front row says confidently.

"Good guess, but no. Anyone else?"

"The lungs?" says the Women's Collective meeting girl. "Are they one organ or two?"

"Actually," says Professor Rettig, "it's the skin. Your skin is one big organ, with three distinct layers. These guys"—she gestures to the bodies on the screen—"don't have any. But it's an extremely important organ."

Anna Lisa writes down "skin." She studies the palm of her hand, with its tiny crosshatches and deep destiny lines. It makes sense: the thing that covers you and holds you in, the first thing people see. Of course, it is huge.

"Your skin, for example, is not just a body part—it's made up of many small cell bodies. And the organs work together to form ten systems. Who can name a system?"

Anna Lisa likes how Professor Rettig throws questions at them. So many teachers hog the spotlight, asking questions only to find out whether students did their reading or not.

"Muscular system," says a well-built young man.

"Musculatory. Good, that's one."

Anna Lisa tentatively raises her hand. She's almost surprised to see it there, as if her nervous system sent a message directly to her arm without telling the rest of her.

"Skeletal system?" she says.

"I'm sorry, Miss, could you speak up?"

"I'm Anna Lisa Kristalovich. I said, um, skeletal system. Bones."

"Of course—the great clothes hanger of the human body. Thank you, Miss Kristalovich."

"The beauty of the human body—well, at least to science types like myself—is that all the systems are interdependent. If your digestive system is impaired, what happens? Your stomach aches—because pain receptors send messages to your brain, following the avenues of the nervous system."

Anna Lisa likes the words Professor Rettig uses: clothes hanger, avenues. It's strange to think that she is not just one thing, just Anna Lisa Kristalovich. She is cells that could live on their own in a Petri dish. She is maps of veins and nerves. She is her father's brown eyes and her mother's need to nest. She is the black-framed glasses she's recently started wearing. She is every scar and freckle that the world has etched onto her since she first ran barefoot through her prickly childhood yard. If she gains the key to all these maps, she'll be able to heal people. If other people and organisms are a part of her, does that mean she's part of them, too? That the things she does—or doesn't do—create who *they* are?

Anna Lisa is studying for her first test a few weeks later when the phone rings. *Fibula*, she memorizes, *fib-you-lie*. Professor Rettig explained that first they would learn basic anatomy, then they would zoom in to the cellular level, then pull back again and take the systems one by one.

"I'll get it!" Anna Lisa calls out. Terry is in the family room, a world away. Anna Lisa has made the spare room her study space. The cradle is full of books.

"No, I'll get it, you're studying," Terry calls back. Is there annoyance in his voice? Terry is encouraging, but he's already asked whether she can take summer school and finish a year early. That way she'll only be 28, still fertile, she supposes. She doesn't like how he presents the timeline of her body, like forecasting sales figures for The Quill Pen.

"I could use a break!" she says, but he's already answered.

In a few minutes, Terry is in the doorway of the spare room. "It's someone named Michelle? She has an accent."

"Really?" Anna Lisa doesn't know anyone named Michelle, but she picks up the phone in the master bedroom, sitting up straight on the edge of the double bed.

"Hello, this is Anna Lisa," she says. She hears a click as Terry hangs up the extension. The laughter on the other end of the line cuts through all the systems of her body.

"Al. It's me. Meg. *Mee-shell*," she says with a French-ish lilt.

Anna Lisa remembers the big logs at the sawmill, the ones that got sliced into huge discs, each with hundreds of rings. She feels as if that's what's happening to her body. Someone will pick up a cross-section of Anna Lisa, of Al, and see a bit of lung, a knot of vertebra, a slice of stomach. *See*, they'll say, *here's how old she was. Here's what happened to her. Here is the drought that lasted and lasted, and here's the time, in 1971, that Meg called.*

"Oh my God," she whispers. "I... how did you find me?"

"I called your parents. Don't worry. I told them I was your friend Michelle, too. Not that they remember who Meg is, I'm sure." Anna Lisa can't gauge Meg's mood. For that, she would need to touch her. She would need bones and eyes and skin.

"Are you okay?" Anna Lisa asks.

"I should ask you the same. Was that your husband who answered the phone?"

"Yes." Anna Lisa feels ashamed, but when she thinks about Meg in Terry's presence, she feels just as awful. She is a chameleon, matching the morality of whoever is in the room.

"What's he like?" Meg wants to know.

Anna Lisa studies the bedroom, the comforter with its small brown flowers. They're not the type of couple to bother with throw-pillows, but there is a painting of a sailboat at the foot of the bed. She does not want to talk about Terry. "He's very nice, he's… well, how are *you*?" *Tell me you're fine and that I didn't abandon you,* Anna Lisa thinks. *Tell me you can't live without me.*

"I," says Meg, "am fabulous." It sounds more like a trait, though, than a mood. There, Anna Lisa would have to agree. Meg's fabulousness, her proud broken nose and loud laugh, washes over Anna Lisa. The quickness of her and the truth of her. The quilt on her bed was soft, and Anna Lisa—Al—loved to roll up tight in it Sunday mornings while Meg made coffee.

"A lot has changed in Lilac Mines. Shallan and Edith moved to Chicago. Caleb the bartender got drafted."

"But I thought… I mean, they don't let homosexuals in the army, do they?" Anna Lisa keeps her voice low and shuts the door quietly. She hopes Terry won't take it personally.

"I guess they're getting desperate. Cradle to grave and all that," Meg says. An edge creeps back into her voice. "And I guess some people would rather get shot by Communists than admit they're gay."

Anna Lisa swallows. "What about Jody and Imogen?"

"Oh, they're still around. Jody's still at the mill. They've let the old church be practically overrun by all these college girls who spell 'women' with a 'y.' "

"Yomen?"

"No," Meg laughs, "instead of the 'e.' "

"Oh." Anna Lisa laughs at her own ignorance as loudly as the thin walls of their house permit. She wants to keep Meg laughing.

"You should see these girls, Al. They dress like Indians, and everything you do or don't do is symbolic of how you're oppressed, or how you're fighting oppression."

There is a tap at the door. Terry pokes his head in. He holds up his watch and mouths, "*Sonny and Cher* is on." Anna Lisa nods. Terry closes the door. Why did she ever leave Meg and Lilac Mines? She honestly doesn't remember. She wants to keep Meg on the phone forever. Each word she speaks weighs so much. If anyone could shatter a bowling ball, it would be Meg, the weight of her pressing down. But the longer Anna Lisa talks to her, the more questions from Terry she'll have to answer.

"Why did you call me?" Anna Lisa finally asks. "I mean, why now?"

"Truth is I need your help. I was dating this butch, Kay from Beedleborough, and, well, she was alright at first, but then she got to be a drag. Real bossy and jealous, you know? She kept accusing me of seeing someone behind her back. I kept saying, 'Lilac Mines is so small—who would I be seeing?' But she wasn't the type to listen to reason. Finally I thought, what the hell, I'll tell her what she wants to hear. I said, 'It's true, Kay. I'm seeing a butch who makes you look like a fag, she's so tough.' I… I said her name was Al."

Anna Lisa remembers a few things about Meg. The way her voice can teeter at the edge of the world.

"Aren't you going to be flattered?" Meg asks, a little hurt.

Anna Lisa looks at the avocado-green receiver. She looks at her sock feet and listens to the heat come through the overhead vent. It's just started to get chilly in the evenings. She looks at her reflection in the mirror, her nearly shoulder-length hair and the crinkles at the corners of her eyes, as if she smiled a lot in her youth. "We both know I'm not actually tough," she sighs.

"But could we pretend?" Meg asks sincerely. "I mean, do you think you could come up for a weekend, just to give Kay a little scare?"

"Meg, that's absurd," Anna Lisa balks. "What am I supposed to do, beat her up? I've never fought in my life."

"I know," Meg says coldly. Then she turns soft and watery. She's no longer an oasis but a flood of hot, salty tears. "Come on, Al, you've got to help me. It's awful here. People leave and the ones who stay act like I'm some kind of *situation* to be dealt with, like I'm some old story they're tired of hearing."

"Couldn't you just ignore Kay?"

"That might work in a big city. That might work for you, Al."

"She didn't… I mean, did she hurt you or threaten you or anything?" Anna Lisa asks hesitantly.

"Well, she threatens all the time. She only hit me once, after I told her I cheated. That's when I broke things off. For good this time. I'm not afraid of her, if that's what you're thinking. I know she's too much of a coward to really hurt me, and besides, I wouldn't care if she did. I haven't been afraid of death since I was eleven. All these butches with their motorcycles and their fights. I just keep thinking, 'That's nothing. I could show you what it really means to not be afraid of anything.' But I wear heels and carry a purse, so everyone just thinks I'm a drama queen."

"I don't," Anna Lisa says. But she's not sure what to think. Meg's voice is thick with tears, like the night the two of them broke up. Something is different, though—Meg's plan is fanciful, not the work of a rational 27-year-old. And why didn't she call for *four years*?

For the first time, Anna Lisa sees her choices laid out like the systems of the body, each printed on a clear cellophane page and layered on top of one another. She could tell Terry she has a field trip for school. She could go to Lilac Mines and be the butch that Meg always wanted her to be. She could find out if Kay is a real threat, or if it's something deeper inside Meg herself. But then what? She could stay in Lilac Mines. Again. Forever. But that would mean no family, no Terry, no money, no nursing school. School is the first thing she's ever done that has made her excited about the future. The first thing that might help other people, but doesn't put her at their mercy.

"I can't," Anna Lisa begins. She hates how familiar this feels. Here she goes, getting ready to be none of the things Meg needs her to be.

"But you can, you know you can." Meg's voice climbs higher, "That's the problem with you, Al, you don't know what you're capable of."

"Why don't you just tell Kay you lied, tell her you can't see her anymore? Get Jody to come with you," Anna Lisa says.

"I don't need *Jody*." Meg's voice is icy again. It boils and freezes over so quickly that Anna Lisa can't keep up. "So that's it? You're not going to help me?"

"I want to," Anna Lisa says, but it sounds weak. "It's just, I have a whole life here. And I like it. At least, I like parts of it. You make things sound so black and white, and they're not." But Meg is right. Anna Lisa is capable of making choices. So she makes one. She chooses black. "I can't..." She stops and starts over. "I won't save you. It's your life, and this is mine. If you had a family, you'd want to..."

"You don't know anything about what I'd do." Meg does not call Anna Lisa on her cruelty. She's too proud to use her dead mother and estranged father as pawns, even if everything else is fair game.

Anna Lisa looks down at her free hand. It too has a life of its own, trembling to the beat of a frantic and silent drum.

"Well then, enjoy the pretty good parts of your life with your nice husband, Al," Meg says, "*Anna Lisa*." The way she says it makes it sound like the ugliest name in the world.

Anna Lisa sits down on the couch, at the opposite end from Terry. A woman on TV is talking about soaking her hands in dish detergent. It actually makes her skin *softer*, she says, as if she is divulging a great secret. Anna Lisa wishes she could feel so happy about dish detergent. She wishes she could plunge her hands into boiling water till her body's biggest organ was numb.

"Is Michelle a friend from school?" Terry asks, without taking his eyes from the TV set.

"No." The easier answer would have been yes, but tonight Anna Lisa doesn't feel like lying more than she has to.

"Oh. Well, she sounded very exotic."

"Mm. She's just an old friend."

"Really? Does she live in Fresno? Did she go to high school with you and Nancy-Jane and Walter?" Terry scoots closer to her end of the couch. Anna Lisa hates his skinny limbs, his hairy fingers, his eyes that look deep but have nothing difficult to contemplate.

"No, okay? I'm not in the mood to talk about it right now."

"I'm just making conversation," Terry says, dejected. "I'm just curious."

Anna Lisa glares at him. He should be better, if she is going to stay with him. If she is going to leave Meg crying and lost and maybe beaten up. They're silent as the credits role. *All those people to make one stupid show,* Anna Lisa thinks.

"Look, I don't know about this school idea," Terry says finally. "I was for it because I thought you might finally get excited about something—and it seemed like you were—but now look at you. Your first test and you're a wreck."

"You know nothing about why I'm a wreck," Anna Lisa says, doing her best to mimic Meg's meanest voice. She wants a new word to hurl at him. One that she never heard her mother yell at her father during one of their squabbles. She wants to link Terry, instead, to all the larger, more terrible things in the world. "And you—you are just *oppressive*, Terry."

"To who? To whom?" he calls as she walks out of the house and into the backyard, the sliding glass door closing behind her.

She sits down in the middle of the vegetable garden. The mud soaks through to her skin in seconds. She is feverish and shivering. The squash turn their shiny yellow faces in the moonlight, like old, wise relatives. Her first test. It's not Terry's fault he doesn't get it. How could he know when she's worked so hard to keep him away, the particulars of his maleness, the rudeness of his curiosity? She will get an F when it comes to saving Meg. And what about saving herself? Is that what she just did, or what she doesn't even know how to do? She picks a squash and takes a small bite. It doesn't even taste like squash. It's bland and turns to mush so quickly.

Terry stays inside. He's not the type to charge outside late at night. Neither is Anna Lisa.

Something is poking her lower back. She touches her hand to her back pocket and pulls out the blue ballpoint pen she was using to underline *tibia* and *fibula* and *femur*. She pushes up her sleeve. Her arm is covered with goose bumps. The flipside of her forearm is paler than the inside of a squash. She uncaps the pen and touches it to her skin. She has to press hard to make a mark. *Meg*, she writes. Below it she draws a plus sign. The pen is a dull blade. *Al*, she writes. Around the two names, she draws a heart. She is a tree and her biggest organ is bark, and she can whittle it away. She presses so hard that her skin welts up beneath the blue lines even before she's done with her message. Then she rolls her sleeve down. It's not as if Terry will try to undress her tonight.

INGA CLARKE
Jody: Lilac Mines, 1974

"We're dinosaurs, Jo," says Meg. "You're that one with the big teeth, and I'm a stega… what are the ones with the plates on their back? I'm one of those. Nice accessories and a small brain." She tips her head back and finishes her wine. The argyle pattern of her sweater does resemble a stegosaurus's plates, sort of. "More?" she asks Jody, picking up the empty bottle.

"That's the last of it," Jody says. They're at Meg's house because Jody can't handle the colony seven nights a week, and Meg can't handle being alone every night. "I should go home now. Imogen's waiting up." At least, she hopes Imogen is waiting up.

Meg looks at the green bottle, drained of cheap red wine, and repeats, "That's the last of it. That's the last of us!" Her dark eyes widen, glistening in the dim light of the kitchen. "That's what Petra said, right? We're dinosaurs. It doesn't matter what we think because we're all going to be dead soon. We'll just be a bunch of bones in a museum, and people will look at our insides and think they know what we were like."

Meg and Petra have had plenty of falling outs. But lately their spats have gotten colder and meaner. The more successful the colony gets, the more convinced Petra becomes that she doesn't need Meg, even though she wouldn't be in Lilac Mines at all if not for Meg. When one of Meg's butches stole four tabs of acid from Gapi, Petra called her a chauvinist pig and told Meg that neither of them were welcome in the colony any longer. Jody is not a fan of Petra either, but she knows she can't wrest Imogen from the church, and she is afraid to make her girl choose.

Jody stands up. Spotting Meg's car keys in a small glass bowl on the counter, she slips them into her pants pocket while Meg is busy thumping the bottom of the wine bottle. Meg is prone to late-night drives through the mountains. "G'night," Jody says. "And you're wrong. They would never build a museum for us."

It's past midnight. Jody knows she'll be exhausted at work tomorrow, but for now she enjoys the peaceful walk. January snowflakes meander down from the clear sky, as if the stars themselves are falling on her shoulders. She loves the snow, when it's just right like this. She's always amazed by how quiet it is. Rain rattles windows and tap dances on rooftops, but snow just goes about its business. It reminds her of Boston, of eight small ears glued to the living room radio in hopes of hearing that school would be closed for the day. But she can never think about Boston or her family for long. Snow days make her think of mugs of hot cocoa crammed with marshmallows, but that reminds her how she used to steal her scrawny older brother's marshmallows. He would cry, and their father would storm in. Ostensibly he was mad that they were fighting, that Jody wasn't sharing, but they both knew he was mad at the order of things. If a bossy older brother had stolen his helpless sister's food, he would have been gently reprimanded, and she would have been given more marshmallows. These memories lead to stinging cheeks, slammed doors, cold beans for dinner, exile that becomes wider and wider: to her room, to her grandmother's house, to we-don't-want-to-know-where-you-are.

Jody keeps walking. Imogen took the car to the Lilac Mines Green Grocer earlier in the day. By now their cupboards will be lined with cans of baked beans and diced tomatoes. In the refrigerator there will be apples and bricks of cheese, and jugs of milk so heavy that the metal shelf sags in the middle. For a night they'll feel rich. When Jody reaches the corner of Gemini Street and Redwood Road, she debates which route to take home. If she heads down Redwood, it's just a short walk to Moon, where the church is. But that route would require her to pass a once-grand Victorian with peeling blue paint and a stream of young male boarders, where last week a man had yelled at her from the porch, something about her clothes. It wasn't even dusk then. She pulls her coat tight around her body and heads west toward Calla Boulevard.

At Calla and Silver Street, a little sliver of an avenue that tapers off into dirt road after less than a mile, two men are felling a street sign. That's what it looks like—one is hacking away at the wooden base with an ax. Jody debates whether crossing the empty street would just draw more attention to herself. But she sees a yellow city truck parked nearby, floodlight in the bed, and decides it's not vandalism, though that doesn't necessarily mean she is safe.

"Evening," one of them says. The one holding the sign for the chopper. He has a big handlebar mustache, like stagecoach robber in a western, or maybe the town banker.

" 'Lo," she replies.

The other one looks up. She knows him from the mill, Tom North, one of two Toms. He looks a little like what she imagines her youngest brother must look like by now, with deep red hair and a face that's just starting to lose its baby fat at 29.

"What're you doing?" she can't help but ask.

"Just a little freelance work for the city," North says proudly. "Mayor Clarkson himself wants these old signs replaced."

"In the middle of the night?" Jody asks. The man with the mustache glares at her from beneath his hard hat. She is questioning the city, and he sees himself as the city.

"Guess he didn't want us disrupting traffic," North says with a shrug.

Jody nods and looks up at the old sign. *Calla Blvd.* is carved in relief on the plank of wood, the raised letters painted white and peeling. *Silver St.* juts out at a 90 degree angle. The new sign lies on the sidewalk, a thin metal pole and two metal signs, white letters on a blue background. One sign says *Silver St.* The other says *N. Main St.*

Tom North *would* hammer the wrong sign into the ground.

"Hey, North, no offense," Jody says, "but Main Street is down that-a-way. We're on Calla."

He looks over his shoulder and says, "Shit." But the bank robber says, "We've got the right sign, lady. Or whatever you are. They're changing the name."

"You're joking, right? What kind of town has two Main Streets?"

"*This* kind of town," says the stagecoach robber. "Or the kind it's gonna be."

Jody has always liked the name Calla Boulevard. She doesn't know where it comes from, but she remembers the story about calla lilies filling Lilac Ambrose's empty coffin at her funeral. The street has always seemed beautiful and sad to her, like her mother singing "Molly Malone."

"But why are they changing it?"

Tom North's face brightens in the yellow floodlight. He has remembered something, she can tell. "Mayor Clarkson said—well, the deputy mayor actually, Bill Heib, he said we ain't gonna have a street named after some dead girl no more, it's bad luck."

"But we have a whole *town* named after a dead girl."

"No, not Lilac," North says patronizingly. " 'Nother dead girl, I guess. Someone named Calla Holmes or something. Bill Heib called her 'Lilac's little friend,' but I don't know if he meant it like they were really actual friends or they were both just, you know, dead."

"Shut up, North," says the stagecoach robber. "You're gonna get us in trouble."

"Yeah, what's *she* gonna do?" huffs Tom North.

The men pant in the thin, cold night. She's still not sure why they're out so late, why they're chopping down the old sign instead of digging it up at the base. They're phantom workers, urging her to forget she saw them, laboring for a different world governed by odd rules.

"I'm not doing anything, fellows," she says in a low voice. " 'Night."

She walks briskly up Calla—up North Main—past the shuttered shops and cooling bars. Is Calla Boulevard really named after a second dead girl, she wonders? Or is Tom North just getting things wrong, which wouldn't be new for him? Of course, every town must have plenty of dead girls, when you think about it. In the 19th century, people died of the flu and infected hangnails, not to mention a catalog of diseases that

Jody can only name in her grandmother's voice. Smallpox and scarlet fever and consumption. Children starved and swooned and were buried without anything being named after them.

It's as if the town is preparing itself for a big date, polishing its shoes and practicing its how-do-you-do's. In February, Petra gets a phone call from Mayor Clarkson. When she hangs up, she says, "Can you believe it? They want to sponsor the festival. *Our* festival." The women gathered in the main room of the church are silent as they try to picture Mayor Clarkson up to his elbows in tie-dye. They don't know whether to be flattered or frightened.

Essie drives to Berkeley and, on her way back, sees a highway billboard that says, *Come to Lilac Mines for Old-Town Charm and Modern Convenience!* There's a cartoon of a haunted house with a ghost girl oozing from one of its windows, next to a map and a bubble announcing, *Just off Route 49!* "Poor Lilac," Essie reports. "Pimped by Clarkson and his goons."

They discuss the possibility of a protest—"Of what, exactly?" Jody asks—but by early March it becomes clear the date is off, with no help from them.

Jody is at work, studying her eye in the bathroom mirror. The skin around it is the color of the sky after a storm, purple-gray with swells of yellow. Last week, when Zeke Espey's fist hit her cheekbone with a solid *thwack*, it was a red, puffed-up fish, then it turned into a blue flame threatening to start a wildfire.

She only wishes she had been fighting *for* something in particular. Imogen, say. Not that most of the men she works with know about Imogen. But it was just a bar fight at Lou's. The boys were restless because the mill hadn't hired anyone new in months, not their friends or brothers or sons, and everyone was overworked, and there were rumors that something worse might be around the corner. Jody knew that times like these were not good for people like her. People like Zeke started to look at the handful of strong, callused women who'd worked beside them for years and think, *Hey, what's she doing here?*

There's a restlessness beneath the town's new sheen. Like the rivers of capillaries that pulse beneath the stone-smooth skin of her eye. She presses her index finger against her swollen eyelid, wincing. The small mirror in the washroom at the mill is flecked with paint and grime. The men share a larger bathroom just off the main work hall, but the mill was built without a women's room, so Jody and Gapi and Jennifer—who also lives with them at the old church—use a converted outhouse five minutes and a foot of snow from the building. At breaks, they tromp over together and pee fast while the men drink coffee.

"Hurry up, Jo! We have got one minute left," Gapi calls. "Remember what Rig say about the next person who is late."

The three women cast short shadows as they make their way back to the main building. Like Jody, Gapi is tall, with wide hips and torso. She's a little lazy, smokes pot almost every evening, but she does what she has to do without complaining. Jennifer is Linda's cousin. She moved to Lilac Mines with her baby last year, leaving her alcoholic husband in Sacramento. She's their first real straight girl, although she talks a lot about lesbianism, like it's a book she just hasn't gotten around to reading yet. She is small but tough, with a tight twist of dark hair and crowded teeth that look like they could take a gleeful bite out of anyone. When the three women approach the hall, they're surprised by silence, not hearing the sound of saws or talking and laughing men. The sun burns distantly above them, and the snow squeaks beneath their feet. They exchange glances. Jody opens the door as quickly and quietly as possible.

"...Damned environmentalists," Rigby Clarkson is saying. He's standing next to Wayland Clarkson, his younger brother and the president of the mill. The workers are crescented around them.

"Hang on, Rig," Wayland calls down to his brother. He is standing on a stool, looking ridiculous in suit pants, dress shirt, and tie. "As I was saying, a team of environmental scientists, some guys from the government, recently discovered that this part of the Sierras is home to a rare type of moth. Little green thing, has some long Latin name. And apparently it *only* lives here, in these sugar pines, only breathes this type of air. According to these scientists and the government, we're destroying this moth's 'habitat.' The short version is—I won't mess around with you here—the mill's closing."

Wayland's fists are balled in his pockets. He studies the rafters above where the workers are standing. No one speaks for a minute. Then everyone does. Questions and shouts and shoves. They are a bear shaking off months of hibernation.

"Folks, folks!" Wayland calls out from his stool, but no one hears him. Rig puts his fingers in his mouth and tries to whistle, but only air comes out. He settles for yelling, "Shut up!"

"Folks," Wayland continues, "I want you to know you'll all be given a generous severance package. Two weeks of pay."

Jody's heartbeat slows slightly. Her grandmother gave her two weeks, years ago, and she found a job at the umbrella factory in one. Moved to a boarding house in ten days. The workers try to hook Wayland, but he's out the door, their questions rolling off his body like water off a freshly waxed car. Jody keeps her eyes, the good one and the blackened one, on the sawdust-covered floor. She is sure that if she looks at any of the men right now, she will see what she saw on Zeke Espey's face last week magnified ten times.

"I think I will hurl," Gapi whispers.

Jennifer blinks and blinks. Jody knows that the long days at the mill have kept her sane over the past months. It was the slow, hard rhythm of pushing log to blade that kept Jody going two years ago, when she learned that Imogen was sleeping with Petra. At home she was a witness to what seemed like a crime—Imogen's low chuckle snuggling up against Petra's young, nonchalant body—but at the mill she was exactly who she was supposed to be. When Imogen eventually chose Jody, the mill stayed the same. That was its beauty. "Let's get our stuff and go," Jody says.

When everyone is home, the church is too crowded. Jody and Imogen bicker; somehow the subject of Petra always comes up. And then she comes up literally, smiling in a doorway, spilling an armful of groceries onto the kitchen counter.

"Brie?" Jody says. "We can't afford *brie*."

"How else am I supposed to make *quiche au fromage?*" Petra asks. She is 25 years old, but Jody has decided that college girls don't age the same way other people do. Jody remembers her mother at what must have been the same age: a flurry of efficient hands, chopping carrots, stuffing small limbs into winter coats. Mrs. Clatterbuck kept her hair under a scarf. She lived off leftovers—chicken necks and potato skins and reused bacon grease—and she looked like it: pieced together but undeniably useful. Petra, on the other hand, still opens her eyes wide when she asks questions, still giggles, still spends slow mornings braiding her buttery hair.

Nine people live in the church. A couple have left. Marilyn took a job as a professor up north in Washington, and Emily left after she and Essie broke up. In Emily's absence, Essie has blossomed into a real person. She revamped the chore chart and struck up correspondence with other women's groups in Oregon and Massachusetts, bringing back tips on gardening and mediating fights. She was like a proud fisherwoman, presenting her catch and frying it up. In addition to Jennifer, there is Jennifer's daughter Christy, and a woman named Athena—not her real name, but one borrowed from a goddess she does a fairly poor job of emulating.

With the three mill workers home all day, the church is claustrophobic. Heat doesn't circulate well, and Jody spends her days moving from hot patches to icy ones. Christy toddles down the hall, away from her irritable mother, drooling on raw yams or handmade toys and howling when Jody or one of the other women trips over her. Linda brings home a cat. Petra complains because it is male, Jody complains because it eats and eats. The baby loves the cat, but the cat hates the baby.

"Think of it as a good thing," Imogen says one Saturday night, over the too-loud chords of Athena's guitar. "It was a shame cutting down all those trees anyway. We've been wanting to be independent for a long time." She unties her hair, and her Afro bursts out of its ponytail, glad to be home from the office.

"But we're not independent, we're just poor," Jody says. She feels like she's always saying this. "You still work for Dr. Tracy, and he's still a pervert. How does *that* help our independence?"

"I know," Imogen sighs. "But I'm the only one of us who has access to any kind of medicine. I like knowing I could score us some antibiotics in a pinch, you know?"

In the main room, an argument between Gapi and Linda competes with Athena's guitar. It's not long before Christy starts crying, and Jennifer yells at Gapi and Linda for upsetting her daughter.

"I can't take it anymore," says Jody, retrieving her coat from the old refrigerator they use as a wardrobe. "I'm going out."

"Can I come?" Imogen smiles, but she doesn't move. She takes in all the chaos of the colony like she's watching a sitcom: sort of silly, not especially like life, but worth tuning in for again and again.

Everyone is at Lou's. Everyone except those who are at Lilac's, who make a point of avoiding Lou's, especially in groups large enough to draw attention. There are still a handful of gay girls that the colony has not lured in and the town has not driven away, but Jody doesn't feel like seeing them tonight either. She keeps her coat and scarf on, and slides onto a stool at the end of Lou's recently refinished bar. Her hands are stiff from the cold. She rubs them together and wonders if the calluses will disappear or if work is now inseparable from her body.

She recognizes a few guys from the mill. They've clearly been drinking for hours, and she decides not to say hello. When someone taps her on the shoulder, she turns around reluctantly. But it's not a mill worker, it's Luke Twentyman, who Meg has worked for on and off over the years. He's wearing a brown suit and a tie, and stands very straight. The mill guys wear jeans and stoop to phantom logs.

"Sorry to bother you, ma'am," Mr. Twentyman says. Jody has never liked being called "ma'am." She's not sure if it makes her feel old or excessively female. "Aren't you a friend of Meg Almond's?"

Jody looks around. She's not sure how much Mr. Twentyman knows about Meg. "Yes," she says slowly. Also, she and Imogen haven't seen much of Meg recently. It's hard to spend time with her and not fall into the halo of intensity that burns around her. Always something with a girl, some adventure, some injustice.

"Well, I just wanted to see how she was doing, what she was up to," says Mr. Twentyman. "Thing is, she was supposed to do some work for me this week, but I haven't seen her. That's not like her."

"No offense, sir, but that *is* like her. Lately, at least. She's gone off a few times on trips with—friends."

"Sure, sure," Mr. Twentyman nods. His dark eyes dart about the bar. He's around 50, Jody guesses; his tan skin is smooth over probing cheekbones, but his hair is almost white. "Too bad. I coulda used Meg this week—she's so organized, and I've got a lot of work to do. *Lot* of work," he adds, and Jody can tell he wants to talk about what he's working on. She remembers Meg's stories. Mr. Twentyman always wanted to expose some corrupt local official or investigate some ancient mystery. Usually nothing came of it. He would move on to the next scandal, or people would get tired of talking to him.

"What sort of work're you doing?" Jody asks. She nods for the bartender to refill her glass.

"Interesting you should ask. I can tell from your hands and your manner of dress that you work at the mill, no?"

"Worked."

"Right. Worked," Mr. Twentyman says, narrowing his eyes. "I've got a scoop that would be of interest to you… to a lot of folks here. But that's exactly why I can't discuss it."

"Okay then." Jody wonders if the colony has quieted down for the night. She wants to crawl in bed beside Imogen. Their room—there are real rooms now, built by Jody—is one of the ones that overheats. She'll strip down to boxer shorts and slide her hands up Imogen's dark brown thighs, warm and waiting beneath the cotton sheet. Imogen has one of those bodies that thickens with age but doesn't lose its shape; she is a delicious second helping of herself.

"Well, I suppose I could let you in on it, but we can't talk here." Mr. Twentyman takes Jody's arm like a gentleman and she follows him to the alley behind the bar. Jody feels the glassy eyes of the guys watching the old Indian in the suit and the woman with the blonde crew cut walking as if they're on their way to the dance floor. She clenches her free fist. The alley is gray with sludgy snow. The sky is clear and full of stars, as if pleading innocent to ever having inflicted foul weather on the town.

"It's freezing out here, sir. Tell me quick."

"*Inga clarkei*," Mr. Twentyman says. At first Jody thinks he's talking about one of the Clarksons, a female maybe. After a dramatic pause, he continues, "Western sugar moth. Little bugger likes to hang around our trees. Feeds off the flowers that grow at the base of sugar pines, those little white wildflowers you see all over the mountain every spring. Sucks up that nectar like it's a dry martini. When they're drunk they curl up on some bit o' bark and snooze a while."

"Right," says Jody, still confused, "except I guess we're cutting down the trees, and now they're endangered, 'cause that's the only place they can 'snooze.' "

"No!" Mr. Twentyman shouts triumphantly. He quickly lowers his voice. "No. That's the northern bark moth. *Inga lunaris*. It actually eats pine needles. But more importantly, it's only found in Oregon, Washington, and the southwestern part of Canada. I caught a couple of our little green moths myself, snuffed them out good. I figured they weren't too endangered yet. But then when I compared them with field guide photos of the northern bark moth, I discovered our boys, *inga clarkei*, weren't endangered at all."

Snooty environmentalists still traipse through Jody's head. They all look like Petra in a lab coat. She pulls her jacket tight around her, and clarifies, "So they closed the mill to save a moth that doesn't even live here? That just has a twin here?"

"Bingo."

Jody can hear faint music coming from Lilac's around the corner on Calla Boulevard. It's "The Night the Lights Went Out in Georgia." "That's *great* news!" she says. "You just have to show the Clarksons, or the scientists or whoever, and they won't have to close the mill!"

"Not that easy, I'm afraid. Let me ask you something: Did you sign any papers when they canned you?"

"Yeah, some stuff to make sure we got our—what did they call it?—

our severance pay."

Mr. Twentyman shakes his head. "I won't bore you with the details, ma'am, but you're not getting your job back. None of you are. Truth is, the wood and the work are better and cheaper up in Oregon. The mill owners want to move there, but they knew if word got out, they'd have the whole town to answer to."

Jody has never felt a kinship with the guys at the mill. She stays out of their way, and they respect her thick-for-a-girl biceps. But suddenly she wishes they were large enough to be a union shop. She wants to spill the news, to rally with them in the cold dark night. They'll storm the Clarksons' big house on the western edge of town, chop it down like a giant tree.

"And so what if it gets out now?" Jody asks.

"If it gets out now, it's just a story," Mr. Twentyman says. "But what a story. I'm working on it." He pats her on the shoulder.

Something about the gesture makes Jody ask, "Mr. Twentyman? You do a lot of research about things that happened in Lilac Mines, right?"

"Surely do."

"Can I ask you a question? Have you ever heard of someone named Calla Holmes? Who might have been Lilac's friend?"

Mr. Twentyman looks at the black sky. His face twitches as he pages through mental files. "Calla Holmes? Oh, well, there's a Calla Hogan, of course. The Hogan newspaper family's girl. I've got a picture of all of them back at my office. Good-looking family, although the first wife— Calla's mother—died of scarlet fever, but quite a family. Newsmakers, literally. Wise not to seek their fortune in mining. Mining is so unreliable. But the news, that'll always be there, good or bad. And if there's no news, you just make something up!" He laughs. "They were the Clarksons of their day. Almost."

"But you don't know whether Lilac and Calla knew each other?"

"I don't know that they didn't," Mr. Twentyman says. "Hard to prove a negative."

"Well, thanks."

"You give me a call if you hear from Meg," he says. "I'm listed." He leaves, walking down the alley, looking over his shoulder in fear of spies behind trashcans, or in hopes of them.

Jody has just promised not to tell Mr. Twentyman's secret, but it seems that it is her secret, too. She is the one with a troublesome shoulder and torn-up hands. And no job. Maybe she could discuss the matter with one person, someone reliable. Maybe it's not too late. She slips back inside the bar and scans the room. A man she recognizes but doesn't know well is kissing the old Bettie Page poster that hangs over the row of tall tables at the back of the bar. His friends are egging him on. He tongues the glass and sloshes beer. She keeps looking. Zeke Espey is hunched over an empty shot glass at the bar. She hopes he hasn't seen her. A couple of guys are here with their wives. They're the most likely to behave themselves, but Jody isn't sure what to do with them. Is she supposed to greet the wives as one of their husbands' co-workers or as a fellow female? Finally she spots Tom Barratucci sitting at one of the shorter tables near the front of the bar. Tom is part Indian, part Italian, part something else. A mix of dark things. He's sort of the de facto black man at the mill—the guys alternate between baffled reverence and overly barbed ribbing. And Jody, in turn, watches him from afar. They could never be friends—that would be asking for trouble—so *she* alternates between empathy and calculated distance. But tonight she says, "Hey Tom."

He nods. He doesn't offer her the other chair at his table. There are two empty glasses in front of him, and she wonders if he's here with someone. "With" is ambiguous in Lilac Mines. You can go to a bar alone and find yourself with everyone you know. Tom's eyes are red beneath long lashes that Jody never got close enough to notice before. Curls of dark hair are matted against his forehead, like little Christy's hair when she wakes up from her nap. "What do you want, Clatterbuck?" he asks gruffly.

The baby-fine hairs on the back of Jody's neck act as antennae that sense hostility, people who are insulted by the mere presence of a dyke. The hairs have gotten coarser over the years, but they still know things before her brain does. She takes a step back from the table, but continues. "I heard something about the layoffs is all. About how the 'endangered species'…"

Tom's lips peel back, and she sees that his teeth are long and yellow. "You know who should be an endangered species, Clatterbuck?" He says her name like an epithet. "Fucking dykes. You think the Clarksons wanna stay in a town that's turning into a hippie commune? I know you live with them. You think folks like it that you're taking over the mill, bringing more and more of your hairy girlfriends there each year?"

Jody thinks about how she urged Linda and Essie to apply for work there, even as receptionists or bookkeepers. But they sided with Petra. Their environmental consciences would let them spend the money Jody bought home, but not actually *see* a tree slaughtered.

"We're not taking over, we're just working, same as you," Jody says, but she's seen this look before. It's a no-turning-back look. Tom's hands are shaking. He's had to work up the courage to be mean, and now that it's turned him into something else, he will run through the forest, biting.

Jody can bite back. She knows how to let words like Tom's blow past her like a wildfire, just hot enough to singe her skin and get her mad, not close enough to burn her. She gave Zeke Espey a fat lip that made him lisp like a sissy. But tonight she doesn't have the energy to fight for the same thing she always fights for, which is nothing at all. Not with quiet, distraught Tom Barratucci. Tonight she is 36 years old and her shoulder hurts. "Never mind," she says. "See ya around." His snarl follows her out the door.

Jody makes her way through brown snow-sludge to her Edsel. She has never been as riveted by Lilac as others are. She went to Petra's ridiculous séance in the woods a few years ago because she knew Jean wouldn't be able to stand being the only butch there. But the past has never seemed particularly useful to Jody. It's either painful or pointless, stuff for college professors to debate as they polish their thick glasses.

Now, though, she wonders why Lilac got a whole town and Calla— if she was really Lilac's friend—just got one street. And what she died of. Jody wonders why the northern bark moth is worth saving, but the western sugar moth is just a pawn. She thinks of environmentalism as another hobby for people with too much free time, but on a logical level she wonders: if the western sugar moth is *not* endangered, but they keep chopping down the trees it naps in, will it *become* endangered? Will the western sugar moth be punished for surviving and reproducing and not complaining? Except it won't be, because it's masquerading as the northern bark moth. It's pretending to be something more precious, and whoever decides these things has decided to save it.

THE PATRON SAINT OF TRAVELERS
Anna Lisa: Fresno, 1974

Anna Lisa comes home late from her hospital nursing internship at Saint Julian's. She chose the hospital after her classmate Letty Quintero told her, "Saint Julian the Hospitaller is the patron saint of travelers and hotelkeepers and murderers and clowns." It has proven to be a good choice, leaving her too tired to think at the end of the day.

Terry is late too; he's grading tests again. Two years ago, he sold The Quill Pen and started teaching elementary school. He just had to take a couple of exams, having minored in primary education in college, a fact Anna Lisa didn't know until he announced his career shift. He took on 25 fifth graders and stopped bothering Anna Lisa about having a baby. She was relieved, of course, but also saddened. She missed him having hope in her. She takes a TV dinner out of the freezer and puts it in the oven and waits. The house is quiet. She wishes she had a dog. Outside a layer of thick Valley mist muffles her May flowers. There are ten minutes left on her meatloaf in the oven when the phone rings.

"May I speak with Anna Lisa Hill?" The woman's voice is deep, and awkwardly formal.

"Speaking... Well, it's Kristalovich now, but, yes, that's me."

"Al?"

"Meg?" The voice on the other end of the line is not Meg's, but this is what Anna Lisa says, as if she's playing the word-association game that terrified her in Psychology 100.

"Did you hear, then?" says the woman.

"Hear what?"

"About Meg. Al, it's Jody Clatterbuck." As if there might be other deep-voiced Jodys in her life these days.

"Jody! Wow, are you still in Lilac Mines?"

"Yeah, but not for long. The mill closed in March, and no one here has any money. Imogen and I are gonna look for a place in San Francisco. It'll be weird to live in a real city, but I dunno, maybe it'll be okay. Everyone's getting outta here. Even Petra… the girl is stubborn, but she ain't strong."

"Who's Petra?"

"That's right, she came after your time. Anyway, Al, I called because Meg… so you didn't hear?"

"No, hear what? Who would I have heard from? Meg and I haven't talked in years."

"Right. Well… Um…. God…."

Anna Lisa watches the clock above the oven. In six minutes her meatloaf will be done. The green beans, the nubbly corn, and the chocolate pudding that will burn her tongue because she'll try to eat it first. Except in six minutes she might never feel like eating again.

"Al," Jody says quietly. "She killed herself."

Because there is something growing inside of Anna Lisa. It was planted a long time ago and Jody's words are a bullet, puncturing the bulb and releasing the thing that wanted to grow. It fills her stomach and climbs her throat. She makes a choking sound into the mouthpiece of the phone.

"She hung herself. We should've seen it coming. I mean, sometimes she was fine and all, but…" Jody's voice is full of anger and regret. But it's the "we" that Anna Lisa hears. There's a group of them, out there in Lilac Mines, to hold each other up as their limbs turn to liquid, to keep each other from washing down the mountainside.

"When did it happen?" Anna Lisa says finally. This seems important. She cannot grasp certain things right now, not yet, so she will focus on the details.

"Last week. Thursday night, we think. We would have called you sooner..." Her voice trails off. Meaning, *but no one thought of it.* Anna Lisa had been gone almost eight years. What was five more nights? Anna Lisa works backward. Last night she studied for her cell biology exam. Sunday night she and Terry ate seven-seas casserole in front of the TV. Friday and Saturday nights she spent assembling wedding decorations with Suzy, who is in town for her wedding to an engineer named Martin Ketay. And Thursday night Anna Lisa stayed late at the hospital, hanging bright prints she'd found at the Salvation Army on the walls because she thought the place could use a little cheer. During each of those activities, Meg was already dead.

"What time?" Anna Lisa asks. She wants it to have been when she was doing something meaningful. She wants to have felt a chill in the hushed hospital corridors, or to have been hanging a picture Meg would have loved.

"No one knows," Jody says. "We saw her at Lilac's on Wednesday. She was her regular self, kind of drunk and quiet."

Except this is not Meg's regular self, as far as Anna Lisa is concerned. Meg is talkative. Meg dances.

"Essie went over there, 'cause, well, actually Meg and Essie had sort of been getting together. They weren't a couple or anything—Meg would only go for butches—but Essie got this haircut a couple of weeks back and, who knows, maybe Meg started to look at her different. Anyway, Essie went over there Friday morning. She had some zucchini bread that Linda made. She could hear some music inside, but Meg didn't come to the door. So she opened it. Meg never locked it—we always told her that was stupid, living alone in the mountains. So Essie found her—" Anna Lisa doesn't know who Essie is, or Linda.

Jody's voice trips over itself. It has been trotting along on the details, but now it slows, as if climbing a steep trail. "Hanging from... you remember that wardrobe she had? I guess she tied a rope... somehow... and she was... stiff. Essie said her face was blue and her neck had... Anyway, we think it happened Thursday night."

The timer on the stove buzzes. An alarm going off in another world, where time still exists. Anna Lisa lets the vibration bore through her as she stands still, feet rooted to the linoleum, hand gripping the yellow receiver. All these years, she's pictured Meg as she was in 1965. A fitted dress made of some slightly rough material that might make Anna Lisa's skin break out if she touched it. Wavy brown hair begging to be mussed by sex. Bessie Smith spinning. Pulp novel splayed on her soft patchwork quilt. Meg frozen, not at absolute zero where molecules stop moving, but a commonplace sort of frozen, where they buzz about but don't really change. It occurs to Anna Lisa that, in this way, she has already killed Meg. Made her hover there, a memory.

"Was there a note?" she asks. She wants to hear that there were pages and pages addressed to *My Darling Anna Lisa*. She'd accept the guilt in exchange for proof of her own existence.

"No," says Jody. "No note."

And what happens now? Anna Lisa is moving through something thick, like water or a dream or smoke. What do people do when someone removes herself from time?

Anna Lisa chokes, "Funeral?"

"A funeral? No. I mean, we had a little service for her here at the colony. Sunday night. But Petra got a hold of Meg's father—they grew up in the same town, you know—and her... body was shipped back there."

Anna Lisa thinks of Meg flying over the thawing mountains, Midwestern farmland, places Anna Lisa has only seen in pictures.

"I guess they'll have some kind of funeral for her there. She hadn't talked to her father in years. Petra said he yelled at her, as if she was the one who made Meg come out to California. Even though Petra was in fucking junior high school when Meg left."

"And what did you do at, uh, the colony?" Anna Lisa asks.

"Oh, it was nothing, I'm sorry we didn't call, Al, really. God." Jody pauses. "This woman, Athena, sang. I hate her songs, actually, they're sissy songs, all about flowers and peace. Meg would have hated it."

Jody's voice is pulling Anna Lisa through a burning building. She has to keep calling "Marco" to Jody's "Polo" as her lungs fill with smoke. "And you... you're moving? You and Imogen?"

Jody takes this as a cue to return to a tougher cadence. "Yeah. She's sadder about it than I am. Her heart was more in the colony. But no money is no money, you know? At first the city tried to make all these little improvements—new street signs and stuff—but then I guess the Clarksons decided it would be easier to just start over somewhere else. There was a fire at the Lilac Mines Hotel a couple of weeks ago. People are saying someone did it for the insurance. Who wants to stick around Lilac Mines now anyway?"

A small voice inside Anna Lisa says, *I do*. "Could I visit you and Imogen?" she asks. She says it humbly, but she's sure that Jody will say yes. It will be as it was a dozen years ago, Jody's strong, thick arms welcoming her, initiating her. "Either at your new place or before you go?"

There is a silence. The thing in Anna Lisa's stomach and throat pushes and pushes. Jody says, "I don't think that would be a good idea." Anna Lisa recognizes it as the voice Jody used to talk to men at the mill, the ones she feared and did not respect.

"But it's been so long," Anna Lisa protests. "You can't still…"

"Al. You *left*. You left Meg and Lilac Mines and us. That's fine, okay, I mean, that was your decision." Jody pauses. "Anyhow, I thought you should know what happened. I'm calling all Meg's exes."

And so while Jody has stayed the same gruff nurturer in Anna Lisa's mind, Anna Lisa sees that she has changed in Jody's. She arrived in Lilac Mines an innocent, the victim of a world that never even gave her a word for what she was, but now she has Meg's blood on her hands. Jody is calling to fill her in on a part of the story she has missed, out of respect for Meg's past, but she's not inviting Anna Lisa to join the next chapter. Shakily, Anna Lisa puts the receiver back on its hook. She waits to begin breathing again.

When she finally takes her dinner out of the oven, it is small and hard and black, and the gust from the oven is so hot she thinks her eyelashes are melting. She is disappointed, in a way, that the smoke is a result of something so mundane. That the world has not bent and burned as a result of Meg's departure from it.

She eats two slices of plain bread. Although she can't quite taste them, she marvels at how the chewed up food slides down her esophagus. It seems as if her throat should collapse, in sympathy. But all the proper valves open and let it into her stomach, where it sits patiently, waiting to be broken down by a pond of yellow bile. All these functions work, as if Meg is not dead. She keeps waiting for the world to end. While she waits, she flips through pictures of eggs and bunnies in *Woman's Day*. She turns the TV on and then off. She makes a wobbly list of names on a crumpled supermarket receipt: Gertrude, Isabella, Persephone, Carmen, Natasha. She goes to the bathroom and vomits her chewed-up food into the toilet. Terry is still at school. He stays and stays. Until 8 o'clock, 9 o'clock.

Anna Lisa studies the picture of Meg that she keeps between eggplant and bell pepper in *Jewels on the Vine: Exotic Vegetables that Anyone Can Grow*. She took it that day they drove all the way to Columbia. They drank sarsaparilla at the old-fashioned soda fountain, then whiskey at a biker bar. It was happy hour, but almost empty. Anna Lisa had to pee on the way back, so they pulled over to the side of the road. She found a tree skirted by tall, soft new plants. Then she found her camera in Meg's trunk and took the picture. Meg smiles brilliantly into the mountains. Not at Anna Lisa. Not then, not now.

Maybe, Anna Lisa thinks, *the world is not ending because it is waiting for me to end it.* If she carries on like usual, Meg will never be dead; she'll just remain another thing Anna Lisa is deprived of. It would be so easy to keep Meg at her cool, back-of-the-mind temperature. But for the first time the thought of carrying on like usual seems unbearable. *Why should Meg have all the fun and all the tragedy?* she thinks bitterly. She cannot let the world progress without her any longer. More than she needs to be part of the gay world or the straight world, she needs to be part of the turning world, the one that spins and shakes and explodes under the weight of history. A surge of energy replaces her bread-and-magazines numbness. She begins to pull clothes from her closet. Jeans and tops and coats and scrubs. The blouse with the billowy collar that Terry loves, the mannish brown button-down he hates. The sea-foam bridesmaid dress she's supposed to wear at Suzy's wedding next Sunday. She piles them on the bed like dozens of flat, sleeping bodies. In the back of the closet she finds a duffel bag, crumpled and dusty from years of not traveling.

Ending the world means finding the end of the world. Going to it: the mining town that's always threatening to slip down the mountain. It is running to, not running away. She will no longer hide in the world's crevices, where she is dry and safe but so constrained that her bones have grown to match the shape of her cage.

It's just after ten when she arrives at her parents' house. Suzy answers the door with her hair half straight, half curled. She is wedding-thin, dressed in a bright pink, flowered nightgown. She manages to radiate maturity and youth at the same time, the trick of a 27-year-old bride.

"Oh, hi," Suzy says. "I'm worried my hair won't hold the curl long enough to take pictures and everything. What do you think?" As if there's nothing strange about her sister showing up unannounced so late at night. As if the hair gods heard her prayer and summoned an advisor. Anna Lisa pushes past her and into the living room, where Martin is tying bows on bunches of dried flowers. Weddings are like funerals: the flowers and the expensive cloth and the longing.

"Hey, Anna Lisa," Martin says, his face displaying a resigned sort of surprise.

Anna Lisa sits on the arm of the couch. She doesn't want to let herself get too comfortable. "I came by because, uh, remember when I lived in Lilac Mines all those years ago?"

"Sure." Suzy wrinkles her eyebrows. She's just beginning to take in Anna Lisa's puffy face and mish-mash of clothing: pink nursing pants, Fresno State sweatshirt, snow boots.

"Well, I just got some news. My... my girlfriend, from back then, she died." She said it. Girlfriend and Died. The good thing that led to the terrible thing that could, maybe, lead to another good thing.

"Oh, Nannalee." Suzy's voice is sweet and sunken. It's the first time she's ever called Anna Lisa "Nannalee" to comfort her, rather than to be comforted. She hugs Anna Lisa so tight that she teeters on the edge of the couch, and it seems that she knows Anna Lisa didn't mean "girlfriend" the way that most girls would. "What was her name?"

"Meg," Anna Lisa says. The name bursts from her mouth and

crumples as soon as it touches air. Is this the thing that was growing inside her, demanding to live in the world? It's taken everything to say it. She is exhausted by the effort, and slumps against Suzy's tanned shoulders. Anna Lisa's parents are in the doorway, groggy from near-sleep.

"Not more wedding hysterics," Eudora Hill sighs. She is happy and relieved that her youngest daughter is getting married, but she has declared frequently that she's too old for the fuss of a big wedding. The implication is that Suzy should be too old to *make* a big fuss as well.

"No, mother, it's Anna Lisa. Her—friend—passed away."

"My girlfriend died," Anna Lisa repeats. The two words seem linked now. As if her freedom and her tragedy cannot exist separately from one another. *My husband Terry is alive,* she thinks. The ugly reciprocal.

"I'm going away. Back to Lilac Mines, I'm not sure for how long," she announces.

"After the wedding?" Anna Lisa's father says, still sleepy.

"No, now. Suzy, I'm sorry. But I have to go."

"Is there a funeral?" Eudora asks, puzzled.

"No, it's not that…"

"It's a friend from a long time ago, right?" Eudora continues. "Maybe you could send some flowers. People will understand that you can't miss your sister's *wedding.* Not when you're the matron of honor."

"But I loved her," Anna Lisa protests. "And it's more than that—"

"Well, your friend isn't going anywhere now," Gerald Hill grouches.

"Gerald, don't be tasteless," Eudora says. She takes Anna Lisa's hands in hers. Her arthritic fingers are knobby and reassuring, like the exposed roots of the black oak tree in their backyard. "Surely you could wait a week," she says to Anna Lisa.

"All I've done is wait," Anna Lisa pleads. "Please understand. I was in love with Meg."

She watches her mother's face. Something moves behind her eyes, like a fish swimming far below the water's surface. She puts her lips together. She drops Anna Lisa's hands.

"Meg. Was she the one who gave you that strange present at your shower?" Eudora asks searchingly.

"Yes! The desert glass." It was the last thing Anna Lisa put in her duffel bag. It was like dragging her heart to the car.

"Well." Eudora is quiet. Anna Lisa can see her face hardening, second by second, and she wants to tell her mother, *Don't think that way. It's so much work. It will rip you apart.* "Well," Eudora says again, "obviously Meg was a troubled young lady. I don't know what kind of shenanigans she talked you into as a teenager, but I hardly think they're worth missing your *sister's wedding* for."

Suzy's face is torn up, blotchy beneath her half-halo of gold-streaked curls. She understands: this is Anna Lisa's turn. "Mother, Daddy," Suzy says, "it's really okay." She guides them to the couch. Martin blinks and moves over. "Nannalee needs to go. I'll still have Marla and June. Marla will be thrilled to be promoted to matron of honor. Anna Lisa is so good, she always does such nice things for all of us."

"Like run away and leave us to worry about her for more than a year?" Eudora demands.

"Mother, please," Suzy replies calmly, "that's old news."

Eudora's eyes are pond-blue and ready to spill over. "And what does Terry think about all this?"

Anna Lisa doesn't answer. She understands the ache of old news. It's why she lets Suzy do the explaining, and walks slowly and decisively out the front door and into the night.

Chester A. Arthur Elementary is just two years old, a squat, mustard-colored building guarded by topiaries in the shape of zoo animals. *One of the Forgettable Presidents,* Terry explained, *that's what they're actually called.* The night is mild too. The air feels delicate, as if it could easily be pushed toward summer-hot or icy-cold. Terry's classroom is in the first of three short hallways, between a hippo and a giraffe. There's a yellow glow coming from the high windows. So he's here. Anna Lisa half thought he wouldn't be. In a way, she's relieved—the world is spinning around her, but Terry is still Terry, a man who pours all his unfulfilled desires into red smiley faces at the top of arithmetic tests. The door is locked, so she knocks. "It's me," she calls.

"Annie, what a surprise," he says. The classroom is chilly, but Terry's cheeks are pink above the beard he's recently grown. He keeps it neatly trimmed and the effect is distinguished, as if he teaches college students rather than fifth graders. *He'd be a good catch for someone,* Anna Lisa thinks. She feels very far away from him, although he's inches from her face. He kisses her lightly on the lips. She hasn't gotten more than a peck on the cheek in a while. He smells like Windex, or maybe the whole classroom does. He looks at her expectantly.

"I got a phone call," she says.

"Is it your father?" Terry would never admit to being superstitious, but he has a habit of calling out bad fortune before it can manifest.

"No."

"Is it…?"

"Terry, just listen. It was Jody, she's an old friend of mine from Lilac Mines."

"From where?" Terry always forgets. She's given him a vague account of her year there, but for him it holds the same weight as the year she took Latin. It might be any year, just a handful of days.

"Lilac Mines, the town I lived in."

"Right. I'm sorry, Annie, these tests have made me really preoccupied." The big teacher's desk behind him is empty except for a blotter and a pencil holder decorated with macaroni. "So… Jody."

"She called and told me that another friend of mine, Meg, that she, well… committed suicide." When she speaks, it sounds like blasphemy. "She killed herself, and… and actually, she was my girlfriend."

"Annie, that's terrible." He takes her burning face in his hands. She feels like she's trapped in a vice.

"Not my girlfriend like Nancy-Jane," Anna Lisa says quickly. "I mean, she was my…" Anna Lisa can't bear to hurt him. "She's dead and I have to go back to Lilac Mines."

Terry's hands fall to his sides, a gesture identical to her mother's. His lips are a small O lost in the forest of his beard. Anna Lisa resists the urge to comfort him, to tell him that it was so long ago; Meg was the only one; he has been good to her. She concentrates instead on the timeline stapled above the blackboard: 1776 to 1945 in ten feet.

"Why didn't you tell me?" Terry begins, bewildered. So many conversations have begun or ended this way. Terry, always waiting for a story Anna Lisa can only tell in a language he doesn't speak. Now they're both exhausted. Terry takes hold of Anna Lisa's chin again, but this time his grip is tight. It gives her something to struggle against. "Was that it all this time?" he asks angrily, voice tighter than his fingers. "You were a *dyke?*"

Her ears ring. She hears it spelled DiKE, like on the slip of paper attached to the braid flung at Meg's house years ago, when it was her house, too. His voice is mean but contained, a neat scroll that will write her out of existence: not *you are a dyke*, but *you were*. Not just *you used to be a dyke*, but *you used to be mine*. She's already receding from Terry's life the way she disappeared from Meg's. She might as well be dust. She jerks her head back and escapes his grip. She watches him search for the cruelest words possible. He can't do worse than *dyke*, than the past tense.

"Pauline!" he yells suddenly. He's shouting into the quiet nighttime classroom. His eyes seem loose in their sockets. Anna Lisa has never seen him this way. She's been craving it, she realizes, the same way he has longed to un-tether her. "Pauline! Come out, I want you to meet my *wife!*"

Slowly, the door connecting the two fifth grade classrooms opens. From the darkened classroom emerges Miss Ernst, the other fifth grade teacher. Anna Lisa met her once, at the school's Open House night. *Your husband is a wonderful teacher,* she had gushed. Her red-brown hair is messy now, and there's a streak of frosty lipstick on her chin. She's wearing jeans with a bright yellow scarf threaded through the belt loops. She looks slightly wild, like a carefree college girl—student to Terry's history prof persona—as opposed to the polite girl Anna Lisa met at Open House. It irks her that Terry might be attracted to all the qualities she so carefully erased over the past eight years.

Pauline Ernst composes herself in a matter of seconds. She looks nervous, but not ashamed. She stands with her hands clasped in front of her. "I'm so sorry you had to find out this way, Annie, honestly. And just after your lover died, too." She says "lover" too easily, like she grew up with the concept. She says it the way a young woman who lounges in the dark while her own married lover talks to his wife might say it. And she says "Annie" in a way that connects her, casually and deeply, to Terry.

"I'm going to Lilac Mines," Anna Lisa repeats, not looking at Pauline Ernst. "I'm not coming back."

It is only later, when Anna Lisa is willing her exhausted body to sleep for a few hours at a motel on Route 49, that she thinks about Terry's version of the evening. Did he think that she announced her permanent departure because of Miss Ernst? Did he think he was powerful enough to be the cause of things?

She eats the remainder of her truck-stop sandwich in her pajamas on the bed. Crumbs fall on her lap. She still can't taste anything. It's as if her tongue has left her body to go live with Meg in some vague but flavorful ever after. During her years in Fresno with Terry, she learned to be patient, to endure the absence of sweet and salty and sour. Now she will wait in Lilac Mines for her sense of taste to return... for something.

But what if Terry was right? What if circumstance rather than will is pushing her, even now? She hates him for spoiling her gesture, for being so pure in his own transgression. He is part of an ancient and romantic myth: man with unloving wife falls for passionate young woman. There will be rumors at the school and he will have to face Anna Lisa's family, but he'll always have the myth.

She crumples the cellophane wrapper and tosses it in the metal wastebasket by the bed. She opens the drawer of the nightstand, and removes the Bible. It smells like fake leather, stiff and inky. She doesn't open it, just lets it sit on her lap, appreciating the weight. She hasn't prayed in years; she's not sure if she's *ever* said a sincere prayer. She's cast little nets of hope into dark nights, yes, but she's never asked God for anything and promised something in return. It always seemed easier just to brace for fate. But now, with her shaking hands on the motel Bible, she says a prayer to Saint Julian. "Let me be a traveler," she whispers, "not a murderer."

ANYONE COULD LIVE HERE
Anna Lisa: Lilac Mines, 1974

She drives at night, in the world of 18-wheelers and white moths that turn to pancake batter on her windshield. One moth, brown-speckled and half the size of her palm, affixes itself to her driver's side mirror. It hangs on through Ragby, Rawhide, Peppermint Creek, Angels Camp. She sees it every time she switches to a faster lane. It is a grotesque and unnerving creature, with its hunched thorax and fuzzy antennae, but she develops a reluctant admiration for it. She's not entirely sure that it's alive, but how could it cling to the car if it wasn't?

Anna Lisa reaches Lilac Mines in the purple pre-morning, seven hours after leaving Fresno. The buildings are soft-edged against a slow burning sky. The streetlights are off, and her headlights sweep the gray road lazily. Here's a bit of boardwalk, a flash of sleeping department store, a low-flying Steller's Jay. She cracks her window and inhales the Sugar Pines: that old, thin, hopeful scent. Her eyes sting, she's home. How could she ever have left?

Her car climbs Calla Boulevard. Hills are an act of faith, pinning her lungs against the back of her ribcage. But as she grows accustomed to the angle, she slowly becomes aware of a sleepiness around her, something that can't be entirely attributed to the early morning hour. Maybe it's the broken window of Lilac Mines Green Grocer, yawning like a geode. Maybe it's the deep, severe quiet: no cars, no factories, no spring wind. It's a town painted in absence. She passes Redwood Road, the turn-off for Meg's house. What used to be Meg's house. She can't go there yet. She drives past the main mine entrance. The road turns to dirt, still dark and damp at this time of year. When she reaches the smaller mine entrance, she stops. An old car rots in front of the boarded-up entrance. Four flat tires and pale green paint spotted with rust.

Anna Lisa climbs out of her own car and stretches her stiff legs. She has no idea what she'll do here. Find a job, she supposes, that's what she always does. But Jody and Imogen are gone. Meg is gone. Shallan and Edith are in Chicago, Caleb is in Vietnam. Maybe he's back now, or maybe he's dead. There are the new women that Jody mentioned, but Anna Lisa is only connected to them indirectly.

The mine is still halfheartedly boarded up. Anna Lisa gives one of the planks a wiggle, and the weight of it falls into her hands. She lifts her feet and enters the tunnel, where the air is chilly and hushed, so intimate it makes her shiver. She runs her fingers along the ragged rock wall. She holds her breath until she finds it: *A + M Forever.* She was worried it wouldn't be there anymore. The only proof that there ever was a forever. Weather and, perhaps, other fingers have smoothed the letters. She craves roughness.

Removing her car key from her back pocket, she poises her shaking hand in front of the support beam. The key glints in the half-light. What is there to say, now, about *A + M?* She adds the first phrase that comes to mind, the one Meg finger-spelled on her thigh that night:

LET'S GeT OUt oF Here.

Anna Lisa fights a knot in her throat. She will need to do this in pieces. This is how she's survived, even if it hasn't always felt like surviving. She leaves the mine and looks down the dawn-hazy mountain to the sprawl of Lilac Mines. The concentration of buildings is shaped like a cross, or maybe a starfish. Cut a leg off and a new one will grow.

When the sun is up, Anna Lisa stops at the Blue Corn Diner for breakfast. She has money this time, enough to support her for a couple of months if she's careful. She withdrew it from the joint checking account, a modest, non-vengeful amount.

The diner looks like an Airstream trailer that has grown roots. A sign in the window says YES, WE'RE OPEN, but everything else about the place says *No, we're closed*. Anna Lisa wrestles the door open, and finds two employees inside, an older man and a girl in a pink waitress dress. They're wrapping white dishes in newspaper and putting them in boxes. Both look startled to see her.

"Your sign says you're open," Anna Lisa says apologetically.

"Oh. Yeah, we haven't taken that down yet," says the man. A curl of greasy gray hair has escaped his comb-over and begun a journey across his forehead.

"Are you closing for good?" Anna Lisa asks. It seems clear that they are, but she's craving a blueberry muffin.

"Who isn't?" says the man. "Gold rush is over."

"Everyone's leaving," says the girl in the same tone she might say, *Everyone's going to the David Cassidy concert*. "This place is spooky. It's like, without all the people here, there's only ghosts left and they outnumber us. My pop here doesn't believe me, but a couple nights ago I heard the door to the old barn behind our house rattling, and you know how there's been no wind lately." As if Anna Lisa has been here the whole time, observing nuances in the weather.

Her presence finally hits the girl's father. "What're *you* doing here?"

"Passing through," Anna Lisa says. "On my way..." Her voice trails off. The girl stares at her like she's a ghost.

"You're not one of them hippie hitchhiker types, are you?" he says, eyes narrowed. " 'Cause even they're hightailing it out of here. They say they like wilderness and all that, but as soon as they've driven the real, hardworking folks out of town—the folks who kept the town going—they're done with this place. And they accuse *us* of environmental whatchamacallit."

"Destruction," his daughter says triumphantly.

The man grunts. Anna Lisa isn't sure exactly what he's talking about, but she's heard this general lament dozens of times from people in Fresno. From her parents and friends, even Terry. *Damn hippies.* Anna

Lisa can never quite chime in. She can never condemn what she's too afraid to be.

"I guess I'm not one of them," she says, and backs toward the door.

Anna Lisa makes her way down the hill, clouds peeling away to reveal a yellow-pink day, full of wildflowers and buildings in near-ruin. The windows of the Washoe Street shoe store are covered with fresh plywood, imitating the post office next door which was boarded up even when Anna Lisa lived here, boards now dark brown and splintered. The drugstore is closed, a laundromat is closed, Lou's and Lilac's are closed. The things she knew and the things she never got a chance to know. While she is sad to see Lilac's shut-eyed and dusty, it's more disturbing that businesses have been born and thrived and died in her absence, that entire lives have happened without her. She finds an open gas station, but the lone attendant working there tells her they'll be closing next week.

"There's a pattern," he says. He is maybe 23, a thin but muscular boy in a Calaveras Petrol shirt. He has large brown calf eyes. A dimple hides in the stubble on his cheeks. "First the expensive restaurants close, then the stores that sell anything but groceries. The bars stay open a little while, 'cause people like to drown their sorrows. The places like this one, close to the highway, selling stuff that people can use even if they're just passing through... we stay open the longest."

"How do you know?" Anna Lisa asks. "You're awfully young for an old-timer."

"I've lived in Calsun and Dynamite City. The highway was diverted away from Calsun, and they paved right over Dynamite City. I'm starting to wonder if it's me," he adds with a weary laugh. He tops off Anna Lisa's tank and screws her gas cap back on.

"What can you do, though?" she says.

"This time I'm going to college," he says. "Somewhere big and solid like New York City. Some place that won't just blow away."

At one point, Anna Lisa thinks she's on Calla Boulevard, but she finds herself looking up at a metal sign that says North Main Street. Has she forgotten so much? But she locates a few landmarks—Lilac's, a burger joint where she and Jody and Imogen once split a cheeseburger three ways after Imogen burned dinner—and decides that the street has been renamed. North Main Street sounds soulless. She had assumed she would stay at the Lilac Mines Hotel. Not only is it closed, but most of the upper half is charred black and sinking in. Only now does she remember what Jody said. Fragments of their conversation replay in Anna Lisa's head almost hourly, but others are lost completely.

In spite of the evidence, Anna Lisa tries the door of the hotel. This time she's not trapped. She has a car and money. She could turn around right now, or head on to Reno or Salt Lake City. But she wants to be inside the Lilac Mines Hotel. The door opens easily, as if the building is saying, *What can you take from me that hasn't been taken?* The lobby has a wet, moldy smell. Water stains map out mythical lands on the light green walls. She makes her way to the restaurant and bar, where Jody once sat looking like a man. Toppled bottles litter the counter like bowling pins. A warped yellow newspaper says it's less than six months old, but it looks bad for its age. The carpet on the stairs leading to the rooms is dirty and matted. The air here is thick with mildew. It feels slightly poisonous in her nostrils. She wills more of it into her lungs. She would never do what Meg did—she couldn't—but she can let this dank, spiked thing into her, let it change her and eat her.

She wades deeper into the burnt part of the hotel, stopping in room 312. Layers of damp wallpaper sag away from the walls, but only the outside of the door is charred. The fire must have stopped here, found the room shut, and moved down the hall. The bed is molding but neatly made.

And on the bed lies a dress. It is old-fashioned, cream-colored, and it looks brand new. Set out as if some high femme were showering in the next room, prettying up for the ball. It is a gorgeous mess of strings and buttons and lace, shaped like a woman on top and an umbrella on the bottom. Beauty created by extremes: tiny waist, giant skirt; garlic bulb shoulders, skinny arms; pearl buttons the size of baby teeth, high lacy collar.

When Anna Lisa touches the crunchy fabric—satin? taffeta?— something overtakes her. She unbuttons her plaid cotton shirt and drops it to the floor, a melted witch. She doesn't even shiver. The dress fits perfectly. She looks down at the milky folds of cloth. Yards and yards— the dress announces its extravagance, the money spent in the name of feminine beauty. She looks across to the splotched mirror and expects to see an impostor: a short, frumpy woman in a princess dress.

But she *is* a princess. A bride, a heroine. It is as if her body was water and she has slowly, compliantly filled this dress, this self. In the splotchy mirror is a pale-cheeked maiden, curls falling across a slightly stricken face. The sort of heroine who has formidable adversaries: wicked stepmothers and cruel spells. She is a heroine not from a Disney movie, but from the original tale, recounted to children after the candle was blown out, scaring them into staying in their beds and out of trouble.

She can imagine herself running through the woods in such a dress, and suddenly that's what she wants to do: run. And so she takes off down the dim hallway, fabric swishing around her legs and brushing the floor. She tries to remember the last time she wore a real dress. Her wedding? It was a small ceremony, she didn't even want one, but all the parents insisted, their smiling teeth nibbling her identity into a new hourglass shape. This dress doesn't restrict her movements as much as she would have expected. If anything, it holds her up, even as it threatens to trip her. *Is this what Meg felt like, a woman in a dress, running?* She travels the length of the third floor, scampers up to the fourth.

"Lilac!"

She stops. It's a girl's voice. Somehow it sounds far away, although it's not quiet. Anna Lisa stands as still as she can in the hallway, her lungs pushing against the stiff bodice. Who would call out "Lilac" as if it should be followed by "Wait!"? So Anna Lisa waits, as the hotel transforms around her into something sinister. The drapes might smother her. The charred furniture might re-ignite. But the hotel is determinedly still. As she catches her breath, she tries to think. She realizes that she's already assigned the voice an owner. It is Meg, back from the dead to help that other unfortunate dead girl, Lilac Ambrose. Meg would do that.

It could be someone else, of course. Some kid, or even some other ghost. She looks around for petticoat-thin vapors. She promises to be a capable messenger, to translate what is written in the ether. But there is nothing that holds up to a second glance, and there is certainly no one on the floor or nearby. Aren't ghosts supposed to smell like something? Sulfur? But only mold and mildew tickles her nostrils. Is it possible that this ghost—Meg or other—is only sound? A ghost made of words?

Maybe she made it up. Maybe her desire for a girl to call out to her is so thick that it has become tangible, like moist air condensing into rain. Her ears await clarification. But the one word never becomes more. Anna Lisa turns it over in her head—"Lilac!"—applying different punctuation and nuance each time until only her own internal voice remains. It's too late. She only had one chance

The dress and the ghost embolden her to visit the parts of town that she had been avoiding. It's late afternoon now. The days have just started to lengthen, and the pale yellow sun seems noncommittal.

From the outside, the church looks roughly the same: the same brown boards that have been struggling to stay upright for a hundred years, the same steeple and rusty bell, the same purpled tin roof. There are a few shriveled plants arranged in rows. She recognizes this space as a vegetable garden and wonders, with a pang, if this is what her garden will look like in a few months. Will her former husband Terry let the plants die to spite her?

Inside she's surprised to find the drafty openness of the church she knew replaced by small rooms, populated by church pews painted yellow, lavender, bright pink, and joined by the occasional sagging mattress or writing desk. In the largest room there's a beanbag chair bleeding beans and a wooden sign as long as her body. It's propped on the raised platform that used to hold the wood-burning stove that was once, she supposes, the spot from which a preacher delineated heaven and hell. The sign says LILAC WOMYN'S COLONY in hand-carved letters. The space it occupies, central as an altar, makes Anna Lisa think that someone took it down from the outside of the building and placed it here, sadly, gently. A body on display for mourners.

Anna Lisa touches its splintery letters reverently. This was the colony that was born and died while she was elsewhere. This is the cousin she never knew, whose waxy face she examines in search of a family resemblance.

She drives down Silver and Washoe and Gemini Streets. They're all the same: boarded-up buildings that won't quite look at her, plus a business still open every four or five blocks, like gravediggers in a plague-town. Anna Lisa marvels that the residents have left so quickly and cleanly. The mill closed just a few months before Jody called her. There's something cruel about their efficiency.

She reaches Meg's house at two miles an hour. The small brown house is nothing like Meg. It is compact and unassuming. There are faded blue-and-white curtains in the living room window, off-white ones in the kitchen. The feeling that grew inside her—that sprouted small white buds when she put on the dress in the hotel—curls up, dehydrated. Meg's house looks like all the other boarded-up houses. Anyone could live here.

Anna Lisa sits in her car and wonders if she should go home now. To Fresno. To Terry. Suzy and Martin won't even have left on their honeymoon yet. Except she's already done that. She's already turned around when Meg and Lilac Mines failed to eclipse the rest of her universe. So, for the sake of difference, she steps out of the car, climbs the porch, and tries the door. It's locked, as if Meg is standing on the other side, keeping her out. Anna Lisa feels a rush of red anger. She remembers how Meg did that—got mad or weepy and wouldn't tell Anna Lisa why. She was like a wild animal smelling something on the wind that humans couldn't sense. Anna Lisa becomes more determined to get inside.

She tries all of the windows, but they're either locked or stuck. At the back of the house, she finds an old shoe. One of Meg's? It's a silver lamé heel; the outside toe is scuffed black. She feels like a silver miner: *Eureka!* She could use a rock, of course. It might be more effective, but she feels stronger, more womanly, smashing the silver heel against the back bedroom window. The glass smashes easily, like it was waiting for her. She pulls the sleeve of her brown leather coat over her fist and clears the wreckage. Glass falls inside and outside the window.

When she hoists herself over the ledge, she finds herself on Meg's bed. It's facing west now. She and Meg used to watch the sun rise through the eastern window. And instead of the pale quilt Anna Lisa remembers, there's a bright red comforter. Did she really think Meg wouldn't have gotten a new blanket in twelve years?

Nevertheless, she searches the house for pieces of Meg, of herself. Her record collection is fatter. A paperback called *Sappho Was a Right-On Woman* lies atop a pile of laundry. Anna Lisa vaguely recalls that Sappho is a poet. Did Meg like poetry? There are a few dishes and a painting of a mermaid that has fallen from the wall. It's signed *Essie Brenner.* A flowerpot the size of Anna Lisa's fist holds spare buttons. Why does it grab her attention? It take a few minutes, but Anna Lisa finally recognizes the little terracotta pot as the party favor from her bridal shower years ago. Why didn't Jody and Imogen claim any of these things? What about Meg's father? Were they all too heartbroken to go through the house? Too busy? Then again, the rooms are fairly sparse. Maybe they already took what they wanted.

The dark, hulking wardrobe where Meg kept her clothes has been pulled away from the wall. It looks like a lunging beast, as if it attacked Meg rather than stood stoically as she looped rope over its doors. If that's what she did. Anna Lisa doesn't know the mechanics of hanging. The act belongs to another era, one of high-noon shoot-outs and executioners in black hoods. It makes sense, in a way. Meg was the most Wild West girl Anna Lisa ever knew. She left snowy Kerhonkson, New York for a mining town so dry and impatient it nearly crackled. Did she feel like it was her last chance? When Lilac Mines started to crumble for the second time in its history, did she see no choice but to crumble with it? Maybe she felt like the town abandoned her, or maybe she felt like the town *was* her.

Holding her breath, Anna Lisa opens one of the wardrobe's creaky doors. The smell of Meg engulfs her like roused bats. Soap and sweat and the vanilla that Meg put behind her ears. *It's not like I'm going to bake a cake,* she would laugh before they went out. It's the smell that summons Anna Lisa's tears. She is surprised by them. She's been waiting a week, and she'd almost given up, decided that real tears must be reserved for real relationships. But here they are, salt in the vanilla cake. And here is sound: deep belly-sobs that climb her esophagus and jab at every corner of her body. She sobs as she sifts through Meg's clothes: a dress in bedspread-red, blouses in wild prints, pink slacks, orange slacks, a lime green skirt that kisses the floor of the wardrobe.

She sobs as she puts Meg's jewelry on her own body: fake pearls, glass beads, plastic beads. She finds a lone earring, a hook with a translucent circle of dangling shell. Her own holes closed up when she stopped wearing the gold studs Terry bought her, but she stabs it through her left lobe. The pain makes her gasp, a break in her sobs. She starts up again as her ear begins to throb.

She sobs when she discovers the one item of clothing that is clearly not Meg's: a black leather jacket with lacing up the sleeves and a row of fringe halfway down the back. There's no name sewn inside, nothing in the pockets. She puts this on, too, to see what it would be like to be Meg's last butch, and it is heavy. It's not until she takes off her own coat that she sees the streaks of blood like switchbacks on her arm.

Anna Lisa cries and cries. Short cadences and long howls. She sinks to the floor and leans against Meg's bed, bleeding and crying. When she looks up from her folded arms, it's completely dark. She doesn't know if a few minutes have passed or an hour. She's not sure whether she's still crying. Something is happening to her body. It reminds her of the dry heaves she sometimes sees from patients: more jarring and terrible for the lack of substance in their stomachs. She presses back into the floor and cries until she falls asleep.

When she wakes up in a thin shaft of gray light, her muscles ache. She stands up and looks at herself in the mirror nailed to the back of the bedroom door. She's still wearing the motorcycle jacket and a garland of necklaces. Her eyes are swollen and strange.

She unlocks the front door and goes outside. There is a bench on the porch that looks like it was stolen from a park. Sitting with her feet on the porch railing, looking at the pines through the morning mist, she feels almost tranquil. Last night she saw the plainness of the house and thought *Anyone could live here.* It was a letdown, a reminder that her gaze and her love were not special. But now the words begin to transform into something like possibility. Anyone could live here... Even a cowardly, mousy divorcee.

MAYOR OF AN IMAGINARY TOWN
Anna Lisa: Lilac Mines, 1974-1976

Anna Lisa leaves Lilac Mines just long enough to buy what she will
need to stay in Lilac Mines: a camping stove, a stack of wool blankets, a
propane heater, two kerosene lanterns, packets of seeds, cans and cans of
food. She walks the aisles of a Beedleborough grocery store, remembering
her fourth-grade teacher instructing the class on how to survive a nuclear
attack. *It's not just ducking and covering that are important,* she said, *it's what
comes after, how we'll live out those long, lean years.*

The spring of 1974 does not feel lean. The mountainside erupts
with wildflowers. Deer and owls and coyotes wander freely through her
backyard—Anna Lisa comes to think of it as hers after she plants pale
peach dahlias there. There are no cars or residents with shotguns to scare
them away. Each species has its own time of day; when there's overlap,
someone gets eaten. Anna Lisa rises from Meg's red bed at dawn and
returns when the sun drops behind the mountain. She discovers that she
has to be very purposeful about certain things—food, warmth—and that
she has to just ride with others, like the hours the sun chooses.

Without electricity, she pumps water from the well behind the house
manually. Her arms are sore at the end of each day. She collects rainwater
in a bucket and pours it on her seeds. The toilet, which feeds into a septic
tank somewhere down the block, flushes with a little encouragement.
After four weeks in the house, she gets a notice that mail delivery to Lilac
Mines will be ending; she'll have to get a post office box in Beedleborough

if she wants to keep in touch with the outside world.

When the day grows too hot to garden, she wanders the empty streets, mentally placing Meg and her friends in various spots, like paper dolls at a tea party. Here are Edith and Shallan dancing at Lilac's. Here is Jody at the drugstore, resisting the urge to touch Imogen's shoulder when she sees her favorite shampoo on sale. Then Anna Lisa realizes that she is the mayor of her imaginary town—why not make it friendlier? Here are Edith and Shallan dancing at Lou's. Here are Jody and Imogen holding hands among the shaving cream and aspirin.

She takes refuge in the dim, dusty buildings. There are all sorts of objects that might be valuable if she had electricity: refrigerators and lamps and coffee pots. But without energy pulsing through the town, it's just a giant museum. She leaves the abandoned buildings in the late afternoons. The sun burns her neck and freckles her arms all the way back to the little house on Gemini Street, where she reads whatever books she can find. Recipes from Meg's unstained cookbooks start to sound like poetry: *Cracked wheat is whole wheat kernels broken into fragments... Yeast is a living organism killed by high temperatures... To sift or not to sift.* In her imaginary town, *Sappho Was a Right-On Woman* (which is not about poetry at all) would be the book in hotel nightstands.

Sometimes she uses the remainder of the hot day to take a cold shower. Other times, she just lets herself ripen. Her body becomes both strange to her and somehow more familiar. Long, light brown hairs grow on her legs. The hair on her head passes her chin and then her shoulders until she has to tie it back with one of Meg's stockings while she works in the garden. She smells like the sun and dirt. She wears clothes, but not in the same way she used to. Now she thinks, *This necklace will catch the light,* and she'll put it on but not bother with a shirt that day. *This is what people must have looked like and smelled like in the cave days,* she thinks. The things she always thought of as normal and natural—furnished houses and ironed clothes—seem like bizarre creations. So perhaps the things she thought of as terrible and unnatural are not what they seem either. When she drives to Beedleborough to buy supplies and pick up letters from her sister, she enjoys seeing people in the streets going about their quaint business but she has no desire to talk to them. Her tongue feels thick and used-up.

In early October, though, the toilet breaks. She knows no plumber willing to drive 30 miles of mountain roads to fix what might be a larger problem with the sewer lines in an eroding town. Also, it's starting to get cold, and Anna Lisa can't imagine spending all her days beneath six layers of blankets. And she is running out of money. So this time, when she drives to Beedleborough, she stops at a bakery with a "Help Wanted" sign in the window. She eats a cherry danish and fills out an application.

Sometimes she thinks about Saint Julian's—the wounds she's not cleaning, the blood she's not taking. Maybe she'll look for a job at a doctor's office in Beedleborough at some point. The town is bigger than Lilac Mines; now there are two large grocery stores, a mini-mall, a campground. But there's no real hospital. Beyond that, though, Anna Lisa believes she cannot take care of anyone right now. Her life is too rich with loneliness.

So she learns to bake from a fat, quiet man named Sid Olney. She learns how much butter to put in a crust to make it flaky but not oily. Slowly the language of Meg's cookbooks is revealed to her, *knead* and *marble* and *zest* becoming manifest. Her biceps and forearms harden from kneading dough and stirring batter in giant metal vats. Cooking is not femme work, or maybe femme work is not easy. She coils her long ponytail into a net. She discovers mornings, waking at 4 a.m. when Lilac Mines is a black icicle, driving on sporadically plowed roads, and slipping her white paper hat on her head when Beedleborough is still foggy, not quite real.

Sid has a soft donut body and a straight, flat nose squished between chubby cheeks. Despite his girth, he seems delicate. Resigned to a life in the off-hours, he rarely asks her questions about herself, as if it would be rude. He bakes almond tarts for her, cookies in the shape of her initials. ALH. She has gone back to H. When he presents her with a puppy the following spring—a pink-tongued snowball of a dog—she realizes he is in love with her. It comes as a surprise, that a man could desire her without seeming to want all the things women are supposed to provide:

sex and food and children.

Anna Lisa takes the puppy and names it Chelley, which she spells with a C as in Michelle, even though she never has occasion to actually write the name down. But to fragile-as-meringue Sid, she says, "There's a customer I'm interested in." He just nods and drowns a herd of raisins in the bread dough. And there *is* a customer she's interested in. *Interested in* is the right phrase, because she's not sure she'd want to date her, if she could date her.

Karyn Loadvine is a butch. She's no taller than Anna Lisa, with a slim, tight body beneath her button-down shirts and low-slung jeans. She has short, shaggy hair the color of the caramel glaze on the croissants she orders every day. Sharp cheekbones, boyish nose, thick lips that acquire a gloss of butter as she sits and eats at one of the store's small metal tables.

Chelley makes friends with Karyn right away, flopping around her ankles and sniffing her men's dress shoes. Anna Lisa prefers to study her from behind the counter. She tells herself stories about how Karyn got to this corner of California. Fleeing a crazy, knife-wielding femme. Leaving her own husband and family somewhere cold and serious. Except Karyn doesn't have that wounded look that Anna Lisa recognized on the face of every woman she knew in Lilac Mines. She's just a butch going about her business: unraveling her croissant layer by layer, leaning down to pat Chelley's head or scratch her own ankle beneath her argyle sock.

Anna Lisa looks for clues to affirm her stories. Karyn drinks her coffee black. Moves her small, square hands through her hair stiffly. Usually reads the newspaper but sometimes pulls a book from the blue canvas bag she carries. Never has Anna Lisa watched a butch so closely. She watched Jody—her swagger, the way she wore Imogen's hand in her back pocket like a wallet—but that was a game of follow-the-leader. When she watches Karyn, she feels invisible. That's how she feels most of the time now. It's not a bad thing. She is a ghost, misting through town, not subject to the same rules and disappointments as humans.

But one day Karyn reminds Anna Lisa that she is not a ghost. It's 9 a.m.—late afternoon in the baking life—and Sid has gone home and left

Anna Lisa to watch the counter. Karyn has finished her coffee and pastry and is about to slip the long handles of her bag over her head. She always positions the bag so that the strap crosses between her small, seemingly accidental breasts. But today she pauses.

"Hey," she calls. "D'y'all give free refills?" Anna Lisa has taken her order before, but she's never caught the southern accent in the short strings of nouns.

"Yes, we do," Anna Lisa says decisively, although they don't. The coffee gurgles into Karyn's styrofoam cup. They don't have any real mugs because they can't pay a dishwasher, and most people get coffee to go anyway. But suddenly Anna Lisa longs for ceramic.

"Thanks." Karyn gives her a cowboy nod.

It's dark when Anna Lisa gets home that night. Early in the spring of 1975, the days are getting longer but they're resistant to change. She carries her kerosene lantern into the kitchen. Meg's kitchen. She pries open the cabinets and finds a mug: white with a blue stripe around the top, shaped like an upside-down bell. She scrubs it in the cold water, her hands going numb as the rest of her body heats up.

She presents the mug to Karyn. "I thought you could use this here." She feels brave, buzzing with possibility.

"You some kinda environmentalist?" Karyn laughs. Her voice is deep.

"No, it's just, I mean, since you're in every day almost. Styrofoam can feel weird on your teeth. It changes how the coffee tastes, don't you think?"

"Yeah, come to think of it, I guess it does. Thanks."

"My name's Anna Lisa. Hill."

"Karyn Loadvine." It sounds different when she says it than when Sid told her, *That's one of our regulars, Karyn Loadvine.* Karyn says it *Cairn.*

It's months before they make more than small talk. In April, Anna Lisa learns that Karyn is from Louisiana (*Loosiana*). In May, she learns that Karyn has a two-year-old nephew. In June, she learns that Karyn likes reading Westerns. She stores these bits of information. A brown ring darkens inside the white mug.

July is so hot the air feels dangerous. Every shrub looks like kindling. Anna Lisa hopes there are no remnants of gas leaking from the old lines beneath her house. The sweat that streams down her back and temples is the only moisture around. It is so hot that she thinks, *Why not?* The skin around her skull feels tight. She thinks of Sappho and of Meg, how they were both brave. Anna Lisa has heard people say that suicide is cowardly, but Meg was never afraid of new places. Maybe death was just west of Lilac Mines, as dark and beautiful as the ocean. *Why not?* And so one day she crosses the border from behind the counter to the front of the store. She pulls out the empty chair across from Karyn and says, "Mind if I sit down?"

Karyn's bottom jaw pauses mid-chew. There's a sliver of almond perched atop one of her molars. But she rallies a polite smile and says, "Sure, why not?"

Exactly, Anna Lisa thinks. Karyn's tan hands are curled on top of a headline that says, " 'I Died But Out Of The Ashes I Was Reborn,' Claims Patty Hearst, Alias Tania." Anna Lisa wants to say something about the story, but she is so far away from the world of war and politics and movies. What if she just stays frozen like this forever? What if she can only ever make half a bold gesture before getting scared and turning back?

"I haven't read a newspaper in so long," Anna Lisa blurts. It's a stupid thing to say, but it's the truth and it feels good in her mouth.

"Oh, y'want a piece of it?" Karyn looks relieved. "I already finished Ann Landers."

"No, that's okay. What… what did Ann have to say?"

"Aw, you know, the usual. Some woman wrote in about her husband's gambling problem. She loves him and he's not a bad guy otherwise, but she's worried about their finances. Ann says, 'Are you better off with him or without him?' That's what she always says."

"Mm," says Anna Lisa. "That makes it sound so simple." Karyn's face glows in the heat. Anna Lisa imagines touching the knob of her cheeks, the square chin. She can almost picture it. She can almost reach across the table into Karyn's world.

"It *is* simple," Karyn is saying. "Are you better off with him or without him?" She's so young. Twenty-four? Twenty-five? "What more is there to say, really?"

"But what if 'without him' just feels like a giant, awful weight, like you're not really even without him because he's so…" Anna Lisa sees Karyn's bushy eyebrows knit in confusion. She stops. "There's not many of us in town, you know."

Karyn knows what Anna Lisa is saying. Anna Lisa is sure of it. Karyn narrows her eyes, which are the same gold-brown as her skin and eyebrows and hair. Her eyes warn Anna Lisa not to say more, but Anna Lisa can't help it. She's sweating waterfalls now, and it feels wonderful, purifying.

"Us girls. Us women," Anna Lisa says. Maybe Karyn spells "women" with a Y, the way she spells her name. "It's just, we should stick together, don't you think? Or at least find each other? Maybe you and I could…" Anna Lisa isn't sure whether she's about to suggest a buddy activity like bowling, or a date. But Karyn speaks before she can figure it out.

"Listen," Karyn says, scraping her metal chair along the tile floor as she inches it back. "You're not the first lesbo to come onto me. I know I'm a tomboy. But I ain't like *that.*"

Anna Lisa gulps. "You're sure?" She thought she felt the air crackle between them, not attraction necessarily, but mutuality. She thought they would share stories of their first heartbreaks.

" 'Course I'm sure. How could I not be sure? Look, I got a fiancé in Louisiana. His name's Curtis Ross and he's six feet three with red hair and he works construction. We're gonna open up a company together. I came out here to see if there was a good place to start up a firm. Find some little boomtown in the West. I always wanted to live out here on the edge of everywhere. Except it's just small and dead, and there's all these hoops they make you jump through to get any kinda business permit. And I miss Curtis so bad. And now I'm getting picked up on by a queer."

The word slaps the formica table and flounders there: *queer.* She says it as if she's recounting a rough day, as if Anna Lisa will be sympathetic: poor thing, getting hit on by a lesbian. And though Karyn's pouting face reminds Anna Lisa of a ripe fruit rotting, this life of details *does* take shape. Karyn Loadvine soon-to-be Ross wants to pour wet cement on leveled slices of the mountain, buy matching cowboy hats for herself and her husband. This life is brushing up against Anna Lisa's, and it has nothing to do with her, even as it nudges Anna Lisa this way and that.

"I'm sorry I guessed wrong," Anna Lisa says. Her sweat is finally cooling her skin. Chelley trots out from behind the counter for an update. She wags her skinny tail to say, *So how'd it go?* "Good luck with your business." She stands up.

"And don't try to tell me I'm lying to myself either, alright? Other queer girls have done that, tried to recruit me. Just back off, okay?"

"I'm not those girls," Anna Lisa says calmly. For better and worse, this is true.

She expects another round of heartbreak. She closes the bakery early and drives home in the boiling afternoon, Chelley panting in the seat beside her. Her left arm is brown with a constellation of dark freckles now, while her right arm is evidence of a more sheltered existence: creamy white with just a few peachy freckles.

Halfway over the pass, it begins to rain. Fat warm droplets on her driver's side arm. A surreal summer rain that reminds you anything can happen. Or not happen: Anna Lisa feels fine, even though there are apparently no other lesbians in a 50-mile radius. When she gets home, she curls up on Meg's bed with Chelley nuzzled into her ribs, smelling like everything the two of them have encountered that day: heat and rain, coffee and cinnamon rolls. She wouldn't have guessed that having a dog would be so different from hosting the wild animals in her backyard. There's a Steller's Jay who eats crumbs from her windowsill. But Chelley is so domestic. She has become a part of Anna Lisa's life as if it's the most natural thing in the world, as if the dusty shack is, in fact, a home. Making a nest in the pile of blankets at the foot of the bed, barking at the buzzing propane heater. And Chelley reminds her that she is different when she's not alone.

Anna Lisa props herself up on one elbow and nibbles on a leftover slice of raisin bread with her free hand. Sid's bread is so good it doesn't need butter. He adds things to it that most small-town bakers wouldn't dare: dates or walnuts or pumpkin seeds, and once, pimentos. Anna Lisa admires his ability to just *make* things, to conjure something delicious or strange out of flour and eggs and odds and ends. She wonders if she could do it.

"What do you think, Chelle?" she asks. Chelley makes slurping noises at Anna Lisa's chunk of bread. "Could I open my own bakery and make up recipes? What if I opened it in Lilac Mines? Then I'd stay out of Karyn's hair. What if I did what she and her dumb old fiancé can't seem to do?"

Because she doesn't have to make sense when she talks to her dog, she lets the idea become almost real, a secret between the two of them. She could get a loan, if not from the bank, then maybe from Sid. She could revive one of the restaurants on the edge of town, so that people driving from Beedleborough to San Andreas might stop when they're hungry.

It begins with a piece of old mining machinery Anna Lisa must have passed hundreds of times, but since she's started wearing her glasses all the time, distances are harsh with detail. It's 100 yards or so from the road—a few miles from town—a jut of wood and metal. At first she thinks it's a fruit stand. Even after two years in an empty town, she's always looking for signs of life, with a mix of hope and dread. She slows her car, then stops. It's a huge contraption, taller than the younger trees that partially obscure it from the road. Its skeleton is composed of wooden beams wider than her body. Even when she worked at the Clarkson Sawmill, years before the logging regulations began, there were no trees this size coming in. These are the proportions of another century. What is not wood is heavy, rusted metal: cogs with teeth the size of her fist, cylinders as thick as her torso. She guesses that this was where the ore from the mine was crushed, the silver forced out. It's definitely not a fruit stand... but it does provide a certain amount of shelter from the elements. There's a wooden bench attached to a cement platform. With a little plywood and a portable cooler, it could *become* a fruit stand. Or a baked-goods stand.

"Let's see if we can make them stop," she tells Chelley a few weeks later, as she unfolds the legs of a card table. It has to stay a game. It has to not matter too much if she wins or loses.

She has a large thermos of coffee, two signs that says FRESH BAKED GOODS—one for the side of the road and one that she strings from the rusty metal girders of the converted machine—and a few trays of muffins. They are her own recipes. Following Sid's lead, she's elaborated on the basics of muffin science. She's added shredded carrots, mashed bananas, currants, cherries, lingonberries. The lingonberries were terrible. She sits with her dog and her muffins and her cash box for two days before anyone stops. But on the third day, she gets a whole family. Mother and father, boy and girl. The little boy, who is antsy and smeared with whatever he was eating in the car, devours his blueberry-cheese muffin before Anna Lisa has even counted out the change and handed it to his father.

"Alexander, you are a little piglet!" scolds the mother. He's a scrawny boy, the sort who consumes food like a fire devouring a forest.

"Mmmm, they *are* good," says the father, taking a bite of his zucchini-bran muffin and pocketing the change with his free hand.

"Maybe we should get some extras to take Grandma Tess," the mother considers. "Could you give us an extra dozen of those berry ones, Miss?"

"I only have six of the raspberry," replies Anna Lisa with a smile. "But I could give you those and then six banana."

And so Anna Lisa sells out her very small stock to her very first customers. She assumes that they're just passing through this string of mountain towns—they drive a clean black sedan and have an urban look about them—but somehow, word spreads. Maybe Grandma Tess is responsible. Maybe it's the cold snap that prompts the oak and aspen trees to turn East Coast shades, encouraging scenic drives. Whatever the reason, Anna Lisa sells out of her FRESH BAKED GOODS over and over that fall. She doesn't make a lot of money, but she has almost no overhead, so by the first snow, she has enough to approach Sid about matching her sum and opening a real store.

"There are so many empty places in Lilac Mines," she tells him. "I don't even know who owns them—I guess someone must—but they have to be super cheap."

Sid twists a strand of his flat, gray-black hair nervously. "But who would go there? Lilac Mines is a ghost town." He's stating the obvious, but she nevertheless feels slightly insulted to hear her home referred to as a ghost town.

"I'll find somewhere on the edge of town," she promises. "Somewhere right near the highway."

Amazingly, he agrees to it. Maybe he's still in love with her, or maybe he likes the idea of having a chain, more or less.

Anna Lisa visits the county courthouse in San Andreas, where she descends an ornate marble staircase to a stuffy basement room. She explains to the clerk—an elderly woman with bright red lipstick and trembling hands—that she wants to find out who owns several abandoned buildings in Lilac Mines.

"Lilac Mines? That's a ghost town, dear."

"I know, but I'm thinking of buying some property there. If I can figure out who owns it."

"Well now, that's sure to be a bad investment." Her voice shakes too, but there is no doubt in it. She has dark gray hair that has been braided and coiled tightly at the nape of her neck, and the deep lines on her face remind Anna Lisa of wagon ruts. "Don't do it, dear."

"Can I just see the records, please?" Anna Lisa wipes sweat from her forehead.

The clerk sighs and returns—a long, sweltering time later—with a thick, leather-bound book. The pages at the beginning are filled with slanting, purplish writing inked by a metal nib. The more recent listings of names, addresses and prices are written in small, black ballpoint letters. The column that says "Owner" is a tall tower built of one name: Clarkson Land Trust. Anna Lisa flips backward, and finds that almost every property purchased since the 1940s has been bought by the Clarkson Land Trust. Lou's is there. Lilac's is there. Meg's house is there.

"So all that time we were living on the Clarksons' land?" Anna Lisa says to no one in particular. When they were dancing on Lilac's ancient wood floors, bound breasts pressed to stuffed bras, they were dancing on the Clarksons' floors.

"You'd better believe it, dear," the clerk offers. "I should know, I used to live there. When we 'bought' property, we really bought a 99-year lease. See that column to the right?" She points with a gnarled finger. "Where it says 'Lessee'? That's you and me. Clarkson still owns most of the town. They just sit on it. They get more from the property now as a tax write-off than they would if they sold it."

This too feels like betrayal. How can they just let the town rot? How can they not even care? She realizes that she has already been thinking of Lilac Mines as hers. It is her rebellious teenage child; she will comb its hair and cook its dinner no matter how hard it tries to run away, no matter how much it hates itself. To the clerk, she says, "You lived in Lilac Mines?"

"I surely did. My husband worked for those goddamned Clarksons for 19 years." Her jaw begins to tremble in time with her hands, a one-woman percussion section. "If you ask me, the town is cursed. When a little girl dies and a town shrivels up, you've got to let it rest in peace. But we were at war then, we marched right over the top of things. They say that little girl, that Lilac girl, went looking for gold in the silver mine. She got greedy, tired of being a poor miner's daughter, thought she'd do a little mining herself. Should have been a lesson to all of us, but nope. The town just kept that Wild West spirit, with the mill gobbling up all the trees and folks doing unnatural things in the bars on Calla Boulevard. I don't miss it one bit, dear, believe you me."

Anna Lisa continues to study the ledger. She supposes that, for enough money, she could buy her very own 99-year lease. She supposes everything is tainted, in one way or another. Every night she sleeps on Meg's sheets, the Clarksons' floor, the bone-dust of Indians. Finally she finds a property, at the corner of Washoe and Moon, that is not owned by the Clarkson Land Trust. She maps the address in her head. It's the old church, she realizes. According to the ledger, it was purchased in 1971 by one Petra Blumenschein.

She traces Petra to an address in Berkeley, a rose-pink bungalow with a wild-looking yard. Anna Lisa visits on an October afternoon. She waves bees away as she makes her way down the brick footpath in the pre-Halloween heat. A broad-shouldered black man with only one and a half legs opens the door. A pink scar straddles his upper lip like a wormy mustache. He looks at Anna Lisa with dark, glassy eyes; he looks like he could wait forever.

"Oh, excuse me," says Anna Lisa, stepping backward. "I think I might have the wrong address. There's not a Petra Blumenschein living here, is there?"

"Yeah, you got the right place." He has a soft voice for such a big man. Metal crutches dangle from his forearms. With a clicking gait, he leads her to a yellow-tiled kitchen, where a woman with shoulder-length blonde hair jumps up from the table and extends her hand. She has skinny arms, but her shake is strong. She's wearing an oversized army shirt, presumably her husband's. "You're Anna Lisa Hill, right? I was so happy to get your letter. It reminded me of the letters I used to get from Meg when I was younger." She lets out a nostalgic sigh. "This is Carver McAdams." So maybe he's not her husband, or maybe Petra is one of those girls who didn't change her name.

"Pleasure," Carver nods, leaning on his left crutch to free his right hand. Then he drops into one of the four wooden chairs surrounding the table, exhausted from the effort. Anna Lisa sits down as well.

"I'm filming a documentary about Vietnam war veterans," Petra volunteers. "After the colony thing failed, I started thinking about failure, what it meant, and what people do afterward. Honestly, it was the first thing in my life that didn't work out. I mean, I'd always gotten straight A's… I figured that if I had an idea, it would just happen for me. And then the mill closed and everything else started closing, and I realized Imogen was never going to leave Jody, and then Meg…" Her breathless tumble of words catches in her throat. "God, I miss her. I always felt like she was the moon and I was the sun, you know? We complemented each other. You dated her for a little while, didn't you?"

Anna Lisa does not want to talk about Meg. Petra *is* the sun, forcing everything in her gravity to dance circles around her. She talks like Meg was hers. Nevertheless, Anna Lisa has to ask: "Do you know why she did it?" She stares at framed photo on the wall, a proud-looking, longer-haired Petra linking arms with Imogen and a girl she doesn't recognize. They stand beneath a banner that says *1st Annual Lilac Mines Festival*. Imogen wears her hair in a short afro.

"Personally, I think she was lonely," Petra says. "I always tried to get her to move into the colony with us, but she didn't really get feminism. She was an individualist, which is cool, but you can't take down patriarchy all by yourself. She thought she could manage all her happiness and all her sadness on her own."

Anna Lisa does not think this is why Meg killed herself. More likely, this is the story Petra needs to believe: her colony could have saved Meg. Nevertheless, Meg was an individualist; that much is true. She remembers Meg's long nights on the porch, drinking coffee with whiskey, telling Anna Lisa to go inside when she tried to join her. *I just want some time with the stars, okay?* she would say. Anna Lisa thinks that maybe, finally, she understands that impulse. That feeling that no human being is enough. She clears her throat. "Um, about the church? The colony…"

"Right!" Petra leans forward. "I am so happy you want to buy it. Just name the price. I hate to think of it out there just rotting. You said in your letter you want to open a bakery, right? I think that's so cool. The kitchen's not much—you would need to put in a real stove and a big fridge and whatever else bakeries have—but it's big enough that you could live there too if you wanted. Oh God, I just think it's great. Maybe you can bring back Lilac Mines, Al."

No one has called Anna Lisa "Al" in years. The fact that Petra does means that Meg or Jody or Imogen must have talked about her, at least occasionally.

"I don't know if I can do that," Anna Lisa says hesitantly.

"Oh, I know you can. I think history is so important. That's what I'm learning from this documentary. Most of our country wants to just forget the war, forget that we lost, move on. But I think we should record it all, every little detail. You wouldn't believe Carver's stories about the shit that went on over there. He's let me interview him probably 25 times, and his buddies, too. White guys, black guys, everyone. He's going to edit the whole thing, the bedroom is practically overflowing with film canisters. My girlfriend is ready to kill me."

Carver interrupts, "If you know anything about Petra, you know she's a determined woman. I ask myself once a day why am I doing this. But it ain't like there's a lot of jobs waiting for me." He picks at an invisible spot on the kitchen table with his thick fingers.

Anna Lisa doesn't know much about Petra, and she knows less about Carver McAdams, but she feels like she has more in common with him. The exhaustion, the scars. She wants to put her hand on the stump of knee that juts over the cliff of the chair.

Petra is ready to give Anna Lisa the church. She is a full person, bubbling over. She has a realtor friend who will handle it all for nearly free, she says. Anna Lisa imagines living in the church again. She hopes that the smell of yeast and cinnamon doesn't cover up the woody, waxy scent she remembers.

She has only one more question for Petra, the thing she will need to know to make the church hers. "What was it like all those years? What happened at the Lilac Womyn's Colony?"

Petra beams. She is clearly thrilled to tell the story.

The winter starts cold and fast, but exhausts itself early on, content to drop occasional shawls of snow and light rain on the town. Anna Lisa spends the months scrubbing the walls and re-staining the floors of the church. Her boss-turned-business-partner, Sid, joins her on weekends. It takes all her savings to renovate the kitchen and take out extra walls and turn the front of the church into a café space. The building is too big and poorly ventilated, but the stained glass windows make red and purple shadows that look like magical placemats on her secondhand tables.

By late February of 1976, they're ready to open. They just need a name (and an assistant). "A new Anna Lisa," Sid says kindly. He means the assistant, but Anna Lisa feels like a new Anna Lisa. The freshly cleaned windows open onto snow-speckled mountains and immense blue sky.

"You should call it Anna Lisa's Café, or Anna Lisa's Bakery... something like that," Sid suggests.

She's not sure why, but the thought terrifies her. Anna Lisa shakes her head, "I couldn't do that. How about Fresh Baked Goods, just like my stand? Or how about Sid's Bakery, so people know that it's an extension of your place in Beedleborough?"

"But it's not an extension... or not *just* an extension. And Fresh Baked Goods is too boring." Sid laughs, "I'm not a creative type, but even I know that. It's gotta be something personal."

Anna Lisa sits down on one of the wooden chairs salvaged from Lilac's. She likes having a piece of the old bar in her bakery. If she puts her face close to the wood, she can smell beer and oily skin, and, she imagines, a trace of perfume. Anna Lisa is and is not Al. Now she's a patchwork of Al and Nannalee and Annie. She's okay with that. "I know," she says slowly. "Let's call it... Al's."

"Who's Al?" asks Sid.

"It's a nickname I used to have," she shrugs.

"But Anna Lisa is so much prettier."

She states, "We're calling it Al's," and that settles it.

By spring, Toby's has opened up next door to Al's. Toby Minnitt cuts hair and sells tires, sandwiches, and used coats. So it's just "Toby's" because there's no single noun that could explain all he does. Anna Lisa brings him pound cake and cinnamon buns. He cuts her long brown waves into a feathered fringe that tickles her ears. Lilac Mines begins to stir. Anna Lisa could swear that the trees turn greener, the sun shines a little brighter. Like the town is preparing itself.

Just after Easter, the Lilac Mines Hotel collapses. Anna Lisa is eating day-old bread with jam in the yellow-white patch of sun behind the bakery when she hears a noise that makes her think of ghosts, the sound of something old on the move. She thinks of her first night back, at the hotel. Later that afternoon, she learns that the burnt-out building has fallen in on itself. Bits of dry-rot, ash, and mold were at work all these years, shifting imperceptibly, adding up to something huge.

A month later, a bulldozer rearranges the rubble and a dump truck hauls it away, mountain by mountain. Maybe it's the parade of cement and wood through neighboring towns, but it's as if Lilac Mines is officially open for business, its charred past cleared. A gas station opens. Two gift shops. Soon there are people, moving through the streets and occupying the old houses. New houses grow like toadstools after a rain. They push into the forested west side of town.

When Suzy comes to visit late in 1976, she says, "Nice town you got here." The mattress buckles under the weight of her suitcase.

"You don't know the half of it," Anna Lisa says.

Suzy is 29 years old, but she looks younger. Her hair is nearly blonde and she wears it in two loose braids over her shoulders. She stepped out of the car in a short red dress with white flowers embroidered around the collar and black Mary-Janes, although she's since changed into a pale blue jogging suit. Her legs were tan and thick. Her cheeks are pink, her nose bears a streak of permanent sunburn.

"You look like such a California girl," Anna Lisa says, smiling. "You look like someone the Beach Boys would sing about."

Suzy laughs. "It's my young mother look, actually."

"Young mother look?" Anna Lisa's eyes reveal her surprise.

Suzy just looks at her sister, smiling her big, beachy smile.

"You mean... ?"

"Uh-huh. Oh, Nannalee, I'm so happy. You should see Martin. They say pregnant women glow, right? But I swear Martin glows. He's such a goofball, running around, painting things and talking about how we'll have build an addition on the house for our *second* one. He's already talking about the second one!"

The Hill sisters stand in the gleaming kitchen, grinning dopily at each other. The shared thrill of bringing something new into the world. A person, a town. The shared lie, pretending there is such a thing as new. Anna Lisa congratulates her, and says, "Have you thought of names yet?"

"Well... I want this baby to be a part of me, to already be here before she's here, know what I mean? I think it's going to be a girl, I really do.

And I want her to be... tied to me," she says quietly. "You know how there are words that just stick in your head for years? There's this place where I got a haircut years ago. June of 1965." When Suzy discovered sex and Anna Lisa discovered the girls of 3-B. "Lola Felix's Beauty Shoppe." Suzy sighs, "And I know Felix is a boy's name, but that's what I want to call her. Felix."

WE ALL AUTOGRAPHED IT
Felix: Lilac Mines, 2002

"Wow, that's some story." Felix's butt has fallen asleep. They are still huddled in the woods on the shack's splintery bench, but the rain has slowed to a lazy drip. She's glued here, ready for more stories. "So you really were married."

"Yep," says Anna Lisa, "I spent the most exciting years of the 20th century married to a man in Fresno." Framed by the hood of her sweatshirt, Anna Lisa's face is pale and defeated. "I think I missed my own heyday."

"Forget it, chasing after heydays is a lost cause," Felix assures her. Her body feels like crap, but she speaks with confidence. "That's all I ever did in L.A. and the minute I'd find a scene I thought was cool, it was like 50 people were behind me, ready to use my little niche as a backdrop for a credit card commercial. We always thought—my friends and I—that people were imitating us, but they might as well have been chasing us, we were so out of breath all the time."

The bits of sky showing through the roof are a milky dark blue. "It's probably safe to walk back now," says Anna Lisa, looking up. "I'd better give the mule some water first."

Anna Lisa pours some water into a red plastic cup, which Lilac takes gingerly in his teeth. He then tosses his head back and opens his mouth, pouring the water in without spilling a drop. He holds the empty cup until Anna Lisa takes it from him. "That was amazing!" Felix can't believe what she just saw.

"Ernie says you can teach them anything." Lilac smacks his flappy lips.

Felix is not ready to return just yet. "Was Meg the only girl you ever loved?" she ventures. It sounds so romantic and so depressing.

"No. There was Millie. Millicent Hersch. We were together for almost ten years. She stopped by the bakery for a bran muffin and orange juice—she didn't drink coffee—and she was wearing a pink nurse's uniform and pink lipstick, and I asked her what hospital she worked at," says Anna Lisa.

"When was that?"

"1978. March 4th. You were almost a year old then," Anna Lisa recalls, saying what Felix is thinking. This is the point where their stories meet, the intersection of History and plain old Past.

"Did I ever meet her?"

"Once, when you were four or five. We were at your grandmother's house in Fresno. Your mom was pregnant again, with Michelle. Poor thing, her feet were so swollen I don't think she left Daddy's old green armchair at all that whole visit. Millie and I were just there for the day. Your grandmother didn't ever really know how to act around her, and that only made Millie feel more anxious. We spent most of the time outside on the porch. It was a good thing, too, because that was the day you decided to teach yourself to fly."

"To *fly?*" Felix repeats, incredulous. But as soon as she says it, fragments return to her: the rusty hood of a car, a fuzzy pink blanket, the smell of a thick felt-tip marker.

"I guess you thought that if you jumped off things and flapped your arms hard enough, it would happen," Anna Lisa laughs. "First, it was the ottoman in the living room, but that drove your mom crazy. So you moved onto the porch, then before we knew it, you were hurling yourself off the hood of Millie's car, then the *top* of her car."

"And that's when I broke my arm," Felix finishes.

"Being a nurse and all, Millie's first aid skills were fresher than mine, so she got you to sit still and wrapped you in a blanket and put you in the back seat. I drove you downtown to Saint Julian's. You got this tiny little cast, and we all autographed it."

"I did love that part," Felix remembers.

"To tell you the truth," Anna Lisa says, "that was the day I decided that I wanted to go back to nursing."

"Really? So what happened to Millie?" She remembers that someone drew Hello Kitty on her cast in bold black ink. Was it Millie? She can't picture a face.

Anna Lisa sighs. Is there another tragic chapter in her aunt's life? Felix studies Anna Lisa's compact body and wrinkled clothing. How much hardship can a person wear?

"Well, I don't know, exactly. At first things were good. It had been so long, and I was so needy, I think I practically smothered her. But Millie was a good person. She had a lot of room in her. She was like a well, I could just pour all my sadness into her. You don't really want to hear this stuff, do you? I'm your aunt, I'm old."

"No, really, I do." Felix smiles. "Keep going, I'm listening."

"Millie was great, but I sort of scared myself, after spending too much time alone or something. I started to pull away a little bit at a time. We hung in there because, well, that's what I've always done. And Millie was a good nurse, she was trained to let people heal at their own pace. But she got fed up eventually with all my scar tissue. She was still young; I don't blame her. Eventually she went to medical school in San Francisco, and I wondered if she ever ran into Jody and Imogen. But why would she? The world is really big."

Felix shivers. How much scar tissue does it take to add up to a cave-in, a taut rope, an alley attack? She is sure, now, that hundreds of quiet tragedies lurk behind every headline.

"We should head back," Anna Lisa says again. "I'm getting hungry." She stands up and offers Felix her hand. Felix takes it gladly, the small fingers lifting her to her feet.

Felix is grateful when Anna Lisa insists she ride on Lilac's back. She feels dizzy as they bump down the darkening trail. "My car!" she shouts hoarsely when they hit Moon Avenue. With a white cap of snow on its blue top, the Beetle looks like a pale Smurf.

"We'll come back for it tomorrow. You shouldn't drive until you've had a good meal and some sleep," Anna Lisa says authoritatively. "Let's drive through Taco Bell, beans have a lot of protein in them. Then I'll make you some real food at home. I have some sweet potatoes I've been meaning to cook."

Felix smiles as Anna Lisa helps her into the cab of the truck. She loves that her aunt can be butch and femme in the same sentence.

"So now I know why you're such a good cook," she says as they turn onto Washoe Street. "You single-handedly revived this town with fucking *muffins*."

Anna Lisa shakes her head. "There's no such thing as 'single-handedly'. Thanks, though."

"Seriously, that's totally amazing." Felix is still marveling when Anna Lisa hands her a bean burrito wrapped in paper. They sit in the Taco Bell parking lot. The moon is a perfect half circle at the edge of the windshield, white as a bone and shaped like an ear, listening to everything they say and don't say.

When they pull out of the parking lot and turn onto North Main, Felix whispers, "Calla Boulevard." Her breath fogs up the glass.

SMALL FIERCE ARMY
Felix: Lilac Mines, 2002

The envelope is flat, letter-sized, and adorned with small green squares. *F.I.T. has the most stylish rejection stationery I've ever seen,* Felix thinks. She flops down on the couch to open it, already thinking about what sort of dessert food she will comfort herself with. Her parents are driving up next week. After a white Christmas in the Sierras, they'll help her move home. L.A. will be, at best, weird. She hasn't talked to her housemates Crane or Robbie in ages, and somewhere the men who broke her ribs are still walking around. She had hoped she could go to New York, start a new life in her knitted bones. She runs her finger under the flap of the envelope, and removes the letter.

Dear Ms. Ketay:

Thank you for your application to F.I.T.'s Museum Theory: Costume and Textiles program. The MT department is pleased to offer you a Wesley R. Coates Memorial Scholarship, presented annually to three students who demonstrate unique abilities and are members of historically underrepresented populations. The scholarship will pay for one half of your tuition expenses for both years of the Master's program.

Please note that your scholarship, which is awarded by the department, is contingent on your acceptance into the university. You will be notified of your application's status by February 15, 2003, at which time you will receive any applicable registration information. While we can make no guarantees regarding the university's decision, students who are accepted at the departmental level typically receive acceptance packages from the university as well. Please call the number below if you have any questions. Congratulations on this honor. We hope you will seriously consider attending F.I.T..

Sincerely,

Ellen Doherty
Dean, Museum Theory

By the time Felix finishes reading the letter, she is no longer lying on the couch. She's pacing the room, throwing in a gleeful little skip every few steps. Unique abilities! Historically underrepresented population? In her essay, she'd mentioned that she was "interested in blending masculine and feminine aesthetics in service of a queer sensibility that transcends commoditization; i.e., an empowered and defiantly queer style that is not simply 'lesbian chic.' " She had no idea how she would accomplish this, but she supposes they read between the not-very-subtle lines. Despite the fact that she rallied in favor of affirmative action in college, it feels strange to be on the receiving end. Well, why not? She's spent the past four months confirming that history is not big on representing lesbians. She calls Anna Lisa at work to tell her the good news.

In the weeks since her fight with Tawn, Felix has worked only a handful of shifts at the Goodwill. There's been a lot to do, since Matty is gone and Tawn has been busy with interviews. This has kept them in different rooms. Felix has spent her days in thick, mothball-scented silence.

Today when Felix arrives, a resignation letter folded in her green vinyl purse, the first person she sees is Blanca Randall, Anna Lisa's muumuu-wearing friend, although today she's dressed in a polyester blouse and black slacks. Just what Felix needs first thing on a nerve-wracking Wednesday morning. Felix slips her apron over her head and takes her place behind the counter.

"Can I help you?" Maybe Blanca won't remember her. She hopes she'll be in and out quickly.

"Oh, I'm just waiting for Tawn. She's getting some forms for me. You're Anna Lisa's niece, right? I'm Blanca, in case you don't remember. And I'm your new co-worker." She smiles, forehead wrinkling and tugging on her taut hairline.

Felix pulls her purse to her chest. "Really? Okay. It's really nice to see you again."

Her face must not be very convincing. Blanca laughs and winks. "Don't worry, I won't spoil whatever fun you young kids have here by telling your aunt." Felix's heart pounds. What does she know about Felix and Tawn? Has Felix somehow failed to live up to Tawn's wishes before even getting a chance to try? "I remember my first job. I was a shop girl in Placerville, and the other girls and I… we used to go out dancing until all hours. And how the young men used to flirt with us! That was before I got married to my you-know-what of a husband, of course, and before I really knew what it meant to be a Christian."

Tawn emerges from the back office, paperwork in hand. Felix gives her a how-could-you glare, but Tawn just looks at her blankly. "Oh good, so you guys have met," Tawn says. "Felix, I told Blanca you'd be able to train her on the cash register."

"Sure," Felix says through her teeth. "Um, when you're done with those forms, can I talk to you in the office for a minute?" She heads to the back room and waits in an old, crushed-velvet arm chair next to Tawn's desk. A CD is spinning in Tawn's boombox, a tropical song with snowy lyrics. *I'm the song that my enemies sing*, the Jamaican singer concedes.

"Joe Higgs, right?" Felix asks when Tawn walks in.

"Yeah," she says, eyeing Felix cautiously.

"See, you've educated me," Felix says brightly. "I wouldn't have known that before."

"What do you want?" Tawn asks. Not quite hostile, just pragmatic.

"I can't believe you hired her," Felix hisses. "My aunt knows her. I think she's, like, a huge homophobe. Or at least kind of born-again."

"Well, you can't really ask those things in an interview," Tawn remarks, rearranging the papers on her desk. "There are laws about that stuff, and you might remember that I like to follow the rules. You *also* might remember that we've been short-staffed for weeks and we're working our butts off."

It's a moot point anyhow. Felix opens her purse and hands Tawn the letter. "It's kind of formal. It's not what I would say if I were saying goodbye as a… as someone you were dating. It's an employee goodbye." She waits while Tawn reads. "I got into F.I.T., I'm going to go."

Tawn doesn't look up from the letter. "Congratulations."

Behind Tawn, the front door dings. Customers chatter and hangers slide across metal racks. Tawn seems infinitely strong, as cold and still as a glacier. The brassy, scratchy song admits, *I'm bewildered all the time.*

Felix thinks of her long, icy night in the mine. What does she have to lose? "Okay, well, even if you don't want to hear it, here's what I want. I want to go to F.I.T. and I want to call you every night after class and tell you about all my annoying classmates and my really cool professors. And you can tell me about Blanca and Matty and the people who used to wear these clothes. You can remind me that the fashion world is just *a* world, not *the* world. And I'll fly out and visit you on my breaks, and you can come to New York and stay in my too-small apartment in Brooklyn, and I'll give you the dress I've made you in one of my classes…"

"I never wear dresses," Tawn says, looking at her now.

"Okay, I'll make you a top."

"That whole plan, that would be nice for you, wouldn't it? Then you could have the best of all worlds. I'd be your keeping-it-real girlfriend, and every now and then you'd swoop down and pay me a visit."

"Tawn, I'm saying I *like* you. Why can't you just *get* that?" Felix's voice is escalating. Tawn closes the door to the office. "Why are you so suspicious of everything?"

"Here's what *I* want," Tawn says, thin-lipped. "I want to live an on-purpose kind of life. You have, like, this checklist. You do things because they're Good For You. I do things because they Happen To Me. And I don't want my life to be one big accident, I don't want it to be the sum of what's leftover after I avoid all the things I'm afraid of. But I don't want to be like you either, just so you know. I don't want to be an item on your checklist."

"I'm not saying you should be like me," Felix says defensively, but she's aware, for the first time, that she's walking in on something old and deep in Tawn. She thinks of her aunt, choosing Lilac Mines, the accident that became purpose. "Life is pretty fucking random for all of us, you know."

"You don't know anything about me." Tawn puts Felix's letter in one of the desk's long drawers and slams it shut.

Somehow Felix gets through the day. Tawn leaves early, claiming a dentist appointment, even though she once told Felix that electric toothbrushes made her skin crawl. Felix and Blanca move the $1 sale rack in from the sidewalk and count out the cash register. Blanca tells Felix about her grandchildren as Felix locks up.

"Telly is such a quiet little thing, but he's a good strong reader, so he'll probably do well when he's older. And Mitch, he's in fourth grade this year." Blanca moves carefully across the snowy parking lot. "I'm going to the Christmas sing tomorrow night. Oops, the *Winter* sing. Have to be PC, right? They learn Chanukah songs, too, these days. I'm all for it, actually. It would be awful if the little Jewish children felt left out."

Felix sees Blanca trying to accommodate this strange new time. It gives Felix a feeling that is not un-Christmas-like. She pushes the remote on her key chain and her car beeps at her.

"Uh-oh," says Blanca. "Is that your car?"

"Yeah, why?"

"Look, you seem like a nice girl, so I should probably tell you: my daughter told me that the gays are using rainbows now as a symbol of, well, of being gay. Can you believe they went and made something dirty out of a nice innocent *rainbow*? You ought to be careful. You wouldn't want people to get the wrong idea."

Tough-love concern clouds Blanca's face in the dim light of the parking lot. She is 65, plump, still wearing her blue Goodwill smock. Six months ago, Felix wouldn't have been able to take her seriously, but her newfound respect for small-town residents allows her stomach to lurch. She feels a curling sense of dread that she is about to be told she should not be here, not be her.

"It wouldn't be the wrong idea," Felix says carefully. Is she betraying Tawn? All day no one asked, and Felix did not tell. But now it's after-hours, now it's nighttime, and so much more—good and bad—seems possible.

"What do...? Oh." Blanca's face twitches, takes this in. She takes a deep breath and clasps Felix's hands in hers. "Oh, lord. You know, if this is something you'd like to talk about with people, my church has excellent counseling services."

Felix shifts her weight onto her hip, the strong ground beneath her. "I'm actually just fine with it, thanks." She feels how this is truer than it was six months ago.

Blanca shakes her head. "I never thought I'd see this sort of thing in Lilac Mines. Your poor aunt."

Felix sidesteps the contemporary examples of lesbians in Lilac Mines she might cite. That's Anna Lisa's thing, Tawn's thing. She points to a roof on the horizon, purple-black in the hazy dark. "See that building? That used to be a lesbian bar. Back in the early '60s, back when North Main was still Calla Boulevard. And your church is like a block from where this other church used to be, where a bunch of lesbians lived and God never evicted them."

Blanca frowns. "I don't know where you got a story like that. I've lived in this area my whole life and never heard anything of the sort."

The light is on inside Felix's car. She could go to it, seal herself away from Blanca. It would be so easy to say, *I have to go.* But she's tired of going. It's time to do some staying. She would like to tell Blanca about Lilac and Calla, too, but her theory is so shaky, the story she still cannot own.

"Maybe you just weren't listening," Felix says.

Blanca fishes in her big shoulder bag. "Let me just write down the phone number of my pastor. He could refer you..."

Felix pushes away the crumpled piece of notebook paper Blanca tries to hand her. "No, thank you."

"If you're not comfortable going to church—though I think you'd find it quite welcoming; they didn't look down on me in the least when I got divorced—but if you aren't ready for church, there are books that could help you, Felice."

"It's Felix."

Blanca throws up her hands and looks heavenward. Her town and her God and her own ghosts occupy the same space as Felix's, side by side, battling for the present.

"Well, if you don't want to help yourself, I don't see what I can do. I suppose I'll see you at work tomorrow." She presses her pale lips together and heads toward her own car.

Felix leans against her Beetle, exhaling white puffs of air. She watches as the lights of Blanca's Cadillac switch on, as the car inches across the slick parking lot and into the street. It's not as if Felix could fight off two strong young guys now, but she *feels* like she could, like she has a small, fierce army behind her.

And she knows, suddenly and not suddenly, that she will stay. She's been walking a road made of crushed bits of history: purple glass bottles, rosebud hair ribbons, ivory dresses, rumors, songs, erasures, names. She will stay, not for Tawn or Anna Lisa but for the whispers she can almost hear on the thin winter wind. If she stands still enough, listens long enough.

Felix asks Anna Lisa to help her find an apartment.

"You're really going to give up F.I.T.? That's no small thing." Anna Lisa is concerned.

Felix has the classified ads in front of her. "I *know* it's not a small thing. That's the whole point."

Anna Lisa leans across the table and takes the newspaper. "Alright." She gets down to business. "This place you circled on Moon Avenue? Nora's husband's ex-boss owns that house, and he's a jerk. You don't want to rent from him. This place on Coyote Drive could be nice. It's just a couple of blocks from here. One of the math teachers at the school lives on the 1200 block."

"What about this one?" Felix points to an ad that says, "1 bd/1 bth 470 N. Main St. Call Trevor."

"North Main?" Anna Lisa is puzzled. "That's all commercial, far as I know. Maybe it's an office space."

"But why would they say 'one bedroom' then?"

"I guess we can call Trevor and find out."

Four days before Christmas, they make an itinerary of four rentals to visit. The first two houses Felix and her aunt visit are in the newer section of town. Both are spacious neo-cabins. They're smaller than Anna Lisa's house, but still too big for Felix. The third stop is 470 North Main Street. Counting the addresses as Anna Lisa drives, Felix gasps when she gets to 470.

"Oh my God, it's Lilac's." Actually, it's the Goldrush Tavern. Felix never noticed that the squat bar had a second story. The newspaper shakes in her hands. Could she live above a bar? Would the smell and noise suffocate her, make her feel as if she had moved onto Cynthia Street? Then again, the Goldrush Tavern is not just any bar. It's the current comfort zone of locals and truckers and bartenders in fringed vests, but it also belongs to Meg and Al and Jody and Imogen.

They circle the strip mall in search of a way to the second floor. Felix enters the alley cautiously. Everything is different, of course, from the alley below Sunset. It's noon on a Tuesday, and this alley is banked with slushy brown snow. Her aunt is with her. Still, her heart knocks against her panging ribs. She reaches for Anna Lisa's hand. It is like her mother's but with shorter nails. Anna Lisa flinches at first, not used to being touched, but then she squeezes Felix's hand so hard it makes her knuckles hurt. Felix isn't sure who is protecting whom.

Trevor greets them at the top of a metal staircase. He's a tall Latino man with a frat boy body; he can't be older than 35. He's wearing a blue T-shirt with white lettering that says, "Lilac Mines Festival is Back! 1981. Sponsored by the Lilac Mines Chamber of Commerce."

He extends his hand. "You're the first one who called," he says to

Felix, pushing a strand of shiny hair behind his ear with his thumb. "The ad's been in the paper for weeks. I think people drive by, see that the place is above a bar, and say, 'Hell no.' "

Felix smiles at his candor. "Um, I have a couple of reservations about that myself. But I thought I'd at least take a look. This is my aunt, Anna Lisa."

Trevor opens the door and ushers them inside. The apartment is small and filled with yellow-brown light. Green linoleum covers the kitchen floor and flows into the living room. The light fixtures are all circa 1976, frosted glass with flecks of gold. The bedroom is carpeted in brown shag. But beyond this there are hopeful details—crown molding and delicate skeleton keyholes, a bookshelf built into the wall.

"It could use a young person's touch," Trevor says apologetically. He opens the dusty mini-blinds in the bedroom. "Truth is, my grandmother lived here till a couple months ago. She started talking about how she could hear my grandfather downstairs, dancing with 'some floozy.' He's been dead for nine years. When it got out of control, my wife and I moved her into Foothills Elder Care." He puts his hands in his pockets, his shoulders slumped.

"Who knows what carries up from that bar," says Anna Lisa sympathetically.

"I wouldn't mind having a dancing ghost for a roommate," Felix sighs.

PLAYING WITH ROCKS
Felix: Lilac Mines, 2002–2003

Christmas comes like a snow globe, shaking them furiously, then setting them back down, the flakes falling into place. Suzy and Martin Ketay, who only saw their eldest daughter every six weeks or so when she lived in L.A., make a big fuss over Felix's move and supply her with furniture. Her sisters bring vases and lampshades. Then they return to Hermosa Beach and Glendale and Pasadena. Felix settles into her new home, plugging in her coffeemaker and perusing Want Ads in the chilly mornings.

Anna Lisa comes over on New Year's Eve carrying scrapers and bottles of paint thinner. She helps Felix tear out the green linoleum. Flooring, like ice cream, is not an absolute—it too is composed of ingredients, and it can be changed. Felix has barely freed a corner of the gummy linoleum when Anna Lisa lets out a small yelp from the other side of the room.

"There are hardwood floors under here!" Anna Lisa flings aside a four-square sheet of linoleum. "And they're *nice*. Maple, I think."

"Are you kidding me? Do you know how much I'd be paying for an apartment with hardwood floors in L.A.?"

They pull and scrape throughout the drizzling afternoon, sweating in the unheated apartment, clawing to get to their buried treasure. They don't speak much, and stop only to guzzle water. Ancient black glue takes up residence beneath their fingernails as the tower of linoleum squares grows. The maple floor is grooved near the front door and pockmarked with staples from long-gone carpeting. Islands of glue form a huge map of nowhere. Felix wipes her face with the top of the old scrubs she's borrowed from Anna Lisa. "This is nice?"

"C'mon, don't be a wimp," Anna Lisa says good-naturedly. "This is nothing a sander and a can of stain can't fix. It's the wood itself that's important. Look, do these look like regular wood floors to you?"

"Well, they're a lot more beat-up."

Anna Lisa squats down, and Felix mimics her position. "No, look closer," her aunt instructs. The rectangles of wood have a more speckled appearance than the long stripes of grain she would expect, perhaps.

"It sort of reminds me of, like," Felix hesitates, "if you held a bunch of dried spaghetti, and looked at the end of it. All those little circles."

"Exactly. This wood was cut on the diagonal. Instead of cutting the trunk of the tree like this—" she gestures with her hands, "—they cut it like this. One long piece and a lot of waste. The timber industry is much more efficient now, you'd never see this."

Felix is glad that the timber industry is more efficient. But, as she and her aunt sand and stain through the night, painting themselves out the door on New Year's Day, she is glad for other things, too. For the evil and beautiful past that she will walk across every day, that she will put her new armchair and her new old coffeetable on. For an aunt who can name that past and who owns a belt sander.

"Whew, those fumes!" Anna Lisa fans her hand in front of her face as they shut the door. Now they're standing in the dim stairwell, where the air is cold and fresh.

"But we did it," Felix says triumphantly. "I've never done such a big project before. It makes me think I could learn to sew, too."

"It does look pretty good," Anna Lisa smiles, almost shyly, "doesn't it?" She looks down at her palms, reading her mahogany-stained lifeline. "I have to say, it's… invigorating. All of it. I was thinking that, in the spring, we could build you a windowbox. The bedroom window faces east, so it would get that great morning sun. We could start you off with something easy, maybe daylilies or peonies."

"And you thought you weren't useful."

Two weeks into 2003, Felix stops by the Goodwill. The mannequins crouch on skis, wrapped in cozy sweaters. *Not bad*, Felix thinks. Blanca is working the cash register. Her fingers move quickly now, punching buttons and bagging handfuls of plastic beads for a customer.

"Felice! Have you reconsidered?" It's the same question Blanca asked repeatedly during Felix's agonizing last shifts.

"It's Felix. And I've reconsidered something else," she says. "Is Tawn here?"

"In the back, interviewing," Blanca sighs.

Felix waits until a greasy-haired young man lopes out of the office. "Tawn?"

Tawn pulls her arms across her chest. "My next interview is in 15 minutes."

"That's all I need. Can I come in?"

"Yeah, I guess."

Felix pulls up an old kitchen chair upholstered in naugahyde daisies. "I don't want to bother you, I just wanted to, well, I wanted to apologize for freaking out about you not being out at work."

"I'm not *not* out. I'm not *in*. And not that it's any business of yours anymore, but when Blanca complained about you, I told her that she shouldn't discriminate and that I was pretty sure the sweater she was wearing used to belong to a drag queen."

Felix pauses, suppresses a smile and continues. "In college, we had a kiss-in. You know, like people did in the '60s and '70s. But we had it outside of NBC studios. We thought some guy on a sitcom should get to kiss some other guy on a sitcom."

Tawn listens, her chin tilted to the side.

"I don't regret it," Felix continues. "Will *should* get a boyfriend. But… maybe there's more. Maybe it's not just about pop culture. I know there's this whole other world—"

"And you're just visiting it," Tawn interrupts. "You'll bring your friends a T-shirt that says, 'My friend went to Lilac Mines and both of us would rather have this stupid T-shirt than actually—' "

"I'm not just visiting." Felix hadn't decided if she would tell Tawn this part or not. "I rented an apartment on Calla... on North Main. For the record."

Tawn's mouth is a small O. "Seriously?"

"I figured, what can I learn at F.I.T. that I can't learn at East Calaveras Adult School?"

"Um, probably a lot."

Felix smiles. "At least I'll learn to sew."

"Well... congratulations. I want to say that. Since I'm sure everyone congratulated you on F.I.T. and I'm not sure that anyone will congratulate you on moving to Lilac Mines. So I want to."

"Thanks."

They sit there awkwardly. The distrust has dropped from Tawn's voice, but she doesn't seem to know what to make of Felix now. Felix would like to suggest coffee, at least, but she's not about to grovel. She's not about to relive her last moments with Eva. There is a soft knock at the door. Felix reaches over and lets in a teenage girl, shy behind a curtain of dark bangs.

"I guess I should go," Felix says.

"If any old sewing machines come in, I'll let you know," Tawn says.

Felix dreams of church bells and Sunday dresses, white and lacy. She wakes up early, unsure what woke her until the doorbell rings a second time. It is Tawn, and she is holding a pair of scissors, handles toward Felix the way they were taught in school. Felix is suddenly conscious of her torn T-shirt and in-need-of-a-wash pajama bottoms. "Are you okay?" she asks. The morning is still blue-gray behind Tawn.

"Remember when you said you wanted to cut my hair?"

"Like a million times. You said you didn't like the feeling of it on your shoulders, it made you think of dead people."

"Well, I changed my mind. I want you to do it. But you need to do it now, before I change my mind again." She's dressed in fleece jacket and jeans, her twist of wet hair dripping on her forehead.

"Come in, you're going to get a cold," Felix scolds. "Oh my God, I sound like such a mom." She rubs her eyes. "Um, yeah, okay. Let me just make some coffee and brush my teeth." That sounds like she's planning on kissing Tawn, but she doesn't know how to take it back.

Tawn drops her arms to her sides, retreating into herself. "I could come back later."

"No, no. I think it's awesome. Come in. Sorry about the boxes. I haven't finished unpacking."

"I could help you," Tawn says.

"Don't try to back out of your haircut, lady," Felix grins. "I'll take a raincheck, though." She drags one of her new old kitchen chairs into the bathroom and spreads yesterday's *Lilac Mines Chronicle* on the white oyster-cracker tile. Tawn cringes when Felix picks up the shears. "Didn't you ever cut your dolls' hair as a kid?" Felix asks.

"I hated dolls," Tawn admits. "Especially their hair. I played with rocks."

Felix turns the chair away from the mirror. She gives Tawn's shoulders a squeeze. They are wiry, familiar, and strange. Then she sets to work. She braids Tawn's hair, noticing the threads of brown, copper, and even silver woven into the near-black. Then she chops it off. Except it's not possible to chop, really. The scissors gnaw at the top of the braid, releasing it little by little. She rubber-bands the base of the braid and hands it to Tawn to inspect. Tawn shudders.

"But doesn't your head feel lighter?" Felix asks.

"I guess so," She says weakly.

From the bedroom comes the metallic ring of an old-fashioned phone. "Oh, that's my cell, I better get it," Felix says on her way out of the room. "Don't move. And don't freak out. You're going to look amazing."

Felix picks up the phone before the fifth ring. "Felix? It's Robbie."

"I know, dude. I can recognize your voice." A month has passed since they last talked. "What's up?"

"Happy New Year. We had a party, you know. Genevieve made something called Hopping John. It tastes, um, well, not so great, even though she's a great cook. But it's supposed to bring good luck."

"I hope it works," Felix says quickly. "Hey, can I call you back later this afternoon?"

"Actually…" He takes a deep breath. His voice is a packed box. "Actually, we're going out soon. Crane and Sandy and I. That's what I wanted to call you about. Um. We're going out to dinner with Eva and Kate. They're back in town."

He says it *Eva-and-Kate*. An institution. Something that always was. Felix sits down on the edge of her mattress.

"How did the tour go?" she says, keeping her voice even.

"They're both pretty exhausted. But the Manly Cupcakes played some great clubs, and some British producer is interested in them, that's what Eva said when I talked to her."

"Have you seen them yet? Since they got back?"

"Once," Robbie says guiltily. "At Taffeta Bar. We just ran into them. I'd never even met Kate before. It was so weird seeing Eva with someone besides you. I was surprised how punk-rock Kate was. She's got a mohawk, and a tattoo of a cupcake on her neck."

There was a time when Felix would have protested, *But I'm punk-rock, too!* Now she tries to picture this foreign girl, her drummer arms and pointy hair, with Eva. Eva who is still drawn on the cave walls of Felix's brain. She waits for the pain to come, for that ball of love and need, history and identity to push down on her chest.

She waits as Robbie explains himself. "Eva said, 'I miss you guys. We should all get together.' And Crane said yes before I could say, 'You bitch, how could you do what you did to Felix? Do you even know what happened after you left?' That's what I wanted to say, at first. But I'm kind of a chickenshit, you know that, and so we just had some drinks, and I found myself remembering… I hate to say it, but Felix, I like Eva. And Kate is pretty cool, actually. But I thought the least I could do is tell you. I know you don't like to be kept in the dark."

There *is* an ache inside her, but it's something much older than Eva. Eva is a real girl, back in L.A., and Felix is content to let her do her thing. "Don't worry about it," she assures Robbie. "I'm over her, really."

Over is invented and impossible, but it's the only word she has. She hangs up and returns to Tawn. Tawn asks who called, and Felix says, "Robbie." She pauses. "He's going out with my ex-girlfriend, and he wanted my blessing."

Tawn nods slowly. "I thought Robbie was gay."

"He is. I mean going out like he's having dinner with her and her new girlfriend." It all sounds so strange when she says it aloud. It sounds like a story, not real, raw facts.

"You never told me much about her. Eva, right?" There's something sweet in the way Tawn says Eva's name, cradling it gently so its sharp corners don't hurt Felix. The way she held the scissors.

"Yeah. She's in law school. Her new girlfriend has a mohawk."

Tawn laughs, and this makes Felix laugh. She's not sure why they're laughing, just that these facts are so far away. It's like a joke: a law student and a punk-rocker walk into a bar.

"Let's give you some layers," Felix says, picking up the scissors. She holds the ragged ends of Tawn's now-just-below-shoulder-length hair in her hands. The braid lays coiled on the sink, ready to strike. Felix begins the careful process of clipping Tawn's hair into arbitrary but meaningful sections. She devotes herself to one layer at a time, losing herself in the coarse strands. Layer after layer. No noise but the two girls breathing. Finally all the sections are free, all the plastic clips piled on the sink. Felix walks around to the front of the chair.

"Shit, Tawn. You're a knockout." Tawn spins around toward the mirror like she's pulling off a band-aid. "See," Felix says. "I left it pretty long… small changes."

"It's so short!" Tawn gasps, but she's smiling, her face framed by two J-shaped locks of black hair.

"Hey, Felix?" Tawn is still studying herself in the mirror. "What would you say if I asked you out?"

"I'd say that was a very purposeful thing to do."

Tawn doesn't quite get romantic-comedy banter. She bites her lip. "But would you say yes?"

Felix rolls her eyes. "Yes, I'd say yes."

They fold the 17-inch braid they've freed from its moorings into a manila envelope that Tawn has addressed to an organization that makes wigs for kids with cancer. "I'm so glad I wasn't a kid with cancer," Tawn says, shivering. "Can you imagine wearing someone else's hair?"

"I hope they streak it with purple and give it to some little punk-rock girl," Felix says. And then they send it off into the world.

By February, Felix has sewn two pillows and a drawstring satchel. She has taken a Teaching Assistant job at Lilac Mines Elementary. The pay is low, but she likes working with second-graders. They are at an age when all subjects are art projects: coloring pie charts and making paper-doily Valentines and singing "Oh my darlin', oh my darlin', oh my daaarlin' Clementine." It will do until she opens her own boutique. Or at least until she learns how to sew something with a zipper.

It is a sleepy, gentle winter, full of nights-in with Tawn, wrapped in her naked limbs beneath thick piles of blankets. There is a newness about her whole body—her lack of cellulite and her black, never-waxed pubic hair. Felix loves running her hands down Tawn's spine, reading her vertebrae like Braille.

But there is a hovering blueness in Felix's life as well. She tries to name it. Regret? Winter? Nothing fits. It's not the angsty-empty feeling of her L.A. life. Is it possible for something to be heavy and missing at the same time?

"I can't believe you talked your aunt into trying online dating," Tawn says. She's setting the big oak table in her dining room for five.

"I didn't, it was her idea," Felix says. "All I did was write her profile. Writing about eyeshadow for a living really teaches you how to capture the intangible in concise but enticing prose. It was nice to put my training toward a good cause."

Anna Lisa had worried, "What if no one responds? What if someone *does* respond? What if we go out and she's completely disappointed?"

"Either way, you'll be fine. You always have been," Felix had assured her.

Someone had responded, a woman named Kim, who used a bit

too much Wiccan-esque vocabulary for Felix's taste but seemed decent otherwise. Anna Lisa had been wracked with nervousness; finally Felix had proposed a group date, which seemed to calm her aunt slightly. And so Kim is coming for dinner at the Twentymans' creaky mansion tonight, which Felix expects a Wiccan-esque woman will appreciate.

"I think I made too much food," Anna Lisa says, setting a plate of pita and hummus next to the homemade samosas. With one new cookbook, she has transitioned from casserole cuisine to 21st century fare. "We probably didn't need two appetizers, did we? That will just prolong the meal, and if things don't go well, it'll be agony."

"Anna *Lisa*, stop it," Felix says for the millionth time.

"My grandpa will be here," Tawn reminds Anna Lisa. "If there's an awkward silence, he'll just launch into some long story. He'll probably do that even if there aren't any awkward silences."

They're all dressed up, playing old-fashioned/new-fashioned family dinner: Felix in mermaidy dress and silver heels; Tawn in her newest, blackest jeans; Luke in a tie; Anna Lisa with a dab of gel in her hair. Kim (Felix is happy to see) wears no crystals, just a small silver K around her long neck. She is in her late 40s maybe, or early 50s, with coarse ripples of gray-blonde hair and a black skirt that swishes around wide hips.

A Midwestern accent lingers in her vowels as she answers all of their questions politely. Chicago, originally, then the Bay Area for a long time. No, she didn't go to Berkeley, her grades weren't that good and she needed to earn a living. Engaged once, then came to her senses. She pays thoughtful attention to Felix and Tawn and Luke, but more to Anna Lisa.

"More curry?" Anna Lisa offers, and Kim passes her plate for a second helping.

When Anna Lisa goes to the kitchen to make coffee, Felix follows her. "So?" she demands.

"See if you can find something to serve the pie with, would you?" Anna Lisa's skin is shiny-peachy. A coffee mug dangles jauntily from her crooked finger. "Oh, I don't know. It's far too soon to tell anything. But it's a rush to be out there. It's like… it's like the first rescue of the season."

"Hey, *I'm* the first rescue of the season," Felix reminds her.

Anna Lisa frowns again. "Oh shit, Kim's probably a tea person, don't you think?"

"She said she would love some coffee, you heard her."

"But maybe she just said it to be polite."

"Anna Lisa, stop it."

They return to the dining room, where they eat pie and drink coffee beneath the watchful glass eyes of a dusty moose head. Talk tumbles out like beads from a jar. Crazy patients. That new Pepsi commercial. Flooded roads. Solstice. When Luke tells stories, it is to keep a good night going. He turns toward Felix during dessert. "You find your gal?"

Felix blushes and looks at Tawn. "Um, yeah. Well, I guess she found me."

"No, not that gal. Lilac."

"Oh." Felix looks down at her apple pie. The blueness is back, that little cloud in her peripheral vision. "No, I didn't. I kind of stopped looking. I'm sorry, I wish I had something exciting to report. I guess I decided to, um, focus on the present?" She glances at Anna Lisa, who is studying Kim. "Or at least the recent past. The part that's knowable."

"Old mysteries can be solved," Luke says. "Richard III, for example."

"Gramp's reading this book called *The Daughter of Time*," Tawn explains.

"He was innocent, most likely. Whole societies out there devoted to proving it. They dress up in old English garb."

Before Luke can begin recounting evidence in the king's favor, Tawn jumps in. "When I was little, I used to go looking for our ancestors. You know, the Indian ones. A girl in my fourth grade class called me a halfbreed when I beat her at tetherball, and it kind of made me want to figure some things out. I mean, I didn't really know anything beyond the guys who fed the pilgrims. I found these round, skinny holes in some of the flat rocks further up the mountain. I decided they were grinding rocks, where our people or whoever used to grind corn. I would mash up my Cheetohs in them after school. It sounds dumb, but it was kind of magical." She points at her grandfather with her fork. "Until Gramp told me that they were dynamite holes. Until he spoiled it for me."

"I was just telling you the facts."

"And I'm saying the facts don't always help." She turns to face Felix. "I hadn't been back to my grinding rock in years. It just seemed fake and embarrassing. But you wanna know the first time I went back? It was right after you started at Goodwill. After you told me all those stories about the people and their clothes."

"Seriously?" Felix blushes, self-conscious and proud.

"I went back there and I remembered how real it used to seem. I think I even found an orange Cheeto stain on one of the rocks. Which means now it *is* real. It was *my* grinding rock, at least." Beneath the table, her hand brushes Felix's thigh, light and anxious. "The truth will only get you so far."

"Who is Lilac?" Kim wants to know. "You mean, as in Lilac Mines?" She has driven over from Murphys.

Felix looks around the room, at her girl and her aunt, the detective and the stranger and the moose. They look at her expectantly, waiting for her story. The blue at the edge of her brain fades to ghost-white. "Well, I can tell you who I think she was."

FAIRYTALE
Lilac: East Beedleborough, 1899

They don't know it, but they watch each other. Lilac watches Calla be good, and Calla watches Lilac be bad. Lilac has to pass the post office and newspaper office on her way home from school, except usually she doesn't pass it, she stops there and stays as long as she can.

"Any mail?" she says to Mr. Crabb, the postmaster. Her eyes drift through the big open doorway that connects the post office to the loud, inky room where the Hogans print the *East Beedleborough Examiner.* The oldest girl Hogan wrestles with the printing press like it's some sort of biblical beast. Her sleeves are rolled up, and she straddles as wide as her dress will let her. The late afternoon sun shines through the front window and traces a silhouette of her legs against thin calico.

"You must have a suitor, you're in here so frequent," Mr. Crabb says. He wears what is supposed to be a fatherly smile beneath his wheat-colored mustache, but Lilac thinks he's lecherous. She would tell her father so, but he would just tell her to stay away from the post office, leave the mail-getting to him.

"I do have a suitor," Lilac says. "He lives in Milwaukee and sends me jewelry by post." The oldest Hogan girl finishes her work and, dragon slain, rolls her sleeves down to her wrists and buttons them. She smoothes strands of hair back into her bun. It's a color Lilac has heard called dirty blonde, but everything about Calla Hogan seems clean to her, even the spot of ink perched like Miss Muffet's spider on her cheek.

"Funny, I can't remember seeing any packages from Milwaukee for the Ambroses lately," Mr. Crabb comments. "Or ever, now that I think about it."

Lilac is vaguely annoyed that Mr. Crabb is going to press her for details. She likes lying—the way it speeds things up and rescues her from trouble—but she expects her audience to help her out.

"How'd you meet a man in Milwaukee anyhow?" Mr. Crabb demands.

"My people are from there." This much is true. She was born in sin there: her railroad worker father and her prostitute mother did their thing in a smelly room behind the train station, the same thing Gertie Zaide did with lots of men. But by the time the new branch of tracks was laid, Gertie's flat belly had grown like a white mushroom after the rain. When she stood in the doorway of her room, between her unmade bed and the sweaty summer, the only one of her men she could see was Harry Ambrose. She told him the baby was his, and then she went back to Berlin, thinking of the little black ducks that glided along the Spree. People expected Harry to leave the child—which was noisy and female—with his sister or at the orphanage. But he bundled her up like a potato and took an already-built train and two stagecoaches west, to a place where the mountains had silver skeletons and everyone assumed his wife had died.

To Lilac, Milwaukee is a very useful word. Its truth can be tightened around her father's neck. It can be rattled off in an authoritative lie, tracks that send the Mr. Crabbs of the world puffing into the wilderness. And it can be hummed beneath her breath, a song marking the dusty walk between school and home. Finally Mr. Crabb stops bothering her and hands her a book her father has ordered. Probably one of his Westerns. Lilac doesn't understand why needs to read about the west when he already lives there.

Calla Hogan is nowhere to be seen by the time Lilac leaves. She sighs. The walk back to her tiny house at the base of the mountain is so long, with only jackrabbits and tumbleweeds to entertain her. It is June and already so hot that Lilac has to pull her bonnet forward like horse blinders. She wishes she had a hat, like a real lady. As she trudges up Moon Avenue, her book bag pulls on her right shoulder. There are three books inside: history, arithmetic, and the Bible. The Bible is the thickest, but it has thin pages and good stories about people sinning. History is the heaviest. She looks around. The street is empty. She spots a large shrub in front of a white house with gingerbread trim. She darts behind the bush and buries *History of the Western World* beneath a quail nest. In the book, "west" means England. She'll be out of school in a few weeks anyway, and then what need will she have for it?

When she looks up, she sees two angels on the porch: That's what they look like. Calla Hogan and a smaller, blonder girl shaking out a white sheet. It puffs up, then deflates like a wistful sigh. Then the girls come together, the corners of the sheets still between their fingers. They are dancing with it, some new kind of waltz. Lilac can't hear what they're saying. Her thighs hurt from squatting. She feels small and evil and left out.

Two little children, a boy and another girl, burst out of the house and come running in her direction. At first their chins are tilted up toward the road, but something catches their focus. Soon they are standing right over her. Lilac freezes.

"Meggie, come back! You are not going anywhere with your hair in a tangle like that!" Calla shouts. This Lilac can hear. Her voice is smooth as pudding on the stove. If she lived in a city, she could be a singer.

"Calla, there's a girl in our bush!" announces the little girl gleefully, as if she has just discovered a nugget of gold. She has a turned-up nose with blotchy freckles on it. Big loops of hair have escaped from her white-blonde braids.

"Meggie, what are you talking about?" Calla laughs. She's getting closer. There's nothing to do now but stand up. Calla is just a few feet away. She smells like a sheet that has been waving in the sun. Lilac suddenly wonders how *she* smells. Like sweat and schoolbooks, probably. She feels grimy, childish.

"You're the girl who was in the post office earlier today," Calla says, extending her hand. "How do you do?"

Lilac loves her, then, for acting as if Lilac is not crouching in someone else's front yard at all. As if the world is full of good, upstanding people doing perfectly reasonable things.

"Howdoyoudo," Lilac mumbles. "I dropped my book is all. It was so interesting that I just had to read it on my way home from school, but I wasn't watching where I was going."

Calla nods. The two youngest children chase after the quail family, which is bobbing frantically toward the road.

"Final exams are in three weeks and I want to make straight A's," says Lilac. She has three C's and one B as things stand right now. She talks too much and never helps the younger children with their work.

"You must be a very good student," Calla says.

Lying to Calla Hogan, Lilac is surprised to discover, is not nearly as much fun as lying to Mr. Crabb. "Actually," she says. "I'm a terrible student. The books were making my back hurt, so I thought I'd dump one of them once and for all." She brushes the dirt off *History of the Western World.* "Something happened in 1066, that's all I remember."

"I'll bet lots of things happened in 1066," Calla offers. She has pink lips that make Lilac think of the Valentine Jack Gundersen gave her last year, which she tore up. There is a small brown mole on her chin, and another near her left ear. Lilac can't quite figure out if she's a girl or a woman. Woman, Lilac decides, because Calla knows so much: "You're Lilac Ambrose. And you *do* have trouble with history, though you're not so bad in arithmetic."

"How did you know?"

"You look like you've seen a ghost. You don't remember? I went to school with you for a year." When she sees Lilac's confusion, she tries to save both of them from embarrassment. "I sat in the back, though. I was pretty quiet, I suppose. And it was only a year. You'd just moved here. Then I finished up and started helping out my folks at the paper. But you kept things entertaining, that's for sure. Like when you filled Jack Gundersen's gloves with glue."

Calla says she's just about to make lemonade, and would Lilac like to join her? Lilac thinks that if lemonade were a person, it would be

Calla. They're about to go inside the house when they hear the clatter of hooves and the slap of reins. Moon Avenue is a quiet street at the edge of town, so it's worth sticking around to see who might be coming down the street. The hooves belong to mules, a gray one and a chocolate-colored one. They pull a dead, spotted mule who doesn't make any noise at all on a buckboard behind them. The afternoon holds its breath as death intersects the meeting of two young living girls.

"Do you think they know?" Calla asks in a hushed voice. "When the mules go down in the mines, do you think they know that there's no way all of them can survive down there?"

The team passes by them with a gust of hot animal air. Lilac has seen plenty of mules. She has seen the black substance that lurks in the creases of her father's skin, no matter how hard he scrubbed during his Saturday night bath. But there is something about this dead mule. Its eyes are open, its big head facing them. It stares at Lilac and Calla from beneath long, girlish lashes. Daring them. The other two just trudge along, because what is there to do but trudge along?

Lilac grabs Calla's hand. It is soft and cold. Calla squeezes Lilac's palm: *I know.*

Until this summer, Lilac has never noticed how *new* East Beedleborough is. It's not so different from the other towns she's lived in—Reno and Angels Camp—just higher in the mountains and more hastily erected. Wherever she's lived, she's always been sure that real life takes place elsewhere. Lady So-and-So in her discarded history book might get beheaded, but she would never have to pull apart a chicken and a rooster who were noisily ensuring that there would be spots of blood in her fried eggs.

But this summer East Beedleborough sweats possibility from every pore. Maybe it's because Calla works at the newspaper, and Lilac is suddenly privy to all the curious things happening around town. Lilac watches her set the individual letters backward in thin metal trays. THGIF ENIM NI DERUJNI NAM, LLAH NOSKRALC TA WOHS NOIHSAF 'SEIDAL, *ENIAM* EHT SEGNEVA TLEVESOOR. And the editorial headlines, written by Barrett Lyman under a variety of pseudonyms and meant to stir up just enough controversy: ?YRUTNEC TXEN EHT FO LATEM SUOICERP EHT REVLIS SI, ?NIS FO NED RO NUF SSELMRAH: RETAEHT DRIB REVLIS. Barrett, a red-faced man whose nervous energy makes Lilac want to curl up and take a nap, hovers because he doesn't want Calla to mess up. Lilac hovers because she likes watching Calla's long fingers spell out their secret language.

The town at this moment is a rattlesnake, shaking its tail as it gets ready to shed its skin. Anyone who doesn't heed its warning will be bitten or left behind as the snake slithers into the 20th century. The whole town quivers: hammers pound new buildings into being. Pickaxes carve out the inside of the mountain. Trees fall. Hooves tap out an irregular rhythm.

As soon as school ends—for good, since Lilac is 16 now—she spends every free moment with Calla at the newspaper office. Lilac watches the younger Hogans—Eva, Robert and Meggie—while Calla sails smoothly through her typesetting, pausing only to rub her sinewy forearms. Calla's stepmother appreciates the break, and Calla works diligently and flawlessly despite Lilac's presence, so no one complains except Barrett Lyman, who frequently hints that proper young ladies don't hang on someone else's family like a mosquito on a mule.

"Are you calling the Hogans mules?" Lilac says sweetly, in front of Calla's father, who is Barrett's boss.

Calla usually finishes making tomorrow's news by the late afternoon. There is a two-hour gap before she has to begin helping her stepmother with dinner, and she and Lilac like to see how far they can travel during this golden-pink time. To the school, the Silver Bird Theater, the church. They walk farther each day, pushing against the sinking sun that marks Calla's curfew. One day they make it all the way to the edge of town. They stop and stare at each other, then begin to laugh.

"We don't have to stop here," Lilac says. There are just a few miners' shacks among the sugar pines and tough shrubs. They are all empty—the miners spend their whole lives in the dark, and most of them don't have families.

"Where's your house?" Calla asks. "Is it nearby?"

"Further up the mountain," says Lilac.

"We ought to go there. I'd like to see it."

"There's nothing to see," Lilac says, not for the first time. Calla lives in light: in a whitewashed house with a yard perfumed by jasmine, on a street that the city promises will be lit by real gas lamps within a year. Lilac likes leaving her small, dark house to visit Calla there.

"Does it look like this?" Calla points to the nearest shack. It is built of plain brown boards, with two droopy-eyed windows looking out over a small porch. A second room has been tacked on the back, so maybe this particular miner does have a family.

"Actually," Lilac admits, "it looks almost *exactly* like this." The curtains in the window are made of mattress ticking, just like the ones Lilac sewed for the house she shares with her father. There is a pile of silvery tin cans at the side of the house, a shiny inside-out mountain. This, too, matches the Ambrose residence.

"It's odd, don't you think?" says Lilac. "Almost as if there's only so many ways of being in this world. Some nights I go to bed, listen to the coyotes yap at the moon, and I feel so lonely. But probably two houses away is some other girl thinking the same thing."

"Or at least a couple of miles away," says Calla with her half-smile.

The sun turns the forest into a checkerboard of light and shadow at this time of day. Calla is sliced into pieces by the shadow-branches of a young black oak: a hollow cheek, a sliver of eyelet, a curve of bustled breast. Lilac wants to gather up all the pieces in her skirt and carry them inside the house. "Cal?"

"What is it?"

"Let's go inside."

"But why? It's not our house."

Lilac can't say why. To determine whether she has a double? To see if Calla will hold up in such a scruffy structure or crumble to gold dust? To escape the ticking sun? "Come on, let's just pretend it's our house... please? It's so hot out here."

To Lilac's surprise, Calla follows her in. The house is not the same as the Ambroses' on the inside, but it belongs to the same set of circumstances.

There is a metal-framed bed, sagging in the middle, a table spotted with wax, newspaper wedged between the boards. Nevertheless, it is someone else's bed and wax and newspaper, and being here is exhilarating.

"I remember this day—a big typo on the opinion page," Calla says, examining a corner of insulation. "I was so embarrassed, but I guess it doesn't matter much now."

"You could read this whole place," Lilac marvels. "You could write this whole place."

And so Calla gives Lilac a tour of the cracks. She runs her inky-clean fingers over the newsprint, spotting bits of words that lead to stories. "JAM," she says, poking at a bit of paper next to the stovepipe. "Now that could be about the log jam at the mill last fall, or it could be about Mrs. Burke's prize-winning blackberry jam."

When they have read every non-obscured word in the house, they flop onto the bed, exhausted. The springs squeak beneath them.

"Sounds like my parents' bed," Calla laughs. "My room is just on the other side of theirs. Isn't that dreadful? Believe me, it's no surprise at all that they have three children together."

"Do you think you'll do that someday? With your husband?" Lilac asks.

Calla sits up onto her elbow. "Well, of course, I suppose. I mean you have to, if you want children. That's how the world regenerates itself. Oh goodness—I didn't tell you something you didn't know yet, did I? I forget that you're younger than me sometimes—"

"No," Lilac assures her. "It just seems… unpleasant. And I hate doing things I don't like. I mean, I don't even like cleaning the chicken coop. I can't imagine…" Except, for the first time, Lilac *can* imagine. Lying here with Calla, looking up at the place where her thin neck meets her ample chest, the things adults do late at night seem as interesting as sneaking around someone else's house.

She puts her hand on Calla's face. Calla's mouth forms a Valentine-pink O. She puts her lips on Calla's lips. Difference and sameness are slippery things. Calla is her double and her opposite. She too wears a corset and cotton petticoats and a picture of her mother in a locket (though Lilac has just a snip of red fabric in her own necklace). It's not like kissing a boy, all angles and stubble, and then having to pinch his sensitive parts with the hand he is not pressing against the splintery siding of the schoolhouse.

And yet, Calla is so different from her. Her strong, clean ink smell. Her softness pressing against the armor of her undergarments.

"Lilac," Calla whispers, and Lilac envisions her name on a shred of newspaper: *"LILAC." Now, this could be a story about the flower show at Clarkson Hall… or it could be the story of how two girls invented an entirely new kind of love in a place where new things were happening all the time.*

Calla sits up, then stands. In a dazed voice, she says, "I'm famished. I'm dying for some bread and jam. Do you want to see if we can find some?"

They run. In order to get to the empty shacks and kiss and play house before dark, they have to run from the newspaper office to the edge of town. They walk down the most crowded streets to avoid attention, but it barely seems like they need to. East Beedleborough is full of people doing crazy things: miners drinking in the streets, mail-order brides looking for East Coast delicacies in the most general of general stores, Indians dressed like white men, men dancing with ore-crushing machines that could become bone-crushing machines in one careless moment.

Having a nibble of bread and a nibble of each other's earlobes in some miner's sleepy cabin doesn't seem like such a strange way to pass an afternoon. They rotate houses, each becoming an island of what-could-be. They never eat more than could be reasonably attributed to mice. They always smooth the bed covers after rumpling them.

"We're like Goldilocks, Cal," Lilac says over strips of salted pork in a shack with an uneven floor.

"But it *all* seems just right," Calla puzzles. "And I think there's something more grown up about our particular fairytale. I think we're more like Snow White and Rose Red."

"Which one am I?" Lilac asks. She wriggles her hand between Calla's petticoat and bloomers, searching for the warm bulge of her belly. Lilac is a miner, just like her father, searching for silver in the dark.

"Oh, you're Snow White," says Calla. "You're the one people remember."

One day, a big bear comes home. Or maybe it's the woodsman, depending which fairytale they're in. They are lying on a twin bed with oily sheets, their stocking feet on the pillow and their heads dangling over the foot of the bed, Calla's loose blonde hair swaying next to Lilac's brown braid, tied with the rosebud ribbon Calla gave her.

They see the man's face upside down first. It is as red as Barrett Lyman's, with two large dark nostrils steaming like a bear's would. Lilac feels the blood rush to her head as she sits up, hoping that things will be different when she rights herself. But no, the face is still there and still angry.

The miner coughs as he yells at them. Lilac's head throbs. It's like he's yelling at them through a pillow. He wants to know what the hell they're doing here, don't they know what private property is? Don't they know he could get in trouble if two young ladies were seen leaving his cabin? This has never occurred to Lilac. She and Calla sputter apologies. Lilac tries to shrink to her most childlike. She sews a story about Calla not feeling well; she needed a place to lie down. The miner pushes them out with big cattle-prod hands, coughing the whole time.

The look on his face stays with Lilac. He was coming off his own day, coming home sick maybe, living his own story. And Lilac and Calla weren't supposed to be a part of it. They were not on an island, splashing in sea foam. Whatever they were doing, it was not meant to be done in this place.

The miner keeps their secret, whatever part of it he knows. At least, neither Harry Ambrose nor Danis or Olive Hogan says anything to the girls, but it grows harder to pretend. The heat weighs Calla down, and she staggers under her layers of clammy clothing. She trails behind Lilac, who wears nothing between her brown gingham dress and thin bloomers. She figures no one can call her on this impropriety, since noticing it would be an impropriety on the caller's part. This is one of the benefits of not having a mother.

Now they walk through the woods, picking flowers and kissing in the low branches of trees. But Calla is slow to start and quick to stop. In mid-August, Barrett recruits her to help him with a two-part story on The Life Of An Indian In Calaveras County, so two afternoons each week, Lilac loses Calla to an old Washoe man who tells dubious stories about the cowboy-and-Indian days. Barrett wants to sell the story to a popular East Coast magazine.

Lilac begins to send Calla postcards. She mails them from the post office, to the post office. It is perhaps a bit melodramatic, but she wants to make a point about how faraway Calla is, typesetting in the next room. She inscribes the postcards with plans ranging from tame (berry-picking) to outrageous (mountain lion hunting). She wants all their plans to be true, and writing them down feels like tossing a coin into a well, wishing and staring into the mossy void.

One day Calla crosses into the post office, as Lilac is handing Mr. Crabb a card recalling that fabulous day they caught the stagecoach robber. In addition to fabricating plans for the two of them, she has also started to recall events of the past. The summer is pressing to a close. The heat makes her short of breath. She feels as if she only has a few weeks to create a lifetime.

"Lilac," says Calla with a delicate nod, "I believe we have plans to pick strawberries today, am I right?"

Barrett pops his ugly red head into the post office. An ink pen perches above his ear, and Lilac imagines the sharp end poking him in the eye. "It's not strawberry season," he says.

"Barrett, I believe this concerns Lilac and myself," Calla says with uncharacteristic firmness.

Lilac and Calla walk quickly and silently to the edge of town. Calla's skirts and bosom bounce around her straight spine, like kids circling a maypole. Lilac is almost as tall as Calla, but her legs are shorter, and she walks with a step-step-skip. When they reach the wooded outskirts, they are both panting and drenched in sweat.

"I'm so glad you came out with me today," Lilac says. She doesn't like the hard, worried look on Calla's face, but she's sure she can will it away.

"Lilac—"

"Wouldn't it be wonderful if there were strawberries in the mountains? Your cheeks are so pink right now, they make me *think* of strawberries..."

"Barrett wants to marry me." Something about the way she says it makes Lilac's stomach boil. As if the whole future hinges on what Barrett wants to do, and Calla is just recounting the events objectively, like a good reporter. "We were watching the little Washoe children play, and I said weren't they precious—somehow someone *else's* rowdy kids are more interesting than your own excitable brothers and sisters—and the next thing I know Barrett's talking about having children, the two of us." She blushes beneath her already-red cheeks. "I can't say I didn't see it coming. Some things are just... inevitable."

"Cal! That's not true. What about free will?"

"I said yes," Calla says softly. Her eyes are on the ground, which is crosshatched with pine needles.

"Don't say it like you're embarrassed," Lilac replies. She has already embarrassed herself for love. Mr. Crabb thinks she's crazy. Her father thinks she's lost and wild. She has no future to speak of, having long ago played mean tricks on the only boy who ever showed an interest in her. But at least it was for love.

"Lilac, you know I love you." Her voice is so low it might just be a rustle in the trees. Calla's brown eyes are a question mark.

"Do you know what having a husband means?" Lilac demands. "It means he owns your time, you can't even read a book or pick your nose, or..."

"Lilac!"

"All you can do is raise his kids and cook his supper." She hasn't spent much time around anyone who is married, but she knows they function as a unit. The man with his important business and gaping needs, the woman with her busy hands. Lilac hates work and can't imagine doing it for an entire family, even if she could find one that would have her.

"They'll be my children, too," Calla says.

This causes Lilac to burst into tears. Calla is already embroidering the future, the one without Lilac in it.

"And you won't have any time to go for walks with me," Lilac finishes, her mouth full of salt. This she knows: what she and Calla do, whatever it is exactly, is off the map of what young women in East Beedleborough are supposed to do with their time. It is stolen, hidden, it is an underground river that doesn't feed into any lake or ocean. At least not for thousands of miles.

"Please don't cry," Calla begs. "You'll always be my best friend."

"No," Lilac says. She feels her bones shrink inside her, becoming as small and dense as diamonds. "I won't. It's all or nothing, Cal."

"What does that mean?" Calla wrings Lilac's braid in her hands. Lilac whips it away. "Sneaking around other people's houses with you till we're old and gray? Not living in a nice house with Barrett, who is smart and lets me help with his stories? And if I look at things the other way around, well, it's just as complicated."

"You could be a school teacher," Lilac pleads. "You're smart enough. I could disguise myself as a boy and work in the mines. No one would know, it's so dark down there. I know, I went with my father once."

Calla smiles sadly. "Your plans always involve some elaborate story. Look, just listen to what I'm saying…" Two jaybirds are quarreling in the branch above their heads, so it's hard to do this. There are so many other voices. "Before I met you, I thought I had to be so good all the time, like God was watching me. But that's just as impractical as being bad all the time. What I'm saying is, *you'll always be my best friend.*" Her eyes are two dark knots in the plank of her face. "I'm saying we can still see each other."

Lilac takes this in. It's true: before meeting Lilac, Calla would never have thought about taking her wedding vows with an indiscretion already planned, hidden beneath her white dress like the seed of a baby. But the squawking birds and the boiling afternoon and the cold sweat forging trails beneath her corset don't allow anything like compromise. And so Lilac musters more mean words for Calla, more impossibilities, and then she begins the long walk home, alone.

That night she breaks out in a fever. In the small looking glass above her bed, her eyes look greener than usual. Her face seems long and thin, but maybe that's just because she's so used to looking at Calla's heart-shaped face. Her father paces the cabin. Usually he eats whatever Lilac has made for supper and falls straight into bed. He says he gave up drinking because he plumb got too tired to bring the glass to his lips, but Lilac knows it was because of her, and money.

"I should call a doctor," Harry Ambrose worries.

"No, you shouldn't." Lilac's throat is dry. She knows this is what her father wants her to say.

He studies her in the dim lamplight of their cabin, which is too cramped for two waking people. Harry Ambrose has coarse brown hair that sticks up from his head if he so much as runs his hand through it, which he is doing a lot now. There are deep black lines in every corner of his face: the grooves around his mouth, the place where his nose meets his brow, as if he were drawn with a charcoal pencil.

"Who've you been hanging around with?" he wants to know. "Who got you sick?"

"No one," says Lilac. "Just let me sleep." Though she knows she'll be awake all night.

"I don't have any idea what you been doing since you finished school," Harry realizes. "I recollect when you were only this big and I felt awful leaving you to go work. Now you'll be leaving me any day, I reckon." It's not nostalgia. He too looks vaguely feverish, with the wild look of a man who knows he's already lost his daughter.

It could end here. At a wedding, with wildflowers threaded to a borrowed trellis and a simple gold band glimmering hotly on the small pillow Robert Hogan clutches. There is only one reason Calla would marry so soon, and Lilac's stomach clenches with this realization. She wonders if Calla's is clenching, too, for her separate reason.

It could end here, but Lilac has decided it won't. It happens like a fever dream, a song building in the back of her head and pressing to burst out her mouth. Lilac sits at the back of the church with her father. He bounces his knee anxiously, touches his pomaded head. He has never liked churches. Lilac knows she will never like them either. Her good dress is wilted against her body. The hard, dark pew is the exact opposite of the beds that she and Calla pressed their shapes into. The pew doesn't care if she's here or not. She's almost not.

"So hot in here it seems evil," a voice from another row says. "Doesn't seem right for a wedding."

Lilac tries to think of a word for this kind of heat. It makes her body so real—her prickly armpits and damp neck and warm female parts—that her mind wants to leave town. She wants to become a ghost and float into the cool atmosphere. Calla is so far away. She is a ghost, too, in her cream dress with the mutton sleeves and high collar and rim of pearls. *Barrett looks like the devil, standing there next to her with his red face.* This is a lie that Lilac tells herself. If there is a truth in this airless church, it is that Calla Hogan and Barrett Lyman are a lovely couple. A breath of normal in a hell-hot church.

When Reverend Lake asks the congregation to speak now, Lilac holds her peace. Her mouth opens, but she feels like she's waiting for Calla to enter it, not for words to come out. *Come into the cold cave of my mouth*, she wills.

There is a reception at the East Beedleborough Hotel afterward. The congregation trudges down the road to the hotel, like a pastel funeral march. The couple glides into the dining room from an upstairs room. Barrett is still wearing his black suit but has removed his top hat, and Calla has abandoned her heavy-cream wedding dress for blue cotton with small brown flowers.

"Ladies and gentlemen, I present Mr. and Mrs. Lyman," someone announces, and everyone claps. Lilac thinks about Calla's discarded name lying on the church floor like a block of type.

Calla shakes hands and receives kisses on her flushed cheeks. Lilac waits. Lilac holds her peace in a way she never has before, sitting at the bar even though it garners strange looks. She tries to order a beer, but the bartender gives her a warm glass of water instead. When Calla finally makes her way to the tall stool where she sits, Lilac says, "I liked your wedding dress."

"My stepmother made it," Calla says. "I left it on the bed upstairs."

Lilac doesn't want to think about beds. "I like this dress, too," she says.

Then the fever dream seems to take over. She touches Calla's dress. She finds a loose thread and begins to pull. "It doesn't have to end here," she says. Lilac holds onto the thread because that is all there is to hold onto. No one sees them leave. No one hears the words that change Calla's mind. That convince her the impossible is possible, that there is a world waiting for them.

People will tell stories anyway, of course. They'll shuffle things around, planting the baby in Lilac's belly instead of Calla's, or imaging suicidal thoughts in her head. As for the one who knows only how to be good, they'll erase her altogether. What else is there to do with a person like that, really? History has no place for those who honor its rules.

The mine waits for them. There are things that are real because of facts and dates and hard church pews, and there are things that are real because we need them to be real. We name the need and tonight it is called thread.

The thread is invisible between Lilac's sweaty fingers. She pulls Calla up the mountain. *We'll go somewhere cold*, Lilac promises. Snowdrifts. Sarsaparilla. Ice cream made in a tin can rolled with salt on the damp ground. Lilac pulls for both of them. She pulls and plans. They'll wait till dark in the mine. It's a Sunday, and the mountain is empty as a hungry stomach. Then they'll cross the Sierras on Indian footpaths into Nevada. They'll eat yucca roots and quail eggs.

What's Nevada like? Calla wants to know.

A glass bead, cold in your hand, Lilac lies.

They are at the top of Moon Avenue, the edge of everything. No mules today, dead or alive. They look back at the church. *It's so small*, says Calla.

Like a house and not a church at all, Lilac agrees. *Let's pretend they're our neighbors, a big family we just visited, and now we're going home to gossip about them.*

You are bad, Calla laughs.

The mine waits for them. They will spend just one night there then move on, they tell themselves. It is as cool as they dreamed. They go into it and keep moving until their bodies fill the mountain like silver.

Acknowledgments

This is a novel about community, and I was fortunate to discover a community of writers while I was working on it. Terry Wolverton and the Tuesday-night crew at Writers at Work in L.A. taught me how to turn a pile of scenes into a novel and supported me when such a task seemed impossible. Jen Joseph is a true believer in indie lit, and I couldn't be prouder to be on Manic D's kick-ass roster of writers. I am also forever and indescribably grateful to my mom, Valerie Klein, who read early drafts and provided even earlier encouragement; and my dad, Chris Klein, who, when the grant money didn't come, packed up the motor home and took me on a research trip through the ghost towns of my youth. My sister, Cathy Klein, gave me rave reviews but reminded me she was biased because we pretty much share a brain. Bari Bendell helped with the moths and other plot puzzles. And my girlfriend, Cecilia Ybarra, helped me survive the sometimes ego-shredding submissions process while reminding me to come up for air and enjoy the community I'm lucky enough to live in. Finally, I'm grateful to all the courageous queer women who inspired this story and sometimes suffered burn marks while blazing a trail for my generation.